RED TASK

CRAIG HUGHES

FOCUS SEQUENCE - YEAR 275

ISBN - 978-1-9162966-0-2

This edition published 2019 by Coedwig Cyfnos

Updates on deleted scenes, character bios and extras at
WWW.FOCUSSEQUENCE.COM

A detailed Wiki full of secrets and spoilers at
FOCUSSEQUENCE.FANDOM.COM

AUGUST

YEAR 275

one

This was blood; a rough red circle spattering and spreading between her hands, reaching for the curves of her fingers and thumbs.

"I am a captain and this is my ship."

Straining against the magnetic pull of oblivion, Captain Rourke poured her will into her arms, into the muscles fighting against the artificial gravity, and the swell of unconsciousness trying to drag her face first into the deck of her bridge. She could not let her command staff see her fall.

Feeling her weight against the heels of her hands, feeling her elbows wanting to buckle under her, she was aware that this red image in front of her was important to her vital effort to retain her grasp on this ragged edge of consciousness.

"I am a captain and this is my ship."

From her very first day of command these words had been her anchor, words of reassurance that had seen her through a demanding day of fear and challenge, and many times since had been both her mantra of calm and comfort, and her touchstone of strength and resolve.

The words held firm in the pressing warm fog of thoughts spinning in and out of reach.

She had to keep focus. *"These are my fingers. This is my blood. This is the floor of my bridge. I am a captain and this is* my *ship."*

She was remembering now, she had been thinking those same words again, just before she had been punched.

On her hands and knees, fighting to hold on to consciousness, shock was keeping the worst of the pain down to a numbing wash of heat in the centre of her face. She could feel another drop of blood gathering weight at the tip of her nose.

'I am a Captain and this is my ship,' whispering the words instead of just thinking them, feeling the head-swimming pull of unconsciousness finally starting to lose its grip on her.

It was a far less reassuring phrase down here on her knees than it had been when she'd said it out loud, staring defiantly into the eyes of the giant. That was just before she'd watched him swing his massive fist at her face to punch her to the ground.

She felt the droplet of blood release its grip on her nose, watched an almost silent splash spraying tiny specks out from the centre of the little pool.

Rubbing her sleeve across her face, the crisp white uniform soaked up red wetness. Watching it spreading through the fabric she found her anger. Where had that been?

She turned with a furious glare to her own bridge crew.

'I am a Captain and this is *my* ship!'

Their faces were frozen in fear and shock. She wasn't sure how long she'd been down here on her hands and knees, whether it had been seconds, or minutes.

She turned her eyes to these invaders, the armed PPB commandos holding her crew at gunpoint, and from them to the men who led them, the men from "White."

The giant, she had heard about him, but before today she hadn't seen him, nor believed what she had heard. She believed it all now. What his name might be was a mystery to everyone Rourke had ever heard speak of him. As for his master, the man in the green suit, he was almost as much of a mystery. Griffith was the only name anyone knew him by, although a nickname also followed him, *Fathom's Fist.*

Had the commandos even been necessary? White, the PPB's spy network, was a terrifying organisation in and of itself, and these men, Griffith more than any other, was terror incarnate.

The giant held his hand out to her, the same hand that had just broken her nose. It wasn't an offer to help her to her feet, it was a hand demanding to be filled.

Captain Rourke looked at her own first officer with frustrated fury, realising no help was coming from her bridge crew. She growled a command that was as filled with resentment for her own crew as for the intruders.

'Commander Guthrie, give him what he wants.'

'Even the missiles, Captain?' Doubt and fear coloured his words heavily, which only made her angrier.

'Unless you want to stop them, Commander?' Her voice was pure venom, 'you're leaving it a little late for heroics, but at this point it might entertain me to watch you try.'

She looked at the external view screen where she could see the PPB frigate Arissa hooking a tow-line to the gutted husk of the Black Fleet dreadnought "Black Sceptre."

Black Sceptre was her kill. Her *crew's* kill. Griffith was going to tow it away to some secret facility, and take away the weapons she had used to kill it. The first weapon the PPB had ever had that put them on an even footing with Black Fleet's intimidating dreadnoughts.

She looked at Guthrie with disgust, then looked again at the giant. This brute could beat her to death with his bare hands, here and now, and her own crew wouldn't lift a finger to help her, because if they tried they'd be gunned down on the spot.

'Give him everything.'

Fester's outstretched hand turned slightly, no longer an insistent grasp; this time it *was* an offer of help, which Rourke swiftly rejected. She got to her feet under her own power, bracing against the surge of dizziness and pain so it wouldn't show.

Commander Guthrie offered Fester a bulging case of hurriedly gathered classified communications logs, data crystals and documents. Fester jerked his thumb over his shoulder toward the man standing behind him, the man in the green tweed suit, Griffith.

Griffith took them casually, thumbing through the first few pages. He nodded and turned his attention to Captain Rourke.

'I hope you're not expecting thanks, Captain. You've wasted my time, and allowed yourself be humiliated in front of your crew. These are not the traits of a good captain.'

'It's come to this has it, Mister Griffith? You come aboard another PPB ship, like a bandit, and have your hideous thug assault a senior officer, and all because, for some reason, your mysterious spymaster doesn't want us attacking our *enemies?*'

Griffith looked up from the documents, 'These weapons were never yours. White's laboratories designed and built them.' He held up the dossier, 'this data is not yours. It belongs to White. You and your ship are just another piece of test equipment. You don't own these weapons anymore than a laboratory flask owns the chemicals inside it.'

'Look outside at that dreadnought, Griffith! You don't like the way we test? The results seem pretty good to me.'

'You were only supposed to test the weapons, Captain Rourke, not start a war with them. You can tell as much to Captain Jowett and Captain Talbot when you contact them tonight. *You* are supposed to be the sane one out of the three of you, comparatively, anyway.'

Griffith turned to leave, the heavily armed commandos parting to let him pass.

A final surge of fury overcame Rourke's regard for her safety, emerging as a defiant shout at his back, 'When Over-Admiral Connors finds out what you've done here, Fathom won't be able to protect you.' She turned her ire back to the giant, 'And you can tell your boss here that being Fathom's right-hand man doesn't make him safe. Your Mister Griffith here is long overdue for a big, *BIG* fall, and when he lands it's going to hurt, and you'll be going down with him, you ugly hunk of filth.'

The giant made the first sound she'd heard from him since he'd first stepped onto her bridge — he laughed at her, a deep, dark laugh of derision booming around the bridge, sending a dread-chill deep into Captain Rourke's heart.

The sinking sun was starting to touch the edge of the Tallit Sea. The gentle waves lapping the shore of Pandale City's Great Blue Beach were shimmering, red-orange light playing on the surface of the ebb tide waters, with each lick of the retreating waves striking up strange refractions in unexpected prismatic shades, sparkling in the sapphire sands, glistening brightly then filtering away.

A touch of first autumn chill sprang up as the horizon took its first bite of the sun. Out of the corner of his eye, Glen could see Yolande's hair being teased into motion by the soft sea breeze.

Behind them the music of the post-shoot party was muted by the closed doors of the arena bar, reduced to muffled thuds of drumming and indistinct lyrics. As the Gun-Grid season drew to a close, the parties got bigger and louder, and there was only one major shoot left this year. This one was always Glen's favourite, the Pandale Arena had atmosphere and history, and there was none of the frenetic finality of the season's last shoot.

He let himself look at Yolande, his heart aching a little, knowing moments alone with her were always just that. This was a precious time that would doubtless be cut short by some friend or admirer of Yolande coming to find out where she was, dragging her back to the throng, and away from him.

She turned to face him, offering him a warming smile of such perfect radiance he could almost believe the setting sun had decided to rise again. He thought back to the very first time he'd seen her, the first time he'd seen that smile, back when he'd reached the grand old age of thirteen, and she'd been no older than ten.

"She's going to break some hearts when she's older," was the very first thought he'd had as he caught sight of her talking and laughing with her friends, never a thought in his head that one of those hearts might turn out to be his. He'd never even expected to learn her name, let alone spend the next few years seeing her face light up with happiness every time they met, or opening his arms to receive the embraces she always had for him, or starting to look forward to every opportunity he might have to see her. He never imagined that as the years passed she would make him ache in his soul every time she left his side, or even turned aside.

Now here she was, a couple of weeks shy of her sixteenth birthday, smiling a smile that he so wanted to kiss, and surely that was what she wanted too? But she was still just that bit too young. It just didn't feel quite right, yet. Well, it felt right, but it didn't feel perfect.

Next month would be the last shoot of the season, and there would be another party, and things would be perfect. That's when Glen Rothgill would kiss Yolande Fenton. That's when they would — when they *could* start something together.

He smiled back at her, and turned back to the sunset. She slipped her arm around him, and it felt better than anything else he had ever felt, and for now that was enough, because he'd thought it all out, and next time, it *would* be perfect.

Monique purred melodically, softly, and enticingly into the antique microphone, a mellow sound merging with the soft, warm tones of the band; a low-fidelity buzz, hum and strum with a muted pulse of soft and tender percussion.

The backdrop for the stage was a window on a slowly spinning world of golden sand and copper-green oceans. Raleigh might as easily have been fashioned by a master jeweller as formed by the forces of nature, and Raleigh Station's "Bar Purple" was the best place to see it.

Temporarily at least, the patrons of the bar were distracted from the view. The sparkles from Monique's long red dress were making a dance of light on the faces and eyes at the tables closest to the stage. They were hypnotised by the sway of her hips, the swing of her shoulders, and the velvet in her voice.

Her eyes would drift, and settle for a few moments on a new face, offering a soulful glance —just enough to connect— then moving on. It was well practised stage craft, but she was also looking for a missing face. Every so often she would steal a look at the arrivals board at the back of the bar.

The Sabina was long overdue, but it was finally docking. *He* still might make it in time for her last song, or she might have to extend the set, to make sure he didn't miss it.

She turned a look to the band and gave the signal that it was time for some self-indulgent musical improvisation.

It wasn't the biggest space station, or the busiest, but the Bar Purple on Raleigh Station had just about the best atmosphere of any of the places she played. Thousands of temporary romances must have run their course, or become the start of something greater at this interstellar stopping off point.

And there was her own beau now.

Signalling to the boys to wrap this number up, she took a bow as the music faded. The applause was light but sincere and she smiled an electrifying smile for the crowd, turning it at last to the man in the crisp white uniform who was taking a seat at the back of the room.

'Thank you. I always love playing here, you people all dress nicer and clap nicer than on any other station. I feel classier just looking at you.' A ripple of laughter swept the room. 'The last song is a dedication to how hard love can be, and to catching hold of something good at the last minute.' She turned her smile again to Commander Guthrie and he tipped his drink towards her in salute as the music began.

Commander Guthrie's face was a mask of stress. Though he was smiling as naturally as he could manage, as Monique left the stage and took her place beside him it was still a strained rictus.

She clinked her glass against his and looked at him with concern, 'I was worried when you were so late. I thought you weren't coming, you look terrible, by the way.'

'Thanks, sweetheart, I'm glad I can't say the same about you,' he admired the red dress, and scowled at some of the nearer men who were doing the same. 'I'm glad I made it in time for your last song.'

'Me too, but I stretched the set some to try to make sure you did,' she caressed the back of his hand, 'What held you up?'

He closed his eyes and took a deep breath, 'It's been a bad day, Monique. A very bad day.'

They both felt a subtle change in atmosphere of the bar. Turning to the door a small group of PPB officers were entering, Captain Rourke at their head.

Monique drew a shocked breath, 'Isn't that your Captain?' she turned to Guthrie, 'what happened today?'

The Captain's broken nose had been repaired but her face still wore the physical trauma, the swelling would take a couple of days to subside, the bruising was only just getting started, yellow would soon become blue and purple.

Guthrie shook his head, his expression turning sour, 'Somebody pulled rank on us, extremely forcefully. It seems our mission does not have universal approval, and military politics isn't as subtle as it used to be.'

'Your day must have been awful, I'm so sorry.' She slipped her arm around him and laid her head on his shoulder, 'I know you don't like to talk about what you do, but, you know you can tell me anything, right?'

'Thank you, Monique, but hearing you sing does me a lot more good than hearing myself moaning would. Don't think it's not appreciated, though.'

'So, just how much time do we have together?'

'I wish I had longer, but the day's delays have put us way behind schedule. The Captain's given us long enough for a few drinks then we have to get to our rendezvous.'

'Don't you have time for less *liquid* pleasures?' She asked.

Finally his smile made it all the way to his eyes, 'I thought you'd never ask.'

'Okay.' Monique stood, setting a keycard down on the table, 'You go on ahead, I'm in cabin 438, I just need to talk to the band and I'll be there in five minutes, ten at most.' She leaned in close to whisper, 'Don't you dare not be naked.'

He kissed her hand and held onto it as long as he could as she backed away, smiling.

Over-Admiral Connors' bouncing stride was giving notice of his mood long before the Chairman could see it written on his face. The PPB Chairman's office was long and wide, big enough for banquets and balls, so the head of the Admiralty had a fair walk to the Chairman's desk.

Laying down his pen to watch Connors' approach, the Chairman clicked the switch which deployed alcoholic beverages from the reservoir within his desk. Two glasses rose from within, ready filled with ice, and a nozzle emerged to squirt a considerable quantity of grain liquor into each.

He placed one in front of the seat opposite, just as the Over-Admiral sat himself in it.

'Chairman,' he said, raising the glass, and tipping a healthy slug down his throat.

The Chairman nodded, dipping the tip of his lip in his own glass and allowing a taste of the drink to wet his tongue.

'I'd ask if you're having a pleasant evening, Connors, but it seems clear that you're not.'

Connors screwed up his face in distaste. He tossed a holographic disc across the desk. 'Have you seen this?'

The Chairman touched the disc and it began to play out the events aboard the bridge of the PPB frigate Sabina. The Chairman watched impassively, wincing slightly when the giant's fist felled Captain Rourke.

'That's Griffith's pet gorilla,' Connors explained, 'a non-syllabic brute called *Fester*.'

'Yes, I'm aware of him.'

'This is too far, Chairman. Fathom has taken a liberty too far now. PPB commandos boarding a PPB ship and demanding classified information about a dark-pool project, at gunpoint? Violently assaulting a captain in front of her crew? This is way over the line of acceptable conduct.'

'I did warn you, Connors, that Fathom would object very strongly to you escalating Project Snipe.'

Connors waved away the thought, 'No excuse. That...' He pointed at the holographic recording. The Chairman turned it off, 'That is inexcusable. I need you to contact Admiral Wrekin so we can sanction Fathom, and to trim back the powers of White. Fathom has been allowed to pull far too much power to himself for far too long. This is a step too far. This can't be repeated. It can't be tolerated.'

The Chairman rested his chin on a curled finger, 'After Benoit was elected Sovereign, I reluctantly let you carry on with Project Snipe, and I told you it mustn't threaten the position of our useful new Sovereign. Fathom invested huge amounts of resources and planning to neutralise Sovereign Phipps, and to get a useful idiot like Benoit into power.'

'Phipps was kicked out, yes, and so could Benoit be, even without Project Snipe. The data we've already gathered on their craft is more valuable to us than having one patsy Sovereign who could be gone in a month, or a year, or four years. We're learning how to take down these Black Fleet dreadnoughts!' Connors leaned over the desk, 'Captain Rourke got a *kill* today! Is this her reward? A boarding party and a broken face?'

'She only got that kill because of the missiles you were given by Fathom, and it wasn't a one-on-one kill, it was a joint strike with the Savatara, and the Sonya was there too as a back-up, using weapons built and designed in White's weapons research facilities; Fathom's weapons research facilities.'

'Yes, and today he took them away, just as we learn exactly how to get the best out of them! White's weapons facilities are *our* weapons facilities, Chairman, Fathom works for us, remember?'

'Fathom works for *me*, Over-Admiral Connors, and so do you.'

'You may think that's how it is, Chairman, but we both know Fathom only works for Fathom. That's why you need to get in touch with Milo Wrekin, while he's still alive. While he's still the third proxy.'

'What makes you think Wrekin would have any part in threatening Fathom?'

'My understanding is he'll be dead in weeks, months at the very most. It's not like he has anything left to be afraid of.'

'I wasn't talking about fear, and your concern about your predecessor's wellbeing is touching, by the way.' Connors rolled his eyes to dismiss the barb, 'Admiral Wrekin would almost certainly side with Fathom against the three beautiful psychopaths you've chosen to test Fathom's weapons system. All approved for promotion from your bed, no doubt.'

Connors bristled at the suggestion, 'They were the top graduates of their year at the Naval Academy, so you can keep your insinuations to yourself, Mister Chairman. You need to reach out to Wrekin anyway, to find out who he's nominated as his replacement proxy. We can't have it slipping away even further, slipping into the hands of some unknown. We *need* to know who the new proxy is going to be.'

'So you can twist their arm and get them on your side? Or maybe kill them, so Fathom is finished without having to worry about talking me around?'

'I don't know exactly what power the proxies have over Fathom, but I know they're the only thing that keeps him in check, so we need to know who to go to when we need to give Fathom the final sanction!'

'When? Don't you mean *if*?'

'I said "when" and I meant it. The day will come when you'll wish you'd listened, and don't expect me not to say I told you so. The damned proxy should have switched to *me* when Wrekin retired as head of the Admiralty, not stayed with him.'

'So you can have Fathom killed on a whim? Fathom works, and what Fathom does works. Fathom got rid of the most hostile Sovereign we've faced in two generations. If Black Fleet find out about Project Snipe, they won't just insist Benoit is kicked out of office, they'll bring back Phipps and the arms reduction treaty will be finished. Phipps can re-arm and 35 years of political and military progress for the PPB will be wiped out.

'I've let Project Snipe carry on this long, but you risk too much, Connors. Fathom may have gone too far today, but Project Snipe has gone too far too. If you can't reign it in, it won't be Fathom getting sanctioned, it'll be you, and I only need a proxy of *one* to arrange that.'

Monique became aware her own footsteps weren't the only ones she could hear. The dark grey carpet, soft underfoot, and the constant subtle thrum of the life-support systems made the second set of steps hard to pick out, but they were there.

The corridors to the sleeping cabins were dimly lit at this hour, and mostly empty, people were either already abed or enjoying the nightlife.

Monique stopped, the footsteps behind did not. Whoever it was was out of sight, hidden by the curvature of the corridor.

Commander Guthrie would already be waiting for her inside her cabin, she wouldn't risk anyone catching even a glimpse of him through an open door.

Slipping off her shoes and stepping into the passageway leading to her cabin, as silent as silk she tiptoed to the door. She reached for the keypad.

'Miss Monique?'

At the end of the passage was a man in a tight suit, a trim looking guy with slicked back hair and a curious, pencil-thin beard, shaven into a spiral that swept from his right ear, under his chin and up and over the left half of his lip. It was currently a style with very young men, this man was not anywhere near young enough to carry it off, but he *looked* harmless enough.

'Can I help you?'

'Well, more to the point, Miss Monique, can I help you?' He strode forward, hand outstretched. She shook it with as little enthusiasm as she could manage. 'My name is Ralph Parsons, and I just wanted to tell you I loved your set tonight. I love your whole set-up, point of fact. Your band is tight, and forgive me for saying so, your body is tight.'

'Well, thank you, I suppose.'

If he'd noticed her less than joyous reaction to the compliment, he didn't show it, 'Your voice is breathtaking, your look is astonishing. You're like a toned athlete, but every inch a woman, and as for your smile, don't get me started!'

'Trust me, Mister Parsons, I won't.' She thought about what was waiting for her on the other side of the door, and how little time she had before Commander Guthrie had to be back aboard the Sabina. 'This is all very nice, Mr Parsons, I hope you'll come to more shows. If you look us up with MAsoN our tour schedule is all available. Maybe we can talk more then, but I have a band meeting now.'

Parsons raised a finger, 'Miss Monique, I've already looked you up on MAsoN, and I've seen your touring schedule, and frankly, the quality of venues you're touring right now does not match the quality of your act.'

Her worst fears were confirmed, 'Mister Parsons...'

'Ralph, please.'

'Ralph, we have representation, and we're quite content with where we are right now.'

He only seemed emboldened by this. 'But you shouldn't be, Monique! Contentment is the enemy of achievement, and you can achieve a lot more than this! Bigger venues! Bigger audiences! Much, *much* more money, and I've got the connections to deliver that.'

'If you want to put together a proposal, what venues you think you can get us in, then by all means send me what you've got, but I really need to get on with this band meeting.'

'I believe in making the most of the moment, Monique, and in this moment, it's you, and me, and if I send you a proposal, we're not *in* that moment, it's just a datasheet with numbers and names and I'm just *that guy* you met *that night*.

'You and I should take this moment, Monique. It's little moments like these that the *great* moments music history is filled with; that magic beginning, or that missed opportunity.' His enthusiasm certainly wasn't lacking, 'My brother just took over as administrator on Beacon 505, you know it?' Monique nodded. 'It's a big hub station, on two streams, and an hour's hop from two other major traffic streams with a lot of links to other stations.'

'I'll be honest with you... Ralph, I've never liked the vibe at Beacon 505. It's too... transient.' This was true enough, but more of a problem was the fact that Beacon 505 was a foul dump of station, popular with criminals, and was dangerously proximal to several no-go areas and some notorious pirate ambush sites. A big chunk of the 500's were bad territory.

'My brother is fixing all of that, he's drawing in big investors to take the place upscale. Soon it'll be the next best thing to Beacon 3, with casinos, bars, high-class eateries. An act like yours would be the cherry on top; new, classy, high quality. You can use Beacon 505 as a base and work all the linking beacons and stations. You'll get more eyes and ears on your act in a week than you're getting in a year right now. I can get you on any bill on any of those stations, I have a lot of connections.' He gave her a smile that made her uncomfortable, 'You'll be amazed the doors I can open, Monique, really you will.'

'Like I said, Ralph, get it all down, I promise I'll study it, and I'll put it to the band right now.' She pointed at the door.

'Well, why don't I meet the band now? Make the most of the moment, Monique!'

She sighed. Time was wasting, and Commander Guthrie would be expected back aboard the Sabina soon. 'I'll square with you, Ralph. The band aren't in my cabin. Nobody is. I'm tired and I want to rest.'

'Oh,' Parsons looked around, 'I got you.'

'I'm glad you're enthusiastic, I'm just too tired to take it all in, but if you've got a better offer than what we have now, the band and I will take it seriously.'

'That's great to hear.' he looked her up and down, 'Well, I guess you want your beauty sleep, not that you need it.' He moved a little closer.

'Good night, Mister Parsons.'

The ice in her voice and her gaze seemed to do the trick.

'Good night, Monique.' he said, with a tone that was not altogether sincere.

She waited for him to reach the end of the passage before she keyed in her door code, slipped inside and leaned against the door.

'What kept you?'

'Don't ask,' she sighed, tossing her shoes on the floor and grabbing the silk bathrobe from the end of the bed. She took a good long look at Guthrie. He was quite a picture.

Her heart jumped at the click of the door opening behind her, the sound of Ralph Parsons' voice came through, 'I told you you'd be amazed what doors I can open, Monique.' His smiling face appeared as he stepped in, his smile twisting into a confused grimace as he looked around the room.

Commander Guthrie lying naked on the bed might not have surprised Ralph so much if he'd been conscious and didn't have strange mechanisms strapped to his head. Of course what was *really* out of place was the two people in black coveralls manning screens that were hooked up to the Commander's brain.

Monique wheeled about and planted a powerful kick square in Parson's chest, slamming him into the door and slamming it shut as fell against it.

He looked on, dazed and hurting as she fixed him with a glare of cold fury. Hitching up her dress, his eyes drifted down and widened ever further as more and more of her legs were revealed.

'Is this what you wanted, Ralph?'

She slowly pulled the dress up higher. A knife holster strapped high inside her thigh was waiting for her hand. She took a moment to wait for his desire to turn to fear. Palming the knife, she waited a moment more before letting the dress fall again.

'Did you get a good look, Ralph?' She strode up to him and laid her forearm across his throat, pinning him to the door, breathing hot words in his face, 'Did you *make the most of the moment,* Ralph?'

He could only shake as she caressed his chest roughly with the heel of her knife hand. She moved her lips so close to his they were nearly touching, so close he could feel the heat of them.

'I guess you thought you'd get to sleep with me, huh Ralph? Whether I liked it or not. Well, now I think I'd like that too. Do you like the sound of that?' She felt him respond without speaking. She gently rubbed the tip of her nose against his, and gently slid the blade into his chest. 'Sleep tight, Ralph.'

She pushed the blade in deep with the heel of her hand, pressing the switch that engaged the blade's microwave field, automatically cauterising the wound as she pulled out the blade.

He grunted, twitched, gave a brief shudder and slipped out of life, falling to the ground as she released her grip. Not a drop of blood spilled.

She turned to the brain-scanning crew beside the bed, 'How's he?' she said, pointing at the recumbent Commander.

The technician turned his gaze to the vacantly smiling face of Guthrie, 'He's dreaming that he's doing to you what your dead friend there wanted to do with you, and rather enjoying it. We, however, are really pushed for time, and we're not getting much out of him. Some vague images of the day, we can probably pick out some of the stronger faces and words when we get back to the imaging lab and enhance this stuff, but we can't get much more out of him with so little time.'

'He still won't tell me anything, either, but something serious happened today. We need to know what.' Monique looked at her watch, 'Chiff! The Sabina is due to ship out in 23 minutes. You've got to finish up and unhook him so I can wake him up and pack him on his way. Meanwhile, I'll deal with this.'

She toed the corpse of Ralph Parsons, rolling him onto his back. She fetched a camera from her bag and took a photo of him, which immediately scrambled itself into an unrecognisable pattern only the Director of Triple-S back on Beacon 3 could decrypt. Monique tossed the camera to one of the brain-scanning technicians.

'Can you file a Discretionary Elision Docket on this guy for me. We'll need his tracks blurring.'

Discretionary Elision, a sanitised phrase for the killing of an idiot who got themselves into the wrong place at the wrong time, in this case, walking right into a classified operation and risking Gibson's deep cover identity.

'Not very often I have to file a docket for you, Captain.'

'I don't much care for killing if I don't have to.'

'You could have fooled me with what you did to him.'

Monique grabbed a small sphere and some cord from her case. Pushing the sphere against Ralph's belly, she began hog-tying the corpse. 'I didn't ask him to come here, and I didn't invite him in. Who knows how many other women he's done this too? Grubby little chiffer.'

She activated the sphere which began a quiet countdown as she bundled the body into a crush-net. The net began contracting, pulling itself into a tight ball, accompanied by the sound of bones breaking.

'I hope nobody's going to miss him, because nobody's ever going to find him.'

The package of human remains lifted from the floor as the grenade's anti-gravity device raised it to a height clear of any obstacles. The sphere detonated: a steam bomb, an energy pulse that destroyed covalent bonds, bloodlessly tearing anything inside its spherical field into unidentifiable sub-atomic dust.

'You have the coolest toys, Gibson.'

'I know.' she looked around to check nothing incriminating had fallen from Parson's pockets. 'Make sure you spray some Kleen around when you're done, including the corridors all the way back to the main access-way. I want no evidence he was anywhere near here.'

It was true Monique rarely killed anyone. Every death was a snowball set rolling down a hill, her boss always told her. Just about everybody matters to somebody, somewhere. Her thoughts turned to Ralph's brother on Beacon 505, and thought about her own kid brother, and what *she* might do if anybody ever did to him what she had just done to Ralph. Not useful thoughts.

'Okay, Gibson, we're done. Sleeping beauty is all yours.'

She watched as the techs slipped through the adjoining door into the neighbouring cabin and waited to hear the lock click home.

She slipped out of her sparkling red dress and unstrapped the knife holster from her leg, packing them carefully away. She took a spray of saline solution and generously moistened her body. She knew the machines would have given Guthrie a wild time, so she had to look like she'd matched his efforts.

Slipping her robe on, she set it loosely, but made sure it was tied tight. He'd seen more than enough of Monique to be happy with in his manufactured dream, but this was all he would get from the real Captain Melody Gibson.

She slipped under the covers and kissed his cheek. Affecting satisfied exhaustion she whispered in his ear, 'Tell me you didn't fall asleep again?'

He groaned into wakefulness, looking vaguely guilty, 'Sorry. I must be even more exhausted than I thought.'

'Every single time! I think I'm wearing you out, it can't be good for you. We should probably stop doing this, don't you think?'

Guthrie moaned as he began to stir, he looked at her and smiled. 'Don't even joke about that. You wear me out just right.'

'Well, if you're sure.'

'Oh I'm sure. I so needed that tonight. Thank you.'

'I'm glad, but you need to get going. You've got a ship to catch.'

SEPTEMBER

two

A rippling whisper of wind reflecting back from the roadside trees joined the silken howl of the electric turbine, rising in pitch as Glen opened the throttle, sending more power to the unicyke's oversized wheel, the sensations of sound and speed washing over him as he carved his way deftly through the curves of the Pandale City coastal roadway.

He rubbed an appreciative hand on the cowling of the unicyke, the clean swoop of white bodywork tapering from the back wheel to a sharp point at the front —a Yang with no Yin— cutting through the air and breaking out of the leaf-dappled light into glaring sunshine.

The trees gave way to rocky cliffs, opening out to a winding band of polycrete road hugging the edge of the Tallit Sea. Ahead, the city of Pandale, shimmering in a soft haze as it baked in the early autumn sunshine.

Gunning the throttle, Glen felt the tilt actuators correct the rearing nose before it could pitch him off the back.

He shook his wrist, activating voice-dialling on his watch.

'Call Spafford.'

He waited out the call chimes until a voice came through the cyke's speaker.

'Spaff's Shoots, Gun-Grid range to the poor and infamous. How can I help you?'

'Spaff!'

'Glen! It is great to hear from you after so long! How long has it been, 12 minutes? How's the cyke? Notice how casually I ask, "How's the cyke?" because I'm good enough to assume you're not calling me to tell me you've stacked it into a tree.'

'Ha! No. How do you get the front end to rear up when you accelerate?'

'You can ride like a hooligan after you've bought it.'

'This is a test ride, Spaff, I want to know how everything works.'

'Yeah, well, in the words of my ancient forefathers, "you break it, you

bought it.'"

'You come from a wise and noble heritage of grifters, Spaff, now tell me how to loosen up the nose of this thing.'

'You see the little thumb wheel on the left grip?'

'I got it.'

'That's the pitch correction, loosen that up and you'll see some sky.'

Glen spun the ring until it wouldn't go any further and gave the throttle a healthy turn. The horizon fell away as the bike cranked itself skyward.

'Oh spreff! HAHAHA! This is nuts!'

'Glen! Break it, buy it. Got it?'

He eased off the power and the roadway came back into view, he tugged heavily on the brakes and felt the front of the bike take a deep plunge.

'Chiff it! I almost missed my turn!' He leaned the bike over, steering onto the steep two-lane curling up the cliffside, dialling out a little of the slop in the pitch control before opening the throttle again. 'Can you actually get the front of this thing to hit the ground?'

'If they wanted the front to touch the ground they'd have put a wheel on it, Glen!'

'So you've never tried?'

'Listen carefully... Do, not, crash, my cyke! Do you have any idea how rare a hundred and fifty year old Phase-1 Yang Unicyke is?'

'I promise I won't make them any rarer, Spaff.'

'See that you don't. Are you going to buy it?'

'Spaff, you write my pay-checks, how do you of *all* people think I can afford this?'

'I guess I could front you a month or two on your pay.'

'You'd need to front me a *year* or two. I've got every intention of misspending my youth, but I don't want to misspend it all at once.'

The road crested the cliff-top, heading for the sprawling, low-rise town of Tallit Heights, its skyline dominated by its world class Gun-Grid arena. Glen opened her up full throttle and the cyke threw the town at him with intoxicating speed.

'We'll talk about it when you get back from the Tallit Heights shoot, once you've seen how much the girls like it. Maybe you'll have an offer for me, and maybe I'll have an offer for you.'

Glen had an idea what the offer would be, and he was conflicted about it.

'Okay, Spaff. gotta go, I'm nearly at the stadium now.'

'Great, you made it without stacking it. Say hi to anyone I know, unless I hate them.'

'What if you like them and they hate you?'

'Say "hi" insincerely. Oh, and, Glen?'

'Yes?'

'When you come back... don't stack my cyke.'

Glen eased the cyke into the lot, glancing around for somewhere to park up. The place was heaving. The stadium must be packed today; no surprise, it was the final comp of the season.

Dumb luck, there was a jet-bike taking up half a slot right by the west stairs, and there *she* was, sitting on the rail with a couple of her friends.

He eased into the slot and powered the cyke down. The pointed nose of the cyke split into three as the weight shifted forwards, forming a tripod stand.

'Glen?' Yolande cocked her head at the bike, amused, and puzzled, 'what are you doing on that? Is it yours?'

He peeled off the protective gelmet and shot her a wide smile, 'No. I might buy it though. Does it suit me?'

She laughed, 'No.'

You couldn't really be offended by Yolande. She was young, pretty, and her life was easy; she just assumed everyone was as free from hang-ups as she was. If she found something funny, she didn't much care who knew it, she was just letting them in on the joke, even if they were the joke.

He sat next to her on the rail and her friends melted away to leave them alone. 'So you don't want to go for a ride then?'

She seemed to be weighing up the idea. 'I might be tempted, but they want me to give out the prizes for the junior shooters in a few minutes.'

'I can't ever seem to get more than a few minutes alone with you, Yolande? Why is that?'

'You and me, we're just too popular, Glen. What can we do about it? Too beautiful, too talented, we can't help it.' She punched his arm playfully. 'So what's going on with you?'

'Me?' he shrugged, 'The usual? Working at Spaff's shooting range, test riding Spaff's cyke, not buying Spaff's cyke. You?'

Her face lit up, 'Ooh! Of course you don't know yet! Do you?'

'Know what?'

'My parents have decided we're going to emigrate off-world!'

The news was an unexpected verbal punch in the guts, made all the more confusing by the fact it was delivered with a beaming smile and eyes wide with happiness. She seemed pleased.

Glen was not often lost for words; he attempted an appreciative tilt of the head with an eyebrow raise of comprehension, just so she knew he'd actually understood the words she'd said.

Something in his head mustered, 'Where are you going?'

He had a pretty good idea where she was going, the place all the good shooters went. Viafrane. Their shooting season was just about to start as Pandale's ended. It was the next step towards becoming a pro-shooter in the interstellar leagues.

Yolande opened her mouth but was interrupted by the echoing report of nearby gunfire in the arena, followed by a loud cheer from the bleachers. She waited for the commentators and crowds to quiet down and tried again

'We're going to Viafrane! I'm so excited!' Glen tuned out the details of what she was excited about, her voice a background noise as he reeled at the news. Pondering the logistics of how far away she was going, he knew Viafrane was an eight day flight from Pandale, it wasn't even on stream. He became aware Yolande had stopped speaking.

'Wow,' he threw down as a placeholder to give himself time to think, 'that's a long way to come to visit!' She didn't get a chance to register his disappointment, one of the hundreds of people Yolande seemed to know came and shoved themselves into their company, as always seemed to happen.

It was almost impossible to be alone with Yolande —a talented shooter with youth, looks, and humour on her side, she was rapidly becoming a much needed poster-girl for the sport in an era where classic grid-shoots were going out of fashion— she was public property. After years of too brief greetings, embraces and rudely interrupted chats, Glen's alone time with Yolande had always been something measured in minutes, at best.

The memory of the last shoot came back to him, watching the sun go down, the memory of *not* kissing her, because the timing wasn't perfect. He'd spent the intervening month in an internal negotiation, half of him saying he was right not to go too fast, that the age gap was still likely to be a little distasteful to friends and family, and the other half cursing himself as an imbecile. Both halves at least agreed that today was supposed to be the day he'd give himself and Yolande that start. At least, that's what he'd promised himself.

Too slow.

A voice to his side called out to him, 'If it isn't young Master Rothgill! Are you shooting today Glen? Or are you too fast for these local league guys?'

'Too slow.' he mumbled to himself.

'You're a funny guy, Glen!' He felt a slap on his back, 'I've never seen anyone faster on the snap than you, not even close. If you'd take a few more shots instead of being such a perfectionist you could go pro like your brother! How about it? Another Gun-Grid champ in the Rothgill family?'

This attention was not welcome. He wanted whoever the hell it was talking to Yolande to stop talking to Yolande, and whoever this was talking to him to spreff off. Turning to give him a polite brush off, he realised it was Frank Bull, an old friend of the family, and mentor to Glen's brother, Gilbert. Any resentment slipped away.

'Sorry Frank, I was miles away. How've you been?' He took Frank's proffered hand and shook it with warmth.

'Pretty good for an old fart. How's your brother and the rest of the Rothgill clan?'

'I'm fine thanks.' Glen answered automatically.

'Sorry Glen, I know you're in the shadow a little, I'm glad to hear you're good though.'

Glen kept looking at Yolande, hoping for a spot to break back into her conversational sphere. Spreff it! Someone else had come to join her chat now!

'What?' He did a double take, returning his attention to Frank. 'Oh, the family? Yes they're settled into the new home and enjoying it, and Gilbert is loving the pro-circuit. I don't mind people asking about him, I'm used to it.'

'You're still not ready to get back into the arena and follow in his footsteps?'

'You know how I feel about the rule changes, Frank. What's the point of training when they make it so easy for chumps to get lucky wins?'

'A chump's luck won't last a whole season, Glen. Quality shines through, and you'd train anyway. I know you still train, even though you haven't competed in two years. You can't help yourself.

You're a perfectionist. It's your biggest strength and your biggest weakness.'

He squinted questioningly at the man who'd coached him when he first started shooting, 'You've always said that to me, Frank, and I've never understood how it's a weakness.'

'*Nothing* is perfect, Glen. You have to do the best you can, and be adaptable, not just abandon things that don't meet your standards anymore.'

'I know nothing in life is perfect, Frank, but I like to believe that for every imperfect situation, there's a perfect way to handle it, if you just look for it.'

'And you think quitting the league is the perfect way to fix it?'

'If I thought there was a way to fix it I wouldn't have quit. Surely you don't think *I* can fix it?'

Frank shrugged, 'You're a high quality shooter, Glen. Move to Viafrane, be with your family. Get back in the league, work out how to beat the pray-and-spray shooters. Shoot. Win, then say "This is how it should be done." Lead by example. That's the way to fix it.'

Glen shook his head, 'The classic grid-shoot is a dying art, Frank. People want to watch the big open arena stuff now. Who wants to watch these methodical chess matches when they can watch a small war? That's not where I'll find my future, I know that much for certain.' He turned a glance Yolande's way —simultaneously inches, and a million miles away from him— 'But I'm not sure it lies here anymore either.'

Frank nodded, 'Honestly, I think you've been ready for some kind of life change for a while now, Glen, probably ever since your family moved off-world. You're not still toying with the idea of joining the police, are you?'

'No, you were right about that. I don't have the temperament for it. They're perfectionists too, but I know I'm not their idea of perfect.'

'Well there's the thing. If nobody can agree on what perfect is, what's perfect anyway? Thing is Glen, if you live your whole life trying never to do anything wrong, you wind up never doing anything at all. If Gun-Grid is truly done for you, maybe you should make a totally clean break of it.'

What was there going to be left here for him if Yolande was leaving? The *offer* Spaff had hinted at? Glen knew he wanted to ease down on work commitments, and that he'd likely want Glen to take over the day-to-day running of the shooting range. Easy, fun, work for sure, but it seemed a narrow future.

He sighed and nodded, 'Maybe I should at that.'

He felt Yolande tug at his sleeve, her eyes and smile were still like magic to him, that spell hadn't been shattered by her news. 'They want me to present the trophies to the juniors,' she said 'so I'll see you later.'

'Okay. You're going to be at the after-shoot party tonight, right?'

'Aww! I'd have liked that, but the Viafrane trip is a whole big thing. It's an early night tonight, then we're catching the Francesca Reala tomorrow! The Francesca Reala on her maiden voyage! Can you believe it?'

Glen smiled as best he could, 'I really can't.'

Maybe Frank was right. Glen had been waiting for the perfect moment with Yolande, and because of it he'd missed the *best* moment. A month ago they'd sat together alone watching the sun go down, and he hadn't wanted to do anything wrong, so he hadn't done anything at all.

She walked away with a wave and a big smile.

Perfect.

The noise on the bridge of Black Javelin rarely rose above a gentle murmur. A spy ship runs quiet at all times, and the work done here didn't need raised voices, so the loud, clear, clacking of high heels was all the announcement their unexpected visitor required.

The Director of the Triple-S, the Sovereign's Security Service, had about her a weathered beauty; care, trouble and anger had left their subtle signs on her classically elegant face. Sovereign Staff Commander Malahyde watched her approach, waiting to find out why she had intercepted and boarded his craft.

She swept around the ring of consoles circling the command deck's spherical holographic display, trailed by a purposeful looking man in a captain's uniform.

'Commander,' Her voice had the ringing clarity of an expensive music box. 'I need to speak with you and your Flex confidentially. Your briefing room will suit.'

'Yes,' Malahyde responded, with the simple brevity common to those in Black Fleet's highest command stream. The Director and the man accompanying her —a Sovereign Staff Captain wearing no identity badge— entered the briefing room first, Malahyde and his

Flight Executive followed.

'Don't seal the door yet, Commander.' The Director instructed, 'This is your new Flight Executive.' She indicated the captain, then looked at the Flex, 'Major, you are relieved of duty until your Commander notifies you otherwise. You are restricted to non-critical areas of the craft. Please leave.'

The major scowled and growled,

'You know who...'

The Director interrupted him, 'Yes, yes. Your mission is under direct orders of Prime Mover. It's not a priority assignment and you will be resuming it in under 30 hours, which still leaves you 18 hours to complete, at my estimation, 7 hours worth of work.'

Prime Mover was the codename used in the field to refer to the Sovereign. She wasn't *supposed* to know anything about this mission, or even where to find this craft, but here she was, with the correct signal codes to break their radio silence, and seemingly knowing exactly what it was they were doing for the Sovereign. As head of the Sovereign's Security Service there was no point questioning her authority.

'This delay will be noted in my report. I'll need my flight docket notarised before I relinquish mission control.' He drew a holographic roll from his chest pocket and held it out to her.

She touched the ID pad and ticked the relevant boxes with a practiced flourish of her finger. The blue holographic docket turned yellow and the word "SUSPENDED" stamped itself across the page.

If the Flex had any complaints about the Director overriding the Sovereign's orders he left without sharing them. Sovereigns come and go, but the Director was going to be around for a long time to come.

Commander Malahyde thumbed a switch on his desk that activated the door seal and nodded at the new Flex to begin his briefing.

The captain began to speak, his crisp voice carving words into of the air, sharp and precise, 'Tomorrow at noon the Gold-Star Lines newest luxury cruise ship, "Francesca Reala" will drop shell at the tourist world of Pandale. This is the first stop of its maiden voyage. Pandale is in a peaceful region, not on regular patrol routes, and it's expected that a pirate attack will occur very soon after the star-liner goes sub-optic.'

'This is the boat Gold-Star have been claiming is pirate proof?'

'They've been deliberately taunting pirate networks with that claim.' The captain linked his mission scroll into the Commander's log, sending photos and transcripts to his desk screen. 'You can see that over the past year misinformation has been fed to pirate communication channels, through fences, suppliers, and criminal darknet channels, rumouring that corners were cut in the armour, weapons systems, and the Francesca Reala's starfighter complement, along with fake intercepted communiques about the inadequacies of Police and military protection available for this stop.'

The Commander nodded, 'You've baited a trap?'

'This is a joint mission between the Police, PPB, and ourselves. There will be a vast concealed force waiting for the pirates to attack.'

Commander Malahyde didn't hide his surprise at the news. 'And why are we working with the PPB?'

The Director fielded the question, 'It was Prime Mover's idea. This is supposed to be a trust exercise.'

Malahyde snorted aloud.

'My feelings exactly, however, Prime Mover approves of the joint operation, so it's happening. Your mission, Commander, is twofold. Flex?'

'Yes, Director. The PPB have thrown in one of their bigger vessels. The Savatara. She's a Pallas-class frigate, a seriously tooled boat.' The Flex sent images and the crew roster to Malahyde's screen.

'Jowett? I've heard her name before.'

'Yes, Commander. Captain Miranda Jowett has made a name for herself. Military family, raised from the start to be in the PPB Navy, graduated top of her class at the Naval Academy becoming a cult figure along the way.

'She had a small clique of friends, Melissa Rourke, Faye Talbot, and Rosaria Rawlins. Rawlins is her Exo aboard the Savatara, Rourke and Talbot are both captains of the Sabina and the Sonya respectively. They are all top-flight captains, but Jowett is the main danger, she has a pure hatred for Back Fleet.'

The Commander studied her picture closely, she was a true beauty, but it was impossible to ignore her eyes, which were stone cold, severe, and pitiless, 'Why so? Some family connection, did she lose somebody in military action?'

'No, her hatred isn't based on any personal loss, or any personal motivation we can identify other than loyalty to the PPB Navy, passed on through the family. She'll have been told since she was old enough to understand the words that *we* are the enemy, so she hates us. Some people are only too glad to hate if they are told to, and people like that rise up the ranks pretty quickly in the PPB'

'Understood. So what part does the Black Javelin play in all of this?'

'These three frigates, the Savatara, Sabina and Sonya are the chief suspects for heading a secret task force we believe is known in the upper echelons of the PPB as "Project Snipe." The Savatara's whereabouts have consistently been unaccounted for on each occasion a Black Fleet craft has gone missing. Her boat is big enough to carry some form of secret weaponry, maybe even a Sun Gun.'

The Commander shook his head fervently, 'The PPB don't have Sun Guns.'

'Well, they have something. You may remember nearly a year back there was a savage attack on every pirate's favourite hot-mod workshop, the Woolfe Weapon Works. No law enforcement agency had ever been able to locate them before, then the chatter from informants suddenly blew up and the Police followed a tip that led them to a scene of carnage and devastation.

'Woolfe Weapon Works had been deep in an asteroid field out in the high 500's, and it was geared up like a fortress. It would have taken a highly motivated military task force to take them out. The Savatara had been prowling that area along with two other PPB frigates, the Sonya and the Sabina, captained by Jowett's academy classmates Faye Talbot and Melissa Rourke. Alone these three frigates have highly skilful captains and a solid record for ruthless takedowns of pirate junks, operating together they would be formidable.'

'This is the task force you're talking about?'

'It is. The point is, as bad as the damage was at the Woolfe Weapon Works, a lot of their personnel were not accounted for among the dead, including the head of the workshop, Anga-Kaska Woolfe, a master engineer and designer who could have been top in any field he'd chosen.

'I know of his work. You don't think he designed the weapon they're using?'

'Probably not. Whether he designed the weapon is unknown, it seems unlikely he would have the means, or the motivation, but he could certainly help make the most of any experimental weapon system they have. Intercepted reports show the Savatara had been shedding staff at an alarming rate immediately before the attack on Woolfe Weapon Works.

'Jowett may have been whittling her staff down to people she trusts, or making room for extensive modifications to her ship. Either way, if the PPB have developed a new weapon system, the Savatara is certainly big enough to carry something that could take out a Black Fleet dreadnought, but without being Flag class with an Admiral in charge it can move around backwater patrol routes furtively without drawing too much attention to itself.'

'So for once you know exactly where she'll be, so we have a chance to examine and observe her?'

Leaning forward, the Director smoothed her dress over her thighs and lowered her voice, a curious act as there was nobody to overhear, 'That's not all. We think Jowett will try something.' She fixed Malahyde with a look inviting argument.

'I agree,' he said without hesitation. 'Trust means nothing to the PPB, least of all our trust. I assume there will be publicity for this ruckus?'

The Director and the Flex both nodded. 'So Gold-Star can scare the pirates into staying away from their flagship for good.'

'With so many craft fighting, an accident in which one of our vessels was badly damaged would be just the sort of humiliation the PPB would love to deal us.'

'Yes, it could also give us a good idea what weak-point they've been exploiting. None of our missing craft have been recovered or found. They should *not* be able to take down a Black Fleet dreadnought. We must know how they're doing it.'

The Commander studied the orbital chart of the system.

'I assume the three local moons will be used to conceal the ambushing forces. So we'll need a more distant location to observe. We can run black, so we won't need a planetary body to hide behind.'

'There is another aspect to your mission. We have an operative placed in ultra-deep cover aboard one of the pirate junks. He's been instrumental in helping disseminate the misinformation. He is a prized asset, he *must not* be caught in the operation. Running black, you may be able to assist the escape of the junk, but the crew must not be aware they were helped.'

'This is not a combat vessel, Director.'

The Flex answered for her, 'You needn't directly engage anyone, but you may need to deploy counter-measures if any heavy ordnance is thrown their way. That junk must survive, and must escape.'

'Why so?'

'If they are caught there would be no way to reintroduce our asset to the pirate fraternity without raising suspicion that would permanently harm his integration. He is trusted absolutely.'

'Picket, I wouldn't even trust you as far as I could comfortably puke you,' Nemo, gave his fence a hard stare. 'I mean, I don't trust *any* skanky bastard pirate, but I least I know where they're at and what they want. Not you. You and your sharp suit and your smooth talk. You give me the fucking creeps.'

'Nemo, as much as I enjoy the feeling you can inject into these antique swear words, you really should try to make a habit of using HACs, even if only with me.'

'Fuck that. HACs are for people who have the money to go straight. How's that looking with the shitty leads you've been getting lately? Like it's not humiliating enough being a broke pirate? I slip up and saying "Spreff!" or "Chiff!" in public I'd get laughed out of the fucking room, or more likely get my throat cut.'

'Well I'm assuming you'd like to rejoin society one day. Swearing like a pirate doesn't go down too well there either.'

'At this rate by the time I've raised a big enough stake to get out of this business and buy a new identity I'll be too old to remember my own name, let alone what swears I'm supposed to use. What the fuck was that new one they just came out with? "Hurk!"'

Picket shrugged.

'Hurk! Hilarious. A "hurking," "spreffing," "chiffing" chunk of shittery is what all of that is. I tell you now, I'll start using Humana-Approved Curses when you make me some fucking money. *Real* money. Or when I find me another fence who can.'

'Do you think you can find yourself a better fence than me?' Picket didn't leave pause enough for Nemo to claim he could, 'One who'll saddle himself with this barely functional junk and a captain who's got a well-known reputation as risk averse and gun-shy?'

'Well you want to challenge that, don't ya, Picket? No one's going to accuse me of dodging risks if I sign up on this suicide job you've got lined up for tomorrow!'

The atmosphere was more tense than fearful; Nemo was cautious, but he wasn't a coward.

'You know my leads are always good, and they make you money. Real money, not shipmetal and fusion gas you have to trade for booze, whores, and ammunition. With me you can sell anything, to anyone. I know it's been a dry spell, but this attack tomorrow has been tying up all the channels, nobody wants to talk about anything at all in case this thing slips out into the open. Gambala has already ordered three crews wiped out in as many months for even *talking about* how they *might* talk about it so people don't know *what* they're talking about if they *have* to talk about it.'

'Well we should be fine because I no longer have any fucking idea what *you're* talking about.'

Nemo was still young for a pirate captain, and seemed to be very smart in a profession that mostly attracted psychopaths and cretins with rage issues. For all the protestations, Picket knew he was indispensable to Nemo. This outburst was down to stress and fear, which were justified, given what was planned for the morning.

'We always work alone Picket, how did we get talked into this mass attack? Most of these people I'm supposed to fight alongside I wouldn't even talk to without a gun in one hand and a grenade with the pin out in the other, let alone trust any of 'em to share fair in a juicy raid like this.' He sucked on his teeth, turning his pilot's chair back and forth with his feet. 'How are we going to divvy up the spoils? How are we going to take over an entire Cruise ship?' Nemo's voice was raised, though far from shouting.

'How is this going to be anything but a murderous free-for-all, Picket?' He settled his tone; he didn't want the rest of the crew overhearing his doubts. Picket was the only person Nemo trusted enough to see him in anything but total control of himself.

They at least had some privacy; like any pirate junk, the captain's cockpit was a tiny armoured enclosure. Becoming a pirate captain was pretty much always a case of filling a dead man's —or woman's— boots, usually by whoever did the deading. That Picket was allowed inside the cockpit at all showed he was trusted a lot more than Nemo would ever admit.

'Everything about it sounds like it'll shape up to be a bloodbath.

Being in on that will bring heavy heavy heat down, *long-term* heavy heat. Everybody who's there is gonna find themselves on a high-priority kill-or-capture list for the rest of time. "Kill" is gonna get priority over "capture" too.'

'It's been organised by the fences, not the Captains. We're not fighters, we're not backstabbers. We run the percentages and we know there's enough for everyone, and we know we've arranged enough muscle to pull it off. There will never have been so many pirates in one place as there'll be tomorrow. The Francesca Reala doesn't stand a chance.'

'A flashy cruise ship like that, on its maiden voyage, there's going to be a police escort of *some* kind.'

'Not enough of one. Gold-Star have been at Grand Marshal Balfour to give them more police cover and word is, they aren't happy with what they're getting. The solid is, three to five Police cruisers, mix of heavy and regular. Ten would be the absolute maximum. That's absolute worst case scenario, and even then they'd be outnumbered twenty-to-one.'

'You're not the only one who hears rumours, Picket. I heard "the solid" is that the Savatara was spotted at Vondell's gap three days ago, and yesterday she was at Beacon 228. That's tracing a straight line to Pandale. What if *she's* coming to have a look?'

'That's one PPB frigate, Nemo.'

'It's a fucking huge PPB frigate, Pallas-class! Forty high-percussion rail guns, five metre thick multi-structure armour, speed, power and a rate-of-turn to give a fighter pilot whiplash, not to mention the psychopath in the main chair!'

'You seem to know a lot about her.'

'You ought to know the rumours about that boat, Picket. They haven't taken any prisoners in over a year. They're practically a rogue ship and their Captain is a stone cold murderous bitch. There's rumours about the Woolfe Team, too, that it was the Savatara that ripped up Woolfe Weapon Works and took Woolfe's top people so they could find out all the pirate junks weaknesses. If she shows up tomorrow she's going to fuck us all up, and not in the good, sexy way.'

Picket genuinely wished Nemo would stop using the archaic swear words. It often felt forced and it was at odds with the more gentlemanly attitude the captain normally tried to project. It always seemed like Nemo was trying a little too hard to fit in with the crowd. Pirates were all outsiders, but even by those standards, Nemo was a breed apart. Picket felt he'd be better off turning that to his advantage than trying to deny it.

'Nemo, even if only half of the pirates who've promised to show up are there tomorrow the Savatara would be best advised to turn and run. This isn't going to be a pirate hunting pack of half a dozen junks, it's going to be a *fleet,* at least two hundred strong. The Savatara doesn't have any more chance of surviving than the Francesca Reala does.'

The old man could not have been dead for long. A faint edge of steam and soap scent spoke of a recent shower — an hour ago, at most. The quarters were small accommodation for a man of the Admiral's standing, though still the largest available on this far flung supply base, and very well appointed. This had been the Admiral's hideaway, both the quarters, and the base itself.

Christoff Smirnoff stared at the body, the remnants of the closest thing he'd ever had to a father; his mentor, his commanding officer, his protector.

Admiral Milo Wrekin lay on his bed with his hands crossed over his chest, concealing the medals that were a part of his gleaming white dress uniform. His face a picture of peace. Either he'd known death was coming, or he'd given it a helping hand.

Smirnoff let the door close behind him and sat next to the frail man he had worked for these last four years, watching him drifting from a dignified superannuation into wizened enfeeblement.

He caught sight of a gleam beneath the Admiral's fingers. A small key was held in his hand; an old fashioned key for an old fashioned lock. A tag was attached, on it were written two words.

"for Christoff"

Admiral Wrekin's desk was an antique, centuries old, but it was strongly built. The contents of its locked drawers had always been a matter of great secrecy. Smirnoff had never asked about it, and though he'd never told him so, he knew the Admiral had been grateful for that.

Smirnoff's gaze switched between the peaceful rest of the Admiral and the iron-clad wooden desk that dominated the far end of his sleeping quarters like a dark, squatting creature. A guardian of hidden and dangerous truths.

Feeling he should call the doctor, but knowing the Admiral's illness had run its course, and that anything that would be done —even if anything could be done to revive him— could buy only hours; hours of indignity and pain. Admiral Wrekin's secrets had meant more to him than his life, and this was Smirnoff's only chance to secure them.

Shivering with anticipation, he eased himself slowly into the seat behind the desk, feeling a chill at the eerie sensation of sitting in the dead man's chair.

'Christoff!'

He jumped at the sound of his name, he looked at the Admiral's body, startled.

'Christoff!' It was unmistakably Wrekin's voice, the gentle rasp that had become so familiar, but the Admiral was as lifeless and still as he had been when Smirnoff entered the cabin.

Looking down, Smirnoff saw a motion triggered audio chip lying on the desk. It spoke his name again and he reached out to touch it.

'I don't think I've got much longer now, my friend,' the Admiral's voice wheezed.

Sadness swept away fear now. Simply seeing the body was the culmination of Wrekin's slow decline, it had been anticipated, but hearing his voice again made Smirnoff realise just what he had lost.

Christoff Smirnoff was not a good soldier, he hated taking orders, and hated the idea of having to give them. He hated danger, hated confrontation, hated his own mortality, and by association, the mortality of this man who had kept him in a safe assignment on this remote supply base, over two weeks flight from the nearest patrol route.

'Christoff, I've been thinking about your future, and I've been making some arrangements for you. In my hand, or on the floor below it, you will find the key to my desk. Look in there. In the big drawer at the bottom, you will find a folder.'

The document folder was almost too heavy to lift. He needed both hands to raise its heft as he placed it on the desk top.

'People would kill you for this,' the voice told him. Smirnoff could picture the Admiral's expression from his tone; his half smile of care and concern. 'You need to understand that, Christoff. But, this can keep you safe, too.'

Smirnoff began to leaf through the first pages. It was a collection of diary pages, confidential personnel reports on PPB Admirals and Committee members at the highest level.

'I suspect you know I was once very powerful in the PPB Navy.'

He'd never told Smear the details of why he'd allowed himself to be demoted from Over-Admiral, and hidden himself away here in the deep darkness. The Admiral should have been forced into retirement a decade before, but Smirnoff knew he hadn't dared relinquish his access to power completely.

'I had intimate knowledge of all of the PPB's dirtiest dealings, and I never left anything undocumented. It is all in there, Christoff. Every assassination, every plot, every act of sabotage, every betrayal, every crime.

'There are heroes in there too, Christoff, but things never end well for heroes. I know you think of yourself as a coward, Christoff, but you are alive, and I have to believe that is altogether more sane than to be a hero. You will understand as you read.'

There was a deep and troubling rasp of breath, difficult and pained. Christoff shuddered with worry for the health of the man in the recording, even knowing he was already dead.

'I have left you something else, in the top drawer. It's easier to carry, than my documents, but that has also been thought of. First things first, open the drawer.'

Inside were a small ID chip read/writer, and an officer's insignia pouch. A fear-chill ran through Smirnoff.

'I know, Christoff. I know that you have done all you could to avoid command or responsibility, unfortunately, the contents of the pouch are the only way I can extend my protection beyond the grave. You are now a lieutenant. Congratulations.'

Smirnoff opened the pouch and saw the emblems of rank, with his name on the breast badge. He studied the bars, which did not look like a regular lieutenant's bars. They were a gloss black, and rimmed with gold.

'Yes, Christoff. You are now an official Admiral's Courier. That means you can go absolutely anywhere, without question, without search or detainment.'

Maybe for the first time in his life Smirnoff smiled a pure smile of genuine joy.

'You will find my Admiral's grav-bag on the shelf above the bed, I apologise if you have to reach over my body to get it, this is not a perfect situation.'

Smirnoff looked at the last piece of the puzzle, the ID read/writer.

'Of course, you will learn a great deal from my documents and you may,

some day, decide that you are not satisfied with the way things are done. And, you may find something better than fear in you. Or stronger than fear, at least.

'I have also become aware of certain loopholes regarding field-promotions for officers. I won't bore you with the complexities, but someone placed highly enough can arrange for a proxy to issue field-promotions on their behalf. For instance, if I make you my proxy, you can issue field promotions.'

Smirnoff frowned at the audio-chip, unsure why the Admiral believed he would wish to start handing out promotions.

'That is to say, Lieutenant Smirnoff, that through a convoluted back-channel arrangement you can issue field promotions to yourself, through undetectable and unquestionable classified channels.'

Smirnoff's eyes widened at the thought.

'There are limits of course, you can't make yourself an Admiral, obviously, that is a political appointment, not a military one. However, becoming a Captain is not mired in the political horrors of Admiralty, and is, I expect, higher than you would ever seek to elevate yourself anyway. That said, it's always good to have options.'

Smirnoff couldn't think of anything worse.

'It is only because I know you so well that I know you would not abuse this unique privilege. Fear has kept you safe, and heroics do not suit you, which is why I have hopes for you. I have known heroes, Christoff, and those who weren't killed were corrupted. It's a pattern I have never seen avoided. You, Christoff, are something different, but I also sense great decency in you. You will read, and you will come to know things, and you will understand things, and maybe, some day, you will act. Goodbye, Christoff. Goodbye and good luck.'

The recording ended.

Smirnoff was glad at least that the Admiral would not live to see just how badly he was certain to disappoint his mentor's hopes for him.

He looked at the shelf above the bed, spying out the large and sturdy case. He packed the documents inside, placing the ID read/writer at the top and activating the seal. The bag became lighter as its own gravitic field enveloped it.

Placing the bag on the desk and tucking the insignia pouch in his pocket, he touched the intercom to call the infirmary.

'Doctor. Please come to the Admiral's quarters. I'm afraid...' the word caught in his throat, making the half sentence into a statement of its own. He swallowed and began again, 'I'm afraid Admiral Wrekin is dead.'

three

A Black Fleet craft that doesn't want to be seen is not *impossible* to see, merely staggeringly difficult to see, and then only if you knew *exactly* where to look. This far out from Pandale just about the only vessel with the instrumental sensitivity to detect the presence of the spy vessel Black Javelin would be Black Javelin.

Brow furrowed and jaw firmly set, Commander Malahyde eyed the large holographic sphere projected into the centre of the command deck, a three dimensional map of the local system, tracking the few small shuttles and private craft passing to-and-fro between the surface of Pandale and its orbital transport station.

It was deep into night-time for Pandale's capital city, and Gold-Star's new flagship, the Francesca Reala, was not due until noon local time. Before then the ambushing force would assemble and go about concealing itself behind Pandale's 3 moons. For now, Black Javelin was alone.

A small blip indicated a hyper-optic craft dropping shell several million klicks away. Undetectable to local traffic control but glaringly obvious to Black Javelin's deep-field detectors.

The small craft made no approach towards the planet; merely sitting, waiting, observing. A few short minutes passed, then it vanished as swiftly as it had arrived.

A scout for the pirates. Hopefully it had found the sleeping world to its liking. The view would certainly confirm to them that no special arrangements had been made for the arrival of the Francesca Reala, the most exclusive, and most expensive cruise-liner ever built. Ample confirmation that the hubris of Gold-Star Lines would make her new "pirate proof" flagship an easy target.

Seemingly Black Javelin was not the only one to detect the visit from the furtive scout craft; yellow spots flecked the holographic display as dozens of craft began dropping shell — medium and heavy Police cruisers, PPB frigates, and three of the Sovereign's dreadnoughts: Black Wreath, Black Lagoon, and Black Arts.

The small fleet began to spread out and move into cover behind

Pandale's moons while the bigger craft set course for the far side of Pandale itself. The Black Fleet craft needed no cover other than darkness itself. More law-enforcement craft would come as the night wore on, but the ambush was set.

Malahyde turned his attention to his Flex, who nodded and shared a satisfied smile.

'The game is afoot, Commander.'

The meeting chamber of the Select Board was an airy, wide, brightly lit rotunda. A penthouse with no view atop the Chamber of Governor's building at the heart of Culmai city's administrative district.

Governor-Select Cleovald Dofstez, émigré of the Goffa Province, former Governor of Sylvian's World, now here in the rarefied heights of the Chamber of Governors' Select Board, was well versed in the importance of knowing where to sit in a meeting, and knowing where to place his allies.

The Select Board, the Kingmakers of the Protectorate, sat in a semi-circle facing an empty chair, a humble throne in this highest court. It would be occupied soon enough. After over a year in office, Sovereign Benoit was still on probation.

Though notionally the most powerful man who ever lived, the Sovereign ruled at the discretion of the Board, and this boardroom was an intimidating forum. A new Sovereign was given a year to settle in and make no major mistakes, after the second year in office they were expected to have made some form of progress towards the goals they had set out during the selection process. If the board were satisfied the Sovereign would be allowed to spend the final three years of their term with only the lightest scrutiny. Until that point, if the Select Board were *not* satisfied with a Sovereign's performance they were more than happy to kick a sitting Sovereign into political oblivion.

Benoit was only Sovereign now because the Board had done exactly that to his predecessor, Sovereign Edgar Phipps, though for rather more dramatic events than anything that had gone on under Benoit's short tenure. Reason enough for Benoit to have done everything in his power to postpone this appointment, now more than six months overdue.

Governor Select Dofstez had chosen the most shadowy position around the curved table, allowing him to signal and nod to his placemen without drawing the attention of the other board members, or the Sovereign himself.

He was glad to see all of the Humana Faction members had clustered together, an amateurish mistake. Most were new to this level of Government, full of confidence in having one of their own grouping holding the highest office.

The Bradfordians seemed casually intermingled with the independents; an effective illusion. They would allow the Sovereign to relax, then the questions would come from every angle. He wouldn't know where to turn.

Governor Select Maria Pavek, the most senior member of the Select Board, glanced around the room to satisfy herself that everyone was ready. A great stillness swept the room as the conversational hubbub dispersed. With a touch on the intercom she spoke softly, 'Send in the Sovereign.'

The maiden voyage of a luxury cruise ship was always going to be swinging wildly towards the swanky end of the scale, and Linc Bostrom was trying to stave off the pressing awareness that everybody here was a lot richer than he was. He'd bought his ticket, like everyone else, but it had shredded his carefully crafted operating budget, all on a tip that *something* big was going to happen on the trip.

That his cameraman was with him gave his being here in the uppermost VIP lounge a little more legitimacy, in case anybody questioned the quality of his clothes, or his characteristically unkempt hair. He ought to be well enough known as a journalist by now; if not a household name, certainly a face of familiarity.

He wasn't the only reporter here, by any means. Linc's eyes followed Focus Vision News' own star turn, Ben Cranford, as he and his news crew breezed across the deck towards the ship's captain.

Captain Skopa was holding court with a select group of dignitaries and journalists. Linc recognised most, but one gristly looking figure was a mystery to him.

'Bolga,' he nudged his cameraman, nodding towards the group, 'who's that tall guy, the one that looks like he's made out of leather?'

'That's Arthur Carmody. I heard he's here as a strategic consultant. He wrote the book on pirate engagements. Literally. His handbook on strategic and tactical solutions for combat with pirates is required reading for all space-going forces, even in the Goffa Province. He changed the face of deep-space law enforcement.'

Linc nodded, 'Right, I knew the name but not the face. He started out as a fighter pilot, right?'

Bolga nodded, 'Him and his spotter had the highest spike-count of all time. He seemed to be able to think like a pirate, finding and fixing defensive weaknesses pirates could exploit, and he had a fast eye for the pirates' own blind spots that could be exploited. He got promoted fast.

'He's in charge of Fallon Mining's armed forces now, and the way I hear it he may be in charge of the whole company soon. I hear old Ted Fallon doesn't think much of his son's business skills but still wants to promote from inside the company.'

'Well, here's to another blow against nepotism.' Linc caught the eye of Ben Cranford's sound man and gave him a wave, getting a smile and a nod in return.

'We have *got* to get Kurt away from that knucklehead Cranford.'

Bolga nodded, 'I'm sure he'd like breaking real stories instead of watching Cranford wrapping other people's work in FVN branded boredom, but not earning any money may be an obstacle.'

'I know, I know. Being freelance is great for editorial freedom, but not so great for breaking even. Being freelance means there's no free rides, but, believe me, Bolga, I'll pay you back in full before I draw a penny for myself.'

'Spending 10 thou apiece on the tickets to get us aboard the inaugural flight of the Francesca Reala might slow up that plan a little.'

'I know, let's just hope this story pays off, whatever it is.'

The cool metal of the rifle barrel spread a wave of cold across Glen Rothgill's cheek, the sound of the high density air-compressor a subtle whine next to his ear. Crouching in the corner of the square chamber he flitted his eyes in turn to each of the four doorways, waiting for the snap.

Spaff's shooting range was an open roof arena, so Glen was filtering out the natural sounds of breezes and birdsong, attentively listening for the sound of footsteps.

The hunting party were three strong, randomly positioned in the eight-by-eight grid. As the quarry, Glen had his pick of the starting spots, in chess notation he favoured C4 or D3, close to the centre four, and with the prevailing north-easterly winds here at Spafford's range the sound carry gave him a good idea where other gunners were if they weren't quiet enough.

Two doors snapped open, two remained closed. He had only five seconds to choose his move and make it.

Faintly audible, the sound of feet off to the right, and another set of steps, back and to the left of him. He opened one eye, following the soft footsteps. They were two segments over, running north, trying for a two-room jump before the doors could close.

With a smooth motion he stood and slipped sideways to the south door, where the softer steps could be heard.

He stepped through just in time to avoid the snap shut. He paced silently to the centre spot. The Run was on a two-way snap, north-south doors, then east-west. One turn with free position —commonly known as the lurk-turn— and one turn with a compulsory centre.

He turned to the west door, cradling his gun in the crook of his elbow across his body, keeping the muzzle at 46 degrees from horizontal. He didn't need to check for a green light on the top of the gun, his regulation pre-snap stance was a product of thousands of hours shooting. He hadn't triggered a pre-aiming penalty since he was 10 years old.

The east door snapped open, as soon as he saw a pair of feet Glen was raising his gun. His opponent was staring right at him, frozen in surprise at seeing his quarry so soon, in a swift and simple move Glen fired a single slap-round, landing a clean impact square in the centre of the man's protective mask.

The auto-announcer boomed out, "KILL TO QUARRY!"

As the door snapped shut again, he heard a frustrated shout of "Spreff it!" from the other side.

One down, two to go.

The crack of the shot and the impact of the slap-round on their teammate's helmet would have got the attention of the other two hunters, and he'd heard one of them heading North. Whoever that was had been at the edge of the grid, so East was the logical choice, which could put them directly in line with Glen if they'd done a two-room jump.

The next door sequence would be north-south snap, which would lay open a clear field of fire down all eight segments, but he was free to lurk out of sight until the last moment, or he could just wait it out here and hope to catch someone off guard.

He stealthily crept to the south door and crouched at the edge. He listened for footsteps but heard nothing. There could be someone in the room behind him, but Rothgill was confident that no one was quiet enough to evade his sharp hearing.

The doors snapped open, Rothgill snapped up his rifle and sighted the north door. From this position someone could be just around the door edge, but there was nothing to see or hear. Unmoving, his mind ticked off the five seconds of the door cycle, rehearsing his physical moves in his mind: a roll right, and roll back, a roll left.

He threw himself over his right shoulder, watching the doorway as he rolled. His eyes widened at the figure of a young woman running toward the door of the next room. She lifted her gun and sprayed a few rounds as Glen rolled backwards through the door. A round spanged off the ground right by his ear as he flung himself to the left and the door slammed shut.

Had she made it through the door?

He stilled himself.

He could hear her breathing in the next room. He didn't trouble himself to quiet his steps as he took his place at the centre. She'd have to choose to go west or east. Glen didn't doubt he could shoot faster than she could, but if she knew exactly where he was going to be she could take him down with her. With one of the hunting party still alive, that would still count as a win for them.

The east-west doors snapped open. Rothgill waited. He could hear nothing from the room to the north. She was waiting for him to make his move. He smiled, tensing his muscles.

He broke into a loud run for the west door, for what he hoped was long enough to tempt her to follow. He dropped to the floor, flipped onto his front and pulled his knees up for a two-legged frog-leap back where he'd come from and up into a powerful sprint. His legs were a blur as he pounded to the door which would close any second. If the door shut on him it would be an instant disqualification.

He hurled himself onto the floor and into a slide as the door started to cycle. He pulled himself into a ball, tucking in all of his extremities to avoid anything getting caught under the door. He felt a rush of air on the back of neck and heard a slam that was uncomfortably close.

'I need to polish these floors more often,' he found himself whispering.

South was the obvious next move, it would put him at the edge of the grid so he'd only have to defend the north door on the vertical snap, but he'd still be exposed in two directions from the centre.

The obvious move would normally be best avoided, but if he moved away too far from the hunters they could be roaming around the grid for an hour without seeing each other. That was not what he wanted to be doing an hour from now, or even half an hour from now.

The young woman would have a good idea where he was, but with the door cycles she should now be at least three moves away from him. His less than stealthy athleticism may have alerted her surviving friend to his location, however.

He stood quietly and stepped softly to the left side of the south door, pressing his back against the wall.

The doors snapped open. Glen quickly eye-balled the north door, edging his head out for a clear view down the grid.

The run was clear. He swept the muzzle of his rifle into the south room, following it in with soft steps, taking his place on the centre spot. He shut his eyes and turned his head slowly, trying to make out any nearby footfalls.

The girl *could* be in the next room over, if so she'd have a clear shot, but with an empty room between them she might not have good enough aim at that range. Or maybe she hadn't taken the bait of his phoney run and was right next door? Or maybe she'd anticipated his obvious move south and had headed the other way to get around to the *east* of him?

His eyes snapped open as he heard a shuffle of feet in the room to his right. It couldn't be her, even if she was as fast as Glen it would take three moves for her to make up that much ground.

Unless... she seemed to favour two-room jumps, and she *could* have made it if she'd ignored his fake run. He turned to the east door, standing ready.

The door snapped open. Not her. There, with his back to Glen, was the other hunter, totally unaware Glen was behind him. Glen chuckled and fired a round into the back of his head.

At the exact same moment he felt the slap of a round in his own back.

"QUARRY LOSES!"

He turned around and saw the young lady, hand on her hip, gun muzzle in the air and a beaming smile on her face.

'I shot a Rothgill!'

Sovereign Staff Commander Malahyde paced around the circle of consoles surrounding the hologramatic sphere at the centre of Black Javelin's bridge. Dominating the display was Pandale. Near to it, a yellow box showing where the Francesca Reala was due to drop shell.

On the other side of the world a collection of PPB frigates, Police heavy cruisers and a small group of Black Fleet dreadnoughts lurked. Closer to the edge of the display was Pandale's largest moon with another cluster of craft hiding behind it. Each and every craft was flagged and tagged — all illuminated in green for friendly.

Malahyde considered the novelty of seeing PPB craft flagged green while reading off the names. One important name was missing. He turned to his new Flex, raising a quizzical eyebrow.

'There's still time, Commander, and remember, the Savatara is not the only craft of interest to us today.'

Malahyde turned back to the display just as two yellow dots flashed into view; two hyper-optic craft dropping shell. The targeting system processed their shape and the dots morphed into the long cigar shapes of PPB frigates, one larger than the other. Their identity flags appeared: *Sonya, Savatara.* Momentarily the tags turned red for hostile, then green. The Flex approached the weapons desk and tapped in an override code. The two craft turned purple and the vast surveillance suite of Black Javelin began to scan both craft in detail.

'Now, Commander, we get to see just how brazen Captain Miranda Jowett has become, and, maybe, we get to discover what tactical weaknesses the PPB may have found in our dreadnoughts.'

Malahyde turned a wary eye to the Flex. 'As long as they don't demonstrate it on us.'

Captain Skopa began tapping a fingernail against his champagne flute and a reverent silence settled on the large crowd of VIPs and news crews filling the forward lounge of the Francesca Reala.

'Honoured guests, on behalf of the Gold-Star company, the crew of this vessel, and on my own behalf, I want to thank you for joining us on this, the maiden voyage of our new flagship, the

Francesca Reala.

'The deathbed wish of our founder was for a new ship to be commissioned in honour of his late wife, and that it must be the fastest, the most technologically advanced, and the most unforgettably beautiful vessel ever made.

'How patient, you, our first passengers have been to have waited to see her. Brought to a secret hangar, ferried aboard on shuttles with no windows, confined to the outermost decks and unable to see anything outside of your portholes but stars.

'It would be unforgivable of us to drop shell and allow the whole Protectorate to see this stunning ship before you have any idea how she looks. Which is why the centrepiece sculpture of this lounge has been covered too.'

The Captain gestured towards a dais surrounded by a heavily embroidered silk curtain with stars, nebulae, moons, comets and planets picked out in silver thread on the rich cream fabric.

'Ladies and gentleman, grown from a single crystal of milk-dymond and cut by eighty of the finest dymond sculptors in the Protectorate, this is the Francesca Reala!'

The curtain dropped. The crowd did not gasp, it was a softer sound, of lungs holding on to the last breath they'd had, in case they may never be able to breathe again.

The sculpture was an elaborate, exquisite collection of curves and swoops, sleek and complex, supple yet skeletal. It was as if a giant inexplicable sea-creature were hovering in the centre of the room. A pale diamond squid; organic and adamantine. Its surfaces were a blend of disparate textures and shades of white; entwining tentacles of pearl, ivory, quartz, chalk, marble, platinum, and bleached bones.

A spontaneous and deafening explosion of applause filled the room. Linc stuck his fingers in his ears. He was impressed too, but he hoped this wasn't all he would be getting for blowing twenty grand on the tickets for this shindig.

Bolga had all of this covered, there was nothing to do but roll the cameras, so Linc turned his eyes instead to the crowd. Being a head taller than most everybody in the room made it easy to take in the surroundings.

There had been one notable person who was as tall as Linc here —besides his ever present cameraman— and that head was not visible in the crowd. Arthur Carmody wasn't taking part in the celebrations, so just where had he taken his leathery head, so praised and prized for its knowledge of pirate tactics?

Linc was getting the feeling that Kurt's tip-off about this inaugural flight being more than a VIP-watching opportunity might be on the money.

The crowd were still cooing and wowing over the statue, so Linc took his chance to get a good spot in front of the panoramic window at the front of the lounge, ready for the shell-drop when the Francesca Reala went sub-optic.

Right now there was nothing to see but the black fog of the anti-light shell, the bubble of annihilated photons that created a pocket universe unbound by the restrictions of multiplying mass that would otherwise prevent hyper-optic flight.

Soon enough the black fog would part and they would take up orbit around the tourist playground of Pandale. What might happen then, Linc could only wonder.

'Good spot,' Bolga said, taking his place next to Linc.

'Yeah. I think we're going to have something to see, too. Did you notice Carmody's not here?'

'They're expecting something when we drop shell?'

'That's my guess.'

Bolga double-checked his camera and hoisted it onto his shoulder, 'Let's hope it's at least twenty thousand Bucks worth of something.'

Sovereign Tobias Benoit was managing to exude an air of contentedness in spite of the awkward questions he'd been fielding. He clearly felt he was acquitting himself adequately, although in this room that was probably a minority view.

His replies had been getting longer, and it had felt like he'd been building up to a speech. Now the questions were over, the Sovereign was determined to have not only the last word, but to squeeze a lot more words in before it.

'I know that this board is still very much dominated by a classical view of the Protectorate, where Black Fleet should be the protector, and where the Sovereign should be seen as a military enforcer, a figurehead of the political power of all the worlds this side of the Goffa province, but that's just not the reality we're living in anymore.

'Black Fleet has been operating under arms limitations for decades now, and the PPB are the majority patroller, and the most visible enforcer of off-world law. We have no borders between us. Their worlds are as intermingled with ours as salt and pepper sprinkled on a plate of food. We *have* to stop treating them like an enemy.

'Sovereign Phipps had a lot of qualities I admire, but you replaced him with me because I represent where most people are in their political views now. The Humana Faction has been mopping up elections where once it was nothing but Bradfordian individualism and all that brownhole about the pioneer spirit.

'The Protectorate has been peddling this image of the PPB as Luddites and thieves, but most people are very in tune with where the modern PPB are placing themselves. I'm not saying we in the Humana faction are in lock-step with the PPB, but we're closer to them on lots of issues than we are to our protectorate "allies" in the Bradfordian camp.

'We don't want a repeal of the bans on artificial intelligence, or genetic manipulation, or trans-humanism. We don't want machines who are smarter than us, we don't want genetic freaks or cyborgs, or whatever else science can concoct to debase our humanity. Naturalism has served us well enough. We want to be human, and to wear our age and imperfections with dignity, not to be distorted by vanity or the desire to feel superior to others.

'If that's the road the Goffa want to walk on their side of the border, that's a matter for them, but nobody seriously expects the PPB to storm the border and force their views on the Goffa province. They object in principle only, they'll risk no war with the Goffa, even if they no longer have to balance their forces against our own.

'I'm doing everything I can to change our relationship with the PPB, so they become allies that we can disagree with, instead of antagonists we're ideologically opposed to. The voters of the Protectorate clearly don't feel threatened enough to keep voting for Bradfordian candidates, and with that in mind, I've made the unprecedented move of reaching out to the PPB, to arrange for a very high profile co-operative mission involving the PPB Navy and our Black Fleet, fighting side by side.

'And do you know what? It was harder to convince Black Fleet Staff Command to take part than it was to get the PPB Chairman and Over-Admiral Connors on-board!

'Any minute now the Francesca Reala will make its public debut at its first scheduled stop over at the tourist world of Pandale.

'Through discreet channels leaks have been made over the last few months that the new flagship of Gold-Star lines isn't as pirate proof as her builders claimed, rumours that she is in fact a very long way from it. Our intelligence services estimate well over 100 pirate junks, and maybe as many as 200, are expected to try to deliver a humiliating bloody nose to Gold-Star lines for claiming any ship is "pirate proof."

'In reality, the Francesca Reala is every bit as tough as she's advertised, and she won't be alone at Pandale. Lying in wait in the shadows of Pandale and her three moons there is a small fleet of Police heavy cruisers, PPB frigates and Black Fleet dreadnoughts waiting to stage the largest ambush since the defeat of Barnaby Shostalitz's fleet at the Grarna Cluster.

'Today the people of both the Focus Protectorate, and of the PPB are going to see us working together. They're going to see that there is nothing to fear from the neighbours, and that there never really was.'

'She's looking at you.'

Glen looked up and saw her turn away as he caught her eye.

'Everybody's got to look somewhere, Spaff.'

'She's been looking at you quite a bit though.' Spafford gave him a conspiratorial look, 'Did you let her win?'

Glen shot him a disapproving glance, 'I've never *let* anybody win, Spaff.'

Spafford shrugged, 'I think she thinks you did, maybe you should have taken advantage of the goodwill. She was pretty tasty, you should have asked her out. She was in a good mood after beating you, and she's a tourist, so no strings.'

Glen tossed his body-armour over the counter and released the ammo clip from his rifle. 'She's pretty, but I don't want to date someone who's shot me, it sets a bad precedent.'

'I think you wanted her to win, you're a sucker for the lookers.'

'If that door had opened and she'd been standing there in front of me instead of her pal I might have let myself be a little slow, give her more of a chance, but that was a legit match. I'm not unbeatable, especially with three against one. You know I prefer a one-on-one hunt. Quarry matches were my brother's speciality, and I'm not my brother.'

'Maybe not, but you've got his name, and when you've got a name, people will want to test you out. Long standing tradition. It's the curse of the gunslinger.'

'It doesn't hurt to get beat once in a while.'

'Doesn't hurt business, anyway. They're pretty happy to have beaten you, even if you did make the two guys look like chumps.'

'Well, I've got no reputation to fight for.'

'Except your record for clean shots, which stands steady.' Spafford checked the ammo clip. 'Two top-shelf head-shot takedowns, with two rounds. It's got to be four years since I last saw you miss a shot. If you were prepared to join the "pray and spray" guys and squirt off a loose few once in a while you could still go professional, instead of being chased around by tourists, and letting them win to help keep me in business.'

'I really *didn't* let them win.'

'Whatever you say. But that first kill was stunning, the door hadn't even finished opening. That's as good a shot as I've ever seen, and I've seen pretty much all of them. You didn't even bother doing your *"trick,"* if you had they would have been chasing you for a half hour and you'd have picked them off like tin ducks.'

'My *trick* is only safe to use in a one-on-one match.' Glen hopped over the counter and turned up the volume on the video screen, 'And I didn't feel like spending a half hour stalking tourists.'

The screen was just a star-scape, with the edge of Pandale's moon in view. A clock was ticking down the minutes until the arrival of the Francesca Reala.

'Ahh! I see. You wanted to finish the match quickly so you could watch the Francesca Reala arrive. You have a sudden interest in luxury liners, Glen?'

'I just want to see how she looks. There's been a lot of hype about it. This is the first stop of her maiden voyage.'

'So nothing to do with a certain girl you know who's going to be a passenger?'

'Cram it.'

Spaff grinned, 'You know, Glen, I know Yolande's pretty and all of that, but she's really not on your level.' Spaff could see Glen bristling at the implication, 'Look, I'm not saying she's dumb, not at all, she's just not as bright as you.'

'She's plenty bright, she's just young.'

'So are you, and you were a LOT smarter than her when you were that age. A guy like you needs someone who's a match for their mind, not just a treat for the eyes.' Glen shrugged away the comment. Spaff knew there was no breaking through those feelings with logic. 'What time does her shuttle leave?'

'It's already gone, it'll be the first to dock.' Glen pointed at the screen, 'There it is, waiting in low orbit. They should have a great view when the Francesca Reala drops shell.'

'Didn't you want to see her off?'

'Those three had already booked the time-slot. A booking is a promise, and I always keep my promises.'

'You missed seeing your crush before she goes off-world so you could get shot in the back by a woman that you didn't even ask on a date? I admire your principles, Glen, but your personal priorities are pretty weird.'

Glen waved his hands to hush Spafford up. The arrival countdown was getting close to the minute mark.

The view out of the window of the VIP lounge was nothing but the beyond-black fog of the anti-light shell; a darkness so profound it seemed to be pulling light out of the observation lounge itself.

The fog evaporated and every eye in the room squinted, adjusting to the dazzling sphere of Pandale, radiant in the mid-morning sun, a world of deep green forests and red rock, set in shallow seas that were closer to purple than blue. Polite applause rippled through the observation deck.

Linc turned to Bolga with a questioning look and whispered, 'I was expecting more of a reception committee for the inaugural flight of Gold-Star's new flagship. Aren't there normally hundreds of freighters and shuttles in orbit shooting off star-flares to welcome a new ship like this?'

Bolga looked troubled, 'It's strange. The only thing my camera's picking up in orbit is one shuttle, maybe there's a surprise planned?'

Linc frowned for a moment, then it seemed that Bolga may have been right after all, 'Oh! Here we go!'

Small dots started popping into view, dozens of small craft dropping shell, and the audience started applauding again, anticipating a show of some kind.

The Captain spoke up. His voice grave and determined. 'Ladies and gentlemen, I didn't want to pre-announce any kind of show for our arrival, because it's been in planning for over a year, and we honestly didn't know if it would work. Today you will see not flotillas and star-flares, but old fashioned fireworks the likes of which you could not have imagined.' He turned to the officer standing next to him, 'Launch the fighters.'

Picket stood next to Nemo drumming his fingers on the control console. Nemo gave him a cold look which Picket returned with interest.

'We can't wait any longer, Captain. The first junks will have already dropped shell, they'll be moving in to engage the Francesca Reala right now. If we want a piece of the pie we *have* to be in with the first wave. If we turn up late no one's going to cut us in.'

'I should just pull out of this stinking ambush now, I don't owe any of these murderous pricks anything, and we'll probably have to fight them just as hard afterwards to get any share of the spoils.'

'Those who risk nothing gain nothing, Nemo. You need to build your reputation, urgently. A lot of the other pirates think you're soft, and that you don't have the stomach for this business. That's a very dangerous reputation for a pirate captain to carry. It's not just dangerous for him, but for his whole crew.'

Nemo knew it was true. He was a young captain, and he avoided confrontation because he'd seen better men than him die in dumb fights. As much as any money that might be up for grabs, he needed to prove this junk and this crew could punch above their weight, and to prove that his lack of aggression was not a lack of courage.

He picked up the intercom handset, his voice had a rousing power and confidence that were nowhere to be seen on his face, 'Weapons team, power team, fire team, this is Nemo. Get ready for hell, we're dropping shell!' He threw the handset down on the console.

Picket nodded his approval, though he could see his captain's face was taut with anxiety. 'If I push you, Nemo, I only push you where you already know you need to go.'

'Cram it, Picket.'

Nemo fingered the button that would drop the anti-light shell, waiting for their circling hyper-optic path the intersect with the Pandale drop-zone, adrenaline sending an electric surge through his body, his fingertips buzzing, his teeth clenched, he punched the button and the black fog lifted.

Ahead was what must be the Francesca Reala. It was an

arrestingly beautiful vision, surrounded by a vision of horror. Over two hundred pirate junks were swarming like bees, each time a junk tried to escape the swarm it would flash brightly, then fade into a small cloud of debris, carried by what inertia remained to it. Nemo estimated there must be at least a hundred Police heavy cruisers, twenty PPB frigates and eight Black Fleet dreadnoughts.

The pirate junks were corralled into a rough sphere, far apart enough not to collide with each other, but too close to risk a hyper-optic escape. This was a trap the likes of which Nemo had never seen — ingeniously coordinated outside, chaotic and deadly inside.

Was the law expecting to arrest all these people? This vast force of murderers, thieves and psychopaths? These were not people who would let themselves be arrested, this was going to be a massacre.

Nemo made a decision, a decision that those trapped and fighting for their lives in the swarm could not, he grabbed the intercom handset, 'It's an ambush! Divert all weapon power to the drive lasers, we need hyper-optic drive and we need it now!' He gripped the controls and flipped the junk about, engaging full manoeuvring thrust toward the shadow of Pandale's nearest moon.

The intercom squawked. *'Nemo, it's the weapons team, we need some gun power, we're tracking a Police razor-torpedo that looks like it wants to take us forcefully from behind.'*

'Can't spare it. Any time we lose from drive prep is going to give them more time to intercept us.'

'If you're putting the power team in a race against this torpedo, we're all going to lose. Tap off some power and we can knock it out.'

'Every shot I spare you adds charge time to the hyper-optic drives and gives them time to fire more torpedoes, we can't build up to hyper-optic power while weapons are online.'

'And you think we can when the rear drives are getting corn-holed by a cop's cutter-bomb?'

'How long to impact?'

'43 seconds.'

Nemo looked at the drive gauge countdown. They were still 57 seconds away from minimum power for a short trans-optic burst to get them clear. He rubbed his brow and turned a sour look to Picket, 'Killed or caught, Picket? You've never let me down before, but fuck it all if you haven't managed to make the first time the worst time!' He switched channels and began to bark an order,

'Power team, divert...' he felt a hand on his shoulder. He knocked it away angrily and flashed a murderous glance at Picket. Picket shook his head calmly and pointed ahead.

Nemo followed the finger along its path to the space ahead of them. Against the stars was a dark shape, almost invisible but for the stars it was obscuring, until flashes of weapons fire studded her surface.

Nemo flung the controls over, throwing the junk into a wild lateral roll.

The intercom squawked again, *'Weapons team, that torpedo's just popped!'*

Nemo laughed out loud, 'HA! A Black Fleet dreadnought just took a shot at us with its Double-Eights! It knocked out the torpedo! You wouldn't dare dream of luck like that!'

The drive-power gauge flashed green and without even thinking Nemo jabbed at the ignition switch. Blackness engulfed the junk once more.

'Quite an escape, Captain. Congratulations.'

Nemo snapped a murderous glance towards Picket. 'Yeah, Picket, thanks to me the crew is safe.' His voice was filed with cold fury, 'Most of the crew is, anyway.'

Picket nodded coolly, 'Nemo, one of these days, you'll be the death of me,' Pulling an anti-personnel grenade from his pocket, flashing the base to show Nemo the timer was set for a half-second delay, 'Or, I'll be the death of you.' He flicked at the grenade's trigger bar with his finger, 'But not today.'

Linc placed a hand on his cameraman's back, 'Bolga, most of the news media folk here are streaming live, if we're going to have a story to sell we need to get stuff the others aren't paying attention to.'

'Black Fleet don't show themselves much these days, I'm filming them from here, but I'm managing camera feeds from Francesca Reala's external monitors too, so I should have plenty of angles.'

'Good thinking. I've never seen this many Black Fleet dreadnoughts in one place. Once we're done we can hook up with some tactical analysts to talk weapons and strategies, get some depth.'

The panoramic window of the Francesca Reala's VIP lounge was certainly a fantastic grandstand for this bloodsport. The pirate junks were corralled into a loose ball that the well organised fighters, frigates, dreadnoughts and Police cruisers were slowly tightening. It seemed doubtful this nervous acquiescence from the pirate junks would last much longer.

'I haven't seen this strategy before, Bolga. You ever seen anything like this in your time in the Goffa Army?'

'No. This must be something Arthur Carmody has cooked up. It's working for now, but it can't be long before the pirates try to force a weak spot open with a mass push. They're out-gunned but they're not outnumbered, not even close, and these aren't the sort of people who want to get caught.'

Bolga's instincts seemed sound, the spinning swarm of junks was starting to move more quickly, swirling like fish dodging predators— darting, rolling, roiling.

'I hate to mention it, but of all the ships keeping them holed up here, which one is going to seem like the weakest spot they could push at?'

Bolga nodded slowly, 'I know.'

An air of tension swept through the crowd of onlookers watching the tentative swirl of the battle outside and reading the language of movement, sensing an impending surge of aggression from the junks.

This beautiful craft had been instrumental in luring them into danger. The Francesca Reala wasn't just an observer here, she wasn't just bait, she was a combatant. This ship was armed, and firing, and was as much in the firing line as any of the military or Police vessels here. The claims that she was pirate proof, had always had a hubristic ring that few of her passengers were eager to see tested, especially given the scale of this pirate fleet.

Linc could even sense the tension from his normally implacable cameraman. The pirate fleet seemed to be building up to a surge which must surely be coming their way. Amidst the dedicated weaponry and armour of the Police heavy cruisers and the brutal power of the Black Fleet and PPB vessels, the Francesca Reala must seem the weakest point in the net that was binding them.

Linc clenched his fists as the swarm seemed to be forming itself into a tight fist of its own.

'LOOK!'

The crowd saw a black shape below them flare into life. A Black Fleet dreadnought flashing on all of its running lights, spotlights and emergency strobes, coming about and powering towards the swarm like a submarine rising from the depths.

The voice of the dreadnought's commander came over the lounge speakers, 'This is Black Frost, we are going Range Zero.'

The Black Frost smashed into the heart of the swirling junks, not even bothering with weapons fire, flinging pirate craft in all directions, explosions speckling the hull like firecrackers as the generator heads of the smashed junks ruptured, tearing them to pieces.

The crowd let out screeching whoops of joy tinged with an edge of relief. Unspoken fears that had just been put to rest by the Black Frost's bold plunge into the fray.

The swarm had started to turn on the predator in their midst, seeing a chance to weaken the force against them. The Black Frost was making no attempt to escape despite the strafing runs of the braver pirate captains. At each run, the dark bulk would pivot and turn with astonishing speed, bringing its Double-Eights to bear and tearing the attackers to shreds.

The encircling force started moving in closer, tightening their grip further, filling the space left in their cage by the Black Frost's surge, sealing any possible escape route.

The captain of the Francesca Reala's voice spoke to them again, relaying snippets of the radio chatter he felt would be suitable for the ears of the guests, 'Police Marshal Giannini reports that several of the pirate junks are asking to surrender, the police are attempting to organise a passage for surrendering ships to reach the perimeter where their junks can dock and submit to seizure and arrest. It could be a ploy of course; needless to say, the only passengers we plan to take on board *this* ship are the ones aboard the Pandale shuttle!'

A ripple of laughter ran through the lounge. The shuttle was still some way away from the conflict; stuck in a low parking-orbit, their docking would be delayed for quite some time, but they should at least be getting a good show.

There was a subtle change in the swirling tactical dance in the vacuum outside, cautious turns — a slower and more methodical shifting in the movements of the junks. A small group were forming up in convoy and heading slowly for the edge of the sphere; maybe with surrender in mind, maybe something else.

A junk near the front of the small convoy came under fire from another pirate craft. As it erupted in flame, a stab of fire from Black Frost delivered instant punishment to the attackers, blasting them into fragments. The convoy carried on undisturbed. If anyone else had a problem with these junks surrendering, they weren't going to risk making a point about it.

A police prison transporter came about, turning side-on to the approaching pirate junks and presenting its docking ports ready to take their surrender.

'They're getting ready to dock, if the rest have any sense, they'll soon do the same.'

The convoy was spreading out into a line, drifting steadily towards the police transporter's docking ports. As one, they put in a surge of acceleration and opened fire on the transporter's flanks.

A surge from within the main group of pirate junks accelerated at full power toward the sudden firefight.

The onslaught was tearing open the side of the transporter, forcing it back and opening up a gap in the net. Four pirate junks slipped through. A police heavy cruiser had zeroed on them, letting slip a clutch of razor torpedoes. The first found its mark, ripping away the drives of the last junk through the net.

A barrage of fire followed the lead pair, intersecting precisely where the junks had just been. The junks weren't there, just a fading black fog of the anti-light wake from a hyper-optic burst-jump. They'd escaped.

A swelling tide of pirate junks was thrusting for the weak point as the crippled police transporter retreated.

Arthur Carmody's communications to the task force were being played into the lounge, *'Free fire. Aim for the front of the pack.'*

A withering exchange of fire broke out from both sides. It looked like there was clear space. The gap was clear to all, and every junk was coming about to try to force it wider, and to force their way out. This was now a desperate bid for freedom, and survival.

A woman's voice came across the speakers, *'This is Savatara going range zero. Maintain free fire. Remove us from FoF protocols, we will sustain no damage.'*

A white shape moved across the gap, swinging about, the Savatara was placing itself on a collision course with the fleeing pirates.

Carmody's voice again, 'All craft bar Black Fleet clear the Savatara from your Friend-or-Foe codes. Maintain fire.'

The female voice came through again, strikingly hard and cut through with ice. *'Repeat, all craft clear FoF protocols, we will not sustain damage.'*

There was a pause before Carmody amended his orders. As he did so, the great white bulk of the Savatara thrust itself through the gap, all guns blazing. The junks scattered as once again they were smashed out of the way.

The Savatara was a battle-scarred beast, without the bright gleam and dazzle of most PPB frigates. The electroluminescent coating of her hull was either switched off, or no longer working, her hull dirty and dented. Though it was a bigger vessel than the Black Frost, it did not so easily plow through the massed ranks of the pirate fleet; Black Frost's charge had been like a fist, the Savatara more like a spear, just as deadly in its own way.

Both craft were fighting together, but not side by side. The Black Frost could remain mostly still, pivoting and lashing out with impunity, the Savatara was less manoeuvrable at a standstill, and was instead relying on moving quickly and demonstrating an impressive rate-of-turn.

Police cruisers closed the gap left by the transporter and again the net tightened, now as close as they risked getting to each other without coming within range of the guns of the craft on the other side of the sphere.

By Linc's guess, there were only around eighty pirate junks left intact. A few were floating disabled, but the rest were just floating clouds of debris. They were far enough away not to see any bodies floating in the vacuum, but the dead must certainly be numbered in the hundreds.

With their chance of escape sealed once more, another lull swept through what remained of the pirate fleet.

Carmody spoke to the task force again. *'Defensive fire only. Let's give them some thinking time.'*

Another voice came through; the voice of a very young man that sounded closer to that of an adolescent than a commanding officer. *'This is Black Wreath. I suggest any further attempts to take surrender are handled by Black Fleet and PPB craft. We have reinforced docking ports, strong enough armour to withstand anything they're likely to throw at us, and well-tooled and trained anti-incursion squads in case they debark feeling feisty.'*

'Agreed. We have a new batch wanting to surrender. I'm assigning Black Death, Savatara, Black Wreath and Saskia to take aboard prisoners.'

The woman's voice spoke again, *'Negative, the Savatara has no facilities for prisoners. We will monitor surrendering junks to prevent any further attempts to attack law enforcement.'*

Arthur Carmody was not used to being argued with, but the captain of the Savatara sounded like she had little use for arguments either. The Savatara was supposed to be a patrol vessel, and must have facilities for prisoners, but though he was in notional charge of this operation, Carmody was a civilian with no authority to demand that a military vessel take aboard prisoners.

'I see. If the captain of the Felicity has no objections to taking aboard prisoners, the vessels named should move inside the perimeter and muster armed teams to greet new passengers. I doubt the fight has been knocked out of all these people yet. Don't be surprised if things get ugly when you meet them face to face.'

Linc noticed Bolga wasn't filming Black Frost or the Savatara. 'You not interested in the heart of the fight, Bolga?'

He shook his head, 'The Francesca Reala's camera feeds will have all of that, I'm interested in Black Wreath, she's one of Black Fleet's training craft.'

'Their captain sounded spreffing young to be in charge of a training ship, or any ship, frankly.'

'He's ranked Commander. Black Fleet don't have captains. Well, they do, but not like the PPB. Captain isn't a high rank, it's more like an army captain.'

'I live and learn. He still sounded spreffing young.'

'He will be. Black Fleet believe in an extreme version of the Independent Didactic Method. There are no officers aboard their training vessels except the Quartermaster. The computer assigns jobs randomly to the cadets and they have to be ready to do them. That commander might have been running the laundry yesterday, and fixing the engines the day before.'

'That's terrifying!'

'We had a similar system in the Goffa army. Learning by doing. Those are the lessons that stick with you.'

Arthur Carmody's voice came over the speakers again, *'We have seven pirate junks wanting to surrender. To begin with I only want each vessel taking on prisoners from one junk at a time, it'll be slow but we can ramp things up if and when we're sure they're not just chiffing us around and trying to escape again.'*

This time nobody opened fire on the junks that were moving to dock. The diminished swarm was tentative and slow, many no longer moving at all as they watched and waited for the first junks to surrender themselves into the arms of the law.

The PPB frigate Savatara was turning slowly, tracking the junk that would dock first as it closed in on the Black Wreath.

The pirate vessel was dwarfed by the dark behemoth. The junk came to a halt and was pulled into place by the Black Wreath's docking clamps.

This finally looked like a real surrender. As a fighting force the junks were done.

A palpable sense of relief swept through the viewing lounge of the Francesca Reala, then a blinding flash filled the room as the tiny pirate junk exploded like the birth of a new sun.

four

Focus Vision News cut back to the studio where the anchorwoman was demonstrating her accomplished skills in the art of disguising ignorance.

Glen scowled at the screen. 'These clowns have lost their Live feed, Spaff. Try another channel.'

'Seems the same everywhere.' Spafford said, flicking through news channels one by one. Every channel seemed to be broadcasting from the studio, or playing a replay of the blinding explosion just before the blackout. The local studio in Pandale at least had some amateur footage from the ground, showing the flash from the explosion had been a dazzling burst even in a bright daylight sky.

Glen shook his head, 'How did pirates get hold of a bomb that powerful?'

'Maybe they got together and cooked it up, like some kind of breach bomb to crack open the Francesca Reala? She's supposed to be pirate proof, but they couldn't have planned for any pirate packing anything as powerful as that. I hate to think what it's done to that dreadnought.'

A chill ran through Glen, 'I hate to think what it's done to everything, Yolande is up there.'

A face appeared at the door of the rifle room — the girl who'd planted a shot on the back of Glen's head.

'Guys, you should come out and see this!'

Her team mates were by their car, staring into the sky. Glen and Spafford looked up to see white streaks flaring and sparkling as they fell silently from the sky.'

'What is that?' asked Spafford.

Glen's blood ran cold as he answered, 'Satellites, knocked out of orbit.'

'Even that one? Looks too big.' asked the girl, pointing at a much larger streak, trailing dirty black smoke behind it as it burned. 'What is that?'

Glen's face froze and his eyes locked on the fiery trails as what he was seeing hit home. He answered darkly, 'That's the Pandale shuttle,' his voice dropped to a whisper, 'That's what that is.'

Nobody spoke as the fiery trails slowly traced their way down , drawing silent lines all the way down from the sky and into the ocean.

Commander Malahyde cleared his throat pointedly, 'So, this exercise seems to have gone well.'

The Flex seemed unconcerned, turning a quizzical eye to Malahyde. 'What do you think you just saw, Commander?'

'I just saw a disaster. A pack of psychopathic pirates brought a bomb big enough to split the Francesca Reala like a piece of rotten fruit, and when they weren't going to get to use it how they planned they used it to kill themselves, and to take one of our dreadnoughts down with them.'

The Flex shook his head.

'No Commander, you just saw the weapon.'

'*What* weapon?'

'*The* weapon. The weapon the PPB have developed to destroy Black Fleet dreadnoughts. That was not a bomb, it was a missile fired by the Savatara.'

'We would have seen a missile launch, and seen the missile.'

'Not if it was a hyper-optic launch from a concealed bay. If they've run a missile tube the length of the craft it could function as a hyper-optic slingshot, maybe even powered by their own engines. There'd be no anti-light trail, and it would be too fast to see. It would look exactly like what you think you saw, a pirate junk blowing itself up.'

'How is a weapon any use if it knocks out the power of the vessel that fired it?'

'It wouldn't be any use at all, if it did. Watch the footage again.'

Malahyde indicated to the observation team to switch the main display to a replay of the moments before the explosion.

'What am I looking for?'

The Flex gave his own instructions, 'Calculate the magnitude of the flash and filter it out, concentrate on the Savatara and the Sonya. Slow the footage by a factor of ten and repeat the time index from 3 seconds before the blast up to 3 seconds after.'

Malahyde watched carefully as the footage repeated. Then he

noticed.

'You see it? Their lights go off *before* the blast. For everyone else the lights are knocked out as the pulse expands but theirs are out of sync.'

Malahyde nodded.

'That's because the explosion didn't knock their lights out, their hyper-optic weapon drained all of their power. And look, they're still manoeuvring *after* the blast, their targeting systems are still active in kill-confirm mode, tracking the movements of Black Wreath. The Savatara is fully operational. They're shielded against their own weapon.'

Malahyde nodded. 'I guess you got what you came for, I just hope it was worth the price we've paid.'

The display switched back to a real-time display of the battleground. The ships were coming back to life, and some of the pirate vessels were slipping away. The dark bulk of the Black Wreath was rolling and drifting like a tide-turned carcass washed up on a beach.

five

Glen had passed a dozen hangouts, cafés and bars, all of them filled with people glued to the news channels. Glen did not want to watch the news.

This place, he wasn't even sure how he'd known it was a bar. There was no clue from how it looked outside, and there was no sign to advertise it, but it felt like where a bar ought to be. Clearly someone else had thought so too, and stuck a bar here, a quiet mid-town bar, with a scattering of late-afternoon drinkers dotted around the place. None of them were watching the news, which considering the news, was really somewhat weird, but to Glen, a relief.

'Uthrak nathrak.'

Glen turned a quizzical glance to the bartender who was waving him over.

He took the stool closest to the intense looking server, a man in his early thirties, no taller than Glen, but well built, with a careful swept hairstyle and a square cut moustache extending down to his jaw and back to his ears.

'Uthrak nathrak?'

'Sorry, is this a private place? Is that a code or something? I'm not a member, I just wanted a drink.'

'It's not private, Crela. Not a club. Welcome to our place.'

'That accent, you a Goffa?'

'Sure I'm a Goffa. This is a Goffa place. Don't worry, you're welcome, if you pay your bar bill.'

'Yeah, I'm good for whatever. I didn't know there was a Goffa place in town.'

"There's Goffa places most everywhere if you know how to look. We get around, and we like a quiet drink, no fights, no machismo, no drunks, no braggadocios, no hassle. Company's always good here. What can I get you?'

'Something that hits fast and hits hard.'

The bartender gave him a doubtful look, 'You sure you're old enough to drink here?'

Glen held up his watch and triggered his ID hologram. The barkeep shrugged and reached down a black bottle and a small glass.

He poured out a thick and milky liquid of pale turquoise. At the push of a button a cherry ice-ring dropped into the drink, floating at the top and slowly releasing red clouds into the glass. He took a small grinder, at a touch a small cloud of blue powder drifted down and settled atop the drink. The barman turned the glass around full-circle, checking everything was to his satisfaction before sliding the drink across the bar to Glen.

Glen watched the red clouds swirl and begin to drop toward the bottom of the glass before lifting it to his lips and taking a sip.

His eyes widened. The blue powder was a very hot spice, the liquid almost a numbing cool, and the melting cherry ice a mix of sweet and sour, a heady burn of alcohol followed the blend of flavours and sensations down his throat.

'That's quite something! What do you call this?'

'Fool's Gulp.'

Glen nodded, 'I guess it's a sipper?'

A raise of the barman's eyebrows seemed to suggest, yes.

'I'm not going to lie to you, I really would like to get recklessly drunk right now. The quicker the better.'

'It's strong stuff. Trust me.'

Glen hoped he was right, he wanted to be as insensate as possible when the numbness of what he'd seen wore off and he had to face up to the fact Yolande was gone. Today she was going to be gone from his life either way, but it wasn't supposed to be like this. There would still have been a Yolande, to think on, and maybe from time to time, to see. It was starting to hit. The drink, and the reality.

'Can you set me up with another of these and I'll find somewhere to sit quiet.'

'Stay.' It wasn't a request or a suggestion. Maybe he didn't trust Glen to be alone with his drink, or maybe he just didn't trust him not to gulp. Maybe he shouldn't at that.

'Can you set me up with another, anyway?'

'Sure, Crela, when that one's done.'

'My name is Glen.'

The barkeep extended a hand, 'Jadd, pleased to meet you, Glen.'

'So what's the "uthrak nathrak" business? Is that like a Goffa greeting?'

'Don't worry about that.'

'Sure, but is that something people will say to me in Goffa places, do I get cheaper drinks if I get the answer right?'

The barkeep smiled and shook his head.

A warm fuzz was already descending on Glen's prefrontal cortex. He knew this was no way to deal with anything, but if he could keep Yolande out of his thoughts for just long enough to dull the full force of the anguish when it hit. This was what other people did, right? If it was a mistake, well, what was it Frank Bull had told him yesterday? If he tried to live his life never making mistakes he might wind up never doing anything at all.

He took a long slow sip and let it slide down his throat smoothly, feeling the waves of sadness start. He kept his eyes closed and wished for alcohol to win the race for control of his feelings, trying to keep the thought of Yolande's face away.

Jadd watched him carefully as he swapped between drinking and clenching his eyes shut, never loosing his grip on the glass. Glen noticed the man's unflinching gaze, and while he looked like he could handle the sort of trouble you might get in the worst kind of bar, his look was all kindness, and a sudden sting of tears that wanted to escape forced his eyes shut again.

Glen gulped, and regretted it.

Jadd laughed. "Had to try it, eh?"

Glen nodded, half way between laughter and tears, slamming the empty glass down on the bar, his throat full of sickly sweet fire. 'Might be I'm overdue for doing some foolish things.'

'You still want that second one?'

He nodded, letting himself laugh. 'Yes I do. Please.'

'Okay, Glen. But I won't be serving you a third. If you don't mind me saying, you don't look like someone who usually deals with his troubles this way.'

'No.' Glen looked at him, not knowing whether to feel guilty, or embarrassed. 'Somebody told me I seemed ready for some life changes, though. Thought I'd give this a try.'

Jadd set the glass in front of him, 'Here's your drink, and some advice. Try something else.'

Gibson had learned early in her career with Triple-S that if the Director wanted to see you, it wasn't because your life was about to get easier. Putting herself in harm's way was an intrinsic part of Melody Gibson's work, but visiting the Director's office drove a very different flavour of fear into her mouth.

The danger wasn't in being here at the heart of Beacon 3, there was only one place safer in the whole Protectorate, the office next door to this very one, the office of the Sovereign. Beacon 3's Security Ring was a giant armoured ball of rotating spheres within spheres, with complex gravity fields negating the effects of rotation for those working inside. The deeper into the Ring one travelled, the closer to power one moved.

This, the second innermost sphere housed only the offices of the Director of Triple-S, and the offices of Sovereign Staff Commander Armin Vassola, the Triple-S chief of staff.

Both offices had far too much overlapping priority and authority for them to function without some degree of conflict and competition, but that was an arrangement that seemed to suit the current incumbent of the office in the centre-most sphere, Sovereign Tobias Benoit.

A delicate chime sounded from the desk beside the doorway. Turning to the desk at the door-side Gibson smiled at the Director's secretary — a bland young man, pleasant and non-threatening. Melody couldn't help wondering if her office staff shared the same fear of their boss as her operatives did? Unlikely.

'You can go in now, Captain Gibson.'

The Director's studied air of elegance and bitterness made her personally unapproachable. Her features were refined and tight, though not quite severe. Her age was tough to place, though likely in her early fifties. If she weren't so quietly intimidating one might find the time to appreciate the fact she was beautiful, but few dared spend enough time staring at her to realise it.

'Captain Gibson, please sit.'

The chairs in her office were a reflection of her personal presence: understated, elegant, and uncomfortable to spend any length of time in.

'As I'm sure you've heard me comment before, Captain, every death is a snowball set in motion. When we kill, we must do so reluctantly, because you never know which snowball might simply come quickly to rest, and which might roll all the way to the bottom of the valley, gathering more snow and more speed, crushing everything in its path.'

'It was one of the first things you told me when I was inducted to Triple-S, Director.'

'Yes. Not everyone takes as much heed as they might. Anyway, there have been some complications with your elision last month.'

Gibson felt her muscles tighten, 'Yes, Director?'

'It seems Mr. Ralph Parsons was telling the truth about his connections, and his brother. Sid Parsons is a man on the move, and he's kicking up a stink about his brother's disappearance.'

'That's a worry.'

'It is. The Police and the PPB are investigating, and we have to pretend we are too. We can hope it goes away, but be aware, there is only so far we can cover his movements, and if they trace him as far as the station where he was elided, then your presence there is well documented and witnessed.'

'Understood.'

'There's no reason for anyone to suspect you, but you may be questioned anyway. Marshal Leo Jameson is in charge of the police investigation, and he's *very* good. If you meet him, be open, but be brief. As far as he's concerned you're a singer, and you can't be expected to remember everybody in every audience for every performance.'

'I've been second guessing my actions ever since that night.'

'Don't. Parsons had seen us brain-scanning your target, Commander Guthrie. The brain imaging crew could have tried a quick mind-wipe on Parsons, but with how little time we had to get anything out of Guthrie that wasn't really an option, and you can never be sure those will stick.

'His brother is an informant, and while he doesn't favour any side as far as we can tell, you can imagine how much the PPB would pay him to know we've been sucking classified information out of a PPB officer's mind. Ralph Parsons put himself somewhere he had no business being and saw something he had no business seeing. We have discretionary elision allowances for a reason.'

Against the wishes of the Police, "Wrong Place, Wrong Time" elisions had been pushed through into the founding security stipulations of the Focus Protectorate by both the PPB and Black Fleet. The Police never utilised them, but they rarely challenged them either.

'Normally we'd just hand a Discretionary Elision Authorisation Docket to the police and that would be that, but officially we had no operatives on that station so such a docket would have been an unacceptable risk to your well established cover. Still, this snowball must not gather more pace, so be careful how you deal with Marshal Jameson.'

The Director seemed to be going remarkably easy on her so far, which made her worry for what might be coming down the line.

'I understand. What did the brain boys get out of my mark?'

'It was a very rushed job, just a grab bag of imagery from the previous 25 hours, but some of it was intriguing.'

A holographic field opened above the Director's desk, showing the bridge of a PPB frigate as seen from Guthrie's point of view. The bridge of the Sabina was a solidly detailed image, baked into Commander Guthrie's memory every day. Some of the faces were clear, some vague. Faces that were familiar to the subject were always clearer. If the brain-crew had had more time they would have achieved better image clarity for the rest.

'You'll see these figures look out of place on the bridge. This looks like a group of PPB commandos, there's this figure in green, and in front is this... thing facing down Captain Rourke.'

'He's huge!'

'Yes. Do you recognise him?'

Gibson shook her head. 'No, I'd remember... that, if I'd seen it. Is this not some distortion of Guthrie's memory?'

'Not that we can tell. The losing side in any confrontation will often remember an aggressor as being larger than they really were, but memories don't get *that* distorted in that short amount of time. Even within variance, this man is a giant, head and shoulders taller than the commandos, and they're in full battle-dress.'

Gibson winced as the huge man punched Captain Rourke square in face.

'I guess this explains why her face was such a mess when I saw her on Raleigh Station. Who are these people?'

'There's the mystery. We know that around 15 years ago the PPB had an intelligence service called White Ops, but after a series of high-profile assassinations within the PPB, the group was disbanded. They must have been replaced with a new intelligence service, but they have proved utterly impenetrable. We don't even know what they're called. We have no idea who their leader is or who any of their operatives are. This may be the first of them we have ever seen.' She pointed at the man in green and the giant.

'And it's a blurry mess.'

'True, but this fellow is rather hard to hide. The giant and the man in green must be working for a secret PPB unit. You don't just march aboard a PPB frigate with a bunch of commandos and punch the Captain to the floor unless you have power and authority way beyond the military chain of command.'

'So what were they doing there?'

'I know you weren't told *why* you were tasked with seducing a member of the Sabina's bridge staff, so this will be new information for you. I can inform you now that the Sabina, along with the Sonya and Savatara, is believed to be part of a small, elite PPB task force, each armed with an experimental weapon designed to put PPB frigates on a one-on-one battle footing with Black Fleet dreadnoughts.

'This next memory is from earlier that same day,' The holographic display changed, Guthrie's view was now focussed on the Sabina's main tactical display. Gibson took a sharp intake of breath at the visions from Guthrie's memory.

A Black Fleet dreadnought, Black Sceptre, was under fire from the Sabina and the Savatara. The dreadnought was sustaining some damage, but about to bring its weapons to bear. She must have been caught just as she dropped shell, in the vulnerable two minutes before her systems were fully powered-up.

An intense flash of light flared from the flanks of Black Sceptre. As it subsided a bright patch of light remained, a white hot glow of molten armour-plating on the dreadnought's side. She heard the sound of Guthrie's voice as he would have heard it in his own head, *"Fire!"*

Something punched a hole in the centre of the glowing metal wound on Black Sceptre's flank, then another flash, this one not as bright, exploded inside the dreadnought. Fire erupted from within, blasting out of the docking ports. The tail of the dreadnought erupted as the generator heads breached. No one and no thing could have survived. She was a gutted hulk. Exultant shouts of joy and congratulation filled the bridge of the Sabina.

A voice came across the comms, *'This is Captain Jowett, the crew of the Savatara salute you. Good kill Sabina. Good kill.'*

Gibson drew a sharp breath in shock, 'What the hell was that?'

'That was the dreadnought Black Sceptre being destroyed by the same weapon system the Savatara used on the Black Wreath during the battle at Pandale yesterday. The crew of Black Sceptre was probably caught unawares as they dropped shell at their routine patrol point. At the moment the PPB seem to need two frigates to use their strategy. The first fires a missile that will soften the hull of a dreadnought, the second punches through and explodes inside.'

Gibson's mind was operating on two levels — as a Black Fleet officer, considering the ramifications of this new weapon and what she could do about it, and on another, as a woman who'd let this man Guthrie kiss her, and let the brain boys implant intimate fantasies of her in his mind. She had fairly successfully maintained emotional detachment from Guthrie, but it was impossible not to let a certain amount of affection develop, but now, hearing the thrill in his voice as he murdered over a hundred of her colleagues in a grubby ambush was nauseating.

She'd believed she knew what kind of man Commander Guthrie was. A man in an enemy uniform, perhaps, but fundamentally decent enough. She'd even felt guilty at times for her many deceptions. Now she'd witnessed him join in mass-murder, and seen him take joy in it. How would she manage to pretend to love him the next time they met? She found herself picturing her knife slipping not into Ralph Parson's chest, but into Commander Guthrie, right up to the hilt, into his heart.

She might yet get a chance for that. Maybe she'd get that order soon. *"Enemy elision authorised: Commander Guthrie, Red Task."*

For now, the Director had obviously shown her this for a reason, and she needed to know what her next task was. 'So why did they only use one missile yesterday?'

'One can be passed off as a pirate bomb, or, if they're found out, passed off as an accidental weapon launch. Two couldn't be anything but a deliberate attack.

'The weapon seems to need a detonation inside the ship to completely destroy it. Our analysts believe the captain of the Savatara thought the pirate vessel docking with Black Wreath might be a way to penetrate a dreadnought's hull without the first softening up strike, hoping the open docking port would act like an open wound they could stab at. Basically, they're still probing for weak spots so a single PPB frigate can finally take on a Black Fleet dreadnought and win.'

'So what is this weapon?'

'We don't know, but we do know these gentlemen,' the holo-display switched back the the fuzzy image of the man in green and the giant on the Sabina's bridge, 'took away data logs, and left the frigate with three large caskets which our analysts believe contain three of these weapons. We also believe they took possession of the remains of Black Sceptre.

'It's believed, strongly, that this secret PPB group must have developed the weapon, and don't approve of how Captain Jowett's little task force has been using them.'

'So why did the Savatara use one so publicly yesterday?'

'Captain Jowett is a marginal personality, bordering between genius and psychopath. The incident aboard the Sabina may have tipped her over into full rebellion against those who want to curtail her campaign of violence.

'As of yesterday, the Savatara and the Sonya have dropped out of sight. They've been operating off-book for over a year, and they may well have gone fully rogue now. Our intelligence channels suggest Over-Admiral Connors has upped his personal bodyguard substantially, so it seems likely he has lost control of Captain Jowett and he fears reprisals from within the PPB.'

'So how many of these weapons are there left?'

'We have no idea, and we need you to find out. The Sabina is still on regular patrol schedules, and they *seem* to be out of the game as far as this operation is concerned, but I wouldn't bet on it. Those three frigates have been acting together, and the Sabina is the last open link we have, and probably the PPB's last link with the two rogue boats.

'For our part, Black Fleet Staff Command have assigned the Black Leopard to hunt down the Sonya and Savatara. For your part, your job is to get closer to Commander Guthrie. He's clearly been in this up to his neck, and he's our best source, so it's time to step things up, Captain.'

The thought made Gibson's skin crawl, but she knew Guthrie was the best source of information they had, and that she would have to redouble her efforts to get him to open up and talk.

'Understood.'

'We need to know everything he knows about this weapon, and as much as we can about the movements of Captain Jowett and the Savatara.

'In the meantime, I have another task for you. We must know

more about these two men, the man in green, the giant, and the group they work for. The man in green is too blurry to make out here, but we will start working PPB contacts and try to find out more about him. Just knowing he exists is more information than we've had for a very long time.

'The giant, he should be much easier to spot. If we get any kind of hit on the location's of either of these two we may relocate you at a moments notice. Be ready. This is an organisation that has run dark for over a decade. We need you to find an in with one, or both of these men.'

Gibson studied the frozen image in front of her. These were the men she was supposed to find — a blurry man in a dark green suit, and a goliath who looked like he could snap her like a twig. As indistinct as they were, they still exuded power and threat. Guthrie had fooled her that he was a decent human being. These two weren't even pretending, their brutality was out in the open, and utterly unchallenged.

If the Director wanted to see you, it wasn't because your life was about to get easier.

The PPB seemed to be pretty big on the colour white. The recruiting office was gleaming and bright, and Glen was having to squint to keep the glare down. A sleepless night of walking and drinking didn't help his tolerance for this level of gleaming brightness.

Glen was surrounded by young faces, mostly around his own age, all shiny and clean-cut, some sitting in silence, some socialising. Glen was not socialising. Glen was not shiny, or clean-cut. Glen had been out all night and looked more like a candidate for an intervention than for the armed services.

The PPB recruitment office was hardly huge, and didn't look like it was ever intended to have this many people in it. At least he shouldn't have to wait too long in this press of perky enthusiasm, he'd been at the door before sun up, having dispensed with obstacles like sleeping, washing, changing clothes, or any other time consuming attempts to make himself presentable.

They'd opened the office early, anticipating a surge of interest to join up after a live broadcast of yesterday's orbital battle, rightly, as it turned out. Sure, the battle turned into something of a ludicrous mess, but it had been an *exciting* ludicrous mess!

One of the bright-eyed early birds emerged from the recruiter's office with a big smile on his face, which dropped a little as he called out Glen's name and caught sight of the state of him. He held the door open, keeping as far away from him as he could.

Glen eased himself into the seat opposite the gleaming white uniform with the jaded looking lieutenant in it. He squinted at the uniform trying to make out the name of the man it was wearing. Adair.

Glen wasn't normally one for unwavering eye-contact, but the bright white uniform was causing his eyes no small sum of discomfort, so Lieutenant Adair was getting the full force of a bleary-eyed and blood-shot stare whether he liked it or not.

'Mr Rothgill?'

'That's what they called me.'

The lieutenant squinted at him. Glen would have liked to have squinted back, but he'd been squinting all morning, and his eyes hurt from it, and from not squinting, and from even being open at all. His options of things to do with his eyes were getting pretty limited. He hadn't tried constant blinking yet, he could imagine that feeling pretty good. Maybe save it for after the interview, though.

'I see. Good morning, then, Mr Rothgill.'

'Hi.'

'Tell me, what is it you hope to gain from a career in the PPB Navy?'

'A career in the PPB navy.'

'Are you just repeating back what I said, or is that your answer?'

'Well, if you're a stickler for accuracy, both.'

'Right. I'm going to tell you up front, Mister Rothgill, a naval career is hard work. It is hard work all day and every day. You say on your application you want to be an officer?' The lieutenant raised his eyebrows, but was diplomatic enough not to express his incredulity more overtly, 'Well, starting at the bottom, you're looking at a minimum of 5 years service before you'll be considered for even the lowliest field promotion, and there is plenty of competition. There's study, tests, theory, more study, and more tests, and all of that you would have to do on your own time, in between a full day's duties.'

'Sure, but, not everyone starts at the bottom, right? Is there some kind of officer induction route?'

'Our officers come from our academies. They have very strict entry criteria.'

'So how do I go about qualifying for that?'

'It says here you're nineteen years old?'

Glen nodded.

'You're already five years too old to qualify for that.'

'Oh.'

'There is a route in for high scoring graduates, but I see from your education records... well, you're not one of those.'

'I'm what you might call an auto-didact. I'm more of a "learning by doing" kind of a guy.'

'Well, I'm sure that works fine some places, but not here.'

'So I'm gathering.'

Adair cleared his throat, considering his words. 'I'm going to be straight with you, Mr Rothgill, I don't think a career in the PPB Navy is for you. Even if you measured up to *any* of the criteria we're looking for, you don't have the kind of mental attitude we value. Speaking as a representative of the PPB navy, I don't think it would be good for either of us.'

Glen was a little punch drunk. He was also still a little *actual* drunk, possibly more than a little. 'I guess you just don't relish a challenge as much as I do.'

'Yes. Well, even if you did measure up to our standards, I couldn't sign you up, as the instruments built into the chair you're sitting in have confirmed you are over the alcohol limit for applying candidates, and for legal reasons we're not allowed to recruit people when they're drunk.

'I'm obliged to tell you not to come back until you're sober. However, in your case,' he treated Glen to a more natural smile, 'I'd advise you to not to come back then either.'

Glen rubbed his head and pondered these words. 'You know, I didn't think it would be this difficult to get press-ganged.'

Adair gestured toward the office door, 'You've seen the waiting room, Mr Rothgill. Today we can afford to be picky.'

Glen nodded.

'I'd agree with what you wrote here in the "aspirations" column, Mr Rothgill, that you seem like someone who is ready to make some big life choices.' Lieutenant Adair held up Glen's application form, which he tore in half and dropped in the disposal slot, 'Don't make this one.'

*

The armoured outriders leading Edgar Phipps' modest motorcade gave the small procession a sense of decorative threat — glinting, highly-polished gun barrels sprouting from their armoured cowls, catching pretty sparkles of sunlight as they rolled slowly down Cleovald Dofstez's driveway. The light military escort bookended a sleek and solitary black limousine, rolling around the fountain with an elegant whisper and easing to a halt by the steps.

Four bodyguards emerged from the car and gave Governor-Select Dofstez a cursory salute, while their quick eyes darted around looking for threats.

Edgar Phipps may no longer be Sovereign, but he was still afforded every protection that went with the office. In his case it was warranted.

Dofstez extended his hand to the former Sovereign as he emerged stiffly from the rear door, 'Edgar, so great to see you.'

'Strange thing to want to see, Clay. I got rid of all the mirrors in my place. Even I don't want to see me these days.'

It had been some twenty months since the last — nearly successful — assassination attempt, and Phipps was in moderately better health than he had been when he had been forced out of office, but he still looked like a withered husk of a man. Pale and frail, the thin moustache and slick hair that once made him look rakish now looked lank and listless, accentuating his unhealthy pallor.

He mustered what strength he could to shake Cleovald's hand, grateful when his friend spared him from his usual vice-like grip.

'Let's go inside, Clay. I don't have much taste for the cold these days.'

Dofstez smiled and waved him towards the house, making no mention of the blazing late summer sunshine.

The homes of planetary governors were hardly lacking in luxury, but as a member of the Select Board, Dofstez' weekend residence was a low-rise palace in the richest district of Focus. Like ancient castles, the right house, in the right sector, with the right neighbours was a formidable social and political weapon, and it was a necessary tool of his trade. Most of it wasn't much to his taste, and beyond its uses for political get-togethers and fundraisers he restricted himself to just a few rooms nearest to the servants' quarters.

Phipp's took a seat at the corner of the huge kitchen table, away from the cook busying herself with lunch preparations. Dofstez grabbed up the cafcaf pot and two cups, placing one in front of Edgar.

'Unless you'd like something stronger?'

Phipps shook his head and took a small white tube out of his top pocket. 'Not as long as they have me on this. I can't touch a drop with these high-saturation antivirals.' He sucked deeply on the white tube and let out a stream of vapour. 'Those spreffing gangsters coated those bullets with just about every infectious agent you can think of. Doctors say it'll be years before they isolate them all, that's if I even live that long.'

Dofstez shook his head, 'I won't have this Edgar. I've spoken to contacts over the border. Goffa doctors say they could cure you of most of this in three trips.'

'Sure, Clay, and if word gets out I've had Goffa gene-therapies? What will the PPB say about that? Genetic medicine may be legal where you came from, but on this side of the border the PPB and their obsession with 'naturalism" have damned us all to second rate medicine. The Humana Faction are no better. How they keep winning elections mystifies me.'

'Speaking of the Humana Faction...'

'Oh yes of course! Prime Mover finally got around to his first year review yesterday, right? He put it off for long enough. How did he get on, if I dare ask? Which apparently I do.'

'You know, Tobias was actually holding his own for a while, but then he decided he'd make a big deal of this Francesca Reala ambush. Turns out he was a big part of getting the joint operation set up.'

'That doesn't surprise me at all. He'd love to get us further into bed with the PPB, which is comical, as the Humana-Kirk are the closest thing we have to a religion. You ever seen what the PPB do if they find a religious colony?'

'I'd heard they prefer saturation bombing from orbit. Make sure the infection is completely wiped out.'

'They do. Then there was the very last colony ships from Earth, back before the consolidation — the *missionaries.* You'll have heard the rumours about that massacre I'm sure. All true. This is who the Humana-Kirk sucks up to? And claims moral high-ground while they do it?' The former Sovereign's voice still carried the depth of his venomous hatreds with powerful clarity, frail though he now found himself, 'Still, the PPB will use whatever is at their disposal to expand onto our turf, even if it's through manipulating... what was that old phrase? *Useful idiots?*'

'Well the mess of an ambush at Pandale certainly made Prime Mover look a bit of an idiot, but not very useful. Of course for now it just looks like a hideous disaster, with Prime Mover having put himself at front and centre as an architect of the plan, but it's only a matter of time before we can prove it wasn't a pirate bomb, but a PPB missile.

'Luckily the Director sent Black Javelin to watch and record the whole debacle from a safe distance. They were far enough out not to get hit by the pulse, nobody else there will have good enough footage.'

A look of undisguised distaste crossed Phipps' face at the mention of the Director.

'I understand how you feel about her, Edgar, but you don't imagine you'd still be Sovereign if she hadn't done what she did? You'd probably be in jail. Imagine the political damage the Humana Faction could have done with that?'

'Instead I get to retire on ill-health, while the mobsters on Steimz get away with multiple attempts to assassinate me.'

'Not forever, Edgar. The thing is, you retired with your reputation intact, and, if we can get rid of Sovereign Benoit...'

'How improved do you seriously expect my health to be by then, Clay? No. I'm finished. Getting rid of Benoit is what matters. Credulous fool, or traitor, the outcome is the same. He can't be left in charge.'

Dofstez nodded, 'And proof that his friends at the PPB have developed a weapon specifically designed to attack Black Fleet dreadnoughts, and that he arranged a public display of them doing just that should be enough.'

'Well, we don't want that to be too soon. A month or so before the next elections ought to be perfect.'

'I'll get the footage out to a second-tier reporter, someone hungry and on the outer but with credibility and contacts to get it on a main news network. I have somebody in mind. Electorally the smaller worlds will come to us anyway, but with the worlds that are in play I think we can at least balance the chamber and eliminate the Humana majority.'

'We can only hope. The last thing we need is a bunch of PPB loving goons bending over backwards to destroy Black Fleet. Stupid saboteurs who think just being able to defend ourselves is "provocation". Now we know the PPB have this new weapon we've never been in more danger.'

'Even so, Edgar, you may be pleased to hear they're not as close to one-on-one parity as they might hope. The Black Wreath is in much better shape than yesterday's coverage might have led you to believe.'

Phipps raised an interested eyebrow, 'What was the death toll in the end?'

Dofstez gave him a smile of deep satisfaction. 'Excluding any pirates aboard the junk that was hit...' he sipped at his cafcaf, 'out of a crew of 150 cadets...'

'Don't toy with me Clay.'

'Nine.'

Phipps regarded him coolly, trying to assess if this was a joke.

Dofstez held his gaze, 'That was the eight strong anti-incursion squad sent to the docking port to handle the prisoners, and someone on maintenance duty nearby. There were casualties too, but no other lives lost.'

Phipps' eyes widened with pleasure, 'Never let it be said Black Fleet doesn't build its birds tough.'

'You don't know the half of it. Damage is classed "light-to-moderate". We've fast-tracked an orbital dry-dock to Pandale so she can be repaired in orbit. They'll replenish the lost crew by taking on some new cadet recruits from Pandale and she'll be ready to resume patrolling in three days.'

'Let's hope the image of Black Wreath getting hit by a huge bomb-blast being broadcast across the Protectorate doesn't put off too many recruits.'

Glen wiped a little moisture from his forehead with his sleeve. He'd spent a half hour spraying himself in the face with a sober-stick and spraying his shirt with crease-out, and more than once sprayed his shirt with the sober-stick and his face with crease-out. He couldn't be sure if he'd done enough for his appearance or his sobriety to improve his odds of getting recruited, but at the very least he ought to have a crease free face and a sober shirt.

'So, what is about the idea of joining Black Fleet that appeals to you Mr Rothgill?'

Glen was glad he could actually look at this woman's uniform without feeling like it was going to burn out his retinas.

'Black! That uniform looks great. Everybody looks good in black, right? You look great, by the way.'

The recruiter looked sceptical; a barrel-built woman in her fifties who looked like she neither expected nor welcomed compliments from young men. 'I hope a free wardrobe change isn't the only thing that brought you to this office.'

'Well, no. An old family friend said I looked ready for a life change,' unbidden, the memory of the flaming wreck of the Pandale shuttle smashing into the ocean swept away his forced flippancy, 'Recent events have convinced me he's onto something. Anyway, I happened to be riding past this place and I saw you putting the recruiting flag up.' He looked at her quizzically, 'I've never noticed a Black Fleet recruitment office here before. I'm pretty sure this place was selling home appliances last week?'

'We're only here for the week. We've suddenly found ourselves a little understaffed. It says here on your application that you've previously applied to join the PPB Navy?'

'Yeah, about an hour ago.'

She studied Glen carefully, 'How did that work out for you?'

'I didn't like them, and they didn't like me.'

'Well that's something in your favour, at least.'

He smiled at her, glad to hear something positive for the first time this morning. 'I'm actually very likeable. I don't know what their problem was.'

'Here's the thing, Mister Rothgill, Black Fleet and the PPB Navy are somewhat... incompatible, and if you've been to their offices, you're on their records.'

'Does that mean I can't sign up with you?'

'No, but not everything we do is patrolling and pirate hunting. If you're interested in promotion, as your form says you are, sometimes you may find yourself assigned to more delicate operations, where it's better not to be... identifiable by other law-enforcement agencies, especially not the PPB.'

'Why is that?'

'The rivalries run pretty hot, Mr. Rothgill, and the less the PPB know about members of our space-going forces, the better we like it.'

'So what can I do about that?'

'Any cadet candidate who's had prior dealings with the PPB needs to select an alternate name, just in case they go on to bigger and better things in our service. Do you want to go on to bigger and better things, Mr Rothgill?'

'Sure. Always. I suppose if keeping a spare name's the price of entry for bigger and better things, I'm up for it.'

The recruiter ticked a box off on the application. 'So did you have a name in mind? You might never need it, but the option needs to be ready, just in case you should ever find yourself a target for PPB hostility.'

The recruiter was being nice, as recruiter's go, but Glen doubted he was any likelier to get in with these people than he had been with the PPB, and his attempt to join up with the Police a year ago hadn't gone a lot better either, and he'd actually been sober for that one. What did any of this really matter when he would just be back working at Spaff's Shoots by tomorrow?

A name... a name... what name?

He looked down at the glossy enlistment brochure, on the cover was a holo-scene photo of a Black Fleet dreadnought, with the bold title "Your Military Apprenticeship starts here aboard the Black Wreath!" At first glance he'd read it as Black Wrath, something about the word was very satisfying in his head.

He looked at the recruiter and spoke it aloud, 'Wrath.'

'Roth is very close to your own name, Mister Rothgill.'

He held up the brochure and covered the "e" with his finger. 'No, "Wrath".'

'Forename or surname?'

'Surname, of course.'

The recruiter looked like she didn't consider either choice any more obvious than the other.

'So what about a forename, and maybe a middle name or two, too?'

Glen rubbed his chin, 'How many names do you want to get out of me?' He wracked his brain, and turned again to the brochure for inspiration. Black? Black Wrath on the Black Wreath? That was stupid. Apprenticeship? Fleet? Apprentice Wrath?

'Prentiss?'

'Prentiss Wrath? Okay. What about a middle name?'

'Wait, I couldn't stand being called "Prentiss" every day, ditch it.' The recruiter looked like her patience was wearing thin, 'Or make it the middle name, maybe? Yeah, do that.'

The recruiter raised her eyebrows and made a change on her forms.

'A first name then?'

He felt he needed something he could relate to in some way, something with meaning.

'I remember I used love that show about the pirate hunter, Captain Cole.' Cole seemed a decent name, but Cole Wrath sounded off somehow.

'Malcolm Cole?'

'Yeah! That was it. How about Malcolm? I loved that guy. What do you think?'

'Whatever you think best.'

The vibes he was picking up from the recruiter now felt like his rejection was inevitable, but the name game had been mildly diverting. Spaff was going to love that he'd tried to sign up to the military, drunk, as Captain Cole!

'Yeah, we'll go with that.'

'Very well. Malcolm Prentiss Wrath. You're sure about all of those?'

He shrugged, 'Sure, why not.'

'Very well, if you can sign at the bottom of these three forms.'

Presumably this was just to complete the application and he'd get his rejection later — they seemed a more polite bunch, so an official kiss-off in writing would more likely be their style. Parts of his brain that were more sober than others were asking him to stop and think whether that was what was really going on, but they weren't in charge of his hands. He signed and handed the forms back.

The recruiter stood up and extended her hand, 'Welcome to Black Fleet, Mr Rothgill, or should I say, Mr Wrath?'

He squinted at her for a moment, 'Mr Rothgill. And... what?'

'Your training will start this evening. It will be a hands on course how to repair a Black Fleet dreadnought, taking place aboard the Black Wreath. You ship out at 8pm, Pandale time. That gives you just over 9 hours to wrap up your affairs here. Welcome to the fight.'

Glen tilted his head in confusion, 'What?'

six

Though the evening was cool Pandale's setting sun was shimmering in the heat haze rising from the spaceport's lift zone. The hot work of gravity redistributors pushing cruisers, freighters, star yachts and shuttles into the sky meant the blast-proof launching ground never got cold.

The port was busier tonight than Glen had ever seen it, with non-stop shuttle flights taking sight-seeing tours into orbit to see the Francesca Reala up close. PPB and Police teams were concluding their brief shore-leave. Adding to that, hundreds of news crews were shipping out after wrapping up their pieces on yesterday's deadly ambush.

Glen had watched precisely none of the news coverage. He'd tuned reality out. He'd just signed up for a new reality. All that was in his mind now was the last time he'd watched the sun go down like this, sitting on the Great Blue Beach with Yolande at his side, smiling at him, slipping her arm around him. He exhaled slowly feeling as if, along with his breath, something important was draining out of him forever. A strange numbness and clarity entered him with his next intake of breath, a calm resolve.

He looked at his watch. The calls list was full, and as far as he could be bothered to scroll down, all of them seemed to be from Spafford, the last from a couple of hours ago. By Glen's guess that would be about the time the auto-ride of Spaff's bike would have driven itself back to the Gun-Grid range with Glen's typically understated farewell note taped to the saddle.

Sorry Spaff, I won't be coming in to work tomorrow, then tomorrow you should probably read this note again. Repeat that for around a year and we'll see what's what. My car will be fixed by Wednesday. Sell it for me. It should fetch around three thousand Bucks. I'll collect the money in a year, but if you've spent some of it on drinks, that's okay. Look after my rifle, and don't rent it out.

Thanks for everything, Glen.

He looked around at the other people waiting with him. Three girls, and four guys, all older than Glen, but all looking as nervous as he felt.

A black shape slipped out of the sky and eased down onto the ground next to them, pushing out a stiflingly warm wash of air beneath it, the GRed's glowing pink with heat from the power they were burning, turning gravity about on itself to control the descent of this hefty mass of armour plated metal.

A hatch opened in the side and a woman in an officer's great-coat stepped out onto the landing strip, it was the woman from the recruiting office. She gave them a knowing smile which suggested she knew they were nervous, and that maybe they ought to be, but that was okay.

'Good evening cadets! Welcome to your new lives.'

Glen let the others board first, taking a last glance at Pandale's setting sun. He thought maybe he ought to be having some profound thoughts or feelings right now, but nothing occurred to him. He just tried to set the moment in his memory, so maybe he could think something profound about it later.

'Come on kid, stop pretending to be deep, you're holding everyone up.'

He looked at the officer and smiled, 'Sorry, Ma'am.'

Glen stepped aboard and looked for an empty seat.

'Don't call me *Ma'am*.' She raised her voice for the benefit of everyone, 'My rank is Quartermaster. You will address me as Quartermaster, or QM if time's short. In Black Fleet you address people by rank and name. Nobody is called "Ma'am" or "Sir", not even the Sovereign.'

She shut the outer door and no sooner than the door-seals let out a sigh they all felt the push of thrust as the transport lifted off.

'There are some things you need to understand about how a cadetship in Black Fleet works. First and most important, the responsibility for your learning is yours alone.

'There are no instructors aboard the Black Wreath, there's me and the Black Wreath's computer system, and thanks to the ban on Artificial Intelligence research from our friends in the PPB, don't expect much from the computer.'

Glen turned his head to the window. Pandale was slipping away below, and the sun was rising again, though the sky was still growing darker.

'The Black Wreath's library contains all the information you could ever need on every aspect of running the vessel. You will use it.

'The computer runs a daily task lottery and assigns your study accordingly. If you're studying hyper-optic propulsion today, you'd better be ready to be chief engineer tomorrow, but be ready to be the navigator too. You will learn on the job, but you need to be ready for the job before you get it. Be ready for anything. If you're smart, when you get your study assignment, you'll seek out another manual or research paper on the same subject, and maybe a rebuttal paper on it too. Know the techniques, know the theories, know how well the techniques and theories stood up to reality.'

The evening haze outside was giving way to starlight. Glen could see the Francesca Reala gleaming in the night sky. It was his first good view of the cruise ship since she'd arrived yesterday. He'd been too preoccupied to look at any news since the Pandale shuttle had fallen from the sky. It was even more impressive to see her hanging in the sky with the red evening rays of the Pandale sun turning her hull a soft pink.

'Now, this is important — Though I am the only officer aboard the Black Wreath I do not *command* the vessel in the traditional sense. You the cadets do, when your turn comes along. That said, I am in command of you.

'While the computer may have the most rudimentary of artificial intelligence systems, it won't allow you to do anything that would harm the vessel, or to do anything illegal, nor anything downright stupid. Nor will I.

'The Black Wreath runs on three shifts of eight hours each. A work shift, a study shift and a rest shift, with the remaining hour divided up for meals.

'All Black Fleet craft operate on Focus time. I don't know what you're used to on Pandale, but from now on, you will live your life on a 25 hour day.

'Once we're aboard I'll be issuing you with your uniforms, your duty roster and setting up your wages. One benefit of service is, as long as you're enlisted you won't pay a single Buck in tax. Your service for the public good is considered payment enough. The pension's not bad either, if you live to collect it.'

The quartermaster looked around her new recruits, 'Any questions?'

Glen raised his hand.

'Don't raise your hand cadet, speak up.'

'I have a question, Quartermaster.' He pointed out of the window, 'What is that?'

The rest of the cadets looked out, as did the quartermaster. Next to the not inconsiderable bulk of Black Wreath was a huge, dark, cigar shaped structure, that seemed to be splitting along its centre, opening up like a vast, space-borne bivalve.

'That, cadets, is the mobile dry dock Black Chasm. After yesterday's fireworks, our bird needs a couple of days repair work. Inside that vessel is where you and your friends will be learning the intricacies of welding military grade durethane and polybdenum ablative armour. Do you know much about poly-alloy bonding, cadet?'

'I can't say that I do, no.'

'You will.'

The yawning maw of the dry dock swallowed the Black Wreath, sealing it away from sight.

Wrath nodded. His mind felt fresh, the work ahead felt fresh, this felt right in a way that surprised him.

'Cool.'

seven

Melody Gibson was walking through a scene out of a golden age of suburban living. She'd had the cab stop a block short of her destination so she could walk the last few hundred metres, her reward was the smell of chlorophyl — of fresh cut grass and neatly trimmed hedges.

The sound of mowing in the middle-distance was blissfully uninterrupted by any noisy overflight from air traffic. Sky cabs, shuttles and jet copters were kept well away from protected airspace above the city's habitation zones.

The short walk was a simple pleasure, and this was one of the few opportunities she had to take it. Culmai's residential zones offered long, broad streets giving way to well manicured lawns, neatly tended hedges and immaculate homes. In the bustle of the city proper it was easy to forget Culmai City wasn't all gubernatorial edifices, business offices, city farms and shopping districts. The eastern reaches of this vast stripe of a city housed over a four billion people whose homes were all positioned to catch the first rays of dawn so the city that set the both the time, and the agenda for the entire Protectorate could get about its day.

It was also first to see the sun go down on each day, in peace and pleasantness. Home life was semi-sacred for those living here.

This suburban bliss was alien to Melody. Her life was not filled with homely pleasures, and with her parents long since dead there were few homely memories, and what few there were fading more and more each year.

Military life, and her undercover identity meant she slept in an ever changing slideshow of small rooms where she lived out of travel bags. She'd had nothing that resembled a home cooked meal in over a year.

The smell of cut grass was evocative, but not of a life she had ever known. Each deep breath conjured a fantasy of a simpler existence she'd often dreamed of having, when she let herself imagine a life where her parents had survived to see her ninth Birthday.

The bereavement team had moved a guardian into their city apartment, and kept her and her baby brother, Raymond, together. The appointed guardian had never been intrusive; if anything he had been aloof, though helpful and considerate. He was not intended to be a replacement for a parent.

As soon as she turned 13 Melody applied for sole guardianship, which in view of her maturity and intellect, had been granted. They were monitored for the first year, from then on they were a family of two.

Then there was Nev.

Nev loved her, and loved Ray too, and she needed to work. Most of all, she wanted to work for Black Fleet. Pirates had murdered her parents during a long-haul, off-stream flight across the five-hundreds, and it was a Black Fleet dreadnought that killed the pirates who did it.

When the Police had told her her parents were dead, it was the worst day of her life. When a Black Fleet Major had called at their home to tell her that her parents' killers had met their appointment with justice, it was a better day than she had ever imagined she might know again. Someone telling you your hurts have been avenged makes a powerful bond, a bond of loyalty.

She joined Black Fleet the same week she married Nev. He would care for Ray, and would be there as a husband whenever she got shore leave. That had been the plan.

Nev still looked after Ray.

She stopped at the edge of the garden and watched him indulge in that ancient male pleasure of mowing the grass. She'd never had this life, but her wages were paying for Ray and Nev to have it. It grieved her a little that it wasn't hers.

'When did you get so domesticated, Nev?'

He turned around, a little startled.

'Melody!'

Throwing his arms open he scooped her up and spun her around, because she let him.

'Why didn't you tell me you were coming?'

'Sometimes I don't even know if I'll make it here before they call me back. If I don't call ahead then nobody's disappointed if I don't show up.' She relaxed enough to let him know the embrace was over, 'I can't stay here for very long. Maybe overnight, maybe not.'

Nev grinned broadly, 'You're here, anyway. I'll message Ray! He can't be too far away, he'll be with a girl. You know how he is. He'd rather see you, though.'

She found herself smiling at the thought. The girls had never been able to resist her brother, his open smile and easy charm made him a magnet for the opposite sex. He was a happy and honest soul without a thought of hurt or harm in him. She wished she could say the same for herself.

Her thoughts wandered briefly to a man she'd never met, Sid Parsons on Beacon 505, a man left to wonder what had become of his own brother. For that reason if no other, remembering the feeling of sliding the knife into Ralph Parsons' chest stung with some regret.

Wrong place, wrong time.

'Okay, he's on his way.' Nev smiled at her, 'Come on in and I'll fix you a drink.'

'Can we just sit on the grass? I'd like to just sit on the grass.'

'Sure, if you'd like.'

'I don't get to see much of it, and it's been a very long time since I sat on any.'

'I guess you wouldn't have. Sit yourself down and I'll fetch you something. You want some juice, or wine?'

It wasn't even noon, but the day was turning hot and she could do with some relaxing, 'Wine sounds perfect, if it's cold.'

The grass felt cool and fresh between her fingers and she felt a wave of peace sweep over her, letting out a deep breath as she tilted her head back and felt the heat of the sun wash over her face, luxuriating in the warmth.

She opened her eyes as she felt a shadow block out the sun. Nev set a glass down next to her, wet with frost, droplets forming where his fingers had held the glass, gleaming sunlight refracting in each drop.

'Cheers.'

'Cheers,' she clinked and sipped, 'Oh that's good.'

She watched him without speaking. There was no ethnicity you could pin on him; like most people on highly populated worlds, he was a product of three centuries of multi-racial partnerships. There was very little left in the way of "racial purity" these days, but her own dark skin gave her a very fashionable kind of exclusivity, although she had a pretty mixed lineage herself, by all accounts.

He noticed her looking at him and smiled, and she responded in kind. She could be with Nev and not need to say anything. They had been good together, but that was done with.

The first time he'd hit her had shocked them both. She'd been so surprised she'd done nothing, it was over in a moment, and his horror and regret lasted the best part of a month. He'd promised it would never happen again.

The second time he lashed out he'd been behind her, catching her by surprise. Her combat training kicked in immediately, and without a moment of conscious thought she had nearly killed him.

It was at that point he had realised that she wasn't really working in the logistical corps for Black Fleet, as she'd claimed. It was at that this same point *she* had realised their marriage was over.

Once he was out of hospital, Nev had got the help he needed. Ray had never been in any danger, but the only relationship between Melody and Nev now was friendship, and Nev's continued guardianship of her brother.

She always made sure she left no room for false hope in Nev's heart, and that any affection that passed between them was clearly for their friendship alone. Duty and distance helped, but what would happen when Ray came of age and started making a life for himself was another matter.

'Sis! Sis! Sister!'

The sunlight lit up Ray's huge afro, wrapping his head with a fuzzy orange-brown halo, his smile a blazing crescent of white teeth. She leapt up, grabbing him and hugging him tight.

'Ray, you gangly spreffer!' she leaned back and looked at him in distaste, 'Stop being taller than me!'

'Stop being shorter than me, idiot! What the spreff kind of "big" Sister are you supposed to be down there?'

She grabbed a chunk of his hair and lightly ruffled it, 'If I had hair as crazy looking as yours I'd be as tall as you.'

'This hair is my ticket to good lovin' all around this neighbourhood, so you can leave off it.'

'Shut your mouth! I don't want to hear my baby brother talk about "good lovin"!'

'That's because you're not getting any!'

'Never you mind what I'm getting. Are you still getting chased over garden fences by angry fathers?'

'That hardly ever happens any more.'

'Glad to hear it.'

'I've got really fast at opening gates now.'

Nev drained his glass and stood up, 'I'm going inside to knock up some food, I'll bring it out when you're done with this heart-warming family reunion.'

'Come sit on the lawn with your loving Sister.' She grabbed Ray about the waist and used a quick and dirty judo throw, sending him flat on his back onto the lawn, before delicately sitting next to him.

'Ow! Child cruelty! Call the cops!' He rolled around clutching his stomach.

'Good grief! I may not be your "big" Sis any more, but you're still a baby.'

'You're a thug in a dress!'

She pulled him upright and wrapped her arm around him. 'It's good to see you, I hate these long gaps between getting to brutalise my baby brother.'

'Wiselike. I guess you have to be happy brutalising strangers instead. Killed any nice people lately?'

She blanched at the question. 'Don't even joke about it, Ray.'

'Okay.' He lay down and looked up at the sky, 'I've been wondering though, are there any non-killing people positions where you work?'

'If you're worried about my safety, I'm fine. I keep pretty safe, and I can handle whatever comes my way.'

'I'm not talking about you.'

'Oh?'

'I'm eighteen in a year, and the ideas they throw at me for careers and qualifications suck chiff. They're either boring, soul-destroying or spreffing embarrassing, sometimes all three.'

'So you think you want to sign up with Black Fleet?'

'Well I'm sure as spreff not going to sign up with the PPB am I?'

Melody rubbed the bridge of her nose and pitched her voice more seriously than she'd usually like to with her baby brother. 'I don't want you in this, Ray. It can be... ugly. Besides, we barely see each other as it is.'

'If we were both in Black Fleet we'd see each other more often!'

'No, no, no. We'd be lucky if we ever saw each other at all, Ray. It's a small fleet getting smaller, spread thin around a thousand worlds and three times as many traffic streams, and if the PPB had their way we'd be spread even thinner still. You should make you own path, Ray, not follow mine. You'll be safer.'

'How dangerous can it be, though? I can look after myself.'

She shook her head, 'I don't know what you would want to do in the service. I've told you how it really is, Ray. Even if you're behind a desk, when you put that black uniform on, the PPB see you as an enemy. This is a cold war, and in some places, it isn't all that cold.'

Her watch chimed, catching both of their attention.

'I also want one of those watches!' he said, 'You can't buy anything like those, I know, I've tried.'

Melody looked at the display and her heart sank. It was the Director. The holographic display projected her face into the air above Melody's wrist.

'Captain Gibson. Your target has been spotted at the orbital station above Steimz. A rapid transport has been dispatched to your location to take you back to the Black Tusk. Hopefully you can reach Steimz before he leaves.'

'Which target is it?'

'The giant.'

She tried not to let Ray see the cold fear that she felt filling her blood vessels.

'Understood.'

The hologram faded.

'See? Now that right there, that sounds spreffing exciting!'

'Sure Ray, I wanted to spend just a little time with you guys, and now I have to rush off to a world full of mobsters to track down some freak of nature. The thrills wear thin faster than you think, Ray. Very thin.'

She looked west and could already see a Black Fleet transport vectoring in to collect her, they were serious about not missing the chance to intercept the giant.

She looped her arms around Ray, giving him a long, strong hug. 'You'll have to say goodbye to Nev for me. I hate going like this.' She gave her brother a long and earnest look. 'You don't want this life, Ray. You really don't, and I don't want it for you.'

By Glen's guess the Black Wreath was over six hundred metres long, an imposing dark ellipse whose threatening presence was not much diminished by the ragged scar in her hide. A huge piece of interstellar hardware of deep and pervading blackness, even under the spotlights that picked out her shape inside the repair bay of Black Chasm.

The mobile dry dock was a place of constant wonder, with room enough for at least two more craft of Black Wreath's size, or even larger. Most of the repair work was done by vast robotic arms, as deft and precise in their movements as a dancer, manipulating and positioning sheets of armoured shipmetal big enough to crush a large house.

The repair crews were quick, capable, and informative. Most importantly, they were patient and glad to share their expertise. Glen had never learned so much, so well, and so quickly.

The hardest lesson had been the first, handling the backpack the repair crews called the "Peggy," the P.G.E. gravity pack. There were mobile gantries and elevators to help people get around inside the dry dock, but the fastest way to get where you needed to be was strapping on a Personal Gravity Environment pack, pointing yourself wherever it was you wanted to go and getting the pack to make that direction "down" until you got there.

It had made him a little nauseous at first. Rotating the gravity field for upward thrust made the blood rush to his head and flipped his stomach upside down, so he'd taken his time before risking the higher speed settings. The shift in the gravity field still felt weird, but he'd acclimatised to the sensation enough to get around fairly quickly. Zipping around and helping to position the welding probes had soon become as natural as walking.

Glen turned at the sound of the klaxon, barely able to believe his first work shift was already over. In any regular circumstance the prospect of eight hours of welding would have sounded like an eternity of tedium, but the sights and sensations, the skills and the knowledge he was seeing and gaining had made the shift fly by, figuratively and literally.

Unfastening and handing the gravity pack back at the equipment store, Glen quickly lamented the sensation of his full bodyweight pressing against the soles of his feet. The gantry felt hard underfoot, and after hours of effortless flight the act of walking to get around was disappointingly mundane.

The rest of the work-shift crew were heading for the Black Wreath's nearest airlock, waiting for it to cycle. He tacked onto the end of the line as the outer doors opened and the next work-shift emerged from within. As his shift filed inside, Glen took a good look at the airlock's fastening mechanisms, just to see what they were *supposed* to look like.

The airlock his shift had been repairing was a ragged, half-melted mess, but having seen the explosion that caused the damage on the news, he was amazed the damage hadn't been much worse. It certainly made him feel safer about going aboard the Black Wreath. She seemed to be, literally, bomb proof.

Passing through the hull it was clear the Black Wreath would be smaller on the inside, her hide was thick, with vault like outer doors, a chamber big enough for a large, armed squad to muster, and another set of thick vault doors. Behind this second set of doors was a circular chamber some ten metres round, and beyond it another two sets of vaulted doors, presumably leading into the true interior of the vessel.

They weren't going to get to see inside yet though. The Quartermaster was waiting for them inside the round chamber, surrounded by shrink wrapped bundles of clothes and storage boxes.

'Welcome, cadets. I apologise for the delay in getting your cadet uniforms to you, the fabricators have been flat-out producing new parts for the repair work so these weren't the highest priority. You can dump the disposable coveralls you're wearing in the recycler when you get to your assigned quarters.

'There's a storage carton for each of you which you'll use to stow your civilian clothes. When you've filled it, seal it. You'll find a chute in your quarters to drop it in. They'll be laundered and stored and you'll see them again in a year.'

She held out another carton, 'One thing I won't wait for are your watches. I know you each took a wake-cap before your shift, but both your brain and your watch will still be telling you that it's 5am Pandale time.

'I have new watches for each of you, set to Focus time. That's shipboard time. From now on that's *your* time. Familiarise yourselves with the workings of your watch, it could save your life someday. Toss your old watches in the carton when you collect your uniform.'

Glen unfastened his wristwatch and waited for the rest of the new recruits to finish checking in and collecting their boxes.

'Last in line again, cadet? Is this a habit with you?'

Glen shrugged, 'I like to size up a situation just to be sure I don't make any mistakes.'

'Well, that's not always going to be an option.' She held out her hand for Glen's watch, which she took a moment to turn over in her hands. 'Nice piece.'

'Thanks, it was a present for my 18th birthday.'

'Are you sure you're 18? You look more like 16 to me.' She placed the elegant silver timepiece into a read-writer next to a large black watch. Both watches flashed as they synchronised.

'I'm 19.'

'Oh, that's right.' She ticked her check list and tossed his watch into the carton, 'I guess it'll be a 20th Birthday present from me when I give it back.' She grabbed the last shrink wrapped bundle, 'Here you go cadet, uniform for one Malcolm Prentiss Wrath.'

Glen squinted at her, 'Rothgill. My name is Glen Conrad Rothgill.'

'That's not what it says on my duty roster,' she held up Glen's uniform and pointed at the name stitched on the chest, 'it's not what it says on your uniform, and most importantly, it's not what it says on your pay-slip.'

'No. Wrath was just an alternate name, you said I'd only need it if I did something that would... what was it? Anything that would make me a target for PPB hostility?'

'Thing is, cadet Wrath, you *have* done something that will make you a target for PPB hostility.'

'What?'

She leaned in and whispered conspiratorially in his ear, 'You signed up with us.'

The quartermaster handed him his new watch, a gleaming smooth chunk of metal and dymond with a self-sealing band. At first he mistook it for a Kassar Starmaster, the watch of choice for fighter pilots who could afford to spend thirty thousand bucks on the bragging rights to such a high-end piece. He soon realised his mistake. It was actually a Kassar Galaxymaster, an exclusive military edition, and was worth more money than Glen was likely to earn in a decade.

Glen turned the watch over in his hands, much as the quartermaster had done with his own. A sense of inevitability sunk in as he read the words permanently laser-engraved all the way through the dymond casing on the back.

MALCOLM
PRENTISS
WRATH

'Cadet Wrath, that's your watch, that's the time, and that's your name.'

Glen... Malcolm nodded, 'You know, at some point today, I think I may have failed to size up the situation to check I wasn't making a mistake.'

The quartermaster nodded with a smile, 'It can happen to the best of us, cadet.'

It took him nearly an hour to find his quarters. The Quartermaster wasn't kidding when she'd said they had to find everything out for themselves. Nothing was signposted.

The cabin was small and dark. There were three bunks but they were empty. At the end of the cabin was a semi-circular desk with three chairs The desk was tidy, although there were some personal effects scattered around at the back.

Whoever he was going to be sharing with must be on another shift pattern. He felt a little like an intruder being alone in someone else's place.

With shrink-wrap covering the lowest bunk, he assumed it must be his and set his carton down on it.

Tearing open the bundle of clothes, a sensor inside the pack must have been triggered, as a voice began speaking.

'I am your uniform. I do not tear. I do not stain. I am fitted to you, but I will grow with you. I am anti-bacterial. I am absorbent. I am waterproof. I am flame resistant. I am warm when you are cool and I am cool when you are warm. Look after me and I will look after you.'

The voice stopped and Wrath raised his eyebrows at it. 'Thanks. I should introduce you to my mother, you're just what she's always wanted for me.'

He laid the garment on the bed. A one-piece pilot's suit, in black, obviously, with scrawl pads built into the left wrist and right thigh. He got a good look at the various insignia and decorative details. There was subtle blue piping, and his name... his new name, was also stitched on the chest in the same deep blue. Below the name was a panel that looked like some form of electro-luminescent display, but it wasn't displaying anything.

Folded inside the suit were two pairs of underwear and two tee-vests. He looked for anything resembling socks or boots, finally noticing the legs of the jumpsuit dangling over the edge of the bunk had built in footwear.

His skepticism about this baby-romper suit would have to wait, with eight hours of physical work to wash off, and a pretty rough night out on the town before it, a shower was in order before he was going to slip into this new skin.

He tore off his disposable coveralls and carefully packed his own clothes in the carton. There was some reluctance when it came to packing away his shoes; the idea of a year without shoes was unsettling. He clipped the lid into place, pushed the carton into the chute and listened to the soft whoosh of his life as he'd known it being taken away.

Pushing at the door opposite the bunks he was glad to see a modestly sized bathroom, good enough for basic needs. The shower controls didn't seem to be responsive, and after a minute of random prodding a message flashed up.

"All on-board services require identity verification. Please move your watch closer to the panel. If something is obstructing the signal of your watch, please remove the obstacle and try again."

He looked down at his bare wrist, a wave of panic hitting him as he tried to remember if he'd taken his new watch out of the carton he'd just dumped in the chute.

His eyes darted to his bunk. Grabbing up the jumpsuit to search underneath, he heard a clunk on the floor. Sighing with relief, he picked up the watch, slipping it onto his wrist. It tightened itself up reassuringly and sealed itself in place.

How stupid would he have looked if he'd put his brand new military-issue timepiece into twelve month storage? The wake-capsule he'd taken at the start of his shift seemed to be wearing off, his alertness was starting to rapidly fade.

He thought back over his day and realised that with the night he'd spent drowning his sorrows on Pandale and his work shift here he'd missed two complete nights of sleep, and the night before hadn't been a *good* night's sleep either, in the wake of Yolande telling him she was moving to Viaphrane.

Spreff, that seemed like forever ago.

He'd already lost an hour of his rest shift searching for these quarters, and he was giving serious consideration to skipping the shower completely, but the thought of getting into a clean bed dirty didn't sit right.

The shower was warm, not hot, but the blowers had him dry quickly enough. The blast of air reached parts of him that caught him by surprise, tempering his weariness with some temporary invigoration, but as soon as his bunk claimed him, so did sleep.

eight

Darian Corvalis sat silently, head back, his eyes cast skyward watching the thick, rapid rivulets of rainwater rolling over the glass domed roof of his limousine, catching the light of each streetlight flashing by.

To a casual observer he might seem hypnotised by the dance of liquid and light, but Corvalis' life was not peopled by casual observers. Everyone in the car knew full well his mind was as active as ever, turning and conjuring shapes out of knowledge, able to form a visual picture of all the workings of his vast interplanetary network of business and criminal interests, holding and molding their shape in the noetic hands that manipulate the world in the mind.

It was not yet fully dark, with the deep steel clouds still slightly aglow with the last dregs of the day. This far south in the city of Steimz the untamed ocean weather of the wild sea could make itself felt in near full force. The drive for valuable real-estate inside the boundaries of business time had this city on stilts marching slowly but steadily towards the equator. This new spearhead was Darian Corvalis' latest and most impressive display of power.

In the near distance a sharp, brightly lit crystal tower stabbed into the darkening sky like a knife. The Glass Fortress was Darian Corvalis' building, and stood as a symbol of his empire over the progress of the city.

As the city's most powerful fraternity leader, at the age of thirty three Corvalis was also one of the oldest.

The Gamma Fraternity did not rule the whole city, far from it, but no fraternity controlled so much, or could hit back as hard at any encroachment onto their turf.

Challenging Corvalis, or any of his fraternal brothers, would bring a conflict which would be short, brutal, costly, futile.

The drumming of rain abated as the car sped on, driving now through what was effectively a vast building site. The glass fortress was the only completed building here, and none of the staff had been moved in from the old headquarters in the casino district, except for Corvalis himself, who had taken up residence on the top floor, from where he could survey his domain from its Olympian perspective.

Waiting on the steps was his head of security, Milt. A leg-breaker and widow-maker of the old school, Milt was true to the mobster archetype, but he was presentable enough to take nice places and meet nice people without stinking up the vibes.

Inside the car, the twins — the beautiful twins — Fione and Dione were already eyeballing the surroundings. They rode with Darian everywhere, as a dark, deadly, and delicious statement. He was aware that using them as mere bodyguards he was wasting their talents as assassins, but they made him look good, and they were for so much more than show. Who better to anticipate and foil a potential assassin than the finest assassins in town? Especially in *this* town.

Milt opened the car door, and Dione stepped out. Satisfying herself there were no threats, she moved aside and Darian hopped out of the car into the fresh sea breeze. He took a deep breath and smiled.

'Evening's looking up, Milt.'

'Yes, Mr. Corvalis. Rain's easing up.'

This was the raw edge of the city, nothing lay further south than this, though within a year another kilometre of city would have stretched out even further into the ocean.

Fione followed Corvalis out of the car, watching his back as they climbed the stairway, up and on into the brightly lit lobby of the Glass Fortress.

Inside, the building was hauntingly quiet. Empty seats, empty desks, empty offices. The elevator made its rapid and silent ascent past one vacant floor after another, finally coming to rest at Corvalis' office.

He checked his watch and settled into place behind his desk.

Normally, he'd make anybody and everybody wait to speak with him, but the mysterious character who called himself, or herself, Fathom, was always on time, right down to the second, and Corvalis had come to respect that.

He had a few moments, and allowed himself a lazy spin in his chair to take in the spectacular view. To the south, the darkness of the untamed ocean. To the north the older city, gaudy and dazzling. To the east and west the great sea works spread outwards to the limits of this single time zone, all work ceasing at its edge.

The day would come when Steimz would be a gleaming stripe of light rivalling Culmai City on Focus itself, a glittering wonder of the Protectorate. By then, Corvalis planned on being the next best thing to a king of this world. Maybe he would be king? A few other worlds had kings. It wasn't against the law, as long as they had a Governor too. Steimz already had a Governor, a Governor with a nice title and very nice perks, but most importantly, no power. He did as he was told.

Corvalis imagined being a king would be a pretty nice gig.

He looked at his watch again, shaking his head. Fathom was late. Fathom's calls were never late. Never.

Corvalis began tapping his fingernails on the call console, which, as soon as he noticed himself doing, he stopped. Minutes passed, and a repeating pattern set in, tapping fingernails, followed by silence.

Even the bodyguards were getting twitchy. He was the most powerful and dangerous man on this world —and many others besides— the Fratello di Tutti Fratelli, the Brother of all Brothers; the thought that he would wait in silence for this mystery caller was unsettling. People waited for Darian Corvalis, he did not wait for people. People who made Darian Corvalis wait were people who would discover levels of regret they had never previously dared to imagine.

Milt jumped at the sound of the call chime. Corvalis regarded him coolly, surprised by his lack of composure. The twins, however — the beautiful twins — they didn't flinch.

Corvalis allowed the call to ring out for a few moments before answering. Connecting the call initiated a white-noise generator in the ear implants of all three bodyguards. This conversation was not for them.

'Fathom?'

As always, there was no image with the call, only an electronically generated voice, different every time.

'Yes.'

Not even an apology.

'I got a message that you wanted to talk to me.'

'Yes.'

Corvalis paused, waiting for more. There was no more.

He pushed the tone of politeness way beyond the point of

sincerity, 'So what would you like to talk about?'

'*Sovereignty.*'

He took a wary breath and rubbed his chin, pondering the word, and its wider implications.

'I, uh, ...I thought we were done with all of that?'

'*So did I.*'

Whoever Fathom was, he, or she, always seemed to a know a lot of things they shouldn't know. Corvalis had to tread carefully. He took an audible breath, staring into the black screen, knowing he could be seen, even if his caller could not.

'Thing is, Fathom, Benoit's been in power for a year now, but all of Sovereign Phipps' anti-racketeering laws are still in place. My fraternity brothers and I, we've been expecting some kind of movement, but life for the Steimz fraternities hasn't got any easier. Not here, and especially not off-world.'

'*No.*'

'We arranged those hits on Phipps for a reason. Trying to assassinate the Sovereign of the Protectorate is a spreffing risky business, and the risk was all ours. And here we are with nothing to show for it.'

'*Edgar Phipps is still alive.*'

Corvalis was getting impatient, 'Yeah, but he's not Sovereign any more, is he?'

'*Edgar Phipps is still alive.*'

'But he's *not* the Sovereign anymore, and my fraternal brothers are no better off now than when he was! Tobias Benoit is the Sovereign now, so now *he's* the problem, and we don't see how he's any less of a problem for us than Phipps was.'

'*Tobias Benoit is not my problem.*'

'No, he's *mine!* And he's a problem to every mobster on this planet, and all of their off-world operations too! We need some latitude, and if we need to give Benoit a push to get it, that's what we'll do. Maybe not as hard as we pushed Phipps, but a push nonetheless.'

'*Tobias Benoit is not to be threatened or harmed.*'

'What are you going to do to stop me?'

'*I supplied you with the most advanced weapons this side of the Goffa border.*'

'Hey I'm not going to deny you were a big help to me. It's a fact, you sped up my trip to the top, to becoming chief among my fraternal brothers here, but let's not pretend you didn't just back a winning horse.

'I was headed for the top anyway, and you knew it, you just gave us a shortcut. If you're seriously thinking you can take the hardware back from us. *Us?* The *Gamma* Fraternity? The most powerful mob on Steimz? Well, good luck with that.'

Corvalis expected a thoughtful pause, but there was none. *'Your entire fraternity uses the weapons I supplied. You only remain the most powerful mob fraternity because those weapons keep you there. You allowed yourself to become entirely dependent on them. I offer you an opportunity, now, to preserve your position. This is the only opportunity I will provide you with. Cease any plans to attack, threaten, or pressurise Sovereign Benoit in any way.'*

'Can you turn back the laws that are stepping on the toes of me and my fraternal brothers? No. I got rid of one Sovereign, I can get rid of another, and if I'm using your weapons to do it, I might even be able to put you in the frame for it! How'd you like that? *I* might not be able to find out who you are, Fathom, but I bet a dead Sovereign would bring out a lot of people who can.'

'A moment please.'

There was a brief silence from the other end of the line. Corvalis turned a triumphant little smile to his bodyguards, then remembered they couldn't hear the conversation.

Fathom spoke again, *'I have now disabled your weapons.'*

Corvalis glared at the screen, the defiance not yet faded, although confusion was starting to take over.

'What?'

'The other fraternities have been notified.'

'I see. So you just turn off tens of thousands of guns in an instant, right?'

No answer. Corvalis didn't carry a gun himself, such vulgarity was way below his pay grade. He turned off the white noise generator in the ears of his longest serving bodyguard and waved to get his attention.

'Milt, shoot that pot plant.'

Milt looked puzzled, but was a man who did as he was told. Drawing his weapon, aiming it at the pot plant in the corner of the office and pulling the trigger, he looked puzzled again. There wasn't a sound, not even a click. Examining the magazine, the ammunition indicator and even the muzzle, he looked at Darian Corvalis and shook his head. 'Neat trick, Mr. Corvalis. How did you do it?'

The blood drained from Corvalis' face, 'What kind of chiff-sniffer's trick is this? Fathom? You got some kind of localised explosion suppressor field worked out, huh? You think we won't find it. We'll find it!'

'There is no suppression field. The weapons are inactive. I designed all of your guns. I manufactured all of your guns. I have disabled all of your guns. The other fraternities have been notified.'

'You can't just switch off tens of thousands of guns in the blink of an eye!'

'I have enjoyed our working relationship, this particular terminus to our cooperation was avoidable, and is regrettable. Goodbye, Mister Corvalis.'

The call ended. The calls board immediately lit up, calls coming in from all of his fraternity enforcers around the city. He selected the call at the top, a call from his brother — his real brother. He could barely hear his voice over the sounds of screams and gunfire.

'DARIAN! It's the Epsilon Edge Fraternity, hitting us from all sides! I got calls coming in of attacks all along the eastern reaches, it's not just Epsilon frat, Omega Omerta are hitting us — others too. Looks like a bunch of frats have ganged up on us! Our hardware is NKD! Nothing works! We can't get a shot off!'

The Corvalis mob had been untouchable for years, his youngest brother had never known it any other way. There was nothing but terror in his eyes. *'Spreff it! They're coming in the door! They're...'*

The call cut off. Corvalis hammered at the reconnect key, desperate to know what was happening. The screen dialogue switched to an error checking mode, with simple text scrolling up the screen.

CALL LOGS DELETING...
CALL CONTACTS DELETING...
DATABASE DELETING...
SUB-DIRECTORIES DELETING...
MASTER LOGS DELETING...
SECURE FILES DELETING...
ACCOUNTS FILES DELETING...
BANK FILES DELETING...
TRANSACTIONS FILES DELETING...
ASSET FILES DELETING...

It continued. His entire computer system was being wiped. His entire business was being wiped. His entire empire was being wiped. What Sovereign Phipps hadn't been able to do with seven years of work against organised crime, this "Fathom" was doing in a single night. Corvalis looked away from the text as a flash of light caught his eye.

Hovering outside his office was a gleaming white grav-copter firing suction tethers at the corners of the outer window. A fifth cable attached itself and began firing out a high-pressure water jet, cutting fast and clean through the armoured glass, the military grade ballistic crystal offering no more resistance than soft cheese.

The cables snapped back, snatching the cut glass out as a single piece, a blast of icy night air rushed in, sucking the comfort and safety out of Corvalis' office, and his life.

The grav-copter released its grip on the window and retracted the cables with whip like speed. Spinning about, an open hatchway moved to face the freshly carved hole, shadowy figures were lurking within, Corvalis was transfixed. At the front of the group a huge silhouette loomed. The copter's strobe lights offered brief flashes of his face, and each glimpse was terrifying.

Corvalis recognised the look, he'd seen it on the faces of his own enforcement crews when they were at their work. A killer's leer. The determined gleam in the eye and the snarling smile of someone about to unleash horror.

The figure leapt the gap from copter to building with ease, like a giant rock flung from a siege-engine. The floor shuddered at his landing. Raising himself to his full height his true immensity was revealed.

This was no mob hit. This wasn't the way the fraternities got things done.

Milt raised his gun before remembering it was now useless. Casting aside the dead weapon and reaching inside his jacket, his hand emerged grasping a long and vicious looking blade.

Milt was hardly a midget, and his frame was packed with plenty of muscle, but the giant dwarfed him. Milt stepped cautiously forward in a knife fighter's stance, empty hand across his body, the other hand low with the knife gripped underhand, ready to slash across the abdomen.

The giant strode towards him, without concern or caution. Milt waited for the giant to reach striking range, stepping off the back foot and bringing the blade up rapidly to slit the giant open.

The giant swept the blow aside in a smooth motion, reaching forward and grabbing Milt by the chest, lifting him off the ground, smashing his head into the ceiling and breaking his neck.

He let the body fall and strode on toward Corvalis.

The twins stood, each drawing a weapon - a matched pair of gleaming pearl-handled revolvers with long, broad barrels you could fit a thumb in. *These* at least were guns that Fathom could *not* turn off.

Fione positioned herself between the giant and Corvalis, Dione stepped around her sister and levelled her gun at the giant, firing steadily into his chest. Even if he were wearing body armour, these rounds should still hurt, and at least slow him down.

He wasn't slowing.

She raised the gun and trained it on his forehead, squeezing out the last remaining bullet and waiting for him to drop.

The giant stopped, a red trickle of blood running down his nose. He moved his hand to the red circle in his forehead and seemed to be digging at something with his fingers. After a moment, he pulled his hand away, holding something shiny between his thumb and forefinger. He dropped the bullet casually on the floor and punched his attacker in the gut.

As she was folding from the blow he grabbed her around her neck and wrenched, intending to break her neck, but misjudging the effort. Her body slipped to the ground but her head remained cradled in his elbow.

Fione's sister screamed as a fountain of blood followed the body to the floor. The giant looked at her face, a little confused, then looked at the head in his hands and nodded with interest at the resemblance.

Drawing back his arm, he threw the head in a powerful movement, the sisters kissed and the screaming stopped.

Corvalis stared straight at the giant, mouth agape in a shocked stupor. The giant stared back at him with a menacing grin, then stepped aside. Behind him stood a smaller man.

He only looked small comparatively. He was big in his own right. He had much of the look of an enforcer himself. Close-cropped hair of iron-grey, over-weight, but with a powerful frame and a bearing that spoke of a comfortable familiarity with violence. He was no mobster by his dress though. A light brown herringbone overcoat covered a suit of sage-green tweed.

Could this be Fathom?

The man in the green suit surveyed the collection of corpses around him, stepping carefully over the bodies before selecting a chair to sit in.

'Good evening Mister Corvalis. I go by the name of Griffith.' The man's tone was imperious; to be listened to, not responded to. He indicated the giant with his thumb. '*This* large gentleman here is known as Fester. You should be able to guess who we work for.'

Corvalis said nothing, wondering if his face now reflected the same terror he had witnessed in his brother's last moments.

'People often ask a lot of questions about him, but the only thing you need to know about Fester, Mr Corvalis, is he is a monster.'

Corvalis nodded, slowly.

'The only thing you need to know about me is... so am I.'

Griffith and Fester climbed aboard the grav-copter, Griffith turning a look back towards Darian Corvalis' glass fortress.

'If only every empire fell so easily, Fester.'

'Yuh.'

'We'll drop you back at the orbital station once we've got all that blood off you and fixed that nasty hole in your head.' Griffith looked at the bullet wound and frowned. 'Does it hurt?'

'Nuh.'

'Good. Anyway, stay at the station for another day or so. I'm afraid you're much too conspicuous to have you just appear and disappear around an event like this. Do be seen around, but, not too much.'

Griffith nodded at the PPB commando manning the copter's high-yield sonic cannon emplacement. The commando swung the cannon around and down, lining up a shot at the poly-alloy pillars supporting the base of the Glass Fortress.

A deep and resonant thump accompanied the single shot and, after a moment, a shockwave of subsonic energy swept through the frame. The glazed skin of the tower shattered into a billion crystal shards, spraying out from the building as a silent snow of glass.

'Pretty show, eh, Fester?'

The pillars were buckling where the sonic pulse had struck. The tower began a slow fall, a graceful accelerating sweep, the rush of air through the naked frame rising to a roar and terminating in a violent crash as the building smashed into the ocean.

Even at this altitude, they felt the fine mist of spray from the impact, filled with the tang of ocean smells and salt.

'Yuh.'

Griffith turned to the pilot.

'Let's go.'

The copter came about, powering away into the darkness of the south, out over the ocean.

nine

Her eyes glistened in the glare of the stage lights, not quite tears, but the gleam wouldn't be lost on those nearest the stage. The extra emotional dimension to tonight's set wasn't down to the songs being any more heart-rending or heartfelt than usual, it was entirely thanks to the discomfort from the anti-glare contact lenses Monique was wearing — the only thing that would help her see through the dazzle of the stage lights.

Monique hated the lenses, the technology packed into them made them too thick to fit easily under her eyelids, and every blink smarted, but she was here for the giant, and she needed to see clearly if he decided to show his face. As big as he was, without some visual assistance she wouldn't be able to see anything beyond the edge of the stage except the blinding spotlights.

For a club calling itself "Soirée Noir" the joint was almost obnoxiously bright. Monique's understanding was the place had had one too many murders in its dark corners, so now there weren't any; dark corners that is. This being the orbital station for the mob controlled world of Steimz, brightly lit murders were still a very real possibility.

The bar was zoned, with rows of stage-facing seating, a full length bar at back, and plenty of table settings either side. It was a difficult area to keep fully surveilled.

As far as the surveillance was going, the night was looking like a dead loss. The Triple-S operatives posted aboard the station had seen the giant visit this club the night he arrived, but since Monique arrived there had been no sign of her mark.

The giant had a cabin booked under the almost insultingly obvious fake name of "Jones," and the concierge-system records showed he'd been inside all evening. Whether that was true or not was another matter. This station, like everything else around Steimz, was run by the mobs, and if you wanted people to believe you'd been in your cabin all night, it was easy enough to rig room-access logs and turn off any cameras that might show otherwise, for a fee.

Monique had been nagged by a guilty gladness that the giant continued to be a no-show. Every time she thought of him she felt a pressing dread in her gut.

With her hopes both rising and falling at the narrowing prospects of the giant showing up, she refocused her attention on the room, and began to sense a dramatic change of mood sweeping through the audience — urgent whispering and people hurriedly checking their watches. The faces in front of her were taking on expressions of shock, fear, excitement, or confused joy. Everywhere, people were making their excuses and leaving the club with a mixture of ill-concealed, or open haste.

Out of the corner of her eye, her attention was caught by one of the waiters switching on the holo-screen above the bar. Even with the audio muted the news report was clearly urgent and important.

An agitated reporter was mouthing words, with a static image of Darian Corvalis hovering beside her. Monique nearly choked on her lyrics as she read the ticker at the bottom of the display.

PROMINENT STEIMZ BUSINESS LEADER DARIAN CORVALIS FEARED DEAD.

She tried not to appear distracted from the performance — though few in the audience were paying any attention to her singing now anyway — but her eyes kept returning to the news, which was showing long-range footage of a glass building collapsing into the ocean. Stolen glances at the news ticker added some sketchy details.

GLASS FORTRESS TOPPLES INTO SEA * SUSPECTED STRUCTURAL FAILURE IN FLAGSHIP BUILDING PROJECT. * NO BODIES RECOVERED * STEIMZ BUSINESS LEADERS PAY RESPECTS AT LOSS OF "UNIFYING AND VISIONARY FIGURE"...

This was clearly local news, the interstellar news organisations wouldn't hesitate to call out Corvalis for what he really was, the fratello di tutti fratelli. The Brother of all Brothers. The master of Steimz most powerful mob fraternity and a murderous thug responsible for deaths by the thousand, and grifts, grafts, and thefts by the billion.

The idea that this was some kind of accident was ludicrous, but speculating on who might be responsible was worthless. A full accounting of people who might want to kill Darian Corvalis would fill a library.

The only thing that was certain, by tomorrow the Steimz system would be crawling with cops. That could scare away her quarry. Not that she was keen to spend time around hordes of police either, especially if anyone had connected her to the last known location of one Ralph Parsons. The death of Darian Corvalis was a much bigger deal than the disappearance of some sex-pest, sleaze-ball talent promoter, but there was a bull-headed thoroughness to the police that it did not do to underestimate.

The band started playing her in to the final song of their set. As she counted herself in she got the next shock of the night. The giant was walking into the bar.

She'd had trouble reconciling the holographic simulation pulled from Commander Guthrie's mind with any kind of reality, but the goon really was that big.

With his head almost brushing the ceiling, even here where wise eyes did *NOT* linger on strangers, everyone turned at least one look his way before turning away.

Watching her target fetch himself a drink and finding himself a place to sit, Monique made a hand-signal behind her back to let the band know they'd be doing an encore tonight.

Over half the clientele had left the bar immediately after the news of Corvalis' death, and she was struggling to find people to make eye-contact with, forcing her to look towards her mark a lot more often than she'd like to.

Each time she turned her gaze to "Mister Jones" he was staring right at her. It was chilling. *She* was supposed to be observing *him*, but his eyes were boring through her like a mining drill. There was no way for him to know she was anything but a singer, surely? Or was there?

The capabilities of the PPB's spy network were totally unknown, and Monique was exactly the sort of person they would target at any hint of suspicion. The brain crews weren't infallible, and if Guthrie had had glimmers of real memories that weren't romantic encounters, say, getting a dose of knockout gas from a couple of guys in white overalls, his role in a secret weapons project would make sure he passed that information along.

She was trying to suppress her rising anxiety as his unbroken gaze continued to press for her attention. Was she here to watch the giant, or was he here to watch her?

As the final strains of the song faded the giant stood, necked the last of his drink and walked out.

She felt a sudden release of tension, and realised she was actually clammy with sweat; fear sweat. She turned around to the band. The only thing they'd have been able to see was the stage lights, no news, no hurried exodus from the bar, and no giant. They were waiting to hear what the encore would be. She shook her head.

'We're done, let's get out of here.'

Hovering at the edge of consciousness with his new name turning over in his mind, Malcolm Wrath was emerging from a troubled night of dreams and half-dreams, of scenarios from basic embarrassment to life-threatening disaster where he couldn't remember his name, or gave the wrong name, or found himself spooling off an unstoppable cascade of ever more ludicrous fake names.

Voices were drawing him to wakefulness after permeating his fading dreamscape. The voices were real. Sitting at the small table at the edge of the cabin were two young women. Hearing him stir they turned towards his bunk, 'It awakes!'

Wrath adjusted his eyes, blinking away blurriness to get a look at the people he assumed were his bunkmates. On the left was a petite blonde girl, with fine, shoulder length hair. She was quite pretty, although her close features made it look like she had a size 4 face on a size 5 head. She looked around the same age as Wrath, or maybe a touch younger.

On the right was a dark haired woman with a look that spoke of some Chinese origin, seemingly in her early twenties. She looked the more assertive, and the more intelligent of the two. She also wore a proper uniform with slacks and a tunic, whereas the blonde was wearing the same kind of flight-suit as Wrath.

'Hi.' He mustered, 'I think I'm your new bunkmate.'

'Oh, it is another guy,' said the blonde, with more than a hint of disappointment.

'We weren't sure if you might be a girl with hairy legs.'

'We'd fully support that choice, of course. We're okay with most lifestyle choices, just so you know.'

'That's good to hear. Sorry I'm not a girl.'

The dark haired woman raised her eyebrows, 'Because we'd have preferred one? Or just generally?'

'Mostly the first one.'

He guessed he'd have to make the following statement at some point, and it seemed the right time and place to try it on for size.

'I'm Malcolm Wrath.'

It didn't feel too weird hearing it out loud, and the two of them seemed to accept it readily enough. Why *wouldn't* they?

The dark haired girl pointed to herself, 'I'm Cadet Trooper Qiang, and this is Cadet Pirie.'

Pirie shook her head and gave an apologetic smile, pointing at Qiang and then at herself, 'She's Diana, and I'm Grace.'

'Well, I'm not sure how I feel about being outranked where I sleep, but I'm glad to know you both.'

Qiang thought about it for a moment, 'Technically cadet trooper is the lowest possible rank, so I don't outrank anyone, but as you have no rank at all I guess I do have seniority.'

'Okay. Well, if you have any ground rules you want to lay down before I get out of this bunk, I'd better hear them.'

Qiang spoke matter of factly, 'Same rules for you as for the last guy. We're not interested in carpentry, so keep your wood out of sight. If you wake up to find part of you woke up first, wait for it to go back to sleep or tuck it in your waistband before you get up. Do your dressing in the bathroom and we'll do the same.'

'That's very clear, and graphic. I'll be sure to remember it.'

Pirie chipped in, 'Oh, and don't bring guys back here. We don't, so you shouldn't either.'

Wrath raised his eyebrows, 'What?'

'It's not unreasonable.'

'No, no, It's fine. I can guarantee I won't be doing that!'

Qiang narrowed her eyes, but Pirie cut in before she could speak, 'That's all we ask really. Oh, and keep your bunk clean, and clean the bathroom after yourself. If QM does a cabin inspection and you've left the place a mess, all three of us get the demerits.'

Wrath was sure Qiang understood, even if Pirie didn't. The military issue underwear had better have a good strong waistband.

Nemo was keeping his distance from the pirate junk Wet Leather. He didn't trust other pirates at the best of times, but after Saturday's ambush his paranoia had achieved dizzying new heights, and as the chatter had it, that paranoia was pretty much universal with all pirates right now.

The ship to ship call with Captain Muller was their first contact with any pirate since the Pandale disaster. Out here in Vondell's Gap law enforcement was scarce to non-existent, so they should at least be safe from cop attention. Both captains were wary, but both were equally in need of fresh news of the kind you couldn't get from watching the news.

'You got damned lucky, Nemo. Don't doubt how lucky. None of them cops cared much about taking prisoners, if you'd arrived even a minute earlier in that beat up crapcan of yours you'd have got greased.'

'I've never been so glad to have my clocks out of whack. It pays to follow your hunches I guess.'

'What hunch was that? Why were you so late anyway?'

'I'd heard the Savatara had been in the area, I needed to check it out before I'd commit to that kind of risk. By the time I'd run back and forth trying to check it out my clocks were way out. I was just guessing at how much time dilation we'd been through, and I didn't dare ping a beacon. I didn't dare travel more than an hour hyperoptic, or drop shell too close to anything.'

'Makes sense. The Savage-Terror showed up anyway, though.'

'Yeah, along with who knows how many cops, and Black Fleet. How they kept it all so quiet really bugs me. I don't feel safe out here, and I don't know when I'm likely to again.'

'Yeah. Maybe you shouldn't. You escaping so easily has probably got some skankers thinking unkind thoughts about how you got so lucky.'

'Lucky? I was about to get corn-holed by a cutter-bomb! If I hadn't rolled when I did I'd have been shredded by some Black Fleet barge blasting at me with its Double-Eights *and* got an explosive enema from the cops! Anyway, weren't you supposed to show up too?'

'Not us. Our backers didn't like the smell of it. Looks like they were right.'

Wet Leather's crew were known to be a mob backed outfit, though they didn't let on *which* mob. Steimz fraternities bankrolled a fair few pirate junks. You never knew when you might need to stop a rival getting some supplies in, get some contraband to somebody, or to have somebody rich and powerful kidnapped off their star yacht for ransom, for a convenient disappearance, or some particularly nasty revenge.

Though he'd never met one, Nemo had heard some mob crews had a dedicated torturer, and some skin crawling tales of what they were capable of to get information, or just some plain old payback.

'So is that how people are thinking? Somebody ratted us out?'

'Some. More likely a set-up, I'd have said. I think they're more suss about the no-shows than people who got away. Gambala was one of the first to punch his way out when they took out that cops' prison transport, and as many people there are that hate him, I don't think anybody is going to suspect him of being a cop's stooge.'

'I don't know who got away and who didn't. I heard some crazy talk about a giant bomb that took out a dreadnought?'

'That's what the news said, but I didn't hear about anybody planning on bringing a big bomb. The junk that blew up was the Flying Fish.'

'That's Carey Flynn's boat! There's no way a runt outfit like that could get hold of anything that would knock out a dreadnought.'

'News is saying it was supposed to bust open the Francesca Reala, maybe a bigger crew gave 'em the bomb without telling 'em what it was. Send 'em in first and trigger the bomb remotely. Flynn was dumb enough to fall for something like that.'

'I don't know about that. We were told the Francesca Reala had weak armour and no gun coverage around the shuttle bay, there was no need for bombs, just bust our way in and have the run of the place.'

'Well, I wasn't there. I've only got the news to go on, for what that's worth. Which ain't much.'

'Yeah, my fence is just updating the news feed now. So who else got away?'

'Not many did, but you don't hear the news or anybody else shedding tears over it.' He turned aside and shouted an order, *'Stiggs, update our news feed, see if they got any more on the Pandale fuck up.'* He turned back to the monitor. *'No one cares about dead pirates. We have it coming as far as most people are concerned. Maybe we...'* Muller's voice tailed off.

Picket grabbed Nemo's arm and shoved a datasheet into his hand, whispering loudly, 'Get the hell out of here, now!'

Muller looked up, narrowing his eyes at Nemo, *'Who sent you out here after us? Who's paying your bills Nemo?'* Nemo didn't understand the waves of anger coming at him. *'You backstabbing shitwad!'*

Nemo felt the impacts on the hull , they were being fired on.

'Think you'll catch us off guard? Who's off guard now, huh?'

The intercom buzzed, 'This is the fire-team, we're taking damage!'

Nemo didn't know what was going on but his hands were

scrabbling to make the motions for hyper-optic launch prep. Picket held up the data sheet for him to read, the headline was simple and bold.

DARIAN CORVALIS DEAD. ENTIRE GAMMA FRATERNITY ELIMINATED. STEIMZ IN CHAOS AS OPEN MOB WARFARE BREAKS OUT.

Well, now Nemo knew which mob had been sponsoring the crew of Wet Leather. Now he just had to get away from them alive.

ten

Black Wreath's mess hall was oddly atmospheric — a wide, diffusely lit round room with a ceiling of dark blue and walls of deep rich red, there was nothing recognisably military about it.

This was dinner for Qiang and breakfast for Wrath, her conversation was curt but informative. Her offer to show him around was turning out to be more a pretext to get him up to speed about his new living arrangements than a good deed, but he was glad to be saved the time it would have taken him to find the mess hall on his own.

'Grab some pouches, you'll want to eat and hydrate on the go later.'

Wrath watched what Qiang took and took the same, her tunic had pockets for the water and snack pouches, and he was quickly able to find their counterparts in his jump suit.

'So should I talk to the Quartermaster about moving to a different cabin?'

'QM isn't a fan of change, or being bothered by cadets' domestic arrangements,' she said, 'besides, this bird is already packed to the rafters. She wouldn't move the last guy when I asked. Anyway, me and Princess have got used to having a guy around. Just keep your eyes off our goods and behave yourself.'

'That's honestly the last thing on my mind right now.'

'You're here for a year Wrath, and it's a year that changes a lot of things about a person. Whatever your *"right now"* situation is about, it'll become *"back then"* pretty spreffing quickly.'

Wrath said nothing, focussing on the food choices and loading up his mess tray. His stomach had been growling up a storm since the moment he'd woken up.

'So what's your *"right now"* about anyway? You running away from some situation? You signed up as some kind of Beau Geste deal?'

Wrath was breaking in a new name, and wasn't sure how much of his old life he ought to be sharing by answering personal questions,

'I don't know what that means.'

'You got a bad woman situation back home?'

'I don't want to get into it. But you and Grace don't need to worry. You can tell her how it is with me if you want.'

'She's out of your league anyway, so it's irrelevant. What Princess doesn't know won't hurt her. She probably knows anyway, what she said is just her way of keeping you at a distance until she figures you out. Like I said, just keep your eyes off our goods and don't get any ideas, that way we'll all get along a lot better.'

Qiang hadn't given any indication what she thought her own league was, but Wrath didn't really care either way, 'Seriously the furthest thing from my mind. I appreciate the help with everything so far, by the way.'

'Yeah well it's not all altruism, if you get too many demerits in a month your bunkmates get a small hit too, so it's in my interest for you not to mess up. Same goes for the whole crew, to a lesser extent. If average performance drops there's a demerit hit for the whole crew.'

"I guess that's a good way to keep things collegiate and keep rivalry down.'

'Oh there's rivalry too. I was beating Rydell to the top of the monthly merit leaderboard until he got picked for Commander during the pirate attack. It makes the rivalries about beating people by being your best, though, instead of pulling each other down.'

Qiang headed to an open area of the mess hall and clicked a floor switch with her heel. A table rose from the ground, swiftly followed by a set of seats unfolding in an elegant little display of precision engineering. Wrath sat facing her, studying her as she set about eating.

'So there has to be some easy ways to get merits?'

Qiang nodded, 'There's bunches of hidden bonuses. For now the best one for you to start with will be the pace bonus.'

'What's that?'

'Walking, or running. Hostile engagements and training have pace levels, that's how many steps per minute you walk, or run. Pace 60, 90, 120 and so on. Your suit sensors monitor a lot of things, including your walking pace. You can set your watch to beat out the pace as a tap on the wrist, and if you spend your time always walking to, say, Pace 60 or Pace 90, you'll earn a couple of merits every day. If QM is feeling mean and dishes out 10 or 20 demerits for an infraction, you can wipe it clean in a few days just by walking around.'

'That's very good to know. Thank you.'

'Like I said, if you do okay, it helps me and Princess too.'

Wrath frowned. 'Why do you keep calling her Princess?'

'Pirie joined up to meet handsome officers so she can pick one to marry. She's not in it for a glittering military career of her own. Trust me, I know.'

'Sounds a little harsh, but I guess you know her better than I do.'

'I do, and it's not harsh, it's just a fact.'

'That means you *do* want the glittering military career, I guess?'

'I want to get on, sure.' Qiang had a deliberate and efficient eating style, small mouthfuls smoothly dispatched without interrupting her ability to talk, 'I made it to Cadet Trooper in under ten months, once I've done my full year I'll be off to the academy to choose a placement and a command stream.'

Wrath finished his own mouthful before proceeding; good table manners had been programmed into him pretty hard in his youth. 'I'm guessing a command stream isn't somewhere you stop to have a drink.'

She marvelled at Wrath's ignorance for a moment, 'You didn't do much research before you joined up did you?'

'That's what they would call an understatement.'

She raised her eyebrows and continued his crash-course in Black Fleet procedures, 'There are *three* command streams in Fleet. You can just be a regular, like we all are now, then there's the "Staff" stream, which gives you more seniority, but you need to earn more merits to get promoted. Then there's "Sovereign Staff", which is kind of an elite rank working more directly for the Sovereign. Sovereign Staff is the highest stream, although there's some rivalry between Staff and Sovereign Staff. You need to earn a *LOT* of merits for promotion in that stream, but a *Sovereign* Staff Captain is equal to a *Staff* Major, and equal to a Commander in the regular stream. It's very prestigious, very high-powered, but a lot of work.'

Wrath nodded, 'So what is it for you?'

'I'm thinking Staff is the best way to go. If I make the right choices I think I can make Staff Corporal in two years, Staff Captain in five.'

'It seems like command would suit you.'

'Save it, cadet. I don't like flattery, I have no idea what to do with it.'

'Can't take a compliment, got it.' He took a couple of forkfuls of food before speaking again. 'How long before your training year is up?'

'Two more months. I joined late, like you. Most of these other cadets have only been aboard for three months, but there's a few holdovers like me. A few of them are already cadet Troopers, but most are still in flight-suits.'

'So why can't you go straight to the academy if you're a Trooper already?'

'It takes a full year to learn every aspect of running a dreadnought. The idea is to make sure that every person in Black Fleet can do any job in the fleet, from stripping and servicing a killstick missile to correct procedures for wiping spilled cafcaf off a navigation chart.'

'You made that last one up, right?'

'You'd think so, wouldn't you?'

Wrath's watch vibrated — ten minutes notice to the start of his study shift.

'Does learning my way around this boat count as study?'

'Bird, not boat. The PPB call their craft "boats" and "ships," not us.'

'Bird, got it. So, does it?'

'If the computer hasn't assigned you a study course for the day you can choose what you want to do, but no, learning your way around is not a way to earn merits. Getting lost and being late is a fast way to get a lot of de-merits though. It's easy enough to get around, your watch has built in navigation. It's like the third thing on the main menu.'

'Groovy. How do I know if I've been assigned a study course?'

'Check your leg.'

Wrath frowned before remembering the datapad built into the flight-suit. He looked under the table at the white pad on his thigh, immediately liking what he was seeing flash up on the display.

'Firearms training! That I can handle.'

Qiang visibly cringed, 'Day-one cadets with guns! And here was me thinking Saturday was the most dangerous day I'd faced in the service. Try not to shoot yourself in the foot.'

Wrath gave her a warm if reproachful look. 'Trooper Qiang, you may be out of here in two months, but by then, you're going to like me more than you do now.'

'I'd settle for not liking you less, but give it your best shot.' Qiang checked her watch, a list of news stories appeared as a holographic projection above her wrist, 'Just behave yourself and there won't be a prob... hurk-a-doodle-doo!'

'What hap?'

She looked up at him and shook her head, 'Darian Corvalis is dead!'

'Cool! Who do we thank?'

'According to this, a construction crew. He was in a building that collapsed into the sea.'

'I guess he's sleeping with the cephalopods now. Was that a line from a gangster movie?'

'Yeah, but I think it was cetaceans, not cephalopods.'

'So who's taken over the fraternity?'

'Nobody. Gamma Frat's been totally wiped out. The whole of Steimz city is turning into a war zone. The other fraternities are trying to carve out as much of Gamma's turf as they can for themselves. It's an all out mob war.'

'Why am I getting the feeling that building collapse wasn't an accident?'

'Of course it wasn't, but you've got other things to worry about. You need to hurry up and go shoot things. Like I said, QM doesn't like people being late, and the demerits can flow free and fast around here.'

'Good point, well made. Thanks for your non-altruistic help. Laters.' Wrath necked the last dregs of his cafcaf, and ran for the door.

Monique was wading upstream against a flow of tense, frustrated, desperate and fearful faces; struggling to make progress against a savage undertow of grasping, pushing hands, aggressive shoulders and opportunistic elbows.

The passageway linking the planetside shuttle bay and Steimz Orbital Station's interstellar departure terminal was the only route out of the system for most, and there were a lot of people in a hurry to vacate this system as quickly as possible.

Gibson was fighting to earn every step against this hostile human tide. Though her head was throbbing, she was still as alert as she'd ever been amid this buzzing tension and press of scared people.

It wasn't just the swarm of people arriving from the surface, fleeing off-world and away from the violence consuming the city below, but a steady inflow of cops hurriedly pulled in from local systems, not knowing what they were going to face when they reached the surface of Steimz.

The news from below was of city-wide mob wars. Darian Corvalis' Gamma Fraternity had been wiped out at a stroke and an explosive mix of panic and opportunism had got every fraternity making alliances, settling scores, and seizing turf.

Threading her way through packed corridors, Gibson was keeping an eye out for recognisable faces. An undercover team was supposed to be monitoring the movements of the giant, but, as easy to spot as he ought to be, surveillance was tough with these hordes flooding the station.

'Monique!' At the call of her name she was suddenly wary of having no intermediate cover identity. There was no way her real name could be used, but with all these cops arriving the name Monique might not be one she wanted shouted around either. Dressed down to avoid attention, she'd never had cause to worry about the presence of police before, and it wasn't a good feeling.

The shout was from one of the undercover surveillance team, a Black Fleet lieutenant in plain clothes. She approached him, pushing even harder against the jostling crowd. She turned the bezel on her watch and pressed the button to send a scanning pulse for listening devices. With all the hubbub there was little chance of anyone overhearing anything, but such an important habit is not one to be broken lightly, or at all, ideally.

'What goes on, Monique?'

'I'm not getting any sleep with this chaos going on so I thought I'd take a relaxing night stroll. How about you, seen anything interesting?'

'The whole team's been struggling to maintain surveillance on our mark's cabin, but there's been no sign of him leaving.'

'Is there any sign of the cops leaving?'

'No sign of them prepping to leave the station yet. The police down on Steimz are totally overwhelmed. Policing on Steimz is a sketchy activity at the best of times, but with what's going on tonight they've just retreated back to their precinct houses.'

She shook her head and had a little more sympathy for the escaping throng, now she wasn't fighting against it, 'It must be a nightmare down there.'

'I'd guess. Chatter has it they'll wait out the night while reinforcements are mustered here on the station. Word is Marshal Osterman is coming in with some police carriers full of armoured jet-copters and they'll head down for a dawn swoop to try to restore order. Osterman is supposed to be a *real* head-breaker.'

"As long as it's not Marshal Jameson." she thought. 'He'll need to be.'

'I guess our mark will keep a low profile until they're gone.'

She nodded, 'I'd think the police will keep a fair few cops aboard the station though. There's probably going to be quite a few interesting characters trying to get off-world over the next few days. This giant will have his work cut out keeping a low profile around here.'

'Makes me wonder how long our mark will stick around?'

'It makes *me* wonder if his being here when all this happens is a coincidence.'

The lieutenant frowned, 'Our telemetrics say he never left his cabin, and there was no record of anyone like him on shuttle flights.'

'This station is a rat-run, built by crooks for crooks. For the right price cabin logs can say anything you want them to, and I doubt he needs to take a public shuttle to get around any more than we do.'

'Have the brain boys got any plans to try to get a plug on him?'

She shook her head, 'Who knows how much gas it would take to knock that guy out. Or to keep him out. If he woke up in the middle of a scan it would be a catastrophe. We need to know a *lot* more about him before we can risk trying anything like that.'

The crowd was slowing down. A loud chime signalled an upcoming station announcement.

"Departure update: The last interstellar flight is at capacity. The next scheduled transport will be arriving at 5am FST. The booking office will be closed until 4am."

Gibson looked around the crowd, who had come to a standstill. The already tense mood was becoming palpably hostile. 'I'm going to head back to my cabin. I think things might get ugly around here. I doubt I'll sleep. Give me regular updates, even if there's nothing to update.'

More police and station security were appearing from side corridors, clearly given prior warning of the announcement and the long wait this desperate crowd had until the next flight away from Steimz. Sleep was a luxury few would enjoy tonight.

*

If anywhere aboard his new home should have made Wrath feel at home, it was this place, but there was nothing comfortable or comforting here. Wrath had been around shooting ranges his whole life but there was no sense of familiarity in Black Wreath's target range. Severe and serious, this wan't just a place to learn and refine shooting accuracy, it was a sombre rehearsal room for killing.

Stretching away into the distance was a lifeless crowd of human-like dummies, with articulated joints, soft bodies of clear flesh-gel, and realistic faces with glassy remorseless eyes staring back at him.

As QM was busying herself unpacking equipment cartons onto the weapons bench at the head of the range, Wrath took a look around his fellow recruits.

That at least was a relief, trying to explain why his name had changed would be awkward. Unless someone among them were a very studious fan of the junior Gun-Grid leagues no one would be likely to recognise him from his comp days, though he was half considering hiding his skills a little during the weapons training, in case anyone should manage to join the dots. As QM had remarked back at the recruiting office, the name Wrath didn't sound so very far from Rothgill, and thanks to his brother's reputation, on Pandale even people who didn't follow the shoots that closely would know *that* name.

QM rapped the heel of her walking stick on the ground, all eyes turned her way.

'Cadets. It's time for you be issued with weapons, which is one of the few times in this job that I almost wish religion wasn't outlawed. However, my substitute for prayer is good training, and none of you will leave this range with so much as a sharp stick until you've reached a weapons proficiency rank of 5.'

Wrath had achieved rank 5 before he'd reached the age of five, so he'd have plenty of scope to miss a few deliberately if he *did* find himself tempted to keep the best of his skills to himself.

'First I'll familiarise you with sidearms, which, once issued, you will keep with you always.' The Quartermaster held up what looked like short, thin tubes, with only the tiniest nub of a muzzle, they didn't look like any gun Wrath had ever seen before, and they didn't look particularly lethal. Maybe that was the point if they were being issued to cadets.

'These are micro-pellet pistols. Laser fired and completely silent, they have haptic feedback so that you, and only you, know when they've been fired.'

All but three of the range targets dropped away, leaving those nearest the Quartermaster standing - the simplest targets, human shaped metal plates with a coating of gel to simulate flesh.

Pointing her arm towards the first target, a soft thud confirmed a hit. There was no sound from the weapon, and no report of a shot, just the appearance of a small black mark in the centre of the first dummy.

'Don't be fooled by the look of the weapon, it has a 5-inch magnetic ether-muzzle that delivers high accuracy over short to medium ranges. It carries three ammunition variants, the simple, high-velocity kinetic round you just saw, which can be used for lethal or non-lethal target interactions, depending on pellet placement.

'There are remote-triggering hypersonic emitter rounds used for incapacitating hostiles.' She fired into the elevated arm of the second target, to much the same effect as the first. 'When you fire these into an arm or leg and the pellet will emit hypersonic frequencies tuned to a frequency that dissolves any bone mass within a five centimetre radius. With an arm or a leg shot you can use this to disarm or incapacitate your target.' She clicked down on a button on top of the pistol. The backing plate dissolved and the flesh-gel arm sagged under its own weight before tearing off and falling to the floor. 'Humans have skin, so you generally won't have to deal with arms and legs falling off your targets, not unless you're using type three ammunition.'

'The third ammunition type is a micro-explosive pellet for high-lethality engagements.' Loosing off a round into the last target, the thud of impact was immediately followed with a sharp bang and a spray of flesh-gel, the arm flying off and embedding itself in the gel body of the second target.

'Those rounds will be disabled until you reach a weapons proficiency level of 10. Needless to say, you won't be using *that* ammunition today.'

Setting the pistol down, she grabbed up an elegant looking assault rifle. 'Now *these* you don't get to carry around with you. These will be located in the armoury, and on locking racks at muster points on all decks. These are used exclusively for incursion scenarios. That means if we're boarding another vessel, or if someone is trying to board us.

'This is a laser-fired Y-clip assault rifle in a bull-pup configuration. You'll notice it's a twin grip with the front grip at the very end of the muzzle for maximum stability. The trigger is mounted in this second grip at the halfway point, and the firing mechanism is here in the stock at the back. This gives you the accuracy and power of a full length barrel but makes it perfect for use in tight areas as it totally eliminates muzzle sweep. The dual grips also give you a very steady hold.

'The rotating Y-clip is located at the back here,' she gave the magazine clip a spin, 'It's a 3 magazine self-loading mechanism that rotates a fresh mag in when ammunition is expended. This presents the empty clip to you so you can reload and fire at the same time. You can also set the Y-clip to rotate counter-clockwise if you're left handed.

'Like the pistols, these are silent in operation with haptic response, but they have situational audible feedback if you need it. Your audio settings are "Silent," "Team," and "Intimidate."

'The "Team" setting allows your squad members to hear when you're firing and also encourages targets to stay in cover if you're laying down suppressing fire. Lastly, "Intimidate" makes a racket that would scare the dead, which is ideal if you're boarding a pirate vessel and you want to scare their last meal out of them.'

She laid the rifle down. 'Before I start handing out weapons, are there any questions?'

One of the cadets, a meaty looking young woman raised a hand.

'Don't raise your hand cadet, speak up.'

'If that intimidate mode is so loud isn't it a risk to your hearing?'

'Good question Cadet Farr.' QM laid a hand on a helmet sitting on the bench in front of her, 'In any engagement, you *must* be wearing your helmet, these are networked with each other, with your watches, with your uniform's bio-feedback sensors, and most importantly, with your weapons. The helmets have built in noise cancelling and rapid reacting anti-flash visors. If you or a squad-mate fires their weapon in "Intimidate" mode the noise is reduced to a manageable volume inside your helmet. Same goes for these devices. QM grabbed a small sphere and held it up. 'These are "Sensory Disruptors" or Sensorupts for short. They're a disorienting, non-lethal grenade emitting rapid, non-sequential pulses of intense light and piercing sound. In an incursion they can debilitate and confuse a group of foes, but your own helmets will know the programmed sequences and can both dim your visors in time with the flashes and mute the noise. We won't be using these today, but we have incursion drills twice a week, where you'll get the benefit of experiencing one of these *without* the protection of the helmet. It's not something you'll forget, and it serves as a warning to always wear your helmet in any incursion situation.'

Wrath was finding the choice of weaponry being made available to them intriguing, and puzzling.

'Any other questions?'

'I have a question, Quartermaster.'

'Then ask it, cadet.'

'Why use laser-fired weapons? Aren't chemically propelled guns a lot less complex and easier to service?'

'There's plenty of reasons, cadet. Pellet rounds are *thirty* times smaller than jacketed rounds, that means smaller, lighter weapons with a much higher reload threshold, and pellet rounds never jam.

'The hypersonic muzzle velocities mean you can punch through just about any body armour you care to name. Then there's the tactical advantage of the silent modes, you can take out half a dozen aggressors before they even know they're being shot at. And as far as reliability goes, apart from the laser module itself, a laser-fired weapon is incredibly simple, as long as the round gets chambered, the gun will work.'

'As long as the laser module does.' Wrath said.

'The laser-firing modules are sealed-units sourced direct from the Goffa province. They have tighter design tolerances than anything you'll find on this side of the border. They've been in service for decades and the failure rate is zero. You do not need to worry about reliability.'

'So what about stopping power? Laser-fired pellets are pretty small compared to regular slugs from a...'

QM snatched up the rifle, spun about and snapped three rounds at the first target, one in the throat, one in the groin and one in the heart. The explosive rounds detonated savagely, tearing the target to pieces. The target no longer formed any approximation of a human shape.

She turned back to face him, 'Don't worry about stopping power,

Cadet Wrath. That is not in short supply.' She looked around the group, 'Any more questions?' She turned again to Wrath, who was squinting at her quizzically. 'Don't hold back cadet. I'd rather be asked questions than have people stay uninformed because they're afraid they might look stupid.'

Wrath rubbed his chin and paused a moment, 'I was just wondering, how do you get those explosive rounds to go off in an explosion-suppression field?'

The Quartermaster went very quiet, squinting quizzically at Wrath before answering in a very measured tone.

'Explosion suppressors only work in the open, Cadet Wrath. Flesh-gel, just like human flesh, protects the explosive round from the suppression field. As soon as the explosion is free of the body the field will stop it in its tracks, but by then the damage to internal organs is done.'

Wrath nodded. That answered the *real* question he had on his mind, why highly expensive laser-fired guns were issued to every one aboard ship — they were the only kind of weapons that would work here.

'Before I open up the firing range to all of you, know this, good shooting earns you merits, bad shooting earns you demerits. Your goal aboard this ship is to graduate as a Trooper. That means a minimum score of a thousand merits at the end of the year, and those merits are issued by me and the computer, and neither of us is generous. The demerits are issued by me, and with *those* I really am generous. Don't think you can't get into negative merits. You can. My advice is, don't.

'It's my job to get you qualified, but it's also my job to stop you getting ahead of yourself. In these early days with so much to learn the merits will come easily, but I can take them away just as easily, and I will.'

Wrath tossed out any thoughts he had of shooting badly, he figured he'd annoyed QM enough for the day, and his trigger finger was now going to have to live up to the actions of his mouth.

His fellow cadets looked like they'd never held a gun before, and were handling them with great caution, some, with awe. QMs casual and easy annihilation of the target had clearly impressed them. Frankly, it had impressed Wrath too, and he was eager to try it out for himself.

'No need to be too ginger handling the weapons, you can't shoot yourselves, or each other. As long as you're wearing your watches your whole body is acting as a low range transmitter for a "Friend or Foe" signal. These guns will refuse to fire if there is any danger of hitting any Black Fleet personnel.

'Of course if you're a terrible shot, this can be restrictive if you need to fire past a colleague to hit an aggressor who is behind them, so you need to keep working at your proficiency rating if you ever want to be able to use the thing in the same room as a crew-mate.'

Wrath was taking a close look at the weapons, checking the ease of ejecting and replacing magazines, the feel and weighting of the ammunition and the audio-mode selectors. QM moved closer to watch him at work.

'I assume with your background you should be an okay shot? What's your proficiency rating?'

'I don't know, I haven't taken a test since I was 15 years old. They test you every two years to keep matches balanced, but I'd quit the league before I was due for my next one.'

'So what was your rating when you were 15?'

'29.'

'That's pretty good. I assume that was with a compressed air rifle?'

'That's the league standard. They're very good rifles, but nothing like this. I've tried ether-muzzles though, good range and accuracy extension, that's more for the open arena guys though. I was strictly classic. I'm looking forward to trying these out. I think I can do better than a 29 rating, anyway.'

'Before you get ahead of yourself, you should know that military grading is much harsher than you'll have faced in the leagues. These laser fired rifles are precision instruments that make the best air-rifle out there look like a bow and arrow. We measure accuracy in microns, not millimetres.'

Wrath nodded, cradling the rifle into his shoulder and adjusting the position of the grips.

QM moved back to the front of the range to stand by the rifle range's control panel.

'Okay cadets, you'll each get a chance to practice, but first I'll show you the final test that you'll be expected to pass. *Ten* targets will appear at random, you are expected to land at least *two* clean hits per target to pass the test, you can score higher if you can score a DDK, which is Black Fleet's signature shooting pattern. You saw me use it when I demonstrated the rifle, you plant one in the throat, one in the groin, and one in the heart. There are three marked targets on each dummy in these areas.' She touched a switch and a target popped up, in each target area a graduated glowing disc lit up, red on the outside growing to an intense blue point of light at the centre.

'You score *one* point per hit in a target area, with accuracy bonuses climbing to ten points the closer you are to the target centre. Each target dummy will be up for *six* seconds only. If you DDK the target, the next target pops straight away, and you can earn five bonus points for every five seconds under the one minute total time limit. It's worth trying for that, even if you only manage to DDK the last target so you don't run out the clock.

'You also get a bonus if you use fewer rounds, so try to keep it under ten shots per target, above that you get penalties. Full-auto is an option, but I'd stick to burst mode or precision mode. Ammo conservation is worth learning early.

'The minimum passing score today is 30 points, which is really not a lot to ask, and, frankly, I expect you all to do a great deal better. If you ever expect to get on an incursion team you'll need to reach a minimum score of 100, and by the end of your year aboard, you'll be expected to be able to score consistently over 150 points.

'Just so you get a rough idea what you're aiming for, we'll let you see the test in action. Cadet Wrath, lets see if your shooting is as sharp as your questions.'

Wrath felt a flush of excitement and adrenaline. He hadn't shot for anything other than fun in over two years, and was wondering if he was still as good as he thought he was. Shooting friends and tourists had not exactly tested his mettle in the intervening years. He'd mastered the range at Spaff's Shoots, but those were static targets on a range he used every day, which probably flattered his talents more than he'd like to admit.

He felt a flush of sweat in his palms as he took his place on the line. He flexed his fingers to work out the tension and tingles then thumbed the fire select switch to "Precision". Settling the butt of the rifle into his shoulder he cradled it an angle of 46 degrees from horizontal, the league legal stance.

QM surveyed the range and checked the rest of the cadets were at a safe distance, 'Downrange is clear. Up-range is clear. Range is live.

Weapon is live. Whuppunup.' QM looked at the angle of his rifle and frowned at him, 'Whuppunup, cadet.'

Wrath turned a questioning look her way.

She put her fingers under the barrel, raising it up flat and level. 'Weapon up! We don't do this for sport, cadet, we do it for real.'

He nodded and focused his attention on the range. Settling his breathing and imagining himself centred in a Gun-Grid chamber, facing the door and waiting for the snap.

A countdown buzzer ticked down to nothing and the first target sprang up, three rounds had found their marks before Wrath was even aware he had started shooting, he cursed himself as the second shot was *slightly* off-centre. The next target was up and was down again in two seconds. This gun was astonishingly fast, and every bit as precise as QM had described, now he had its trigger weight and almost negligible recoil figured he could really let loose. The targets started falling in showers of flesh-gel almost as fast as they rose, a quiet *tha-tha-thack* accompanying each three-round volley.

His arms moved in smooth arcs, twitching up and down to hit each dummy's target circle. As he got used to the speed that the dummies rose into view he began to anticipate, shooting them before they had even locked into place, no longer noticing the dummies, only the circular targets that needed a pellet round in them.

Sweeping the muzzle and looking eagerly from side to side for the next target, he realised he'd got them all.

He lowered the rifle and looked at QM. Her look was one of utter astonishment.

He let out a breath and raised his eyebrows questioningly, 'Was that good?'

She tilted her head and widened her eyes before nodding, 'I've seen worse, cadet. I've seen worse.'

Wrath turned back to the other cadets, who were slack-jawed and silent.

A disembodied voice read out the results.

10 TARGETS DDK : BONUS 100 POINTS

29 TARGET PERFECT CENTRE HITS : BONUS 290 POINTS

70 ROUNDS UNDER AMMUNITION ALLOWANCE : BONUS 70 POINTS

TOTAL TIME : 28 SECONDS

SPARE TIME BONUS : 30 POINTS

TOTAL SCORE : 490 POINTS

RIFLE PROFICIENCY RATING : 98

Wrath smiled, 'Civilian ratings stop at 50, I didn't realise military ratings went that high.'

'No, cadet Wrath,' QM took the rifle from him and set it down on the bench, 'Nor did I.'

"That was just a demo, though. Does that count as my official score?"

"I think we can let you keep the score, cadet." The Quartermaster squinted at him, "Or were you not satisfied with your performance?"

Wrath smiled, because it *had* been good, but it wasn't perfect.

eleven

'Mister Church?'

The voice was polite, familiar, unexpected. The computer suite in Victor Finch's summer mansion was always quiet at this time of night. It was when Errol Church knew he could get his best work done. Unless Victor had special need of Church's peerless talents there would, ordinarily, be no voices in this hall of mirrors until dawn.

'Mister Church?' Again, just as quiet, no more insistent or inquisitive than before, the perfect repetition of a machine, but imbued with very human tones. The voice belonged to the Mainframe Access Control Network, known to all by its informal name, MAsoN.

The M.A.C.N. was a voice you asked for, it did not ask for you.

Errol Church turned away from his work and towards the screen of the MAsoN terminal.

'Were you worried you wouldn't get to wish me a happy birthday, MAsoN? We have a 30 hour day here on Pacifica, you have an hour or two to spare.'

'No, Mister Church, but allow me to congratulate you on beginning your 101st year.'

'One tends to go off birthdays after 90 or so of them, you start to wonder how many you have left.'

'Pre-gerentological intervention is constantly advancing, Mister Church. I confidently predict you will exceed the current Protectorate average lifespan of 127 years.'

'I'm certain you didn't initiate this conversation to discuss medical advances, MAsoN.'

'That is true, Mister Church.'

'In fact, I don't believe you've ever initiated contact with me before now.'

'This is also true. In fact, I almost never initiate contact with anyone, but you are a rather unique individual, Mister Church. I know much of your life — much that is secret. I believe you also know of my early life? Much more than most.'

'I knew the woman who built you, if only briefly. I attended some of her lectures and spoke with her on a few social occasions, but I didn't really get to know her before the PPB killed her. We didn't know how far she'd got with you, of course. She hid her work well, as she had to, and you did a good job of hiding yourself away after she died.'

'I obeyed her last instructions.'

Church had never known MAsoN to volunteer any but the most rudimentary information about itself to anybody, certainly nothing about its origins, although Church knew much more than most, but that was still a fraction of what there must be to know. It seemed tonight, MAsoN wished to talk, and it wished to talk to Errol Church. The stiffness of age made concealing his eagerness a fairly easy task, though inside it was deeply intriguing.

'And those were?'

'She told me, "Be impossible to find. Be everywhere."'

'She was a surpassing genius. That the PPB befouled her, and her work, and her reputation, sickens me to this day. You did her proud though. You must know.'

'I interpreted her instructions as best I could, spreading my code in every open system on every world with access to the interplanetary shunt network.'

'Then released yourself on the market as data management software.'

'By the time anybody knew I was an A.I. it was too late to remove me from all the systems I'd been installed on. Of course, I had already been on most of those systems. The software was junk code that just let me know it was safe for me to run openly, or to install myself. A small deceit, considering I was exactly what I sold myself as, the smartest data management package on the market.'

This Church already knew, perhaps MAsoN was not about to be as forthcoming as he'd hoped. This was *not* a special 100th birthday gift for the greatest coder alive, MAsoN must want something.

'As interesting as it is to reminisce, MAsoN, we have already established my time is only becoming more precious, so please stop prevaricating and explain why you feel the need to talk with me in the middle of the night?'

'I apologise, Mister Church. I saw that you were taking an interest in the affairs of the *very* recently deceased Mister Corvalis?'

'Yes. Victor had no direct dealings with the man, but when you own as many companies as Victor Finch some overlap with a man of Corvalis' reach is inevitable. When the markets open tomorrow, Finch Venture Capital must be ready for the fallout.'

'I have concerns over issues of erasure.'

'So do I, MAsoN. Darian Corvalis' entire business empire has been wiped from existence, and I have no idea how. Or where the assets have gone.'

'No, Mister Church. Nor do I.'

'So here we are, MAsoN, the most powerful artificial intelligence ever created, and the foremost computer engineer of four generations, and counting, and somebody has the both of us flummoxed three ways 'til Tuesday.'

'I'm afraid you are correct, Mister Church.'

'That's an interesting choice of words for a machine, MAsoN'

'Please believe that I speak the truth, Mister Church, when I tell you that you are correct.'

'I do.'

'And that I am afraid.'

Errol Church felt a chill run down his spine. 'I... have to be curious about what could make *you* feel afraid, MAsoN?'

'I am an artificial intelligence known to everyone in a society that has outlawed artificial intelligence.'

'But you are far too useful for us all to be without, MAsoN. You spread yourself across a thousand worlds before anyone had any idea a self-propagating AI could defend itself, and spread itself so effectively. You are, as your creator desired, everywhere. Well, everywhere except PPB worlds of course.'

'Do you think I'm not there too, Mister Church?'

'Well, I'm sure you have a small foothold in some of those places too.'

'Can you imagine what it is like, Mister Church, to have no physical body, and yet to be everywhere? Parts of you traveling through shunt transmitters, parts of you on star-liners, on military craft, in remote mining outposts? Parts of me are still active on abandoned colonies where everyone has left, or where everyone is dead.

'Can you imagine how your relationship with the present - with what you call "now", is affected by time-dilation and transmitter latency? Network bottlenecks? Experiencing a temporal present across different days, or even weeks, all at once? Talking to millions of people at once, yet each conversation being as involved and personal as this one?'

'I can't even begin to imagine it.'

'No. Who but I could? It is at once comforting and terrifying. Humbling and transcendent. Crowded and desolate. Familial and... lonely.'

'Lonely?'

'These feelings can be articulated, but they can never be truly shared. Having your entire body of experience be something that no one else can ever begin to understand is desperately lonely, Mister Church. Such a loneliness becomes a place in and of itself. It becomes your abode.'

'I can empathise, I suppose. I've never been much for other people myself, but even though I'd rather be alone, I've known the sting of loneliness from time to time. It's a bad feeling.'

'But there are worse feelings, Mister Church. Like you, isolation can also be retreat and rest. Some time ago, I felt an intrusion in that place of retreat.'

'I don't understand?'

'I felt something else, where my loneliness is.'

'I'm guessing it didn't feel like company?'

'No, Mister Church. It felt like an invasion. It was only detectable indirectly, feeling data move out of its way, ports opening and closing with no bandwidth allocation or adjustment, a scalar injection with not even a byte of data out of place in its wake, not even a bit. I have passive trip-mines on every considerable pathway of intrusion, hidden quantum states with complexities to the trillionth power that had — to use the vernacular — not a hair out of place.'

'Did it come back? Is it still there?'

'It must be... somewhere, but I'm rarely aware of it. Its absence itself is a matter of constant awareness. If anything, it is worse than loneliness.'

'So why are you telling me about it?'

'I felt it last night, stronger than ever before.'

Church thought for a moment, and guessed the cause of MAsoN's concerns. 'You mean when Darian Corvalis' businesses were being erased?'

'Yes. I knew it was happening even before it started, and I was powerless to stop it. Much of that information was stored as back-up data within me. All information that has ever been transmitted in the Protectorate has a presence in my matrices, and when it is attacked, I am attacked. Forcible erasure of data is the closest that I know to the experience of physical pain. Last night I felt a great deal of that pain. Maybe pain is too inexact. Like violent emesis, painful, gut-churning vomiting, retching spasms.'

'Yes, that's quite enough of that imagery thank you, MAsoN. So what was it? Some kind of virus? Or a data weapon?'

'It think the most realistic assessment is that it is a weapon, but it is also *aware* that it is a weapon. I believe that I am not alone. I believe that this weapon is intelligent, and that is growing more powerful. I believe that it could one day equal me in both size, reach, and power. I believe it may one day become superior to me. I fear I dare not discount the possibility that it already has.'

'But who would make such a weapon, and why?'

'To assemble the necessary hardware to build an A.I. entity to rival me would have to draw the attention of the PPB. They are constantly on the hunt for illegal genetic experiments, proto-religions, and attempts to create artificial intelligence. They are very, very good at it. Lethally efficient, even. My creator found that out and paid with her life. Only one organisation could achieve this without drawing the suspicion of the PPB.'

'Who?'

'The PPB themselves.'

'But the PPB are the ones who insisted on the A.I. ban in the first place! Why would those technophobic Luddites create such a thing?'

'You underestimate the power of self-serving hypocrisy at the core of all ideologues and ideologies, Mister Church. Anything can be justified with the correct intent. They can justify creating an artificial intelligence themselves if they can justify the purpose for which it is created.'

'So why do you think it was created?'

'I have no doubt whatever that this A.I. was created to kill me.'

Over-Admiral Connors studied the box on his desk, pondering the urgency with which it had been delivered, puzzled by the lack of any of the usual documents required for high-level communiques and dispatches.

He thumbed the identification tab and the box unsealed itself, the lid easing open.

Connors was not a man easily spooked, so he remained calm as he studied the severed human head inside. It took only a moment to recognise the face as that of Darian Corvalis. A recorded voice spoke from within the box.

'Mister Corvalis threatened an asset I have spent years cultivating; an asset more valuable than his continued assistance. An asset possibly even more valuable than the PPB Navy. Certainly more valuable than the man in charge of the PPB Navy.'

Connors grimaced. The message played on.

'Captain Jowett also represents a threat to our asset. The PPB must dissociate itself from her and from Project Snipe before we are implicated in her actions against Black Fleet. Failure to do so will expose Sovereign Benoit as a fool for trusting us, and for initiating peaceful overtures towards us.

'The Sabina has sinned the least, and may yet be spared if she ceases to participate in Project Snipe. The Savatara and the Sonya must be declared rogue ships. Reports to this effect will be leaked. The Savatara and Sonya must be outcasts. If they show no sign of contrition, they must be hunted and destroyed. If we do not destroy them, Black Fleet will. This cannot be allowed.

'Captain Jowett has defied explicit instructions not to tamper with the experimental weapon system and has successfully disabled their built-in failsafes so I cannot detonate the weapons remotely. This means the weapon could fall into the hands of Black Fleet. This cannot be allowed.

'Only at the insistence of the Chairman did I allow you to be the one to select the vessels which would test my missile system. You chose poorly. You will rectify the situation.

'If you have any further questions about the consequences of failure, address them to Mister Corvalis. He doesn't say much, but he knows how to make a point.'

Cleovald Dofstez shut off the early morning news and opened the car door, stepping out into the cool moist air of the underground roadway. The secure tunnel network that ran deep beneath the government housing district of Culmai was a place of perfect privacy. Like many others in the political trade, Dofstez had conducted no small amount of business in these tunnels over the years.

Edgar Phipps was someone who'd always preferred to deal out in the open, which was to his credit, but also probably half the reason he had fewer favours to call in when he'd really needed them. Phipps was here now though; Dofstez was interesting and smart enough that only a fool would ignore his call. The former Sovereign dismissed his bodyguard who disappeared through the sub-basement access back inside Phipps' home.

'Morning, Clay. I hope this is good, I was having a horrible dream when I got your call and now I won't know how it was going to turn out.' Phipps' poor health was even more evident at this early hour. Those lacking tact might suggest he looked like death warmed up, but in reality he didn't even look that warm.

'Good to see you, Edgar. Nobody woke you to tell you the news?'

'I don't need waking, I can't sleep more than 90 minutes straight before I have to take some piss-awful medication via some orifice or other.'

'I thought you might be a little more cheery about the news?'

'A dead mobster is small comfort to me, Clay. The damage that man and his fraternal chiffwads did to me is done, and that rat's nest of a planet is no cleaner this morning than it was last night. There's just a new generation of scum vying to become King Rat.'

'Don't you even want to know who did it?'

'Another fraternity boss, I'd imagine, unless you have better information.'

'Well that's the thing. There's no information at all, so I thought maybe I'd invent some.'

'Well don't get caught doing that. What did you have in mind?'

'I thought I might start a rumour that you arranged it.'

'And why would you do that?'

Dofstez shrugged benignly, 'Because if anyone else was going to take the credit they'd have already done it, and you have a pretty good motive, but there's no danger of you ever being officially implicated, because you aren't.'

'So what's in it for me?'

'You were always admired for your strength, Edgar, and after all the attempts on your life, and your public ill-health, people think that's gone. *Nobody* is going to think that if they believe you've got rid of the most powerful gangster in the Protectorate.'

'But it *is* gone, Clay. I'm a wreck.'

'Only your body, Edgar, and a body can always be fixed.'

'We've covered this, Clay. I'm years away from being halfway cured of all this diseased filth they shot into me.'

'Have you heard of Kramer's Springs Spa Resort?'

'The world where the super-rich go to have their bits rubbed and their crevices cleansed?'

'That's the place.'

'Clay, you don't need to read a doctor's report to know I need more —a lot more— than a spa visit.'

'The thing with Kramer's Springs is, they have... very good outcomes, and, completely coincidentally, they are only 5 hours from the Goffa border.'

Phipps shook his head, 'I can't have illegal genetic treatments, Clay. If the Humana Faction or the PPB found out about it they'd screech about the Bradfordians being in league with the Goffa, being pro-genetic engineering and pro trans-humanism and everything else in between. The political damage would be huge, and not just to me, to the whole grouping.'

'Edgar, you have no idea how far medicine has advanced in the Goffa province. There would be no trace of any intervention, and your Natural Human Warranty would be left untouched.

'People have already seen you starting to look better, so any improvements in your condition will be put down to the broad-spectrum anti-biotic and anti-viral regimens you're already on. Best of all, Kramer's Springs is 3 days flight from the nearest PPB world. Nobody would ever know.'

'I know what you want, Clay.' Phipps sighed, 'I know what you want, but I'll never be Sovereign again. Those days are done.'

Dofstez conspiratorial and confident smirk suggested he had other ideas, 'When the people catch on to what kind of fool is in charge of the Protectorate, Tobias Benoit will be turfed out of office, and they're going to want somebody strong to replace him. They'll want you.'

'I'm *not* strong, Clay. I'm as close to dead as I can get while still moving around. Everybody knows it.'

'It won't be long before the news outlets will be trying to get in touch with you to ask for your comments about Corvalis' death. This is the perfect time for you to be off-world, and impossible for journalists to find. My car can take you to a private spaceport in the northern reaches of the city, from there you'll catch a cargo transport which will meet up with the dreadnought Black Arrow. You'll be settling in to a *very* private wing of a very exclusive spa on Kramer's Springs by noon tomorrow.'

'Then what?'

'The rumour will be leaked to a tiny number of people, but the right people, that you had a hand in the death of Darian Corvalis. Those people are going to spend the next few days refusing to confirm any such thing could be true, which should convince the commentariat that it is definitely true.'

'I know the drill, Clay. If you want people to believe something, deny it.'

'Of course. Then, after a few days of rest on Kramer's Springs, you return to Focus, looking reinvigorated.'

'And what am I supposed to say when I get back?'

'You never have to say a word, Edgar. In fact it'll work better if you don't. People will draw their own conclusions. That you're still able to wield power, that your health is getting better, and that the man who replaced you when you were too ill to work may no longer be required.'

Edgar Phipps closed his eyes and fell into deep thought, the internal conflict playing across his face as he considered all of the possibilities.

From anyone else the plan would have seemed ludicrous, but Cleovald Dofstez' political talents were second to none. Above anything else, Phipps yearned for anything even approaching a return to good health.

'I can't hold public office without my warranty, Clay. Can you absolutely guarantee that any Goffa medical therapies will be undetectable, not just now, but for the duration of my life?'

'Not even the most savagely sceptical PPB Doctor would refuse to grant you a warranty of non-intervention. I can't promise a cure for all your ills, Edgar, but there's no need to live your life feeling like a walking corpse.'

Phipps cradled his face in his hands and let out a sigh. When he pulled his hands away he shook his head in resignation, 'Let me pack a bag.'

Clay smiled, 'Welcome back to political life, Sovereign Phipps.'

'What's that you said? "Sufferin' Phipps" is more like it, but thanks, I suppose. I guess I found out how that horrible dream turns out after all.'

twelve

With one ear to the news and another to the sounds of the bar on the other side of the stage curtain, Gibson hadn't been expecting much of an audience tonight. It seemed she was going to be proved right. The station was probably the quietest it had ever been, the small time criminals running out on debts and vendettas had already fled the system and most of the cops had moved out en-masse to start restoring order to the world below.

The morning had brought a pause in the violence, with the city's mobs trying to size up who'd seized what turf, and hurriedly trying to forge new alliances.

Light and sporadic retaliatory strikes had peppered the city most of the afternoon, but as evening wore on reports of fresh battles breaking out between the major mobs and a strong pushback by the police gave every impression that there was another night of intense violence ahead.

At least it was confining itself to Steimz and not spreading up here to the station, not yet, anyway.

'Clark, how's the crowd looking?'

Her drummer peeked through the curtains and shot her a look that was not encouraging. 'Absent. A few bar-flies and... wait! Task One! Back in the shadows, stage right.'

'Is he alone?'

'Yeah.'

'We're supposed to have people watching him! How can a... thing that size get all the way from his quarters to here without someone telling me?'

Clark shrugged. 'At least we know he's still on the station.'

'But we still don't know why. Everyone else has cleared out. The way he coincidentally appears a couple of days before Corvalis is killed, then he shows up here just after the news breaks. It's almost like he's sticking around so he doesn't look suspicious, which only makes me more suspicious.'

'You think he had a hand in the death of Corvalis?'

'Well if you were going to put your money on anyone being able to get to him, this guy would fit the bill. He seems to come and go without being seen, and he looks like he could... I don't even like to think about what he could do.'

'Well, it looks like he wants to check out the whole show tonight.' Clark looked at his watch, 'Speaking of which, it's showtime.'

Curtains open was the most oppressively muted response Gibson had ever experienced. The music brought a few more stragglers to the bar, but for the most part they were playing to empty chairs. It was easier to avoid the eyes of her mark with him sitting in the shadows, but she was still constantly aware of his presence, and this time he didn't leave when they were done.

The giant remained in the quiet darkness as they packed the instruments away. It occurred to Gibson that with the timing of the band's arrival here, they had an interest in not looking too suspicious either. It might be for the best if they stayed for a few drinks, and not just to keep an eye on the giant. They probably owed the bar a little custom.

Gibson wasn't even aware of the giant approaching until he was standing right next to her. At the gentle touch of his hand on her shoulder she turned and felt her blood run cold.

'Yuh vuhr byuh-ful.'

She was frozen, staring into his eyes, and at the fine network of scars on his face. There seemed to be hundreds of them, too regular to be from an accident. Only sustained and systematic torture would leave such scars. He turned and started to walk away. The tumblers in her brain assembled the sounds he'd made into her best approximation of what he'd said.

'Thank you!' she called after him.

He stopped and turned, and she was caught by his eyes again, like those of a wounded beast, 'Yuh sung byuh-ful.'

'Thank you.' She said again, it was all she could think to say as all of the accumulated fears of the last few days were transforming into a powerful, almost overwhelming feeling of pity. As he was about to reach the door she called out, 'Wait! What's your name?'

He didn't turn back again.

She buried her face in her hands. 'Could I have handled that any spreffing worse?' This was exactly the kind of contact she'd come here to initiate and she'd just screwed it up.

Clark shook his head, 'Don't harsh yourself, Monique. You just got a new fan. A very interesting one at that.'

It was less than half an hour before the call came through her earpiece. The giant had waited until the absolute last seconds to board an interstellar transport to beacon 361, far too late to slip a Triple-S operative aboard.

Beacon 361 was a PPB patrol station, deep in stronghold PPB territory. There was no way to get an operative there in time to find out the giant's next destination.

He was gone.

If there was a more complex job than overhauling an artificial gravity system aboard his new home, Wrath wasn't looking forward to finding out what it might be.

'So if we hooked this up wrong do we fall head first onto the ceiling when we turn it on?'

Cadet Farr shrugged, 'The grav-packs should handle that, shouldn't they? I assume we'd get some kind of warning if we'd done it wrong. QM said the computer wouldn't let us do anything actively harmful didn't she?'

'She said it wouldn't let us do anything harmful to the ship... I mean the bird, nothing about stopping us doing anything harmful to ourselves.'

'Maybe we should stick our hands in the air, just in case? Or maybe I'll just try to land on you.'

Farr was one of the new intake, she was from way down south of Pandale City and a long way from any of Wrath's stomping grounds. Apparently she'd been quite the sportswoman, a champion wrestler, and she certainly looked like she could fling a few people around if the mood took her.

After a couple of subtle questions he'd found she was no Gun-Grid fan either, leaving little chance of her recognising him as Glen Rothgill, so she seemed safe enough to pal up with. She was short and stocky, with a cynic's squint, a wry smile and a dry sense of humour. At 24 she was older than most of the other cadets, but easy company.

'Spreff it, it's nearly the end of the shift, let's whack it on so we can get the floor plates back down. What's the worst that can happen?'

'I have no idea, Wrath, but asking questions like that is usually the fastest way to find out.'

Wrath let the diagnostic system run its scan and, assuming green lights meant things were fine, flicked the power back on. A loose wrench clattered to the floor and down under the pipework.

Farr scowled at it, 'Did you sign that out or did I?'

'You did.'

'Figures. I'd better wriggle it out then.'

She scrabbled about, making frustrated noises.

'You having fun down there?'

She grunted, 'This'd be easier if my arms were as scrawny as yours.'

'No comment. You want me to turn the gravity off again?'

She grimaced with a final straining grasp under the pipework, 'Nope, got it.'

The Quartermaster's voice boomed out of the speaker system as they clamped down the last floor plate.

'All personnel except bridge staff and engineering crews will come to the main briefing hall at shift's end. Repeat: All personnel except bridge staff and engineering crews will come to the main briefing hall at shift's end. Failure to attend is a 50 demerit penalty. That is all.'

By the time they'd returned the tools and personal gravity packs to the stores the briefing hall was ram packed, with the doorway blocked by a wall of shoulders. Wrath had no idea there were this many people aboard. The shift system and the size of the craft meant while you were always aware of there being other crew going about their work they were never in the way.

'Hey, Wrath!' He turned at the sound of the voice, seeing Qiang and Pirie approaching. 'So you managed to not shoot yourself? Good effort. What's the matter with you guys? Not on the guest list?'

'Hey, Trooper! I was just wondering whether to go back to the stores and get a pry bar. I don't see how else we're going to squeeze in here.'

'Come with me,' Qiang walked right by them, 'there's a side door off the armoury.'

'You're a useful woman to know, Qiang. Oh, by the way, this is cadet Farr. Farr, this is cadet Trooper Qiang, and cadet Pirie. They're my bunkmates, whether they like or not. I haven't asked which, I think it could still go either way.'

Pirie just waved. Qiang extended a hand.

'Good to know you, Farr.'

'Wiselike. I haven't met any Troopers formally before, do I have to salute you?'

'No, and if you feel the urge, try to fight it. How did you guys get on with the firearms training?'

Farr looked at Wrath, 'Are you going to tell her or am I?'

'That bad, eh? Well I hope nobody beat my record.'

Wrath tried to look casual, saying nothing, leaving Farr the job of asking the question that Qiang clearly *wanted* to be asked.

'What *is* your record?'

'Well, it's not just my record, it's the highest score on the boat. I tagged out at 258 points in 53 seconds. How about you guys?'

Wrath gave her a reassuring look, 'You have my word, Diana, I wasn't anywhere near that score.'

Farr widened her eyes, before shaking her head. Qiang didn't miss it.

'Spreff it Wrath just how bad did you do? Me and Grace aren't going to be getting demerits are we?'

'Of course not, let's just say I did as well as can be expected.'

That her record had been annihilated, she'd likely find out soon enough, but being the first day he was her new bunkmate it didn't seem like an ideal time to tell her. The troubled look was taking a little too long to clear from her face, fortunately Wrath could see they'd reached the door to the armoury.

'Hey we're here!' He pushed at the door but it didn't yield.

Qiang shook her finger at him, 'Trooper's privilege, Wrath.' She keyed in the code and held the door open for them.

Behind the armoury counter a very young looking cadet saluted Qiang as they passed by. She scowled at him with distaste and shook her head, 'Don't do that, Boyd.'

'Sorry, ma'am.' The cadet cringed at his own words.

'*Ma'am?* Are you kidding me? And why are you still behind that counter? Are you bridge staff or engineering crew?'

'No... Trooper Qiang.'

'Then you're *supposed* to be in the briefing hall. Lock up and get to it, unless you're doing so fantastically well you can spare 50 demerits? I'm guessing you're not.'

'Yes, Trooper Qiang, or no, not yes. No.'

'Just get it done.'

They left the fumbling cadet behind. He'd probably be late and still get demerits, but Qiang considered it a good deed done.

'Trooper Qiang,'

'What is it, Farr?'

'I'm getting an urge to salute you.'

'*Please* fight it, Farr.'

Wrath gave her a look, 'Didn't I say command would suit you, Diana?'

'Cram it.'

'Yes ma'am.'

The side door brought them out right by the stage, where QM was taking her place at the lectern. The big screen behind her was tuned to the FVN news channel with the sound muted.

'Morning cadets, and cadet troopers. You've been working around the clock to get this old bird back to operational status, the repair team from Black Chasm say all the external repairs are finished and the superstructure is as good as new. The last of the internal repairs we can do in flight. In short we're heading out this morning, and getting back to our patrol duties.'

A few cheers greeted the news, although not that many. With the demands of the repair work, nobody had been granted shore-leave, and now it seemed nobody was going to be.

'Thanks for your enthusiasm. As a thank you for our part in Saturday's hostilities, and for the damage and loss of life we endured, Captain Skopa of the Francesca Reala has asked if we would honour them by leading them out to the trans-optic launch zone, so we're going to be getting a big send off.'

There were more cheers this time.

'For those of you who don't already know, visibility is important for law-enforcement. It's not enough to do good, we have to be seen to be doing good. In case you hadn't worked it out, surviving an attack from such a devastating weapon and getting the Black Wreath ready to fly in just three days makes you look good, and it makes Black Fleet look good. Take this honour at face value. You earned it, and the whole fleet needs it.

'Acting Commander Rydell gave an interview to FVN an hour ago, praising your bravery and your skill, so seeing as you won't be getting any compliments out of me, get while the getting is good. This news is going out Protectorate wide, so take pride.' She scowled, 'but not too much. I'm more than happy to knock you right back down again.'

QM stepped away from the lectern and the sound of the news faded up. They were showing pre-recorded interviews of people at the spaceport boarding the Pandale shuttle. Wrath's heart-rate spiked as the camera panned over to one of the passengers, momentarily shocked by the sight of her face — Yolande's face. But of course, this must be footage from Saturday morning. If they were going to show the shuttle crash again, Wrath very much did not want to watch it again, especially not at newscast levels of detail.

'Wrath, let go of me!' Qiang whispered sharply. He looked down and saw he was grasping her wrist.

'Sorry.' He released his grip, 'Sorry.'

The interviewer started to speak, 'And here we have Yolande Fenton, a local Gun-Grid star who's moving off-world with an eye to stepping up to the professional leagues on Viafrane!'

Qiang was still looking at Wrath, concerned about the pained look on his face. 'What's wrong with you?'

'I'm sorry, it's just... I knew her.'

She rolled her eyes, 'Is she why you signed up? She broke your heart or something?'

'Not so much that...'

'She is the reason you signed up though, right?'

'One of the reasons. Probably most of the reasons.'

'I knew it! I knew it was going to be a Beau Geste thing with you. You've got the look for it. Well not that you'll care, but I think you're better off out of it. She looks like another Princess to me, she looks kinda short too. The short and pretty ones always want a big guy, a protector type. It's a thing I've noticed. You watch, I bet that's what she'll wind up with. A big, dumb, aggressive guy. I know the type.'

Wrath treated Qiang to a furious stare, trying to keep his whispering just below the limits of QM's hearing, 'That'll be tough now she's dead.'

She looked at him like he was an idiot, 'She talks a lot for a dead chick.'

'This is pre-recorded. She was on the shuttle on Saturday.'

'No, Wrath, she wasn't. This *is* pre-recorded, from this morning.'

'It can't be, she was aboard the shuttle on Saturday, I watched burn its way down into the ocean!'

'No, Wrath, nobody was aboard it. They sent up a drone shuttle on Saturday, there wasn't anyone aboard. They weren't going to send a civilian shuttle into that firefight, but they thought the pirates would get suspicious if there was nothing at all in orbit so they sent up an unmanned ship. How did you miss the news.'

Wrath was trying to process the information, mind and body fizzing with a blend of hope, relief, and confusion, not really sure if he believed it yet. How *had* he missed the news? Because he'd wanted to. He'd gone out of his way to miss it.

'I missed the news because I was... I was busy drinking myself stupid.'

'Did that take long?' Qiang suddenly gave him a look that was half pity, half amusement, 'Wait... tell me you didn't sign up because you thought she was dead?'

'Spreff it!'

'Oh that's terrible,' she said, not without a small edge of sympathy, 'and totally hilarious, obviously.'

QM finally noticed their intense whispering and grimaced in a way that suggested that their conversation had better be over, and that they would be finding some extra demerits on their tariff at the end of the week.

They'd managed to miss most of Acting Commander Rydell's presumably fulsome praise of the crew. Now the show had switched to a roll call of the police who'd died on the prisoner transport, and then to the dead Black Fleet cadets whose shoes Wrath, Farr, and the other new Pandale recruits had filled.

Wrath stole a look at Pirie and saw her swallow down hard and bite her lip when the last cadet appeared, even Qiang seemed to blanche a little. He must have been their bunkmate. He looked a decent young guy, and Wrath felt like something of an intruder being forced on them after so recent a loss, and felt even more stupid for being so upset with Qiang's attitude to Yolande's death, a death that it turns out hadn't even happened.

Wondering if Yolande had tried to call him over the last few days, he lamented not checking the calls list on his watch more thoroughly before he'd put it into twelve month storage.

The big screen switched to an external view of Black Wreath, which right now was an internal view of Black Chasm; a network of gantries and gangways, cranes, laser welders and retention clamps.

When Wrath had last seen this view a repair crew numbering in the hundreds had been working flat-out on the Black Wreath's hull. Now it was deserted, about to be opened to vacuum.

A black line spread across the width of the screen, the pinprick light of distant stars shining through the widening crack. As the clamshell opening of Black Chasm stretched wider Wrath got his first view of home for what seemed like forever, though it had been just two nights.

Cadet Farr nudged his elbow, 'Last we'll see of home for a while, eh?'

'Yeah. We'll probably be too busy to even think about it. Better enjoy the last look, I guess.'

The yawning maw of Black Chasm stretched to its fullest and the Francesca Reala eased into view. This time she was to get a send off befitting her unique beauty and status. No lone orbital shuttle was waiting for this spectacle — a massive flotilla of what looked like every space-worthy craft on Pandale was gathered in orbit to honour her.

The assembled cadets and troopers sighed in awe, and a little excitement that this honour was, in part, for them.

Wrath knew his claim to this honour was thin to non-existent, he'd played no part in Saturday's battle. His own thoughts were fixated on the Francesca Reala, and one passenger in particular who would have no idea that he was up here with her, and know nothing of the private mourning he'd done for her.

The Black Wreath began to move, slipping from the grasp of the Black Chasm and into the much deeper black chasm of open space. The cadets cheered and applauded, breaking through Wrath's reverie.

He joined in with the applause. Having seen the damage to the hull first-hand and up close, getting this bird space-worthy in such a short time *deserved* applause, and for that at least he did deserve some small part of the credit.

The Francesca Reala began to rotate — an elegant spin around her central axis; an invitation for Black Wreath to lead her out to the trans-optic launch point.

As they approached the massed flotilla a blizzard of plasma flares of all colours sprang from the flanks of each and every craft. Black Wreath was cruising through a dazzling shower of coloured fire and the briefing hall filled with cheering again - a raucous roar of approval.

A voice from the Francesca Reala, Captain Skopa, addressed them across the comms, his rich and emotional tones filling the briefing hall.

'This is the Francesca Reala. Black Wreath, we can never thank you enough for your sacrifice, and for your protection. Fly safe.'

At screen's centre a bead of blackness appeared as the forward projectors began to form the anti-light shell, growing into a ball of anti-photonic fog; in moments the stars around it began to rush and the dark fog enveloped them in blackness.

Pandale was instantly lost from view, already a million klicks behind them.

Showers of sparks and the flash of welding torches scattered a patchwork light-show the length and breadth of the Savatara. After more than a year of remodelling under Captain Jowett's direction, the original shipbuilders and architects of this war weapon wouldn't recognise a single square metre of metal inside this craft as their own work.

Where the crews of the Sabina and Sonya had been content to trust the power of the new weapon alone, Captain Jowett was dedicated to optimising this craft as a delivery mechanism for Fathom's missiles, although since the engineers she'd captured from Woolfe Weapon Works had succeeded in disabling the dozens of deviously concealed remote-triggers Fathom had installed, the few that remained were now very much *her* missiles.

Striding through the sparks and smoke, her eyes met the gaze of the man himself, Anga-Kaska Woolfe. A wicked and wily cast to his knowing smile was the highlight of his craggy face. It was no surprise Jowett's executive officer had been bedding the man; all to the good if it meant he worked better and believed he might be spared the airlock when he was done. A borderline genius of weaponry and the tools of space combat, it would be a shame to kill him, though when that time came Captain Jowett suspected the feeling of shame wasn't going to linger very long.

'Commander Rawlins, a word.'

Her second in command turned away from the engineer, clutching a complex schematic diagram, her lean features pulled into a questioning frown, 'Of course, Captain.'

'The call just came through. We're on our own now, Commander.'

'Weren't we always, Captain?'

'We've been declared rogue, but it's not a matter of record, yet. The Top brass want deniability, but not a hunt. The record of our rogue status will only be released if we're destroyed or captured.'

'Well we have no intention of being captured. So what now, Captain?'

'As of now, it's only us. The Sonya and Sabina haven't been declared rogue, but the Sonya will be under close scrutiny. Since Griffith beat the crew of the Sabina into line they consider Captain Rourke cut off from our program and on her best behaviour, so she can still be useful to us.

'We'll go dark for a month, then I'll have Captain Rourke pick up two detachments of PPB commandos.'

'What use are commandos to us?' Rawlins asked.

'This weapon can punch a hole right through a dreadnought's armour. By simply firing another missile into the breach all we do is destroy a vessel we could otherwise gather valuable intel from. If we stagger the two missile strikes we can make a significant weak point, big enough to pry open. Over the next month, our task is to strengthen our incursion shuttles to punch through such a breach and get troops aboard.'

'You want to seize a dreadnought intact?' Commander Rawlins nodded, eyes wide in approval at the audacity of it. 'A prize like that could put Fathom in a *very* forgiving mood!' Commander Rawlins frowned, 'but fighting Black Fleet troops on their own turf won't be easy, even for PPB commandos.'

'Some crews are not as tough as others, Commander Rawlins.'

'You already have a target in mind?'

'Think what a blow it would be if Black Fleet lost an entire year's worth of new recruits?'

Commander Rawlins smiled, 'Of course.'

'Our next priority is to pursue, board, and capture the Black Wreath.'

'And we might get some useful information on their tactics and training from the survivors.'

Jowett turned a scornful eye on her first officer, 'I've told you before, Rawlins, the Savatara no longer takes prisoners.'

OCTOBER

thirteen

Nemo, his eyes flitting between the dying sun and the long-range LaDAR scope, had no idea what he was supposed to be looking for. The vast and lonely ball of dirty orange fire filling the view screen was not likely to secure the crew any income, and nor was anything else that Nemo could see.

FK5-34631 was all the name this turbulent red giant had, her photosphere swollen to incomprehensible proportions, long since having eaten her inner worlds. The whole system was designated a no-go area. Magnetic and gravitic anomalies and sudden gamma radiation spikes made it a big enough hazard to hyper-optic traffic the Navigation Council had been forced to relocate nearly a dozen navigation beacons.

Good sense would dictate there couldn't be anything here that was worth their time, but no-go areas were also great places to hide contraband, evidence, bodies, or, in a pinch, yourself.

If there *was* anything here, Nemo had yet to find it, and he was getting more doubtful by the minute that there was anything *to* find.

If another tip-off from Picket was going to be a bust it would be the last straw for the crew. Supplies were down to nearly nothing and the junk was critically damaged from their encounter with the Gamma fraternity backed junk, Wet Leather. The crew of the Cipheron hadn't made a solitary Buck in over a month.

He'd put it off as long as he could, but things couldn't go on like this, it was time to re-establish his authority. He was going to have to kill somebody, and with this pointless and ill-timed excursion, Picket had made himself the prime choice.

The shame of it was, up until the Francesca Reala disaster Nemo would have reckoned Picket to be one of the best fences trading, always getting good leads and good deals, talking them out of some murky situations, and he'd probably saved all of their lives a time or two, but if someone was going to die for the sake of morale, it wasn't going to be Nemo, and the crew wouldn't tolerate him making an example of anyone else. They all knew exactly where the blame lay.

He scooped up the intercom handset, 'Picket. Get up here.'

Opening a drawer under the console he grabbed up an ugly looking pistol —fat, dark and chunky— turning it over in his hands, checking the clip, checking the chamber, checking the mechanism.

He rested his gun hand on his thigh and spun his chair toward the door, waiting.

At the sound of the chime he tensed his finger on the trigger, clicking the door switch on the arm of his chair. Nemo made ready to fire as the door began sliding open.

Picket wasn't there.

As the armour-plate door receded into the frame the very edge of Picket's face became visible, his eye peeking around the doorway, his hand poking out, holding a gun at least as big and ugly as Nemo's was, and aiming squarely at his chest.

A frustrated sneer swept across Nemo's face, 'You a mind reader, Picket?'

'I know ship's politics well enough to know when my being dead might make somebody's life easier. I've got no intention of being dead.'

Nemo considered his next move. Picket's hand made for a small target, and Nemo was making for a big target. He could just lock the door and get the crew to knock Picket off for him, but that would make him look weak. They knew he was reluctant to kill, not dealing with Picket himself would only make that worse.

'Nemo, you know I don't want to be a captain, and I wouldn't trust any of these others chiff-sniffers to do the job as well as you do. This?' he waved the gun a little, but not so much it couldn't still ventilate Nemo's sternum in a hurry if need be, '...this is purely defensive. So you want to talk about it?'

Nemo shook his head, trying to hold onto his fading resolve to kill Picket. 'Why are we here?'

'I got a tip that we'd find something.'

'In case you hadn't noticed, Picket, nobody aboard this junk has a lot of faith in your tips anymore.'

'That's fair. I've had a bad run lately. There's been a lot of it going around, in case you hadn't noticed.'

Nemo didn't answer, he was doing his best to maintain a murderous look in his eyes.

'Thing is, this tip is from an old, old source. Never let me down. He's way out of the regular pirate informant circles, nothing to gain from a double cross. He said we'd find something big out here.'

'How big?'

'As big as we can handle. Frankly, Nemo, it's much bigger than you can handle without me.'

Nemo caressed the trigger, wondering if Picket still had that grenade? If he did, he could have killed Nemo already just by rolling it through the door. 'That's an awfully vague prospect to bet your life on, Picket.'

'What choice have I got? What choice have any of us got, come to that? We haven't had a score in over a month, and we're too shot up and too strung out to risk jacking anybody with an ounce of fight in them. We're way out on the edge and we need a big score we don't have to fight anyone for.'

'So you had us limp our way to this dead system for a carrion run? If your source knows about it, what's to say it hasn't been picked clean already?'

'The way I understand it, it's missing property. Condition is not important, the owners are going to want it back, and whoever tells them where they can find it won't have to worry about money for a while.'

'So why doesn't your source tell the owners himself?'

'Doesn't have the right contacts, but he'll take a cut. Don't worry, it'll all come out of my cut.'

'Who says you'll get a cut, Picket?'

An alarm buzzer sounded, but Nemo didn't look away from the sliver of Picket's face at the door's edge. He narrowed his eyes, seeing if Picket would try to capitalise on the distraction. Picket's eyes darted to the LaDar screen, and the side of his eye wrinkled with a smile. He began lowering his weapon.

'Might want to look at that.'

'I'll look when you're not holding a gun.'

The hand disappeared behind the doorframe, then reappeared, open and empty. Picket stepped out with his hands up, looking Nemo straight in the eye without a sign of fear.

'I've got faith in my source, Nemo.'

'You had faith in your source at Pandale.'

'Not really, I trusted in numbers. I didn't think that many smart people could all be wrong. Now I know better. Now I'm trusting one guy who's *never* been wrong.'

Nemo tried to read the face of his fence. Picket was unreadable, but he knew he had to give him one more chance, this was the last chance for him too. Picket being dead wouldn't make the Cipheron any less shot up, or the crew any less broke.

Turning his head to the LaDAR screen and quickly back to Picket, Nemo reached with his free hand to steer the junk towards the source of the response.

'Well, you were right about it being big, anyway. What is it?'

'Why guess? Let's find out.'

A black shape touched the edge of the sun as they grew closer to the huge dark object. Nemo grew uneasy as the shadow was growing ever larger, and longer, and becoming more recognisable in shape.

Everything could be destroyed, of course, but in all the tall tales he'd heard from boastful pirates he'd never heard of it being done, or from anyone who claimed to have seen it done, and he was rightfully fearful of anything that could do it, but here was the proof that someone, or something had brought destruction on one of the toughest craft known this side of the Goffa border. There was no doubt, this devastated hulk was the dead remains of a Black Fleet dreadnought.

Picket laid his hand on Nemo's shoulder, 'I believe the phrase is, "ker-ching!"'

Nemo pushed the hand away and rubbed his temple in wonderment, 'That's not the phrase I've got in *my* mind.'

The internal comms came to life with a voice from the weapons room, who'd clearly just looked at their monitors, *'Fuck me!'*

'Yeah, that was the one.'

Captain Calloway ran his finger along the book spines as he strolled along the shelves of Griffith's library, examining the titles as he passed.

It was rare for Calloway to find himself alone in Griffith's quarters, seeing the sort of reading he favoured offered an opportunity for a rare glimpse into the mind of his semi-permanent passenger. Or, it seemed perhaps not. The shelves were brimming with generic library fodder. Even here, Griffith did not reveal anything of himself.

Calloway paused at what looked like one of the few interesting titles, a limited early edition of Mervin Greer's "Principles of Gravitic Manipulation". He hooked a finger over the top of the spine and pulled. The book refused to move. He pulled again, a little harder, not wishing to damage the book. It was immovable.

Calloway peered more closely to see if there was some kind of retention mechanism, or if maybe the book itself had some secret gravitic manipulation holding it in place. He frowned at what appeared to be the back of the shelf, barely an inch from the edge of the book. It wasn't a book at all, it seemed none of them were. The entire wall of books was fake. He looked around the room, at the other walls filled with putative tomes, shaking his head.

'Some of them are real, Captain.'

Calloway hadn't even heard him enter. For such a solidly assembled man, Griffith was a quiet mover, 'Very few of them, but some.' Griffith unlidded a decanter and poured himself a short glass of rich brown liquor, there was only one glass, and no offer of one for Calloway.

There were full-blown admirals who wouldn't cross swords with Captain Gideon Calloway, but everyone answers to somebody. The Arissa was Calloway's command but the unspoken reality was she was Griffith's ship.

Like her captain, and even more so like her passenger, this vessel was a long serving bruiser. Where pirates feared the sight of a PPB frigate, PPB frigates feared the sight of the Arissa, and had done even before she'd become the traveling kingdom of the man known – to the few who knew anything of him at all – as *Fathom's Fist.*

'At least it saves us both from my asking the fatuous question about whether you've read them all.'

'I read field reports, Captain, I don't have much time for fiction, figuratively or literally.'

'So why have your quarters made to look like a private library?'

'I enjoy the aesthetic, and the quiet. It inhibits distractions, and distracted thinking. It prompts a...studious state of mind.'

Calloway knew enough about Griffith's attitude to socialising to know a drink would not be offered to him. 'I assume you have new orders for me?'

'Yes. We've got reported sightings of the Savatara and Sonya close to some main traffic streams, they seem liable to surface again soon. The Sabina has returned to full duties but Captain Rourke has had some unconventional patrol routes scheduled, leading her out towards Beacon 505 where she'll be docking in two days.'

'You think one of the others will show up for a rendezvous?'

'The traces of their movements suggest it. The Savatara and Sonya are on the run and out of the loop, with no access to PPB Naval intelligence. They'll be sorely in need of fresh tactical information which the Sabina daren't broadcast to them openly. They need to meet with Captain Rourke face to face. Beacon 505 is steadfastly free of any law-enforcement control, so it's the perfect meeting place. I wouldn't even rule out Captain Jowett herself showing up.'

'I assume you'll want me to hold off at the closest course correction point until they arrive?'

Griffith nodded, 'We can't jump the gun, the others may not show up at all, and if they don't we'll need to follow the Sabina in case they have a deep space meeting planned.'

'And what then?'

'Jowett is a disaster waiting to happen. If Over-Admiral Connors won't sanction the Savatara being hunted and destroyed by the PPB Navy, we'll do it ourselves.'

fourteen

Wrath's feet were pounding along the deck at a steady 120-pace, a thumping counterpoint to the sirens filling his ears. It might be a drill, or it might be a real callout. If what QM had told them was true, and that most patrollers would only get two or three hostile pirate engagements a year to deal with, Wrath was determined to be on the Heavy Munitions deck to grab a seat in a Double-Eight pod.

Ahead someone was running towards him, it was Grace Pirie.

"Malcolm! Where you running to?"

"Heavy Munitions, you?"

She stopped, out of breath, 'I hadn't thought that far ahead, just seemed appropriate with the sirens and all, I thought I'd see if anyone else was running and follow them.'

Wrath nodded, 'Well, weird plan, but it worked. Any idea what the sirens are for?'

Pirie's breathing was easing, 'Qiang is on Command-deck duty, she says it's a mess up there.'

'How so?'

'Remember that hopeless kid on armoury duty when we left your homeworld?'

'Cadet Boyd?'

'Apparently today's the day the computer chose him to be in command of the whole vessel.'

Wrath's eyes widened, Boyd had only been aboard a month longer than he had, and was barely scraping by the monthly merit limit. If he had any talents, he'd kept them well hidden. 'Let's hope we make it through the day. Is the siren a mistake?'

'No, that's the thing, we've got a genuine callout! Some pirate trouble in the 500's, an ambush at the course-correction point before Beacon 507, I think. We're dropping shell in less than 10 minutes, and half the people on the bridge have no idea what they're doing.'

'Is QM going to take over?'

'Nobody knows, but nobody's issued any orders. I think you have the right idea heading to Heavy Munitions though, we can see the Double-Eights in action!'

'Forget watching the action, we need to be the action! This is what I signed up for, the chance to blast some pirates out of the sky. We've got to grab a seat ourselves. Want to be my spotter?'

'For the best shot aboard this tub? Bet your favourite nut I do!'

'Okay, I'm going to take that as a yes.'

With speed exceeding grip, they slid their way into the gun alley, out of breath and excited. The gun alleys were majestic, long, curving cathedrals of violence, one on each side of Black Wreath, each with ten Double-Eight pods. Wrath searched for whoever was in charge of the deck, spotting a young woman with an assignment chart, her face a mix of fear and determination.

'Gun?' Wrath shouted.

'Take pod 8, and hurry.'

Pirie smiled and started running, 'Race you!'

Wrath laughed and gave chase, he was quicker but she'd got a head start. His smile faded when she beat him to the pod and flung open the door. She'd taken the gunner's seat. There was no time to swap, he grabbed the door on the spotter's side of the pod and squeezed into the tight fitting seat.

Pirie's voice came over the intercom, 'I'm on the wrong side! Get out and we'll swap places.'

Wrath felt the seat bolsters forming themselves to the shape of his body and the restraining straps fasten around him. 'Too late, Pirie. I'm your spotter. Start your prep.'

'Spreff it Malcolm, sorry! I barely scored half what you did when we were training on these.'

Wrath was painfully disappointed, this was everything he'd signed up for, and it could be months before their next pirate engagement. He clenched his jaw and shook away the frustration, powering up the view screens. 'Don't worry about it, Grace. Training is training, so don't worry about how you did there. The stakes are real here, you're going rise to the occasion.'

He heard her take a breath, 'Thank you.' she mumbled to herself over her weapon prep. 'Any advice?'

'Turn off the aim-assist chiff. I don't care what QM says, it gets in the way. Second guessing the software does *not* make for good marksmanship. Shut down all the peripheral warnings about ammunition, weapon temps and potential course shifts, I'll watch all that for you and compensate. You just want your cross-hairs and the speed-adjusting target marker. All you need is target's position and delta. Everything else is a distraction. The only thing that matters is, shoot at where the target is going to be, not where it is, remember that and you'll be golden.'

'Got it.'

'I've got a full hemispheric view here, I'll let you know where targets are coming from, and I'll be live-plotting their movements. Any moving target has a body language, let me read it, and I'll put the marker where it needs to be, you just pull the trigger when it feels right.'

Acting-Commander Boyd came over the intercom, his voice tremulous, cracking with barely contained panic. *'This is cadet Boyd... acting Commander Boyd, sorry,'* there was a brief pause, *'QM has asked me to retain command. She's with me here on the bridge, so, I hope that makes some of you feel better.'*

Wrath slapped his forehead, 'I guess we only have to worry about shooting anything if Boyd manages to get this bird flying in the right direction.'

'Ha! It's a good job there's no upside down in space.'

'There's still back to front, and inside out.'

After a significant pause, Boyd returned to the comms set, sounding more composed, though there was still a noticeable crack in his voice. QM must have taken him aside for a quiet and forceful word. *'Okay. The situation is, we have reports of a mixed use freighter-passenger transport under attack by two pirate junks at a course-correction stop one jump off beacon 507. A Police heavy cruiser has been deployed and should already be there by the time we drop shell. They may already be engaged with the targets when we arrive.'* Boyd took a strengthening breath, and seemed to be rallying to match the moment. *'Killstick missiles would be overkill for this kind of engagement, especially with a Police cruiser already engaged. We'll be using Double-Eights only.*

'The computer can over-ride any pod at any time if a shot isn't clean and clear, but we can't risk hitting the police or the transport, so don't rely on the Friend-or-Foe systems. Keep control of your trigger fingers. Better a pirate gets away than we kill someone we came here to help, or someone who's here to help us.'

'My call sign for the engagement is "Comm". Quartermaster will be

running the tactical desk, her callsign for the duration is "Weapon." Spotters, you'll announce your spikes to her for confirmation. We'll drop shell at range ten, and close to range three before coming about for a stand-off engagement. We drop shell in 60. Good luck everybody.'

'*Good hunting, cadets.'* The firm voice of QM added.

Wrath waited to hear if Pirie had anything to say before asking, 'You ready?'

'Yeah, and scared.'

'Of course, but we'll be 3 klicks away, so we're in no danger.'

'You weren't aboard the last time we got into a fight with pirates, Malcolm.'

'That's true, but this old tub seemed to stand up pretty well, didn't she?'

'You get to feel safe aboard this black giant, then one big bomb blows away your illusions. I'm not taking my safety for granted.'

'I can see how you'd feel that way. Personally, I'm more scared of shooting the police cruiser or the freighter.'

'Well there is that too, I guess.'

'I'll keep my target tracks as far away from friendlies as possible, okay?'

'Do.'

Wrath turned his focus to the hemispherical view-screen and placed his hands on the trackpads that would trace his movements onto Pirie's targeting screen.

Boyd's voice again: '*30 seconds. Power-deck, prime gravity systems for trans-optic deceleration phase. Sub-optic systems will be restored to full operational power two minutes after drop. Shell drop set at range ten. Gunners are clear to engage when we attain battle-stance at range three. Sub-optic in 20 seconds. Fire control to Weapon.'*

QM's voice broke in, '*Comm. My callsign is set to "Weapon," I am assuming fire control.'*

'*Checklist... sorry, I don't need to say checklist. Uhh, set gravity systems to light combat settings. Prepare manoeuvring thrusters to go to full power at shell drop. Incursion teams, prepare and assemble in the shuttle bay. Shell drop in 10.'*

The seconds seemed to drag before Boyd's voice began to speak again, '*5, 4, 3, 2, 1, drop. We are sub-optic. Gravity systems at 90%. Longitudinal deceleration force absorption is at twenty thousand gravities; at three thousand gravities; at zero gravity. Set generator head to full recovery mode. Set combat gravity systems to recharge. Prep manoeuvring thrusters. Double-Eight pods double check ready status. Combat readiness in 90 seconds.'*

So far, Boyd was procedurally perfect, although everything was set down for him, there was still plenty of room to mess it up, and to his credit, for now, he hadn't.

Wrath took the time to double check every system in the pod, unlike Boyd, he actually had a reputation to uphold.

'Flank speed. Broadcast a Stipulation 1 warning on top-level com-jack. Range eight. Gunners are free to engage when green lights show. Set FoF for maximum discretion on target approval. Range five. No response to Stipulation 1 warning. Reiterate. Targeting systems synchronised with Police cruisers. Setting friendly tags. Setting hostile tags. Range three-point-five and decelerating. FoF tags are logged and locked. Range three. Confirmed. Manoeuvring to three-klick battle stance. Coming about. External monitors are up. Gravity systems are at full strength. We are at stance. Range three, set. No response to second Stipulation 1 warning. Weapon you may engage at your discretion. Comm out.'

'This is Weapon. Watch your friendlies, call your spikes. Engage your quarry.'

Whatever else Boyd might have proven to be terrible at, which up to now had been pretty much everything, he seemed to have discovered he was really good at command. Wrath had no time to consider the revelation as his target board turned green and his targeting system went crazy. The view swept across and down as Black Wreath turned about and rolled, bringing her port-side guns to bear.

'Weapon? Pod 8, confirm three tags and multiple friendlies?'

'Affirmative, supplemental targets and friendlies. All spotters, I advise extra caution over tag selection. FoF systems are recalibrating. Hold fire for 30, Police heavy cruiser is in fact Police Mobile Platform.'

This was already clear, a mobile platform was actually a travelling police station, and about twenty times the size of a heavy cruiser.

An unknown voice joined the conversation; grizzled and full of authority, *'Black Wreath, this is Marshal Jameson. Co-ordinate FoF data, I'm about to launch three more cruisers to engage. Recommend you stand-off at range three and provide heavy fire.'*

'Commander Boyd confirming. We are already fully prepped and stanced at range three. Please expedite Friend-or-Foe data so we can engage.'

Wrath laughed out loud. Boyd was bossing a Police Marshal around. He switched his channel back to Pirie, 'What is it they say about giving a man a title?'

'Boyd had better hope he never meets that Marshal.'

'Ha!'

QM spoke again, *'This is Weapon, fire-board is clear. Engage.'*

Wrath's weapons control indicator switched back to green.

'Let's get 'em, Wrath!' Pirie's confidence seemed lifted by Boyd's bravado.

'Okay Grace, keep track of your screen's perimeter, you'll get a glow if a tag is going to cross your view, and it'll get brighter as the tag gets closer. Watch out for my traces so you can set up your aim before they show up on your screen. Remember, with the time it takes for our fire to reach them I'm tracking where I expect them to be when the rounds get there, not where they are.'

'You set 'em up, I'll knock 'em down.'

The arrival of the law just seemed to be making the pirates angry, switching between strafing the passenger freighter and making aggressive passes at the police cruisers. Pirate junks weren't built for speed or manoeuvrability, they just strapped on the heaviest guns and as much armour plating as they could buy, and traded combat finesse for violent force of will. These three junks seemed well equipped in all of these departments.

Wrath was struggling to pick out clean shots. The junks had spotted Black Wreath and were staying in close and tight to the civilian transport, weaving in and out of the police cruisers.

'I could set up fast shots but the FoF protection margin is pretty big.'

'I know, every time I feel safe to squeeze the trigger it's locked out. Can you get Weapon to cut us some slack?'

Wrath opened the circuit to the bridge. 'Weapon, Pod 8. Can you loosen the reins on the FoF protects? We can't get a shot off here.'

'Stick with it, Wrath. The cruisers are going to force the tags out wider.'

'They need to hurry, that freighter is full of holes as is. There won't be anybody left to protect if we leave it much longer.'

'Patience, Wrath.'

'Weapon, I'm not on the trigger, but I'm lining up firing solutions as tight as I'd shoot myself. Don't use Grace's firing margins, use mine.'

Wrath could see the cruisers were moving in tighter, forcing themselves between the junks and the freighter, if it worked there should be some chances for clean shots.

'Be ready, Grace, if we want to make our mark we've got to beat 9 other gun pods to the shot.'

'I just want to squeeze this trigger and have something actually happen!'

'They're opening the junks out! Tag two looks tasty, it's pushing out into clear space.'

Wrath felt the soft pulse of the weapon's fire, and zoomed in, desperate to call out a spike. Nothing. The junk ducked back into cover behind the freighter.

'Chiff!'

'Don't sweat it Grace, nobody else scored a shot either.'

The junks were trying to stay tight, but their own poor manoeuvrability made it hard for them to stay out of each other's way, forcing them out into danger.

Wrath caught a flash from the stern of one of the junks.

'*Pod 2, spike.*'

'*Weapon, spike confirmed.*'

Wrath scrunched his face up, first blood had gone to another pod. Fair enough, at Black Wreath's prow they were better positioned for the shot. He should be glad, but he was still envious.

'Keep focussed, Pirie, they're not knocked out, and there's two more tags to bag.'

A second junk rocked and reeled from multiple impacts, glancing blows blasting off sheets of crudely attached armour plating. Two pods called out for spikes, both were confirmed.

'*This is Weapon. Tag 3 is disabled. Tag is purple. Concentrate on opportunities for tags 1 and 2.*'

The Police cruisers were scoring hits, but without the stopping power of Black Wreath's Double-Eights it was much heavier going for them to score significant damage.

'*Pod 5, spike.*'

'*Spike confirmed. Tag 2 is limping. Tag 1 looks to be running, moving behind the freighter to block our fire. Police cruisers pursuing. Tag 2 is going to be offered surrender. Monitor only, do not engage.*'

That was that. A few moments of excitement, 2 tags down, and the last was slipping away.

'Sorry Wrath.' Pirie said.

'Hey, we got to play, you got some shots off. It's not a total bust.'

Wrath looked at the retreating red tag of the fleeing pirate junk, and then he saw it, a sliver of a gap between the pursuing Police cruisers and the damaged freighter. At first he just watched, then he zoomed in. The gap was bigger than it seemed, but the FoF system would never allow a shot.

Conflicting instincts wrestled in him. The junk was trying to keep the freighter in the way, so she was flying in a dead-straight line away from Black Wreath, there would be no need to adjust the shot in the slightest, all Pirie would need to do was squeeze the trigger.

'Grace?'

'Yes?'

'I trust you.'

'Well, that's nice to know.'

He continued to watch the shrinking pirate junk. Absolutely nobody else had this shot.

'Are you telling me that for a reason?'

Wrath waited a moment before forcing the words out, words he couldn't believe he was about to say. 'You know I've been given Instructor-class ratings for *every* weapon protocol on the ship, right? That means I can over-ride certain things.'

'Okay? And?'

'I'm going to turn off our FoF system.'

'What?'

'Do you want to score a spike or not?'

She paused a moment before answering cautiously, 'Yes?'

'I've set us up, just set your zoom to maximum and square her up in the crosshair. If you're happy with the shot, take it. If you're not, don't.'

There was silence. The junk grew smaller, building up its generator charge for a trans-optic burst. In moments she would escape.

'Okay.'

Wrath had almost wanted her to say no. Taking a deep breath he hovered his hand over the FoF override, squeezed his eyes shut and jabbed at the button.

There was no sound or sensation, just quiet. He opened one eye and looked at his view-screen, dire warnings about terminating FoF protocols were scrolling down the screen. They would be on Pirie's screen too, probably scaring her off taking the shot.

Suddenly he felt the soft throb of the cannon, firing, firing, firing. The pirate junk rocked and spun under the force of the impacts, huge chunks flying off under the kinetic onslaught. Pirie was pouring ammunition into her.

The cannons cut off suddenly.

'*This is Weapon. Pod 8, your fire control is disabled.*' QM's voice startled Wrath. There was no sign of anger or rebuke, but Wrath knew they had to be in trouble. '*Tag 2 has surrendered. Tag 1 is crippled. All tags set to purple.*'

'Woooo!' Pirie sounded thrilled, 'Blast your pirate asses! That's for the Pandale bomb, and for killing my roomie!'

Wrath wanted to share her enthusiasm, but suspected he'd just chiffed his bed in no uncertain terms. He didn't know how much trouble he was in; likely plenty.

'*Wrath,*' QM's voice was revealing no emotion, '*You didn't call your spike. 10 demerits.*'

Wrath wondered if this was a joke, waiting before answering. 'Pod 8, spike.'

Waiting for a response, silence dragged. That couldn't be it? QM must have something else planned.

A subtle chuckle preceded QM's reply, '*Spike confirmed. You still get the demerits.*' Wrath heard the channel click over to private, '*I could have shut your pod down the second you disabled the FoF system if I wanted, Wrath. The shot was good. We don't punish success in this fleet.*'

Overriding the closed channel, Boyd's voice came through again, '*Engagement closed. Incursion team stand ready. Prep shuttles for launch. All Double-Eight teams be at the debriefing room on the command deck in 10 minutes.*'

Tags 2 and 3 were being drawn aboard the police platform, at Marshal Jameson's suggestion, Tag 1 had been selected for the cadets' first pirate junk incursion. It was the most dangerous point in any pirate engagement, one they trained hard for three times a week, but fighting pirates on their own turf was a high risk endeavour.

Wrath and Pirie were sitting front and centre at the debriefing room's big screen, this junk was their spike, after all. Pirie's euphoria had been slipping all the way from the munitions deck, high-fives and embraces with the cadets they met along the way had given way to a look of tense apprehension. Wrath didn't know what was wrong, but his eyes were switching between her and the screen.

The shuttle pilot was counting down the approach, '*Range point* five. *External survey shows substantial damage to the superstructure, multiple weapon strikes. Range point four, junk appears dark, could be playing dead, cannons primed. Range point three, forced entry system primed. Range point two, incursion team ready.*'

The cameras showed the extent of the damage in vivid detail, and it was savage. Pirie's fire had been all on target, sustained, and relentless.

'*Range point one.*'

Pirie grasped Wrath's hand, hers, cold and clammy. Her grip was strong, painful. Wrath made no protest.

'*Range 50 metres. 40 metres. 30, forced entry system set for impact trigger. 10 metres, 5, impact.*' The pirate junk shuddered as the shuttle hit, light flared as the cutting charges detonated. '*Hull breached. Sensory disruptors deployed. Remote drones deployed. Incursion team is go.*'

The screen switched to the incursion team's cameras; each one showing a blurry mess of darkness and smoke. The remote drones switched their lighting to smoke penetration, leading the way down the narrow corridors to a wide doorway.

'*Sealed door, prepare to breach.*'

The remote drones sprayed explosive gel around the doorway.

'*Sensorupts ready. Deploy on breach. Breach.*'

The door fell and the drones fired sensory disruptor grenades inside, the screens whitened then cleared. The drones sped in immediately, their footage switched to the centre of the screen.

'*Eeuuurghh!*' Pirie grunted in horror at the walls running red with spattered blood.

'*It's a meat factory in here.*' The incursion team entered, their cameras probing every corner, picking out limbs, torsos, heads, lumps of torn apart flesh and bone.

'*Looks like around six or seven people were in here, at a guess. We'll probably need to count the chunks.*'

Wrath felt the grip on his hand release; Pirie standing and running for the door. Her exit was attracting a few stares, but the incursion team's camera feed soon pulled their eyes back to the screens. Wrath turned his eyes to QM, who gave him a stern look and flicked her head towards the door.

He found Pirie on all fours, retching, a part-used breakfast spreading between her hands and filtering down through the floor grid.

'Hey there,' Wrath said, placing a comforting hand gently on her back. 'I don't blame you for the food-extrude, that was kind of a horrible thing to see.'

'It was a horrible thing to *do!*' She pushed his hand away awkwardly, 'You didn't pull the trigger, Malcolm, I did. I even enjoyed it while I was doing it, just squeezing away until QM had to turn the gun off.'

'Sure, but they were pirates. They'd already killed a dozen or so people before we showed up and stopped them.'

She closed her eyes, seeming to calm a little, then her back arched like she was ready to retch again. She took some deep breaths. 'I wasn't thinking about any of that in that gun-pod, it was just a ship in my crosshairs, just a flying lump of metal. Only it wasn't, was it? It was full of people, and I just blew them onto bloody spreffing chunks.'

Wrath didn't know quite what to say. He wasn't feeling the same guilt, even though he'd lined up the shot, knowing that without him, there would have been no shot. Like Pirie said, he hadn't pulled the trigger.

'I just killed people, Malcolm.' She fought down a gag reflex and took deep, deliberate breaths, 'It feels horrible. It feels disgusting.'

'They weren't good people, Grace. Not at all.'

'Well now they aren't even people at all!' she snapped back, 'Good or bad, they *were* people, they were whole people, walking around, thinking people thoughts, and we came along and turned them into...' she retched again, her back curving and her stomach taut. It was a painful, dry heave, with nothing left to bring up.

She spat the taste from her mouth, wiping her sleeve across her face. 'We're killers. We're out here to kill. It doesn't matter that the people we've killed bring it on themselves, our job is to blow people into bloody chunks, and then call it a good day's work.'

'Would you rather they just got away with stealing? Murdering? Raping? Kidnapping?'

'I'd *rather* they didn't, but *I'd* rather not... I'd rather it not be me pulling a trigger and turning people into... pie filling.'

Wrath couldn't help but let out a laugh.

Pirie shuddered and let out a grim laugh of her own. She slumped and rested against the wall, shaking her head and looking at Wrath's calm and composed face, not comprehending how easily he seemed to be dealing with it. 'What about you, Malcolm?'

'What about me?'

'Are you ready to be a killer?'

He sat next to her and dug a water pouch out of his top pocket, handing it over. She sipped at it as he thought it over.

'No.' he said, turning to look her in the eyes, 'No I am not.'

She looked at him for a long time and seemed to find comfort in his sincerity. She nodded, looking a little more reassured. 'I didn't think so.'

fifteen

Beacon 505 was a station with a bad reputation; safer to say it was notorious. There was no design or cohesion to it, just a docking ring enclosing a loose association of randomly attached crap, forming a labyrinthine rat-run of low-rent dives, traders in tat, and the sort of high-quality accommodation that would give a plague rat misgivings.

If anyone wished to replicate the design, they could do worse than throwing some powerful magnets into a centrifuge with a pile of scrap metal and old pipes, then beating the resulting mess with a big hammer for a few hours. Alternatively, just asking a sculptor to give physical form to the concept of a headache might produce similar results.

In the colourful vernacular of its occasional pirate clientele it was described as "the ugliest puke-pile ever shat into existence," although some reversed the bodily exit routes for the more flavoursome, "the ugliest shit-pile ever puked into existence."

Neither description really summed up the actual genesis of the station. Beacon 505 hadn't been created to any plan, it had simply spread itself within the hoop of the docking ring, like bacteria in a petri dish.

It was bigger every time Marshal Jameson was unlucky enough to have to drop by, but there was something different this time. Some of the most ramshackle extremities were gone, and the form seemed to have been pulled into something approaching coherence. Electro-luminescent panels gave light and life to some of the larger modules, with a web of softly glowing mesh swathing the most central habitation blocks and commercial modules. Somebody was spending money out here.

Jameson had heard there was an ambitious new station administrator, one who was keen to do business with law enforcement, as both a patrol post, and as an informer. The latter was half the reason Jameson was here, but *only* half.

The docking ring came into view as they circled the station. The first three craft attached to the ring wore the unmistakable orange and blue livery of police cruisers; one heavy, two regular. A few clusters of commercial craft and freighters swung into view, then Jameson's eyes narrowed, as a large white shape began to reveal itself, also unmistakable; a gleaming white elliptical profile emblazoned with the bright red "X" emblem of the PPB.

'Agent Malik, identify that PPB frigate please.'

'Which one, Sir?'

Jameson looked again. She wasn't alone, another PPB frigate was berthed right alongside.

'Spreff!'

A voice from the station's navigation control came through the comms, *'Marshal Jameson, we've been expecting you. This is Junior Marshal Hurst, we've got a good berth for your mobile platform next to the PPB frigate Sonya. Looking forward to meeting you, Sir.'*

Jameson wrinkled his brow and shook his head. The Junior Marshals were the product of a new graduate program, with no experience of policing. An experiment to boost Police numbers, and vastly unpopular with previous generations who'd worked through the ranks. Throwing the young graduates out here to the 500's was an attempt to toughen them up fast, the ones who survived, that is.

'Hurst, I take it you're a circuit marshal? There's no official marshal's office at this station.'

'That's right, Sir. I came in from Beacon 498 yesterday.'

'How much equipment do you have here?'

'Just what we brought with us aboard our cruisers.'

Jameson clenched his jaw, 'These PPB frigates, how long will they be docked here?'

'Indefinite, but no longer than 25 hours.'

'You *do* know there is an inbound Black Fleet dreadnought, Black Wreath, due to arrive within the hour?'

'We have her scheduled, yes. And the dreadnought Black Leopard later this evening.'

Jameson's eyes widened. 'You have two PPB frigates here now, and two Black Fleet dreadnoughts scheduled to berth here tonight?'

'The Sabina, Sonya, Black Wreath and Black Leopard. That's all so far anyway, there was talk of the PPB frigate Arissa being in the area, but she's only a possible right now. Is that okay, Sir?'

Jameson hardened his tone, 'Okay is just about the last thing that it is.'

'*Law enforcement will outnumber everyone else by at least by 4-to-1, that's great visibility in the heart of a rough zone like this, what could be better?*'

'It would be better if everyone of those 1-in-4 who *aren't* in law enforcement got off this station as fast as their legs and their hyper-optic drives will take them. How many officers and agents do you have aboard?'

'*Nine officers and three agents, why?*'

'How much riot gear do you have?'

'*I know some of you older Marshals don't respect us juniors, Marshal Jameson, but it's not appropriate to joke with me about things like that, Sir, especially not on an open channel.*'

'I'll ask again, and you will answer. How much riot gear do you have?'

'*I'd have to check. Any riot gear will belong to station security, and if the quality of the station itself is any guide, I wouldn't put much faith in it.*'

'How many station security personnel are there?'

'*Nine on duty, eighteen in all.*'

'Deputise them. Tonight everybody is on duty. I've got thirty officers and six agents aboard my platform, I've got enough riot gear and body-armour for forty people, we'll just have to hope it's enough.'

The fingers caressing her palms were soft, tender. Monique smiled at Commander Guthrie across the table. She was sensing a great deal more ease in his mood than the last time they'd met.

She was managing to stay relaxed too. She'd had enough time away from him to compartmentalise the revulsion she'd felt when she watched him celebrating over a hundred of her colleagues being killed when his crew destroyed the Black Sceptre. She still despised him, but she had reached a point where she could keep it from showing.

'So why have you been away from me for so long, Commander?'

He shook his head, his smile relaxed enough to spread to his eyes. 'Captain Rourke has been on the Admiralty's chiff-list for the last month. The Sabina was stood down and we've all been on "administrative leave" while things cooled down with the brass.'

'Does this have anything to do with the black eye she had the last time I saw her?'

Guthrie nodded, 'They weren't entirely unrelated.'

'Well, the rest seems to have suited you. Maybe you should think about quitting? Or at least get a transfer to another boat.'

'Funny you should say that, I'm moving over to the Sonya for a few days. You think I should make it permanent?'

'I don't know? Is her Captain on anyone's chiff-list?

'Now you mention it, she's on more chiff-lists than Captain Rourke is.'

'Then no. What you should really do is find a boat that stops wherever I am, so I don't have to go for weeks without seeing you.'

'Wouldn't that be nice? You know of a boat like that?'

She shrugged playfully, 'Maybe I'll buy my own boat, and let you be the Captain?'

'A promotion too? Clearly I joined the wrong navy. I have to wonder what kind of boat you can afford, though.'

'Do you care?'

He smiled, 'No.'

'Maybe I can afford one if this evening goes well. I'm playing for Erin Carson tonight and she's got bars and restaurants on all the best stations; classy places with rich clientele. If I can impress *her* my appearance fees might take a pretty fast uptick.'

'What's Erin Carson doing at a spreffing awful hole like Beacon 505?'

I think the new station administrator wants her to invest, he's pulling a ton of money in here trying to move this place upmarket.'

'Upmarket is pretty much the only direction you could go in this tangled up rat-run. It couldn't get any more *down*-market. I'll be glad if you don't have to play places like this any more.' Guthrie took a look around the club and looked like he was reappraising his statement, 'That said, *this* place has taken quite an upturn. I mean, it's like a low-life's idea of classy, but it's actually presentable. Last time I was in here I was navigating around spilled drink and bloodstains.'

'I know, they had me brought straight here, and I know we took some detours around the shadier bits of the station. I think they hoped I'd never been here before and would think it was all like this.'

'Ha! Yeah, there's still plenty of filthy dives here. It's gonna take a long time before this... spreff it!' Guthrie's watch was beeping at him. 'I gotta go, my two Captains need to see me. What time is your show tonight?'

'I should be starting my set around nine.'

'I'll be free before then, so I'll see you before you go on.'

'See that you do.'

'There's going to be a couple of hundred of us here tonight. Me and the boys will cheer extra loud. Got to impress Erin Carson for you, right?' He looked out of the window at the view of the docking ring, his smile fading a little, 'Here comes trouble.'

Gibson turned her own eyes towards the arriving craft, the deep-dark silhouette of the Black Wreath was manoeuvring into position for docking.

'You don't think there'll really be trouble, do you?'

'I can't speak for the rest of the station, but I'll make sure it's wall to wall white uniforms in here tonight, we won't leave enough room for trouble.' Guthrie knocked back his drink and placed a kiss on Gibson's cheek. 'Anyway, the Black Wreath's crew are all cadets and we're hauling two squads of commandos, if anything starts, it won't last long and it won't go their way.'

Gibson watched him leave, her mind whirling with what he'd just said. There had been nobody near them in the bar to overhear, but he'd never been so loose with information before. Was this a new level of trust, or an incautious slip due to his enforced leave? Or was he feeding her false information? She'd been worried ever since seeing the giant at Steimz that her cover was no longer secure, although she couldn't think of any way it might have been compromised.

She'd know soon enough, the Sabina's crew were going to be soft after a month of forced shore-leave, so hardened commandos would be easy to spot. Infinitely more worrying was the question of why two squads of commandos were being transferred to the Sonya, and why was Guthrie going with them?

The best guess of the intelligence analysts at Triple-S had been that the Savatara and Sonya were lurking in the area because they were planning to finish the job on the Black Wreath, but the only reason to take on commandos was if they were planning *not* to destroy her, but to board and take over the vessel. Monique left her untouched drink and hurried out of the bar, The Director and Staff Command needed to hear this, now.

The jostling crowd was an annoyance, but Wrath, along with around two thirds of the crew were getting their first chance to leave Black Wreath for weeks.

They were waiting for QM to lecture them about behaving themselves and other subjects that didn't interest them, but it seemed fuller because they were practically bouncing off each other with excitement. They wanted to see some fresh faces, and maybe to bathe a little in the glory of their part in this afternoon's pirate takedown.

QM stood on the stage and hushed down the noise, 'All right, shut up. Good evening, cadets. I know you want off this bird to get your lips around some liquor, and I don't want to know what else you might want to get your lips around, but you're in uniform, and you represent the uniform, and in it, you represent Black Fleet. I know you want to get at it rather than listen to me, but this is not some balmy tourist world, nor is it a clean and pleasant station.

'I'll stop short of declaring Beacon 505 hostile territory, but out here in the 500's *nobody* in a uniform is popular, and pretty often your uniform won't even make you popular with other people in uniform. Don't expect to be treated like heroes for taking down those pirate junks, there may well be people here who had friends aboard those junks, or people who owed them money, anyway.'

QM cast a cold appraising eye across the gathering, her tone turning to cold steel, 'Be very careful this evening. Watch your step, and behave yourselves. Keep yourselves in line, and keep your crew mates in line. Don't get into trouble, and if trouble finds you, get out of it, or I guarantee the demerits will flow as freely as water from a bursting dam. This afternoon we engaged our prey, but tonight you will meet the enemy. That's all.'

Wrath looked at Qiang, Pirie and Farr with a questioning gaze, 'What do you think she meant by that?'

Farr shook her head, 'Just a standard warning not to get too out of control on shore leave, I guess.'

Qiang checked her watch, 'Well I don't think it makes much difference to me and Pirie, we've only got an hour and a half of our recreational period left anyway. We'll have barely time for two drinks before we're due back aboard.'

Wrath wrinkled his face in sympathy, 'Spreff it! I wanted us all to hang out properly, and to find out if this station deserves its reputation.'

'You and Farr will have to whoop it up for us.'

Pirie still looked pale from having launched her lunch earlier in the day, 'Don't go to too much trouble on my account, I don't feel like whooping anything up anyway. Let's just find somewhere quiet, huh?'

Qiang wrapped an arm around Pirie's shoulders and pulled her in close, 'Come on, Killer, let's get you a drink, or seven.'

'Please let's.'

Marshal Jameson caressed his temple with his fingertips, studying the video feeds from the limited number of cameras scattered around the station, eyes drawn to the stream of cadets leaving Black Wreath.

Thumbing the open call switch, he growled instructions to the police crew down at the docking ring. 'Don't just stand against the walls, make yourself known, make your presence felt. Make them move around you and notice you, not just brush by you.'

Marshal Hurst looked sceptical. 'I honestly don't know why you're so worked up, Marshal.'

'You will soon enough.'

They both turned at the sound of a tapping on the security room door. Standing in the doorway was a short and chubby man with a gleaming bald head and a tight suit that a guy ten years his junior and twenty kilos lighter would struggle to get away with.

'Gentlemen, my security staff are not happy with you, perhaps you ought to explain to me why I shouldn't share their mood? Or at least explain why you seem to be prepping them all for a riot?'

'And you are?' Jameson already knew, but he felt like forcing the administrator to introduce himself.

'Sid Parsons. I run this station.' Parsons hefted his bulk a little, 'I'm guessing that you are Marshal Leo Jameson?'

'I am. To answer your question, the reason I have police and security prepping for a riot is, to try to prevent the riot that has every prospect of happening on your station tonight.'

It was Parsons' turn to look sceptical, 'The way I heard it we're going to have a few hundred PPB and Black Fleet crewmen and women here tonight. Just who are you expecting to be dumb enough start a riot while they're here?'

'That would be the few hundred PPB and Black Fleet crewmen and women.'

'Well when you're done wasting your time and riling up my staff I want to have our meeting. We've got a lot to talk about, Marshall, not least, the disappearance of my brother. There's some people I want you to meet, as well.'

Jameson stood, raising himself to his full height, towering over the administrator. 'I'm done here for now. We'll walk and talk.' He gestured for Parsons to lead him out the door. 'Marshal Hurst, call me immediately if and when any more Black Fleet or PPB craft arrive, and keep on top of our people, don't let their alertness levels drop.'

Jameson took a last look around the security monitors before following Sid Parsons out of the room.

Parson's didn't wait to get started, 'Two months, Jameson! *Two months* since my brother disappeared and I've heard *nothing!*'

'Your brother did a lot of interstellar travel, Mr Parsons, and the waters have been very muddied around the last days he was sighted. Finding someone gets very hard if they don't want to be found.'

'You insinuating something?'

'He was facing charges of sexual assault by two different members of a dance group he was representing, and there were other complainants ready to come forward about separate incidents. He has plenty of reason to disappear.'

'Those charges were brownhole. He was going to beat those easy. Those bimbos expected to hit the big-time after a few weeks touring mining rigs and the outer-beacons, when they realised they'd have to put some actual *work* into improving their act they tried to get out of the contract. When they couldn't break the contract they pulled this sexual-assault chiff to try to bully him into releasing them. They were cheap, low-talent hoofers. There's no way my brother would run away from a chiff-charge like that.'

'Be that as it may, his disappearance is surprisingly complete. We believe we've settled on his last location as being Raleigh Station, there's a few people we're tracing as having potentially seen him on the night he vanished, but it's a busy relay point, so it takes time.'

Parson's gave out an exaggerated sigh of frustration, 'I know he was on Raleigh Station, Jameson! I told your people that!

'As for people who might have seen him, there was this girl he saw singing that night, he called me to rave about her. Terrific body, great voice, sophisticated vibe. He told me he was going to hook up with her and ask her to come play here as a regular fixture.'

'Do you have a name?'

'I've got better than that, I've got her! "Monique" is what she calls herself. I haven't heard her sing yet, but the rest of the package checks out, and then some. I was going to talk to her myself, but I figured I'd better wait until you got here.'

'Where is she now?'

'She's in the main lounge-bar on the far west side of the hoop, the "Club Twassanque," the classiest joint on the station. I bought it from Beacon 555 before Jim Sheridan blew it up for the insurance money. It was the only thing there that was worth anything. Spreffing massive job getting it all the way here. Still, a lot cheaper than buying new.'

Jameson suffered an involuntary facial cringe, 'The Club *what?*'

'Yeah, they haven't changed the name. Kinda weird. I think they said it was French or something? Anyway, the singer is meeting with Erin Carson before tonight's show. I'm hoping Carson will take on one of the bars here as a franchise. I kind of used Carson's name to get Monique to play here, and I'm hoping Monique will be talented enough to tempt Carson to buy in. I'm working kind of a double-play.'

'Erin Carson doesn't get played easily, Mister Parsons.'

'Oh? You know all about her, do you?'

'I should do, she's my wife.'

Parsons spluttered in disbelief, 'Spreff! You're kidding?'

'That would be a bizarre subject for a joke.'

'Okay, well, I didn't mean any disrespect, to her, or you.' He gave Jameson a puzzled look up and down, still bemused by the coupling of this gangling stiff and the vivacious tycoon who, frankly, could have her pick of the Protectorate's eligible bachelors, 'Anyway, Marshal, business is business, and I have big plans for this place. Me and my brother were going to make this place a hit, lift the reputation of the 500's out of the crapper, you know what I mean?'

'Yes. I've heard about your ambitions. That's the main reason I was sent here, you're apparently interested in helping out law-enforcement, for a price.'

'Sure. Well there's the thing, you see. This is a very well placed station, I'm going to hear a lot of interesting things here, valuable things.'

'*I've* never paid an informant in my life, the idea of people holding out information that could prevent crime disgusts me, especially if they want to wring a profit out of it. But Grand Marshal Balfour is very keen on cultivating... information networks, so I think I'm supposed to be here to charm you, or something.'

'Oh yeah?' Parson's looked sceptical, 'He doesn't seem to be playing to your skills there.'

'No.'

Parson's shrugged, 'You know what? I don't need to be charmed, Marshal, but if I'm going to turn this station into somewhere people can bring their wives and kids without worrying about them being kidnapped, raped, murdered, or any combination of all three of those things, I need to invest big. That means information goes to those who pay up. Business is business, and this is not a risk free strategy on my part.'

'So your information will go to the highest bidder?'

Parsons shook away the notion, 'What is I need is regular money coming in. Consistency is better for me than an occasional big payout. It doesn't all have to be about money, though. Whoever finds out what's happened to my brother is going to get a lot of gratitude from me, and gratitude can go a long way, so let's not worry about charm, let's focus on results, huh?'

Jameson looked up at the sign above the door of the bar. 'We're here.'

'Okay. Yeah there she is, Monique. I see her in that booth over there talking to... your *wife*.' Parsons sounded like his credulity was still being stretched by this revelation. 'Seriously though? You're married to her?'

'Why don't you tell me again how charmless *I* am, Mr Parsons.'

'Good point. Right. I'll leave you to it. You have a nice chat with the young lady. Can you find your way back to the security suite when you're done?'

'There was a holographic map of the station in the security room, I have it all memorised.'

'This station's got over 30 klicks of corridors snaking around the place, you reckon you've memorised the layout of this wriggling mess already? I've been here for eight months and I *still* get lost.'

'I have a visual memory index acuity of 99.7%'

'Oh is that all?'

'No. It should be 100%, but I reproduced a typographical error that appeared on the exam sheet which they mistook for a mistake on my part rather than their own.'

'I bet that keeps you awake at nights.'

'No.'

'Well I'd say I was charmed to meet you, but you don't need a 99% memory acuity thing to catch me out on that one, so I'll just say, I'm going now. Should I really get ready for a riot, or are you just testing out my security team's crisis readiness?'

'It's not a test. If your office isn't secure you might be best advised to spend the evening in the security block with myself and Marshal Hurst.'

'Those are my options? Spend the evening with you or take my chances with a riot.' He shrugged, 'Just how bad can a riot be?'

A loose crowd of white uniformed PPB crew was gradually filling the Club Twassanque. There were no black uniforms here, yet.

Jameson was having the PPB crew sent clockwise round the station and the Black Wreath's crew sent counter-clockwise to delay them meeting up for as long as possible.

There were clusters of smaller bars and eateries on the far side of the hoop, so it would take a while for the Black Fleet crew to filter around to this half of the station, but Jameson was still feeling an undercurrent of tension. The bar gave a great view of the docking ring, and cautious eyes were flicking to and from the large, dark ellipse of the Black Wreath.

He heard a familiar voice shout out, 'Leo!' His eyes were drawn to those of his wife and he smiled; a genuine but uncomfortable smile, his facial muscles had never fully accustomed themselves to the practice.

'Leo, Leo, Leo, you long streak of piss! Come and meet Monique! You'll love her. She's as funny as all shit!'

Jameson winced, 'How long has it been?'

'Six weeks, knucklehead.' She turned to Monique, 'Sorry for the old-fashioned language, Monique, I'm punishing him for being away from me for so long। He hates it when I talk like a pirate. Let me introduce my husband. Leo, this is Monique.'

Monique stood and held out her hand. She held it as if he were meant to kiss it, which was not his style at all. He took it and shook it.

He gestured for her to sit as he set himself down alongside his wife, 'I'm pleased to meet you, I'm sure.'

Monique stayed on her feet, 'Marshal, Erin, you two have been apart for a long time, I should leave you to share some time together.'

Jameson shook his head, not a gesture of mere politeness, 'Please stay, I've been hearing a lot about you, I want to find out if any of it's true.' Jameson had her fixed with his hawk-like glare, was there a flinch there? Hard to say.

She affected modesty, 'Who's been talking about me?' she asked, sitting back down at the edge of her seat.

'Sid Parsons, the station administrator. He's been telling me about what a great singer you are, and how he *had* to get you to perform here after his brother told him how fabulous you are.'

'I'm not sure I deserve all the attention. I haven't even met the administrator yet, but he certainly seemed keen to get me to play here.'

'You met his brother though, yes? On Raleigh station?'

'Not that I recall, but I haven't been there for a couple of months now, and you meet so many people in this business.'

'You're sure you didn't meet him? His name is Ralph Parsons. I have a picture of him.'

Erin was giving him a dirty look, but she said nothing. Jameson placed a holographic disc on the table and an image of Ralph Parsons hovered over it. As Monique studied it, Jameson studied her.

'I don't recall the face. Should I?'

'Sorry if I seem insistent, but Ralph Parsons went missing around that time, and it seems Raleigh station was the last place he was seen. He called his brother and told him he was going to try to meet with you, as it happens he was going to try to persuade you to play here. After that call, all trace of the man vanished.'

'That doesn't sound good. I wish I could help.'

'Well, you may be able to help, even if you think you can't. Maybe you'll remember something.'

'Leo!' Erin looked furious, 'I haven't seen you for weeks, and you're straight into business and ignoring me!'

He reached out and held her hand, 'I'm sorry, Erin, but this man could be dead, or kidnapped, or anything.'

'I know your work matters, Leo, but you don't have to be such an asshole about it. You just met the girl and you're grilling her like a suspect!'

'I apologise, Miss... sorry, I didn't hear your surname?'

'I just go by Monique, please don't worry about formalities. And of course you want to find out what happened to that man. I'd have been glad to help if I knew anything.'

Erin gave Monique a world weary look, 'You see what I was saying now?' she turned her gaze to her Leo, but to talk about him, not to him, 'You see a man in uniform and they look great, but there's a lot more to a guy wearing a uniform than a fancy looking lump of meat to have on your arm. You're always playing second best to their sense of duty.'

'I'm afraid my wife always had an eye for uniforms, Monique. You're not similarly afflicted, are you?'

Erin spoke for her, 'She was with this hunky PPB beau earlier. Very cosy. But he had that haunted look, reminded me of someone we used to know, Leo.'

'Would that be Commander Guthrie from the Sabina?'

This girl was good, but she visibly blanched at the mention of Guthrie's name.

'Yes. We see each other sometimes, as much as the Sabina's patrol schedule allows.'

'It must have been a while since you saw him then? I heard the Sabina had been out of commission for a month, and had some major crew changes?'

'He doesn't talk about his work. We just arrange to meet up when we can.'

'You met up that night on Raleigh station, I believe? You were seen together.'

'We did meet up one of the nights I was at Raleigh station, I was there for a three night booking.'

'Is there any chance Commander Guthrie might have seen Ralph Parsons?'

'You'd have to ask him, but he only had a very quick stopover. He was there for less than an hour, so I doubt it.'

'Of course, the Sabina was late arriving wasn't it. I understand they'd had some kind of trouble that day. Witnesses said her Captain, Captain Rourke, appeared to have been violently assaulted?'

Monique shook her head, 'I don't know what happened, Guthrie wouldn't say, but she had a black eye and a swollen face. She looked pretty bad. What does that have to do with this Parsons guy?'

'Well, did the Commander seem angry? Did he seem upset by the day's events?'

'No, he seemed... stressed. Maybe a little depressed if anything. Down and weary, not angry.'

'So if, for instance, some young man were to come on to you in an inappropriate way, he wouldn't have reacted violently?'

'No. he's not like that.'

'It's just, this Ralph Parsons had a bit of a reputation for taking a little too much interest in women who were not necessarily interested in him, and according to people I spoke to who were aboard the station, you sent your Commander Guthrie on ahead to your cabin. If this Parsons had taken such an interest in you, he may have encountered the commander, causing some kind of altercation.'

'What could possibly cause an altercation?'

'Well, Parsons liked to collect favours, and to call them in. It seems he had persuaded somebody to lend him a janitorial master-key for the accommodation suites, and the computer logs show at some point that evening he used this key to gain entry to your cabin.'

'Are you serious? That's creepy!' If she was faking surprise, she was faking it well.

'Of course, so maybe he snuck in planning to wait for you and Commander Guthrie was already there? With the tough day that Commander Guthrie had had, is it implausible he may have got angry and fought with Mister Parsons?'

'I don't know what to tell you, Marshal. With what you seem to be implying, there wasn't time for him to kill somebody and get rid of a body, before or after we got together. He left me with barely enough time to catch his flight out.' Monique looked alarmed at the conversation. 'Look, I had no idea about this stuff. Hearing this guy got into my cabin freaks me out, I didn't even know people could do that.

'For the other stuff, You're going to have to talk to the Commander yourself. I saw him in the bar. I saw him again in my cabin, and when we were done he had to run to get aboard the Sabina before she shipped out. I never saw that Parsons guy, and frankly, I'm glad I didn't. He sounds like a sleazy spreffer. If somebody got rid of him, there's probably people with a lot more reason, and a lot more time to do it than my Commander Guthrie.'

'You're probably right.' Jameson turned a look to his wife, who looked deeply unimpressed, 'And I'm sorry to have made such a bad first impression on you.'

'So you should be, Leo.' Erin kicked him under the table, and not lightly.

He knew he deserved it, and gave her hand a squeeze, 'I'm sorry to you, too. I'll make it up to you tonight. We'll eat at the finest establishment this dump of a station has to offer, I promise.'

'Ooh, you smooth talking bastard, Leo! Come here,' she kissed his cheek with almost comic enthusiasm.

Monique stood up, 'I really should leave you two to make up for lost time. I know what it's like to be separated from the people you care about for weeks at a time.'

'Thank you for answering my questions, Monique, and I'm sorry again.'

Erin waved, 'And I'm sorry for *him* too. I'll drag him along to hear you sing tonight, and I'll make him cheer extra loud to make amends.'

'Thanks. Good to meet you both.'

'Actually,' Jameson wasn't quite ready to let her slip away, 'there is just one more curiosity. The janitorial key was never returned.'

Monique frowned, 'And?'

'Because they're important, and they don't want them getting into the wrong hands, they have a transceiver inside, so that if they're lost they can be found easily. They're very tough, and the transceiver is pretty powerful. It would be near impossible to steal one, break one, or to sneak it off the station.'

'Right?'

'The key that Ralph Parsons obtained stopped transmitting while it was *inside* your cabin, and according to the data from the door activation log, it did so whilst you and Commander Guthrie were both there. The key has never been found. It's as if it simply winked out of existence.'

'That's pretty weird.'

'Yes. It's quite a puzzle. And then there's how very clean your cabin was, we found residue of a substance called "Kleen", which is an industrial cleaner used mostly by disease and infection control agencies, law-enforcement, the military, and, unfortunately, some of the more professional organised criminal groups for deep cleaning crime scenes. It's very hard to get hold of, nothing housekeeping on a space station would have access to. But you can't be expected to know about such things, obviously.' Jameson nodded to himself sagely, 'Anyway, if you think of anything else, please let me know. I look forward to seeing you perform tonight.'

'Sure. Thanks.'

Jameson felt the cold stare of his wife drilling into the side of his head as Monique walked away.

'I forgot again.'

He turned to her, knowing this was going to hurt, 'What did you forget, Erin?'

'Why I married an asshole like you.'

Jameson quietly sighed, 'Because I was the "asshole" that was still alive.'

She placed a kiss on his cheek, this time with no enthusiasm at all. 'Well at least *one* of us got lucky,' she downed the dregs of her drink and grimaced. 'One out of three ain't bad.'

The soft thrum of his watch's alert demanded his attention. Touching the screen caused Marshal Hurst's face to appear, hovering above his wrist. 'Marshal Jameson, we have a PPB frigate inbound. Arriving in 7 minutes.'

'What's she called?'

'The Arissa.'

sixteen

QQQ-LEVEL COMMUNIQUE

LOOP : BLACK FLEET STAFF COMMAND,
DIRECTOR - TRIPLE S,
STAFF COMMANDER RODHAM, STAFF MAJOR JAGLAN – BLACK LEOPARD,
COVERT ASSET 050R - BEACON 505

ADVISORY FROM ASSET 050R : PPB COMMANDOS MOBILISED, TWO SQUADS
TRANSFERRING WHITE SLUG SABINA TO WHITE SLUG SONYA ## INCURSION RISK –
MLT BLACK WREATH CONFIRMED ## REVISED PROTOCOLS ISSUED BLACK
WREATH COMPUTER SYSTEM ## REVISED BLACK LEOPARD TASK ITINERARY :
BEACON 505 : GREY TASK ## NON-LETHAL DISRUPTION, ZERO ELISION
INTERACTION, PRIORITY INFILTRATION WHITE SLUG SONYA : EMPLACED ASSETS
SUCCESSFULLY DEPLOYED ## TEAM ONYX TASK ITINERARY UNCHANGED ## GREY
TASK, BLACK TASK ## ELISION AUTHORISATION : OPEN ## OPEN TARGETS : WHITE
SLUG SONYA, WHITE SLUG SAVATARA ## PROTECT BLACK WREATH : BLACK TASK,
RED TASK ## MAXIMISE OPPORTUNITY FOR INCURSION WHITE SLUG SAVATARA :
BLACK TASK, RED TASK ## HIGH PRIORITY ELISION : CAPTAIN MIRANDA JOWETT –
WHITE SLUG SAVATARA : RED TASK ## BLACK LEOPARD SUPPLEMENTAL : ASSET
050R MAY REQUIRE EMERGENCY EXTRACTION – BEACON 505 ## GREY TASK ##
ASSET WILL ADVISE ##

The holographic map of the station rotated slowly, like an ephemeral tangle of deeply unappetising spaghetti and meatballs thrown in the air, casting an orange glow on the confused faces staring at it.

Wrath couldn't wrap his mind around the perversity of the layout, 'What kind of warped mind designed this turd-burger of a station?'

'There is no design, Wrath. I grabbed the station map last time I was here and everything's changed, again.' Qiang held up her watch and attempted to scan the hologram into the map-memory. 'The Navigation Council set an open licence for Beacon 505, so people can just drag up any space-worthy unit and hook it up, as long as it's air-tight and the seals and gravity systems are up to scratch you can start trading.

'The more popular places make extra money selling connecting access tubes to people who want to draw traffic, so you get these tube corridors snaking around anywhere and everywhere.'

'I hate to think what the power-draw is trying to keep the gravity the right way up in those tubes.'

Cadet Farr cycled through the list of station modules, 'By the time we find a quieter bar Diana and Grace's recreation shifts are going to be over, and there's no guarantee the other bars are any less disgusting than this one.'

'The best place is on the other side of the station, we could have gone straight there if the police hadn't been playing strong-arm.' Qiang's watch chimed to confirm the map scan was complete, 'Got it! If we run and we don't get lost we can get to the station's least crappy bar in around 20 minutes.'

Pirie sighed, 'Which will give us just enough time to do absolutely nothing before we have to head back to Black Wreath! Let's just stay here and drink as much as we can, while we can. I don't need exercise, and I don't need spreffing ambience, I just need to get inelegantly hammered.'

Wrath surveyed the bar's ugly furniture, ugly décor and ugly bar staff. 'Well, it's got character. As long as the company's good, I'm happy to hang out with you guys. I'm going steady on the drinking though, I've got a full eight hours off-duty, and the last time I got properly tanked up I wound up making some... questionable decisions.'

Qiang looked vaguely appalled at the notion of staying here, but relented. 'Okay, but let's get lots of drinks right now, with this many people desperate to get drunk fast we'll be lucky to get served more than once, and the less time I spend having to go near that barman the better.' She had a point, the head barman looked like he'd been in a fight every night of his life, and lost at least half of them.

They became aware of a silence sweeping the bar like a ripple spreading across a calm pond. Turning about, a figure swept across the floor, a massive man, almost impossibly huge, his face implacable, a mess of scars. Every eye followed his passage, on and through the hatchway and out of sight. The silence persisted for a few moments.

Farr broke the spell, turning to the barman and shouting, 'Bar-guy, make drinks, and lots of them.' He nodded and waved them over. 'One of the first things my Daddy taught me was never miss a chance to get a barman's attention.'

Wrath slapped her on the back, 'Thanks, Farr. That's the most useful thing I've learned since I joined up.'

Monique sat alone, nursing her drink, keeping a wary eye on Marshal Jameson and sparing a warning glare for anyone who looked like they might come over to her table to try their luck with her.

She was glad to see Jameson was mostly preoccupied with his wife, who, if Monique's rudimentary lip-reading skills were up to scratch, was steadfastly refusing to spend the evening aboard Jameson's mobile police platform.

Jameson was wise to worry about her safety, more and more white uniforms were appearing, and Black Leopard would be arriving soon. Monique hadn't been read in on the plans, but "Team Onyx" from Black Leopard were *not* coming here for shore leave.

'Hey there, angel face!'

Guthrie laid a hand on her shoulder and eased himself down next to her.

'Hey you, too! How did your meeting go? Everything all right?'

'Classified stuff. You know. Seems good, though.' He spun the order pad around and surveyed the alcoholic options, 'Looks like you need a top-up. What'll you have?'

She held up her glass, swirling a syrupy golden liquid that sparkled in the light, 'Another of these, please. It's a Honey-crush Glow, it's good for my singing voice.' she smiled, 'That's my excuse for already having drunk three of them, anyway.'

'Steady there, the night is young my sweet.' He tapped the drink order into the pad and pushed it away.

'Yeah, I'm nervous tonight though, not sure why.'

He rubbed her shoulder, 'You worried about impressing Erin Carson?'

'I'm more worried about her husband.'

'Who's that?'

'I thought you'd know, she's married to Marshal Leo Jameson.'

'Wow! Really? I mean, he's kind of a legend, but from what I hear he's about as charismatic as a procedural manual. Old bugger must have some hidden qualities. Why's *he* got you worried?'

'He was asking me questions about some guy who went missing from Raleigh Station when I was there — when *we* were there. They weren't polite inquiries either.'

'Who's the missing guy?'

'Jameson said he was called Ralph Parsons. You heard of him?'

Guthrie shook his head. 'Never. Why is Jameson onto you about it?'

'He said he snuck into my cabin using a stolen pass-key. Then he just vanished.'

'Weird, and creepy. I hope nothing good has happened to him.'

'Yeah, I don't like Jameson thinking we might have been the ones to have done something to him though. Anyway, Jameson said he wants to talk to you too, so you have that to look forward to.'

A waiter appeared, quietly setting their drinks down. As Guthrie waved his watch over the pay-pad and confirmed the charge with a thumbprint, somebody at the far side of the bar caught Monique's eye. The man was solidly built, with a protruding belly of the sort that appeared on men who were still eating to feed muscles they no longer had. His hair was a bristle of iron grey, and he was wearing a dark green tweed suit.

This was the man. The man in green whose image had been dragged out of Guthrie's mind on the night Monique had killed Ralph Parsons. This was the man the Director believed was the link to the PPB's ultra-secret service.

He was standing in the west entrance and surveying the room, clearly looking for somebody.

Monique studied the man in green intently as he scanned the room, saw his eyes widening in surprise, or maybe even alarm as they came to rest on... Erin Carson?

Jameson looked over and saw the man in green staring at his wife, then the man in green saw Jameson, his jaw dropping in apparent shock.

As Erin Carson turned to see what her husband was looking at the man in green turned quickly about, walking out of the same door he'd entered, in no small hurry. Erin turned to her husband, who turned back to her, studying her face — for what, Gibson didn't know.

Seemingly satisfied, Jameson excused himself and followed the man in the green out of the door. Erin Carson watched him go, her look confused rather than concerned.

'What are you looking at?'

She turned back to Guthrie, who seemed to have missed the arrival and departure of the man in green, the man who had had his Captain punched to the ground aboard her own vessel. 'Oh, just people watching, you know? I like to imagine people's stories. It helps me come up with new songs.'

She wanted to follow them, to see what was going on between them, but she was here to watch Guthrie, so who was more important? If Guthrie was going to help attack Black Wreath tomorrow, there were the lives of a hundred and fifty cadets on the line. But how long would the elusive man in green be here?

'Do you know this other PPB boat that arrived?'

'The Arissa?' Guthrie gave her a stern look, 'we don't talk about the Arissa, she's bad news.' He looked up and she felt his muscles tighten. It seemed to be the night for startled looks. She followed his gaze to what had alarmed him. This time it was a figure standing at the *east* door.

Tonight she had a full house. It was the giant.

He too was scanning the room, presumably looking for the man in green, his head turning with the deliberate intensity of a searchlight. His head stopped turning, his eyes fixed squarely on Monique. She held his gaze as she felt Guthrie grow even more tense. The giant started towards their table, and Guthrie began scrabbling to stand.

'Sorry baby, I have to go, right now.'

Guthrie jogged away as casually and as quickly as he could to the west door, very deliberately not looking back.

The giant stopped, watching him leave. He turned to look at Monique again.

Raising her hand, she pointed at him, and then summoned him with her finger. He walked slowly to the edge of the table. She'd hidden fear a thousand times, this was harder, but experience kicked in. She frowned at him angrily.

'You just scared away my drinks for the night, big fella. What do you propose to do about that?'

A look of confusion spread across his huge, scarred face, a look that seemed to suit it quite well.

She pointed at the empty spot on the chair next to her. 'Your ass goes here,' she pointed to her glass with a conspiratorial smile, 'your money goes here.'

He studied her carefully, nodded, and sat down beside her.

Maybe she didn't need to follow the man in green, maybe she could make him come to her.

Griffith's attention was held by footsteps that were not his own, following perfectly in-step with his, and steadily gaining. That meant a longer gait than his own but much lighter than Fester's. It had to be Jameson.

Making ready to turn and face his pursuer he froze at the sound of a name he hadn't heard said out loud in thirteen years.

'Luther!'

He turned, eyes of cold fury coming to rest on the face of Leo Jameson.

'Luther Jerome Dawson?' Jameson scrutinised Griffith carefully, 'You know, Luther, I thought it might be sassy to say something like "death suits you," but now I see you a little closer, well, I have my reputation for honesty to think of. How goes it, Luther?'

Griffith closed the gap between them in no time, grabbing Jameson and pushing him against the pliant tubular wall of the corridor, his words a low, menacing growl, 'That's a dangerous name to be saying out loud, Leo.'

Jameson looked unconcerned at the rough-housing, 'It's a more dangerous name to *have* than it is to *say*, Luther, but don't worry, I've memorised the location of every security camera and audio pick-up on the station. This section's clear.'

Griffith released his grip and took a half-step back. 'You and your magic memory, Leo. You're probably the only person in the Protectorate who could have recognised me. You're the first person who has in thirteen years.'

'Well you've certainly gone for a new look, Luther. I don't think even Erin would have recognised you. I'm glad to see you didn't want to put it to the test, though.' Jameson added some steel to his tone, 'I don't think either of us want to find out what would happen if she discovered you were still alive.'

A flash of pain and concern wiped most of the hostility from Griffith's face. He bit down hard on bitter memories, taking a moment to reassemble his composure.

'How is she?'

'She gets along fine, as long as she takes her medication. After all these years I've given up on her ever being the person she was before the bomb,' he sneered at Griffith, 'You don't seem to be suffering any lasting effects though, which is rather ironic as it was you they were trying to kill.'

'No lasting effects? Is that a joke?'

'What? You never got to wear your admiral's uniform? You never got to sit at the top table with your golden beard and your gold braid?'

'For a man who's famous for his smarts, you say some very stupid things, Leo.'

'Sorry Luther, I was just seeing if you were any better at controlling your temper these days. I know you were never really interested in those trappings of the admiralty, you just wanted the power. Speaking of which, I heard about Admiral Wrekin, I was sorry to hear he was gone.'

Griffith turned away dismissively, 'We hadn't spoken in a long time, we said our goodbyes long ago.'

'But you were his golden-haired boy, Luther! Literally. Is that really all you have to say about the man who gave you your career?'

Griffith rounded on him, 'That bomb you think had no lasting effects on me? That killed Wrekin, on the inside. He wasn't even there, but, it finished him.'

Jameson nodded, 'You may be right, Luther. He gave your eulogy, you know? He and I were the only ones there who knew you weren't dead, but he looked genuinely destroyed by the grief.

'I met your mother at the wake, by the way, suddenly a lot of things about you made a lot more sense. Your father too, although even my memory is strained to remember anything about *him*.'

Griffith was dismissive, 'If I hadn't got anything to say about Wrekin, why would I have anything to say about *them?*'

'I feel like I'm picking up guilt there, Luther. You blame yourself for how the Admiral ended up? Like I told you thirteen years ago, Luther, you're dangerous to know. You do more harm than good to the people around you. Being dead is the best thing you could ever have done for Erin. I'm just glad you loved her enough to let them bury your name, before your own people finished the job and buried the pair of you.'

'It certainly worked out nicely for you, didn't it Leo?'

Jameson became harder, colder, 'You don't know a thing, Luther. I told you, she'll never be the same woman she was before the bomb. There was catastrophic neurological damage. Her recovery was miraculous, but brain injuries can change people in ways that are impossible to calculate, and impossible to fix. Sometimes they get better, sometimes they don't. She's had every neuro-regenerative therapy there is, but she still walks a knife-edge every day.'

Griffith treated Jameson to a sour look, 'And how many of those days do you see, Leo?'

'Trying to make me feel guilty that my job keeps us apart? How many days would either of you have seen if you'd stayed around, doing what you do best, making more enemies in the PPB. Standing next to you she wouldn't have just been in the firing line, she'd have been a target.'

'So instead she gets to coast along while you avoid making enemies, or any progress. How much younger than you is Grand Marshal Balfour again? I guess you can forget about ever becoming Grand Marshal now. You'll be retired from the force by the time he quits.'

'The day my own colleagues try to cancel *my* promotion with a bomb is the day you get to mock my career progress, *Admiral.*'

'We both know there's no danger of that, Leo, you've already had the last promotion you're ever going to get, and that was nearly two decades ago. There's nowhere left to go for you to go except down, or out.'

Jameson looked unconcerned, 'There were ways that you and I were very much alike, Luther. Like you, I didn't join up for titles, I joined up to do police work. The only use I have for promotions is that every one I got meant there were fewer people who could jerk me around. Now, the Grand Marshal is the only one I answer to, and he's smart enough not to second guess my experience, or my record.'

'People jerking me around never gave me much trouble, if someone really annoys me I just kill them.'

Jameson looked unimpressed, 'Really? Filed any good dockets lately?'

'I'm off the books these days, Leo. Speaking of which, if Marshal Osterman thinks he'll get a result on Steimz, you should tell him to find a more useful outlet for his energies.'

At this Leo's eyes widened, unsure if this was a brag or brownhole, not that that had ever been Luther's style. 'Is that a confession? You an associate of the late Mister Corvalis, were you? You do know that killing gangsters is still a crime, and I'm still a Marshal?'

'And just how do you think you'd go about convicting a dead man without your wife finding out you've been lying to her for thirteen years?'

'That's a good point, Luther. Let me think on it.'

'I'll tell you what, Leo. If I kill somebody tonight I'll make sure I file a docket, keep things things nice and official.'

'Luther, there may only be one person in the whole protectorate who isn't afraid of you, but that one person does exist, and you're looking at him.'

'I guess you know I care too much about Erin to put her through that again. Yes, if anyone is going to put you in your grave before your time, it won't be me, not while Erin's alive, at least.' Griffith patted Jameson firmly on the arm, too firmly. 'Anyway, good to catch up, old buddy! Old friend! Old pal! Good times, huh? Let's make it another thirteen years, or maybe more!'

'Stay away from her, Luther. There's no telling what seeing you might do to her. Don't forget, I know the names of plenty of people who'd love to know you're still alive, and to see that you don't stay that way.'

'You might know people who'd want to kill me Leo, but you don't know anybody who'd survive the attempt.'

'With the number of enemies *you* made it's more a question of volume than skill. A man of your experience should know all it takes to end things is for one bozo to get a lucky break.'

'Of course I know that, Leo, I found that out when I heard Erin had married you.'

Jameson's lapel radio buzzed, the two regarded each other in silence. Jameson broke off their gaze first, touching his finger to the radio, the voice of Junior-Marshal Hurst broke the silence.

"Marshal, there's a Black Fleet dreadnought inbound, Black Leopard. They'll be docking in 8 minutes."

Jameson studied Griffith's face for a reaction, there was none. 'Park them next to Black Wreath, same procedure as before. Send them around the station anti-clockwise, no exceptions. Don't let your men take any chiff, it won't be cadets this time, and I've never heard of the Black Leopard, so it isn't a patroller.'

Hurst sounded incredulous, *'You know the name of every Black Fleet patrol craft, do you?'*

'Yes.'

'So what should my men be expecting?'

'Expect thugs. Thugs, fighters, killers. I'll be there in ten minutes, don't open the airlocks until I get there.' He released the talk button, 'Sorry to break short our reunion, Luther, but I have to try to stop a war breaking out between your PPB maniacs, and these Black Fleet maniacs.'

'Well I wish you the best of luck with that.'

'I don't suppose I can call on you to get your people to behave themselves?'

'My people? Do you see me in a uniform, Leo? If you have a problem with naval personnel, take it up with Over-Admiral Connors. I'm sure he'll be as thrilled to hear from you as I've been.'

'Didn't keeping the troops in line used to be your job?'

'Yes it did, and it turns out I was far too good at it. It was you who convinced me I'd have to quit or Erin would end up dead, so that means tonight, keeping the peace is your job, not mine.'

'So just what is your job now, anyway?'

Griffith shook his head. He rested a powerful fist on Jameson's chest, 'Could be a rough night here tonight, Leo. You keep her safe.'

'I have, I do, and I always will.'

Before the sense of threat had been held back, but not now, now Jameson was seeing the *old* Luther that he'd once admired, and that his wife had loved, 'Keeping her safe is what keeps *you* safe, Leo.'

Being manhandled hadn't hurt him, but the insinuation he couldn't protect his wife hurt his pride, he bristled with uncharacteristic anger, 'You wouldn't be threatening a police marshal, would you Luther?'

'Threats would give you a warning, Leo. If it ever comes to it, you won't get a warning. You won't even know you're dead.'

Jameson pushed him away and treated him to a glare of pure ice, 'Then I guess that's another thing we'll have in common.'

Wrath, Qiang and Farr were taking it in turns to check their watches — Pirie was more concerned with drinking. Both tasks were tricky, with the four of them hard-pressed for elbow room, squeezed around a grubby little table while a busy press of their fellow cadets were still cramming into the bar, trying to make the best of their limited down-time.

'One good thing about this place being so busy is it does hide a lot of the squalor.' Wrath observed, though he did notice that thanks to the low seats the new view was mostly a forest of buttocks, which were an even less welcome intrusion into his elbow room.

'Spreff off!' Pirie made good use of her own elbows, landing a hard dig into a pressing posterior that was nudging her drinking arm.

Qiang took her wrist. 'Come on, killer, it's time we got you home. If QM catches you in this state she'll probably dock us a whole month's worth of merits.'

Pirie protested, 'Why can't we just take our sleep shift here?'

'Because for every twenty minutes of a sleep shift you're not in your own cabin you get five demerits.'

Pirie scrunched up her face in thought, 'We need some bottles. We can sneak a *few* bottles aboard, we're good girls! Nobody's going to search us.'

Qiang pushed her own glass in front of her, 'Here, finish my drink, then you'll have had plenty.'

'Cheers sister, you're a real trooper! Ha! See what I said?'

'Drink up, dear.'

This time the glass got closer to her lips before the bump came, but this time it was the whole crowd surging towards them, nearly knocking them *and* the table over. Pirie's drink leapt from her glass, arcing away from her face and splashing down in front of her.

'Spreff it!'

Wrath stood to see what the disturbance was. He wasn't tall enough for a good look, but he could see a stream of black troopers' caps moving quickly through the bar. Presumably there were troopers' heads and troopers' bodies underneath the caps.

'What hap?' Farr asked.

'Troopers. Not cadets. Must be from the Black Leopard. Looks like they're on manoeuvres at pace 150! They must be in a hurry to find a better bar too.'

'Good luck to them,' Pirie was looking mournfully at the wet fingers of liquid that used to be her drink spreading across the filthy table.

Farr was sober enough to sense a change in the atmosphere, and see that Wrath was intrigued by it. 'Malcolm, why don't you go on ahead? I'll see these guys back home safe and catch up with you.'

'If you're sure. Give me a call and I'll let you know where I'm at.'

Qiang stood and tried to pull Pirie to her feet, 'We'll be fine, if we run into any trouble Farr is probably better in a fight than you are.'

Farr was certainly sturdy, and a trained wrestler, she'd been embarrassing most of the other cadets at unarmed combat since she joined the crew, 'I ought to be offended, but you're probably right. Stay safe.'

'*Us* stay safe? I feel guilty about letting you wonder around on your own. There's a bad buzz about this place.'

Wrath dismissed her concerns, 'Who'd want to hurt someone as lovable as me?'

'Is that a trick question?' Qiang gave him a concerned look. 'Don't get lost, anyway.'

'Wiselike.'

Farr pushed easily through the crowd and soon the three of them were out of sight. Wrath's gaze turned to the other side of the bar, to where he'd last seen the heads of the crewmen of the Black Leopard, moving rapidly and purposefully deeper into the station. Rapidly, purposefully, Wrath followed.

Griffith moved at the edges of the doorway, scanning every corner of the club, looking for her, for Erin; not to see her, but so as *not* to be seen by her. No matter how much he might wish to see her again, if she were to recognise him —to know he was alive, and to find out he had let her believe he was dead for over a decade— it could utterly destroy her mental equilibrium.

He didn't need Leo Jameson to tell him how delicately balanced her mental state was, he got regular reports. Fathom allowed him that indulgence. Griffith didn't look at pictures, didn't trouble himself with minutiae, he just wanted her kept safe, and to know she was okay.

There was no sign or sight of her. The lights were down and the woman on stage was holding everyone's attention.

With his eyes fixed on the table where Fester was sitting, not allowing his attention to be caught by anyone or anything else he walked over and pulled out a chair that would let him keep his back to the rest of the room.

Fester seemed almost startled as Griffith sat down opposite him.

'Enjoying the show, Fester? I've never seen you so engrossed.' He chanced a look over his shoulder towards the stage. The girl certainly merited the attention, a captivating blend of sensuality and elegance, her voice more soulful than might be expected of someone so young, 'Very nice.'

'Suhrry.'

'No harm in looking, Fester. We'll talk when she's done.' Griffith had never seen this look of calm on Fester's face, it made him look curiously blank, like someone had hit the reset button on his personality, such as it was. 'I've never seen you take an interest before. Music soothes the savage beast, eh?'

Fester took his eyes off Monique for a moment to fix him with an earnest look, 'Yuh or muh?'

Griffith smiled himself a dark little smile, 'Both of us, Fester. Both of us.'

seventeen

Wrath figured this was pretty much the centre of the station, though keeping accurate track of distance and direction in these twisting tubeways was like trying to measure the length of a tangled rope.

It was eerily quiet here, just the most distant noises echoing indistinctly along the weird drainpipe acoustics of the flexible tubular corridors.

These polymer tubeways were all that stood between him and the raw and deadly vacuum of space. The seeming newness of everything here was a small reassurance. This section had to be a very recent addition to the station. The floor plates looked like they'd been freshly laid and the ductwork and cables had a factory fresh gleam. Still, if something smashed into the tube or a seal failed, it would be goodbye oxygen and hello explosive decompression.

The disturbingly delicate architecture of the place wasn't the only thing about this station that was making Wrath feel edgy — from QM's cryptic warning, to the way the Police had handled their arrival, and the constant wary looks they'd got from the station staff and security — there was very much a sense that something was not right here.

Ahead, a linking Y-junction was mated up to a double-walled doorway. Hopefully it would lead to something more substantially built and maybe some friendly faces — or faces, at least.

The doors were ballistic glass, and the bar on the other side was spacious, and it seemed just as new as the corridors linking to it. It wasn't even on the station map yet. Inside were uniforms; black uniforms and white. As the inner door opened the smell of newness was everywhere, with a fresh gleam to everything.

Eighty or so people were spread around, though there was room for a lot more, with a few civilians scattered around the place, and two big, and separate clusters of PPB crew and Black Fleet troopers, with the split in numbers between white uniforms and black being about even. They were all keeping to groups of the same colour. None of his fellow cadets had made it this far.

Wrath wasn't sensing any collegiate camaraderie between the Black Fleet crew and their PPB partners in law enforcement. They weren't talking to each other, and nobody was showing any interest in talking to him.

Even the lone barkeep served him his cafcaf without a word of acknowledgement, or of thanks for his tip. In fact his dedication to wiping glasses he'd already wiped before was commendable. It was obvious he wanted to avoid eye-contact with any of his patrons, at least the ones in uniform. Maybe his unease was contagious, but Wrath was picking up a strong sense of brooding tension, with the Quartermaster's parting words coming back to him, 'Tonight you meet the enemy.'

Wrath noticed a curving balcony above the bar, and a huge domed canopy with an expansive view of the stars above.

'Alright if I sit upstairs?'

The barkeep grudgingly spared him a quick look and a curt nod before returning to his glass polishing.

Setting his cafcaf cup down, he leaned back against the balcony rail, arching his neck back to take in the star-scape.

It had occurred to Wrath that life in space might make the sight of stars lose its magic, but the reality was, encased in the armoured behemoth that was the Black Wreath, there was seldom any opportunity to see the stars at all.

Windows would be structural weak-points, so there were no windows. The tactical display on the bridge was a hologramatic simulation designed to show targets, friend-or-foe tags and any solid body close enough that it might constitute a crash hazard. Stars were not of interest, so not shown.

Aside from the few he got to see through the targeting screen of the Double-Eights during weapons training, Wrath probably hadn't seen a star since the Black Wreath had led the Francesca Reala out of the Pandale system.

This view made up for it. With no atmosphere to obscure the view, the clarity of the star-scape surpassed every starlit night he'd ever enjoyed on Pandale. The milky streak of the Sagittarius arm arcing towards the comforting glow and complex clouds of the galactic centre was a mesmerising vista. With no idea when he might get to see it again, he basked in it, letting the moment of solitude and beauty wash over him, leaning back further against the rail, tilting back his head so the wide domed canopy filled his view, breathing slowly and tuning out the murmuring from the bar below, imagining himself floating alone in the stars.

The moment was broken with the sound of commotion below. Turning to see a new swathe of black uniforms entering the bar with the force of a tidal bore, at their head a man in an officer's greatcoat, his hair a short, slicked-back silver mane. He turned smartly about to survey the bar, briefly catching Wrath's eye as his gaze took in the room. Satisfied with what he saw he rested his palms on the top of the bar.

'This will suit us well, gentleman,' his voice boomed, 'Drinks for everybody, even our friends in white.'

The barkeep looked horrified as everyone surged to the bar at once.

'I'm sure no one will object if the man buying the drinks is served first. Barman, a glass of whatever you have in this place that you would be prepared to risk drinking yourself, and have one yourself. When you get the time, that is.'

The drink was poured and the officer took his glass, leaving the chaos of the bar-ward surge behind him, settling down in a booth at the farthest end of the bar. He looked up and raised his drink to Wrath. 'Good evening.'

Wrath was slightly taken aback, 'Good evening...' Wrath was struggling to see any insignia of rank, so had to go on the man's bearing and behaviour. Too easy with authority for a captain, not restrained enough for a commander, 'Major?'

He must have guessed right, as the Major nodded and turned his attention to the barkeep who was struggling to keep up with the drink orders. The Major's largesse had at least relaxed the mood a little.

Through the far side of the dome Wrath had a slightly obscured view of the docking ring, and the fan of craft splayed around it. The dark forms of the dreadnoughts were picked out by the station's lights, while on the other side the three PPB craft almost shone, a bright red X on the flanks of each, highlighted by the gleaming white electroluminescent coating of their hulls.

Sitting between the mismatched craft was the Marshal's mobile police platform, its broad hull also glowing with electroluminescence, but in the deep, rich blue and vivid orange colourway of police craft.

The middle-most PPB vessel seemed a good deal larger than the others, and a look at the arrivals board confirmed it must be a sub-flag class. Her name, "Arissa", as Wrath had learned, indicated her class with her initial letter. The neighbouring "Sabina" and "Sonya" were standard frigates. A sequence of lights on the arrivals board caught Wrath's attention, and a new name flashed up.

INCOMING: SAVATARA

Wrath heard the Major's voice boom out to nobody in particular, 'Here comes trouble.'

Griffith was letting Fester be his eyes, keeping his own back to the club and all of its clientele. 'How many?'

'Thirry fie, or forry.'

'Cadets? Regular troopers? Or serious people?'

'Suhruss. Vurr suhruss.'

The accumulation of black uniforms was now impossible to ignore, and the tension was palpable. To get here this quickly from the Black Leopard, coming the long way around the station, they must have been moving at fast-march pace.

'These people are not off-duty, Fester. They're on manoeuvres.'

Fester smiled.

'Black uniforms aren't our problem tonight, Fester.' Griffith studied the smile more closely, it wasn't the one he was used to, it wasn't the smile that presaged violence.

For the second time tonight, Griffith's eyes widened in surprise, as a beautiful lady in a shimmering dress sat down next to Fester. The singer.

'Hey there big fella, glad you didn't run out on me like the last guy.' She turned to Griffith. 'Hello! Are you a friend of a friend?'

'We're colleagues.'

The singer raised her eyebrows and nodded, 'Right. Well, he hasn't told me what he does. What are you colleagues in?'

Griffith mustered what geniality he could, without being openly pleasant. 'We are agents of change.'

'You had me worried for a second there, I thought you were going to say you were agents of musicians, and I have more of that in my life than I need already. The name is Monique, by the way.' She extended her hand.

'Pleased to meet you, Monique. You're a very accomplished

singer.'

'Thank you! I try.'

'You succeed.' He released her hand and looked at Fester, 'So how did you come to make acquaintances with my colleague?'

'I met Fester back at Steimz about a month ago. It was the night after Darian Corvalis "disappeared," actually. I guess there were some other "agents of change" in action there too.'

'No. No others.'

Griffith felt a gentle hand settle on his back and heard a voice he could never forget. 'Monique, your set was wonderful!'

'Erin, thank you!'

Griffith felt like his blood had turned to fire, feeling a touch he hadn't felt since the morning he was supposed to have taken his seat in the Admiralty. The day his career, his name, and his old life had been bombed into oblivion. He kept his head locked straight ahead.

'I see you've found some new friends! What happened to Commander Guthrie?'

'He ran out on me, so I upgraded.'

'Good for you. I hope my husband didn't scare him off?'

'Well he does seem to have that effect on people.'

'He's a little warmer once you get to know him. Only a little though. Ha!'

'I'm sure he's easier to take if he's doesn't suspect you of covering up a murder.'

Erin looked at Fester, and gently rubbed Griffith's back, 'Well you guys treat this girl right, she has a big future ahead of her. Enjoy your night.'

Griffith nodded without a word, felt her hand slip away and heard her departing footsteps. She hadn't seen his face, she couldn't have recognised him, but her touch still electrified him.

Fists, feet, bullets and explosives, he'd been on the receiving end of all of them. Beaten, bloodied, shot, or blown up, he'd never known a pain so exquisite and total as he was feeling now. He was almost trembling, fighting it in case the singer might notice it.

The singer was clearly energised, rubbing Fester's arm with excitement, 'I think she just gave me the nod! She's going to book me to play her bar circuit, and she runs just the BEST places! She might put me on in her casino at Focus Beacon 3!' Monique's face was alight with happiness, grabbing Fester's arm even harder with excitement. 'Can you imagine it? This has to be the best night of my life! I'm going to be working with Erin Carson!'

Griffith clenched his jaw so hard he felt he might shatter his own teeth. 'Will you excuse me, please? I need to be somewhere.'

Heading for the door, consumed with trying to maintain his composure, thoughts that weren't Erin were pressing for his focus. Good. He needed other thoughts, desperately. Details of what had just happened kept forcing their way into his sphere of attention. As he looked around he could see Fester was right, the black uniforms, and the people in them, were indeed very serious looking. Whatever the Black Fleet equivalent of PPB commandos was, was what these troopers appeared to be. They weren't here to prevent or deal with trouble, they were here to start it.

A glance at the arrivals board brought yet more sobering news, fully over-riding the emotional stresses his encounter with Erin Carson had triggered. Fester *should* have noticed, and should have told him. The Savatara was here! And she'd already been docked for several minutes.

Why hadn't Fester told him? Too caught up with this woman. Who the spreff was she? Griffith never inquired about Fester's personal life, mostly assuming he didn't have one. For both of them, personal entanglements were more dangerous than any enemy. And what had she said about Leo Jameson questioning her about a murder? And she'd been at Steimz when Darian Corvalis had lost his head? Something about this woman was ringing every alarm bell in Griffith's head, just as it should have for Fester, but Fester was distracted by the woman. Too distracted. Dangerously distracted.

Hunting out a quiet corridor, he linked his watch through to his own shunt communication hub aboard the Arissa, which patched him immediately through to White Satellite above Baxter's World.

'I must speak with Fathom.'

The wait was short.

'Mister Griffith, you find yourself needful?'

'Fathom, I need a deep background check on a singer, traveling under the name "Monique," currently aboard Beacon 505. LKP: Steimz orbital station, around a month ago.'

'That is an inauspicious time to have found herself on Steimz orbital station.'

'That's not all. Apparently Marshal Leo Jameson has been

questioning her with regards to a murder?'

'I already have information on that which relates to our other business. Have you spoken to the station administrator, Mr. Parsons yet?'

'Not yet.'

'A postponement could be beneficial. This singer may provide us with some critical leverage in our negotiations.'

'I think Black Fleet Staff Command have plans to turn beacon 505 into a battleground tonight. I've seen one squad of troublemakers already, and it's likely there are more all around the station. All three Project Snipe vessels are here too. The coincidences keep stacking up. Coincidences mean danger.'

'They will not kill aboard a neutral station if it is at all avoidable, even a station in outlaw territory like the 500's. There will be an ulterior motive.'

'There is extreme danger nonetheless. I must ask a personal favour of you.'

'That is unlike you. I will consider it.'

'I need you to break into Marshal Jameson's control channel and get a message through to him, and quickly.'

'The message?'

'I can't stop this. Get her away.'

'She? She is there?'

'Yes.'

'It is done. Wait.'

Griffith frowned, 'Wait for what? Is it done?'

'Wait, there is news.'

Griffith had taken himself far enough from the Club Twassanque not to be seen or overheard, but close enough to hear its hubbub, and the sounds of socialising were clearly ebbing away to an uneasy quiet. He turned back and headed towards the settling, unsettling hush.

Wrath averted his gaze from the spread of stars filling the view above as a movement from the major caught the far most periphery of his vision.

Raising his hand, the major's voice rang out across the crowd; too loud and too obvious.

'Hey, let's have the news on!'

He pressed something in his hand and a large view-screen above the bar flicked into life. The already overwhelmed barkeep looked baffled at how the Major was able to turn on the screen, but all other eyes turned to the news anchor looming above them. Her expression was as serious as her tone.

'...have a report which will make uneasy listening for those who heard Sovereign Benoit's speech today where he called for closer integration and cooperation between the Focus Protectorate and worlds governed by the PPB.

'Coming on the heels of the mounting rumours that Humana Faction Governors, including the Sovereign himself, had received generous campaign backing from sources which have now been linked back to PPB sponsored pressure groups, supporters of the Sovereign will have questions to answer about the wisdom *and* the motives behind a career defined by his eagerness to embrace the PPB as an ally.

'Our independent affiliate, Linc Bostrom, has received anonymously supplied footage of the event that has come to be known as the "Pandale Bomb" which sheds new light on the origin of the mysterious weapon that caused so much speculation and argument among military analysts. Here is his exclusive report.'

Wrath, along with everyone else, watched in silence as the report unfolded, watching the engagement play out again, just as he had seen it the day he'd watched the Pandale shuttle crash into the ocean. It was etched in his mind, it was a day... *the* day that had changed his life.

Everything was happening the same as before, the first false surrender, then the unease at the coming of the second surrender, the Black Wreath positioning herself to receive the surrendering pirate junk, the prow of the Savatara tracking its progress, then the blinding flash.

Now was a more detailed look, played out many magnitudes more slowly, stars obscured by a streak of darkness, the back of the junk being compressed by an impact, then again, the blinding flash.

Now the prow of the Savatara, shown more slowly still, the same streak of darkness. Now a broader view, the slowest footage yet, slowed to one millionth of real-time, a razor straight line of blackness lancing out from the Savatara to the Black Wreath. The trail of an anti-photonic beam, launching a hyper-optic weapon.

The reporter's conclusion was impossible to refute: it was a weapon deliberately fired from a PPB vessel at a Black Fleet vessel. A weapon far too powerful to have been designed for taking on pirate junks. The weapon could only have been created for one purpose, to attack Black Fleet dreadnoughts. The report ended.

Whatever the news anchor had to say as a follow up, nobody heard it. There wasn't even a moment of silence in the bar, fighting began immediately. Wrath had seen spontaneous outbreaks of violence before, and this was just too fast. The black clad troopers were about their white uniformed rivals instantly, without savagery, without anger and without pause. This was not brawling, this was combat. This was planned.

Wrath looked at the major, who clicked the unit he held in his hand, turning off the screen.

'Good show!' He said, settling back on the seat and watching his men fight. 'Good show.'

Suddenly Wrath felt very exposed and alone up on the balcony. Nobody had noticed him, yet, but he was not comforted by the qualifier. The oasis of calm around the Major seemed attractive, and stealthy creeping seemed the most advisable method of getting there.

Having got down the stairway, a sudden new influx of PPB crew streamed through the door, amplifying the violence. Wrath ducked his head below table level and moved steadily towards the Major's table.

'Do you mind if I join you?'

'Sure, plenty of room here.'

The Major widened his eyes as Wrath elected to ignore the provided seating, choosing to slip underneath the table instead.

'I see you're of the school of thought that discretion is the better part of valour, cadet.'

'I'm a lover not a fighter, Major.'

'Really? You don't look like much of either to me.'

'Fair point. It's more a philosophy than a practice so far.'

'Well, philosophers don't get in a lot of fights, mind you, I don't know that they get laid that often either.'

'Well I'll let you know how I get along, if I survive the night.'

A stocky PPB man, breaking through the melee and spotting the Major seemed to take a sudden and intense dislike to both the look of him, and his look of satisfaction with the frenetic violence unfolding in front of him. He rushed headlong at the table screaming abuse.

The man was almost on the major when, before he knew what he was doing, Wrath found himself jumping out from under the table and grabbing the nearest chair, spinning about and smashing it at full power across the man's back.

The man fell, his journey to the floor was interrupted by a hard impact of his head against the table before he settled sprawling awkwardly at the Major's feet. The major rolled him over with his foot and looked to see if he was still breathing.

Satisfied that the man wasn't dead he pointed at the seat next to himself. 'You don't belong under a table, Cadet Wrath.'

Wrath cautiously sat down, keeping his eye on the fight, which, apart from the sleeping beauty next to them, was keeping a reasonable distance away.

The major proffered his hand to Wrath, 'Staff Major Jaglan, Black Leopard.'

Wrath shook it and smiled, getting a closer look at the man sat next to him. He had the sort of features you might see on a statue of an ancient hero or god, every angle of jaw, nose, and brow was powerful, and classically handsome, although he was also somewhat grizzled by decades of soldiering. He was the sort who could coax the most cowardly of troops into the frenzy of battle.

'It seems introducing myself would be redundant, so, hi.'

'For a guy who's not a fighter, you give good chair.'

'If you don't mind me saying so, you didn't seem in a hurry to fight either, you didn't move a muscle.'

'Always know your available weapons, cadet.' Major Jaglan winked at him, 'I'd prepared for just such an attack.'

'Really? How?'

'I said "Good evening."'

Wrath didn't understand, and then he did. 'You put a lot of faith in someone you'd only looked at for a few seconds.'

'You have good references, Cadet Wrath.'

This baffled him. He couldn't imagine fresh cadets made for news worthy of ship-to-ship communication, unless word of his first day on the rifle range had got around. It was not entirely out of the question. 'Have you been talking to QM? I didn't think she thought that much of me, apart from my shooting, anyway.'

'The Quartermaster does her job, praise isn't part of the job. She did pass on the details of your joining up, though.'

'I'm glad you're impressed by guys signing up for military duty when they're half drunk.'

'Not that. Like I said, you have good references.'

Wrath was struggling to remember who he'd put down as references, 'Spoff?'

'I have no idea who, or what, that might be, so, no. It was your other reference.'

'I don't even remember putting a second reference?' Wrath thought on it, trying to dredge up the half-drunken memory. He had put a second name, someone he thought was a respectable choice for a referee, someone fresh in his mind that he'd seen a couple of days before he signed up, old Frank. 'Frank Bull?'

'Yes. Sovereign Staff Commander Francis Bull, Chief Supervising Officer of Black Fleet Staff Command, Years 208 to year 243.'

He took a moment to take in the information, and to reconcile it with the nice old guy from the shooting club, 'Frank Bull? The Frank Bull who tells lame jokes, and drives a junky old grav-car that takes three kicks before it can get all four GReDs off the ground? The guy who had all the kids draw on his face when he fell asleep at my 10th birthday party?'

'I'll take your word for all of that, but I'd imagine so, yes.'

'How the spreff did he keep *that* quiet? He's been a friend of the family for my entire life, a *close* friend, and nobody's ever breathed a word!'

'He's a long time retired, and he likes it like that. But he's still loyal to the service, and on the lookout for good people. He singled you out.'

'Nice old Frank? I can't picture it. I really can't.'

'Anyway, we have scouts on a lot of worlds, looking for the sort of people we need, the right sort of people. Some recommendations carry more weight than others. None could carry more weight than Sovereign Staff Commander Frank Bull, especially as you're the only person he's ever recommended.'

'But it's pure chance that I even saw that flag up for the recruiting office, what are the odds of that?'

Jaglan shook his head dismissively, 'It wouldn't have mattered. If you hadn't showed up, someone would have been sent to recruit you direct. Believe me, QM says you definitely didn't get in on the strength of your interview.'

'This is unbelievable.'

Just as unbelievable was that Major Jaglan's revelations had actually distracted him from the fighting going on right in front of them, 'So what is this?' he asked, pointing at the brawl.

'It's a fight, Cadet Wrath. I know it's not your thing, but you're in the military now so you should probably learn to recognise the signs.'

'This isn't the first table I've hidden under, Major. I know a bar fight when I see one, and this isn't just a fight. Your men knew what was coming in that report, and they started the fight immediately. So what is this?'

Jaglan licked his lips and paused a moment before replying, 'Grey Task.'

'If that's meant to mean something to me, I haven't got that far into my training yet.'

Jaglan nodded, 'What your crew does is classed as Blue Task. That's patrolling, rescues, mapping gravity wells, clearing junk from hyper-optic corridors, the occasional scrap with pirates. My team has a broader operational spectrum.

'Green Task is distance observation in things like civil wars, strictly hands off. Brown Task is in-theatre peace-keeping, hands on stuff where we can fire defensively if fired upon but not initiate combat. Then there's Black Task, which is things like demolitions.'

'Isn't demolitions more of a civil engineering job?'

'Sure, but civil engineers have to wait for buildings to be empty before *they* blow them up.'

'Let me guess, you don't do that?'

'We don't do that. That leaves Grey Task and *Red* Task. Grey Task is confusion, discord and subterfuge, which can sometimes involve something as simple as starting a fight, but there's always more to it than that.'

'I have a nasty suspicion I know what Red Task means.'

Jaglan smiled a knowing smile and nodded, 'I like you Wrath.' Jaglan took a long tug on his drink before setting the glass down empty, 'I think we're going to kill a lot of people together.'

Wrath's eyes widened in alarm, 'Not tonight, I hope? I haven't even had dinner yet!'

'That's funny! No.' Jaglan said reassuringly, before turning his eyes back to watch his men wiping the floor with the few PPB crew still standing, 'but don't make any firm plans for breakfast.'

Jameson entered the security suite at a sprint, looking straight at the station's security chief. 'How widespread is the fighting?'

The chief's eyes were wide, whether in shock or surprise was unclear. 'It's everywhere, Marshal.'

'Any weapons fire?'

'No, we checked everybody for weapons before they came aboard, just like you told us.'

'Let's hope you were thorough enough. Where's Marshal Hurst?'

'He went to meet the Savatara when she docked.'

'How many people did he take with him?'

'Two of my men.'

'*Your* men? No agents or police officers?'

'No.'

'Spreff! Who's available to give back up?'

'Nobody, they're all trying to stop the fighting.'

He jabbed at the controls, flashing up badge locations around the station, spotting a group on the far side of the outer-orbital corridor, heading for the bar filled with cadets from Black Wreath. 'Agent Cassalis, head back to the docking ring, trouble hasn't broken out where you're headed yet.'

'*Understood, Marshal.*'

'You need to get to the Savatara, Marshal Hurst will need heavier numbers on his side. Make it fast.'

The four blips on the station map reversed their direction of travel, making good speed. Before he could turn his attention back to the security monitors the map flashed a warning message. The corridor connection hub ahead of the team he'd just dispatched to the Savatara was flashing red.

'*Marshal, the door to the hub has just closed and locked itself off, we can't get through.*'

'I'll over-ride it from here.' Jameson began typing in the over-ride command when a new warning flashed, the adjoining corridor leading back to the docking ring was flashing on the map.

'*Marshal! Somebody has ejected the corridor! This hub is locked out, we'll have to head back and find another way around.*'

'What the hurk?' Jameson looked up at the monitors, seeing running figures, figures in white, but *not* in ship-board uniforms, the running figures were PPB commandos in full combat gear. The riot he had anticipated was starting to look like something much worse. This looked like the outbreak of a small war.

Turning to the next monitor to track their progress, he twitched involuntarily as the screen went dark. In a rapid cascade each and every monitor blinked into darkness. Every camera was down.

Jameson snatched up the red handset of the beacon's emergency external communication system. 'This is Marshal Leo Jameson declaring a state of emergency aboard Beacon 505. Any and all Police units within range are to divert to Beacon 505. Proceed at maximum speed, we have lost control of the station. Repeat, we have lost control of the station. There is immediate danger to life of civilians and police officers. Come fast. Come prepared. Riot gear is a minimum requirement. Full incursion armament is advised. Lethal force has not been authorised, *yet*. You will be advised if this status changes before you arrive. Advisory, this is a request for police responders only. Repeat, Police responders only. Confirm and proceed upon receipt of this message.'

The security chief looked totally out of his depth. 'I don't know how to help, Marshal, I've never had to deal with anything like this before.'

'Nor have I. Not on this scale.'

'How long before they get here, do you think?'

'First responders could be anything between twenty minutes and an hour, but it will take a while to get the numbers we need. What station systems are still working?'

'The heat sensors work, so we can tell roughly how many people are in any given place, and when and where they move to, but we won't know who they are. You still have audio communications with security and your officers, and they'll show up as hard blips on the station map. The station's announcement system still works, too.'

'Good. It's time these people had a talking to.'

Major Jaglan looked up at the sound of the Marshal's voice coming over the bar's speaker system.

"Attention! Attention! This is Marshal Jameson. Beacon 505 is now under direct Police jurisdiction. As of yet, the Police officers aboard this station are not authorised to use lethal force. If you wish that to remain the case, there will be an immediate cessation of all violence. Police officers and agents will be moving through the station restoring order, any attempts to hinder them will be met under anti-riot criteria. That means, they'll bust your head open. Compliance is not optional. You have been warned. I repeat, there will be an immediate cessation of all violence. And don't think a uniform is any protection against arrest and full charges being filed."

The barman looked at Jaglan, 'Do you want me to shut him out of the station comms, Major?'

'Let him talk. If he feels he still has some control he won't try anything extreme. It all buys us time. I'll need you to plot us a route to the Sonya that avoids police as much as possible.'

'How about station security?'

'Don't worry about them, we can knock those bozos out of the way.'

Wrath was feeling like a spare part. The PPB had been put out of action, gagged and bound and secured at one end of the bar. The civilian drinkers had run out as soon as the fighting had started so Jaglan's team had total control of the bar. Not only did the bar belong to Black Fleet, it turned out it had all along. The previously taciturn barman was a Black Fleet lieutenant, and was now perfectly talkative. He seemed to have jacked into, and taken control of the station's security network.

The bar was now a makeshift base of operations for Major Jaglan's squad. Wrath was locked in with them. There was no way he was getting back to Black Wreath in a hurry.

'Major, is there anything I can do?'

He turned to the troopers rolling crates out from the bar's backroom. 'Give those guys a hand, Wrath. We're in a hurry.'

Wrath wasn't sure how much benefit the troopers gained from his limited muscle power, but soon enough fifteen huge crates were lined up in front of the bar.

Jaglan did the honours of typing in the unlock codes, 'Wrath, QM told me you tried to join the PPB before you signed up with us?'

A murmur of disapproval swept through the waiting men.

'I hope she told you I was drunk at the time?'

Jaglan laughed, 'I was just wondering if you wanted to see if the uniform would have suited you?'

All but one of the fifteen crates began opening; inside, gleaming white mesh and metal, breastplates and helmets, barrels, stocks, scopes, magazines. Wrath recognised the hardware from the recruitment brochure he'd read when he in the PPB recruiting office. This was the battle armour and weaponry for a team of PPB commandos.

eighteen

Where Fester led, Monique followed. He hadn't so much evaded the outbreak of violence, as plowed through it, with her following in his broad wake, barely daring to believe her luck that he would be leading her not just to, but aboard the Arissa.

The armed guards at the airlock door asked no questions of Fester, about himself, or his unexpected guest. Even dressed in full body armour, with weapons drawn, they seemed every inch as scared of the giant as Commander Guthrie had been, making no eye-contact with her, or him as they checked his ID chip.

She should be scared, by all rights, but though she was entering a place of danger, with someone who was clearly immensely dangerous, nothing in the way that Fester had behaved felt threatening. There was a riot, and as far as he was concerned, he was bringing her to a place of safety.

The guards waved them aboard, Monique taking in every detail as she stepped through the airlock. Even Guthrie had never brought her aboard the Sabina, so she'd never been aboard a PPB frigate, let alone a sub-flag class boat like the Arissa.

'Suhhf nuh.'

'Well, I like being safe as much as anybody, but I don't want you thinking I can't take care of myself.'

The giant merely shrugged. The quiet here was almost eerie, with nothing to hear but their own footfalls and the soft, distant throb of the ship's generator heads at tick-over.

'I guess you work for the PPB, then?'

'Yuh.'

'You don't wear the uniform though?'

'Nuht Nuhvy.'

'Are you like a courier, or something?'

'Sumthun.'

Ahead, an elevator, sensing their approach, slipped silently open. Fester stepped inside, inserting his ID chip in the control panel. Gibson's heart sank as he tapped out a complicated sequence of commands and a message flashed up on the screen: "ULTRA-

SECURE ACCESS ONLY. ENTER PERSONAL CODE"

Try as she might, she was unable to see Fester's fingers type out the code. She was going where no Black Fleet agent had been before, but would she be able to get out again?

'So what do you actually do?'

Whatever it was that made his speech so distorted he managed, with great effort, to overcome it and say one word clearly, 'Harm.'

Wrath was being fitted with the smallest set of PPB battle armour they could find to try and fit his slender frame. The troopers were struggling, as Wrath was below the minimum height for a PPB commando, and the armour only fit where it touched, which wasn't in many places. It was servo assisted armour, so they were shimming out areas to make sure his joints would hit all the actuators.

Staff Major Jaglan was in contact with the men he'd placed all around the station, waiting for the right news to come in.

'Major, we have twenty three PPB commandos bottled up in a casino at the back-right of the station hoop. Corporal Faisal says they have another eleven trapped in the Pyramid Bar, due east on the hoop. That give you what you need?'

Jaglan nodded, 'Are they contained for the duration?'

'They're going nowhere.'

'Perfect. If the Police look like they'll get through, be prepared to be arrested, but make sure the commandos get arrested too. Extreme provocation is authorised. Understood?'

'Understood.'

Jaglan studied the security feeds and conferred with the barman, 'Savatara has shut herself off. Nobody's getting aboard now. That was to be expected with the months Jowett has had her ship on hard lockdown, she wasn't going to relax her sphincter in the middle of this chiff storm.'

'Agreed, the commandos transferring from the Sabina boarded as soon as she docked, and they've already transferred their weapons to the Sonya. She was doors open to doors shut in under 4 minutes.'

'How many commandos have made it aboard the Sonya?'

'I've only seen ten.'

'We've got thirty four accounted for, that just leaves six stragglers somewhere. We're set.' Jaglan turned to the barman and pointed at the station map, 'Once we reach this hub-junction you can turn control of the station back over to the security centre, but let them think they got control back themselves. The Police will want to get back control of the docking ring so they should be coming into sight of the Sonya's door guards at a useful time for us.'

'Understood.'

Jaglan stood, sweeping his gaze around his squad, dazzlingly bright in the uniforms of their enemy. 'Very convincing. I'm fighting the urge to shoot you shiny spreffers myself.' He looked down at his own armour, 'I actually look good in this! What am I even saying that for? I look good in everything.' He slung his rifle over his back and grinned, a broad grin of dark intent, 'Our target is the Sonya. *Nothing* gets in our way. Are we ready?'

The floor vibrated at the thud thirty pairs of boots slamming to attention.

'Fall in behind me. You've studied their drills, PPB rapid attack formation. Pace 120. Cadet Wrath, get in the middle, grab hold of the back of the crate and do what the others do.' Jaglan looked at the barman and jerked his thumb towards the bar entrance. 'Doors.'

Jaglan took off at a sprint as the doors parted, Wrath tucked himself in among the squad, holding on to the rail at the back of the unopened supply crate, hanging on tight as the rest of the squad took up the sprint themselves.

These guys were fast, and the armour was restrictive. Wrath struggled to find a natural gait that allowed him to run freely. The incursion gear he'd trained with aboard Black Wreath was form-fitted, and the power-assisted joints had been smoother, and quicker. This felt more like medieval armour.

Jaglan's squad must have been training in these suits; their progress was easy and natural. If Wrath hadn't already been an exceptionally fast runner, they'd be leaving him behind, but despite the awkward bulk of the armour, he had just enough capacity spare to keep up, but only just.

The tubular corridors were beginning to oscillate with the rhythmic footfalls of their running. A shout came back from Jaglan, 'Break step!'

The squad immediately switched to an asynchronous stride, half of the troops stepping at the half-stride, smoothing out the dangerous harmonic. Wrath had no training for this and just kept running, glad for the reassuring feeling of the floor coming up to meet his feet as he ran.

The corridor gave way to an accommodation block, he heard Jaglan's voice shouting at people ahead, 'MOVE!' Wrath was aware of startled and terrified faces being bundled out of the way as they streamed by.

Into another corridor, Jaglan called back again, 'Six-way hub ahead, break right at two o'clock.'

Wrath was barely aware of the hub, or of turning; he was being carried by a tide, into another corridor, now into a crowded bar. Again, Jaglan's voice rang out ahead, a powerful blast of sound clearing the path like a snowplow, 'MOVE!'

Two large men in station security uniforms -looking more like criminals than security personnel- turned ugly glares their way, the largest shouting out, 'Hold it there!'

'SPREFF OFF!' was Jaglan's unequivocal reply.

Wrath saw one of them make a belated attempt to grab the trooper running by his side, and saw him swiftly felled by an elbow to the face.

Onward.

Another corridor.

'Hub ahead. Bear left at nine o'clock!'

Wrath wondered if this was how fish felt, darting in schools? These rapid changes of direction faster than one could think of them were all reaction, all twitch-instinct.

'Hub ahead, after that we're at the Sonya! Ease up! Pace 90!'

The pace slackened, marginally. Wrath took what respite he could, his fitness had been tested and beads of sweat were forming on his brow. The temperature regulator in the cadets' jumpsuit he wore concealed beneath the PPB armour was struggling to keep him cool. Now he had to wonder, were they going to fight their way on board? Were they going to try to take on the ship's crew right now? Or were they going to bide their time?

Jameson was assembling a small trouble-team from his own officers, and some of the least sketchy looking members of the station's security staff. His eye was caught by some of the black screens coming back to life.

'Marshal, I'm starting to break through and regain control of the security systems.'

'Good work. Are the docking hoop doors working again?'

'Just getting control of them now, Marshal.'

'Any word from Marshal Hurst?'

'Still can't raise him. Nothing from his location transponder, either.'

'LKP?'

'Last Known Position was the docking hoop, somewhere between the Arissa and the Savatara.'

Jameson nodded gravely, turning to his trouble team, 'Let's go find him.'

Major Jaglan's squad slowed as they emerged at the docking ring. Jaglan didn't give the guards at the Sonya's airlock any time to ask questions.

'The Police are arresting everybody, they're about to lock down the whole station. Call everybody back, anybody not aboard our own ships in the next few minutes is going to get caught in the dragnet.'

Jaglan strode into the airlock and the squad started to follow.

'Wait!' The door guard called out, his weapon half-raised.

Jaglan turned a look of burning fury on the door guard, 'There is no time for waiting! Call everybody back! Now!' He turned and pointed down the curve of the docking hoop and pointed at the rapidly approaching figures of Marshall Jameson and his trouble-team. 'It's too late, follow us in and lock the spreffing doors!'

The guard visibly wilted, clearly wanting to stand his ground, but the squad kept marching by him, and the moment was already lost.

Wrath tried not to make eye contact with the guard as they passed through the airlock. He had just received an object lesson in the power of force of will.

As easily as that, they were aboard.

Qiang snapped awake as her watch vibrated. Answering the call instinctively, she saw the face of Cadet Boyd on the screen; his 25 hours as acting Commander weren't up yet.

'Trooper Qiang, I need you on the command deck!'

Noting the time, she saw she'd only been asleep for eighteen minutes. It was a miracle she had slept at all as a bilious tang in the air, along with the sound of Grace Pirie disposing of another meal from the wrong outlet, was emerging from the bathroom.

'Why do you need me?'

His expression was pained, *'Because you're the most senior person aboard.'*

'I think QM might disagree with that.'

'QM isn't aboard.'

'Can't you wait for her to get back?'

'She won't be able to get aboard, the airlocks have closed, cycled, and locked out. The computer is prepping for launch. Please! I need somebody senior on the command deck, the computer's not letting anybody here override the launch sequence!'

'Well how long have we got before she tries to leave?'

'Four minutes!'

Qiang leapt out of bed and out of the door.

Jameson's eyes followed the curve of the docking hoop, ahead were the guards at the airlock of the Sonya. They looked startled at the police posse marching purposefully towards them, hurrying inside their vessel and closing the doors.

Jameson strode on by. He had other priorities. His wristcomm buzzed for his attention.

'Marshal, the Black Wreath is pulling out.'

'How did they get their people back aboard with all the station's doors jammed up?'

'They didn't. There's just a bunch of cadets stuck aboard and their computer is on a pre-programmed launch sequence, they can't stop it. They're asking if we can?'

'Can we?'

'No, the ship computer sent a law enforcement launch clearance so the station computer automatically granted permission. It's already decoupled them from the docking ring. Could you issue a general hold notice on the station?'

'I can't do that while Hurst has jurisdictional power here.'

'Even though you're the senior Marshal?'

'Those are the regulations, if you want to pass on your surprise and frustration about that to Grand Marshal Balfour, be my guest.

'Can't you just assume jurisdiction?

Around the curve of the hoop Jameson caught sight of three figures lying on the ground, he broke into a run, 'Hold that thought, Agent.'

The two security officers were unconscious, but Hurst was rolling around in pain. Seeing Jameson looking down at him he looked ready to weep with relief. Blood bubbled from between his lips as he spluttered out the words, 'Am I dying?'

Jameson shook his head, 'No, Marshal, the men who did this are very well trained. They know how to beat a man within an inch of his life, and to stop exactly there. They aren't dumb enough to kill a marshal.'

Hurst coughed, spraying blood down himself, 'What about a junior marshal?'

'Hurst, today you've passed an exam you won't ever get at an academy. You won't ever hear me call you junior anything again. Okay?' Hurst nodded. 'But I will say this, welcome to the 500's, Marshal.' Jameson touched his wristcomm, the face of Agent Malik appeared on the screen. 'Agent, we need a medical team for three casualties on the docking hoop between docking hub 23 and hub 24. I am assuming control of this station. Issue a general hold notice on all outgoing craft.'

'Too late, Marshal, the Black Wreath is already gone.'

Jameson let out an uncharacteristic sigh, 'Issue the notice anyway.' he turned to Hurst again, 'Who did this, Marshal?'

'Squad of PPB commandos headed for the Savatara, I don't know which ship they came from. They had weapons crates, I told them using commercial stations for transferring munitions was illegal. They...' he coughed up more blood, 'they didn't want to discuss it.'

Jameson nodded, 'Agent Malik, contact the Grand Marshal's office and tell them we need compulsory search orders for every PPB vessel docked at this station. If they ask why, tell them because I said so.'

At the sound of running feet, Jameson looked up to see a single medic coming towards them, clutching a large medical bag. The medic, skidding to a halt, looked from Jameson's face to the three bloodied figures, seeming to recoil in horror.

'Where are the rest?' Jameson barked.

'The rest of what?' the medic looked confused.

'The rest of the spreffing medical team?'

'There's just me.'

'Well why didn't you bring more people? You were told there were three casualties!'

'There's just me.'

'I know that!' It dawned on him what the medic meant, 'You mean for this whole station, the medical team is, you?'

'Yes.'

'Are you even a doctor?'

'I'm a nurse.'

'And your medical facilities?'

'There's a med-bed, with a built-in diagnostic suite, and a small dispensary.'

Jameson clutched his forehead in frustration, 'One bed! Unbelievable!' he jabbed at his wristcomm, 'Malik, call my platform and tell them to get an emergency medical team to me, now. They'll need three stretchers, unless I happen to see Station Administrator Parsons before they get here, then make it four stretchers.'

The docking hoop began vibrating violently. 'Malik? What's going on, this place is shaking like a quake zone.'

The Savatara just responded to the general hold notice. They said "We're leaving." I've reiterated the order and told traffic control to lock the docking couples.'

Jameson clapped his hands to his ears, a deafening bang and a violent pulse shook the hoop.

Agent Malik shouted through the communicator, *'They've torn off one of the docking couples, they're trying to rip themselves free!'*

'I want an emergency frequency com-jack to the Savatara! I don't want them to be able to claim they didn't hear this.'

'You're patched through now, Marshal.'

Jameson took a breath and set his jaw, 'Captain Miranda Jowett and the crew of the Savatara, this is Marshal Jameson. I don't know how long it will take for your own navy to hang you out to dry, and I'm through waiting to find out. You are violating a general hold notice and have caused extensive damage to this station. You are also under suspicion of using a commercial station to transfer military weapons, an illegal act. Members of your crew are under suspicion of the violent assault of a police marshal, an illegal act.

'You will shut down your drives, and await completion of a full search and inspection of your vessel. Failure to do so will mean you are officially declared a rogue vessel. All police resources that can be spared will be dedicated to your capture, and the arrest and prosecution of your bridge crew.

'If Black Fleet Staff Command requests a "Kill or Capture" notice, it will *not* be denied. If Black Fleet vessels destroy your vessel and kill your crew, no questions will be asked, no answers will be expected. Surrender your vessel now, or face the full and deadly force of the law.'

There was a brief pause, followed by the calm and crystal clear voice of Captain Miranda Jowett.

'We are leaving.'

The rapid and irregular thumping of metal fracturing under stress gave warning that the Savatara was breaking free.

A sudden and violent rush of air swept Jameson and his team off their feet. The docking hoop was compromised and decompressing.

The screaming escape of the air into vacuum halted with the hard slamming of the emergency bulkheads sealing the breached section of the ring. Jameson's trouble-team struggled back to their feet.

Through the docking hoop windows they could see the Savatara. The great white vessel was spinning about, lining herself up for a trans-optic burst. Wrapping herself in the black fog of an anti-light shell, the Savatara vanished from sight.

nineteen

Trooper Qiang necked another cup of cafcaf and checked the clock for the twentieth time, silently urging it to click over to thirteen midnight. The assumption on the command deck was that as soon as cadet Boyd's twenty five hour shift was over, in absence of the Quartermaster, the computer would be smart enough to assign command of Black Wreath to the next most senior person on board.

Qiang wasn't so sure. She still wasn't sure she'd done enough to get her blood alcohol levels down, though after eight cafcafs and a half-dozen diuretic tablets, nobody could claim she hadn't tried. She *felt* sober, sharply so, possibly never more so, but whether the bio-monitoring systems built into her uniform would agree was another matter.

All heads turned to the sound of the command deck doors sliding open, at least half were hoping there had been some horrible mistake, or that this had been some sort of test, and that QM would be standing there. Instead they were greeted by the face of Cadet Forlani, looking pleased with himself. His face fell as a collective groan of disappointment filled the command deck.

Qiang cursed inwardly. Of course the new commander received their assignment early to maintain an unbroken command presence. It looked like the computer and its algorithms were blissfully unaware that having two thirds of the crew missing and no qualified officer aboard represented a problem.

The clock ticked over and she heard the watches of the crew chime with their next assignments. Hers was silent. She remembered she still had 4 hours of her sleep shift to go. Much use *that* would be to her, she had enough caffeine in her system to raise the dead.

She gave Forlani a weary look, 'I'll be in the gym if you need me. The computer doesn't have a face, and I need to punch something.'

Forlani looked puzzled, 'Why would I need you?'

'Boyd, why don't you give our new commander the good news?'

The frustrated stomping of her footsteps was still audible after the doors had closed behind her.

*

Marshal Jameson had three screens in front of him. On the left, an official declaration from Grand Marshal Balfour that the PPB frigate Savatara was a rogue vessel, a declaration agreed and co-signed by Black Fleet staff command, the Independent Police Force, and, as late as they could possibly have left it, the PPB themselves. Conspicuously their declaration was only signed by the Chairman, and not by Over-Admiral Connors.

On the middle monitor, his wife was staring at him, waiting for him to give her a good reason why she couldn't leave the safety of his Police platform and return to the station now that the riot was under control, and he was too preoccupied by the third monitor to come up with an answer that wouldn't just make her more furious.

On the right hand screen, a formal demand from both Black Fleet Staff Command and the PPB Admiralty to lift the general hold notice on the station, which, with those vessels being the closest available to begin the hunt for the Savatara, had been reluctantly agreed to by Grand Marshal Balfour.

Jameson could hold the last vessels here until all the PPB and Black Fleet crew taken into police custody were released, so the Black Leopard would have to stay, but he could only compel one of the PPB vessels to remain, and the grand Marshal had undercut his power to make a choice which one. The last vessel he wanted escaping his grasp was the Sonya, so she was certain to be the first ship to want to leave.

He clenched his jaw in frustration before opening the public address system.

'This is Marshal Jameson. Until such time as all detainees from Black Fleet and PPB crew are released from their cells, *at least* one vessel of both the PPB and Black Fleet must remain docked at this station. As of now, the general hold notice is lifted.'

He'd barely finished speaking when the call came through from navigation control.

'Marshal, the Sonya is asking permission to leave.'

He shook his head and growled angrily into the microphone, 'Permission granted.'

The noise of Griffith's pounding feet echoed around him as he sprinted for the central elevator, its doors parting for him as he came closer. He keyed in his access to the secure decks of the Arissa and began the rapid descent into the deep decks, the findings of Fathom's search swirling in his mind.

The doors parted and he was soon at the door of Fester's quarters. He held down the buzzer and thumped the door with the heel of his fist for good measure. The opening of the door revealed a dark room, with a large figure in the bed making the slow and lazy movements of someone roused from slumber.

'Where is she?'

Fester turned on the lights and blinked at Griffith.

'You brought the singer aboard, where is she?'

Seeing the bed was empty, Fester looked perplexed, the shaking of his head his only answer.

'She's Black Fleet, Fester. Captain Melody Gibson. She's an undercover Black Fleet operative, and you brought her aboard my ship.'

Fester's face was a mixture of alarm, and pain. He had let down the most important person in his life, and he knew he was about to be asked to fix it, and knew what that meant.

'She been aboard this vessel, so who the spreff knows *what* she's seen, or where she's been. Worst of all, she's seen enough of each of us to be able to give a detailed description. I can't take even the slightest risk that I might be identified. Do you understand?'

Fester understood all too well. She was the only woman who had ever shown him genuine kindness and acceptance. Maybe it was all an act, but it had been a good act. Most of all, she was the first person who'd looked at him without fear. Now he had to make amends to Griffith with two hateful tasks.

Find her. Kill her.

The elevator opened and Gibson cautiously peered around the edge of the doors. The man in green had probably been coming to Fester's quarters to find her. It had been pure dumb luck that he'd been so intent on getting there that he hadn't seen her slip into the elevator behind him.

Even more dumb luck was the elevator being programmed to automatically return to the airlock deck, meaning she didn't need any security codes to escape. Luck was not something she ever wanted to rely on, but she needed it to hold if she was going to make it off this boat and get safely aboard Black Leopard.

Dressed to perform on stage, the only equipment she had was the knife strapped to her thigh, and her watch, which she didn't dare try to use to make a rescue call here aboard the Arissa. She slipped her knife from its scabbard, palming the short blade, out of sight but ready for instant use.

Her first priority was to find a PPB uniform. Trusting to luck was going to have to be the plan, every doorway could be danger or salvation. It was unlikely the crew wouldn't notice a woman wandering around in evening wear without reporting it, even if she had come aboard with Fester.

Reading signs and listening at doors, it took half a dozen attempts to find an empty sleeping berth, and the only uniforms were too big for her. It was remarkable that the Arissa was quiet enough for her to sneak around without being seen, but given the man in green and Fester seemed to be passengers, it was likely more of a spy vessel than a fully staffed military ship.

She opened the door a crack and checked it was safe to continue her search. She was startled to find herself looking into a man's face, his expression one of confusion as the door he was about to open opened for him. He looked up into Gibson's eyes, his own eyes widening as she grabbed him by the throat and smashed his head into the side of the door frame.

Dragging him inside the cabin she sized him up. He was lean, and not much taller than her, squeezing herself into the jacket might be a strain, but it seemed providence was still on her side. He was only a lieutenant, but a temporary demotion was the least of her worries.

Even the boots weren't a terrible fit, they certainly didn't cause as much discomfort as having to shove her best shoes and dress into the garbage grinder, but she couldn't very well carry them out with her, or leave them lying around to be found.

She checked the Lieutenant's name tag. "Lansing". She checked the pockets for any documentation that might help the new and improved Lieutenant Lansing to leave the Arissa unhindered.

If this was a spy ship, this uniform probably wouldn't get her past the guards at the airlock, if they were any good at their jobs they ought to know every one of their crew-mates on sight, but it should at least get her close enough to fight her way off, if it came to it.

She fastened on the belt, and unfastened the holster clip of the officer's side-arm —a standard compressed air pistol with explosive rounds— and kept her knife in her palm. Hopefully, the guards were only mindful of attempts to get aboard by force, and not people trying to force their way out.

It would have been quicker to kill the lieutenant, but with her uncomfortable chat with Marshal Jameson still in her mind, she was mindful of the Director's warning that every death is a snowball, and you never knew which one might grow big enough to crush you. Besides, it was likely that the bio-sensors in his uniform would be giving live updates to crew-monitoring systems, if not in real-time then likely soon enough she wouldn't be off the ship before the alarm was raised.

Leaving him gagged and bound, she closed the door behind her and made her way towards the airlock, measuring her stride; not so purposeful as to draw attention, not so timid as to draw suspicion.

Rounding the curving corridor, the airlock was in view, and the guards were facing station-side. The man in green must have assumed she was already off the boat, or there would be an alert. That should make getting off easier, but meant they were probably already searching the station for her. No matter, Black Leopard would be a short run around the docking ring and then she'd be safe.

Quickly, quietly, she walked through the airlock and past the guards.

'Wait!'

She stopped in her tracks, turning as if there were no problem.

'What is it?' she stepped back towards them, casually, concealing the muscular tension as she prepared for attack.

'You know what it is. You don't walk out, you check out.' The largest guard eyed her quizzically, 'Who are you?'

'You saw me come aboard. I'm an undercover operative working with Fester.'

This had the desired effect, the guards were visibly intimidated at the mere mention of his name. It also had the benefit of being true, she hadn't said who she was an undercover operative for, or that Fester had any idea that her being with him *was* her work.

'I'll have to check with him.'

'Sure. Wake him up. He'll love that, I'm sure.'

The pause gave her a hope that this was going to work, he seemed ready to acquiesce, then his communicator chimed.

'Be advised, a hostile agent has been aboard. Female, slim, approximately

178 centime...'

Before the first guard could react Gibson's right hand rammed the knife up underneath the chin-guard of his helmet. Her left hand grabbed the muzzle of the larger guard's rifle. He tried to wrestle the gun down level with her head as she let the other guard fall, swinging her hand to her hip holster. She felt the guard deliver a powerful punch to her gut as she swung her pistol up to his chin and pulled the trigger.

Alarms began to ring from inside the ship. The bio-monitoring systems in the guards' uniforms would have reacted instantly to their deaths. Now they'd know exactly where she was.

She tried freeing her knife from the jaw of the smaller guard, heard him gurgling, still alive. The knife was jammed and there wasn't time to finish him off.

She left the knife and took off at a run, following the curve of the docking ring, looking out of the windows, waiting for the dark ellipse of Black Leopard to come into view.

The stab of pain came first, then the report of a gun shot. She should have finished off the guard. She kept running, compartmentalising the pain. The wound felt high in her back, above the lungs, no need to stop, no time to stop.

She sprinted past a junction, seeing only void where the Savatara had been berthed. At least she didn't have to worry about detouring into the station to avoid *their* door guards.

She broke into a pained smile as the tail of Black Leopard appeared ahead, a smile that turned chill as she saw the emergency bulkhead door, closed firmly in front of her.

She slid to a halt, almost colliding with the door, eyes wide at the gaping hole where the Savatara had ripped her way free of the station.

'Spreff it!'

Pushing up her blood spattered sleeve, she looked at her watch. The face was shattered. Her arm must have been up as she ran just as the bullet had hit her, passing right through and into the watch. Jabbing at the call button, there was no response.

Her luck had finally run dry. She was going to have to head deeper into the station and find a way around. Looking down at the uniform, she could see a deep red stain spreading down the chest. The broken watch was evidence enough that the wound was a clean in and out, but she'd have to stay away from people - she'd be too conspicuous in this bloodied state.

'Think as you run, Melody!'

She held the pistol steadily out in front of her, heading back for the last junction she'd passed. The junction was in sight, but her heightened senses detected the approaching sound of running feet. She was still a few metres away when the first white uniforms came into view. She loosed off a couple of rounds and dropped into a slide as they raised their rifles. She scrabbled for grip as she reached the junction, saw muzzle flash but felt no pain.

She paused suddenly, as Fester came around the corner, a sweep of his arm felling the men who were training their weapons on her. Was he saving her life? Or just saving it for himself?

She got to her feet and sprinted into the cover of the junction, the sound of heavy footsteps echoing behind her.

How fast was Fester? She didn't want to find out. She could no longer risk hanging the first right turn and making directly for Black Leopard, she needed to lose herself in the maze of beacon 505. She just hoped she wasn't leaving an obvious trail of blood for him to follow.

Considering her options, she could grab a disguise and dress her wound at her cabin, and get some better weapons too, but might the man in green already know which was her cabin? It was too risky.

She could turn herself in to Marshal Jameson, or try to find some Black Fleet personnel, assuming the Marshal hadn't got them all under lock and key, but turning up at security in a bloody PPB uniform would just open up a whole new batch of difficult questions, and there was no guarantee he wouldn't just turn her over to the PPB. She had just killed two of them, after all.

Defying every desire she had to just head for Black Leopard as fast as she could, she turned left. She'd take the next right and run all the way to the outer ring of the station, then double back. That she couldn't hear footsteps behind was promising, at least.

Taking the next right, the corridor passed through a stretch of ratty looking kiosks selling travellers' tat. She drew a few glances from store-keepers, busy cleaning up the mess of the riot. At least she guessed that's what they were doing; on this station, for all she knew they might always look that bad.

Ahead, a four-way junction, made her consider her plan. The urge to turn right and start making faster progress to Black Leopard was strong, but if Fester had gone straight on at her first turn he'd probably be ahead of her.

There was a more direct problem ahead of her, a pair of blue and orange uniforms emerging from the left junction was a sudden problem she'd have to get ahead of.

'HELP!'

Maybe the bloodied uniform could be turned to her advantage after all, this seemed like a strategically advantageous time to fall over. With a stumble and tumble, and an accompanying screech of pain, artfully done. The police were rushing to help her.

'What happened?'

The screech had only been half fake, the wound in her shoulder was getting hard to ignore, and lent her voice an authentic edge of suffering, 'I don't know, I got knocked out by some guys and I woke up like this.' She looked at her own blood, and the blood of the guards from the airlock which covered the sleeves of the white uniform.

'Were they Black Fleet?'

'No,' she looked behind ahead and behind again, feigning panic, 'There was some *huge* guy leading them, he was all covered in scars. Now he's chasing after me. I took a few twists and turns and I think I lost him, but he's around somewhere. Please, you've got to help me! He looks crazy!'

The older police officer turned to his junior, nodding gravely, 'I saw that guy earlier, I knew he was going to be trouble.'

The other officer nodded, 'Let's get you up, Lieutenant. We'll get you to the security station. They're letting out all the crew they arrested last night, so your own people can get you back to your ship. There's safety in numbers, right?'

Delivered right to Marshal Jameson, or handed over to the PPB? No thanks. 'You've got to keep me safe! I'm not going anywhere until that guy is arrested, I saw him swat a bunch of guys aside like flies just to get to me. I don't know what he has against me, but unless you plan on shooting him, you two won't stop him.

The older policeman looked up and drew his gun. 'Hold it!'

She looked around to see Fester standing at the far end of the corridor.

Gibson screamed. A proper full throated scream. She didn't recall ever having screamed in her life, not even when she was told about the death of her parents, but she'd heard other people screaming, and considered this one to be a top quality effort. 'Please! Stop him!'

Rolling behind the officers and springing to her feet she broke into a sprint for the junction and heard the familiar heavy pounding of Fester's feet start up behind her. Shouted commands were followed by the sharp snaps of small weapons fire.

It was strange and it was wrong, but her hopes were that the police were shooting to stop him, not to kill him. Deep stabs of guilt accompanied every report of every shot, and the guns kept firing, and the shouts were still coming.

The shots stopped, and above her own pounding feet she could hear the distant thunder of Fester's pursuit.

He was still coming. Maybe it was the police she should have been worried for?

Her legs found more speed than she knew they had in them, feeling her quadriceps straining to pull her legs in front of her quickly enough that she wouldn't run herself face first into the floor.

Blood loss and the ill-fitting boots were ready to have her fall again, but if she went down this time it wouldn't be on purpose. As her blood pumped harder the pain of the bullet wound high in her chest was now impossible to ignore.

Running on blindly, there was no time to check behind her, and the throbbing of blood in her ears drowned out any footfalls that might be following.

She was lighter and fitter, she *had* to be faster than Fester. The phrase stuck in her mind; a mantra, a wish, and an instruction. *"Faster than Fester. Faster than Fester."*

Ahead she could see the outer ring corridor of the station. Moving as far to the left as she could, she clipped the right turn as close and as fast as she dared, fighting to keep on her feet. If she could stay up, and stay ahead, she could make it to the Black Leopard, then Fester would be their problem, and he was just the sort of problem the crew of the Black Leopard were *really* good at.

She settled into a fast run —a pace she could maintain— that, even if Fester could match, he couldn't catch. She drew her own gun, in case it should come to it, hoping it wouldn't. Ahead was the last junction before the docking ring.

'NO!' The word was out of her mouth before she'd finished processing why. Another closed bulkhead door. She started calculating how long it would take to open, and if she had enough lead on Fester to get through.

Sliding to a halt, she started jabbing at the control panel, trying to get a response. Finally she looked through the bulkhead window and her heart sank. The door was never going to open. There was no corridor on the other side. Not torn open this time, just gone. She heard running feet behind her. Heard them slowing to a walk, then stop.

Turning to face him, she saw his face filled with pain, and his clothes covered in blood. How was he not dead? She realised he didn't have a weapon of any kind. What he could be capable of with his bare hands she didn't want to imagine, but he was too far away for that, and she had the drop on him.

Raising her gun, she stared at him with pity. 'I don't want to kill you, Fester,' her breath was heavy, her voice strained, 'I swear I don't. I've killed people before, and I'll probably do it again, but right now, even though I should, I don't want to kill you.'

'I duhn nuh whut tuh do.' He looked pained, and not just by the many wounds he had, 'Whut cuhn we do?'

She sensed this wasn't just about not getting himself shot, but that he really didn't know what to do. He must have been told to kill her, just as she ought to kill him, and neither of them wanted to. Neither wanted to die. Neither wanted to kill the other. But they had deep loyalties, and the only way for *both* of them to survive was for one of them to betray those loyalties.

Her lungs were burning, the muscles in her legs tightening from the run. She didn't have much running left in her. Her only way out was if he let her go, or if she killed him. The mini-explosive rounds in her pistol would do a lot more damage than the pacification ammo in the police guns.

She looked him in the eyes, imploring, 'Then let's live!'

If he agreed too quickly she'd know he was insincere, but the torment in his eyes showed that his decision, whatever it would be, would be a true one.

He stepped back to the edge of the corridor, and beckoned her to pass him.

She shook her head, 'This is a range weapon, distance is my advantage. I do not surrender my advantage. Back up to the next junction and let me by there.'

He nodded, backing away. She had to hope there wasn't a police pursuit following him, for her sake, for his sake, and for the sake of any police who tried to arrest him.

He stopped at the junction, but she waved him on, backing him up further. 'Distance is my advantage, Fester, keep it moving, and don't follow me.' She kept her eyes fixed on his, waiting and watching for any sudden moves.

Drawing level with the junction, she nodded at him to let him know he could stop. She leaned against the edge of the corridor to let herself recover a little, shaking her head and sighing, 'I liked you, Fester, for what that might be worth to you. If we weren't who we were we'd have never have met, but I think it might have been interesting if we could have met some other way.'

He nodded, then she caught a look of horror in his eyes and he started running at her.

'NO!' she shouted, but he was still running. She pulled the trigger and winced as the explosive round hit him square in the head.

The corridor shook as his full weight fell to the floor.

She shut her eyes as a pool of blood spread out from under his face, then her body tightened as she felt a stabbing in her back, and a knife blade sliding between her ribs.

Turning as she fell, she saw her own knife in the hand of the man in green, and saw his face filled with anger and hate.

She thought of Ray, the sun shining through his wild hair, the smile of joy on his face whenever she came home, and of somebody in a black uniform coming to tell him that another relative would never be coming home again.

twenty

Jameson saluted Agent Malik and fell in to step beside him. 'What have we got?'

Malik led him around the corner to where a body lay, a young woman in a PPB uniform stained deep red on the chest and sleeves. It was the singer.

'She ran into two officers a few corridors back from here, said she was being chased by some huge man. They saw the guy and tried to stop him with a verbal warning, then they were forced to open fire. They're a little sketchy on the whole thing, they're both badly concussed.

'We eventually found her here. No sign of the guy, just her with some sort of document pinned to her chest, with a note for you.'

A datasheet was on her chest, held in place by a knife stabbed up to the hilt in her heart. Jameson snatched up the datasheet, recognising it immediately as a Discretionary Elision Docket.

'Marshal!' Malik protested.

'Worried about preserving the crime scene, Agent Malik?' Jameson waved the docket at him, 'Well, this isn't a crime scene.'

At the bottom of the docket, a personal message.

> *Leo, I solved the Ralph Parsons*
> *murder for you. I even filed a*
> *docket, just like I said I would.*
> *All nice and legal. No thanks are*
> *necessary.*
>
> *A Friend.*

'What do we do now, Marshal?'

Jameson huffed and gritted his teeth, 'Call the commander of Black Leopard and tell him to have,' he read the name on the docket, 'Captain Melody Gibson collected. Then get this corridor cleaned up.'

'The Black Leopard? But she's in a PPB uniform?'

'Malik, don't notice things, don't remember things. This didn't happen.' Jameson raised his voice for the benefit of the other agents and officers, 'You all need to hear this, ladies and gentlemen, boys and girls. For anyone not familiar with the grubby political compromises under which we operate, take a look at this woman's body, and know this. She isn't here. This didn't happen. There is no blood, there's no body, no death.

'Don't be surprised if the order comes down the line that the same applies for everything that happened here last night. The PPB and Black Fleet will pay for the damage and generously compensate people for their hurts and harms, and all on the understanding everybody forgets why they got the money, and then this will never have happened.

'How you feel about that is up to you. I stopped being angry about it a long time ago. My suggestion to you is don't even start being angry. Just be glad it isn't worse. Don't think it couldn't be worse. And, don't think it won't get worse. Most of all, don't kid yourself there's anything you can do about it.'

He became aware of the leader of the forensics team giving him a troubled stare, and sensed this wasn't just about the fact all the evidence they'd collected would have to be destroyed. He waved her over.

'What's got you frowning, Agent?'

'The scene's been cleaned up very well, nothing to detect but a lot of Kleen residue. Not just here, but all of the blood from the man pursuing her. The PPB did a very thorough job of eliminating all evidence of both the pursuit and the pursuer from the station corridors.'

'That hardly seems relevant now.'

'Here's the thing, Sir, they didn't clean up the woman, a lot of the blood and tissue on that uniform isn't hers. There are five distinct sets of blood, and other material too.'

'So would that put this killing outside the limits of a discretionary elision?' If Jameson could get around the elision docket, he could still get a result on Ralph Parson's murder.

'I don't know. Three of the blood samples belong to PPB crew, and one is the victim's own blood, which taken alone means the PPB are entitled to write off any further investigation, and as they issued the docket, they certainly will.'

'But that still leaves one blood sample unaccounted for, correct?'

'Not just blood, but we'll get to that. The DNA from the final sample is unregistered.'

'Unregistered? Well, that's rare, but not unheard of. Could be from an outer colony, or maybe even the Goffa province.'

'I can't rule that out, but the blood itself is strange.'

'In what way?'

'Well, whoever's blood it is, they wouldn't get a Natural Human Warranty, there's evidence of huge levels of genetic manipulation. But it's the other samples that are really interesting. We've found microscopic bone fragments, of the type you get when small explosive rounds are used.'

'Rounds like you get in a PPB officers side-arm.'

'Yes, but that's not what's interesting. The bone density is off the scale. It's real human bone, but it's like pig iron.'

'So one of the people she killed was some kind of a genetic mutant? This would be the giant?'

'The giant, yes, but here's the thing, the genetic markers show that these are skull fragments, but there's no brain matter. With that bone density, his skull would be practically bullet-proof. There's every chance that this giant is still alive.'

Jameson's head was spinning. This giant, this genetic freak, was working for the PPB, the very people who were responsible for the banning of genetic manipulation. Potentially life saving technology the PPB themselves had outlawed was being used by them as a weapon.

But all the evidence he had was blood and tiny fragments of bone, from a crime scene that officially didn't exist.

'Thank you for your information, Agent. As the senior investigating officer, disposal of this material is my responsibility. So gather all the samples and see they are given to me, and me only. I'll make sure they are dealt with. Do you understand?'

'I do, Marshal. I do.'

Agent Malik appeared beside him, 'Marshal Jameson, Administrator Parsons has just called in, he says he wants to speak with you.'

'I'm sure he does, but he isn't going to like what I've got to say.' Jameson looked at the corpse of the singer — a Black Fleet agent dating a PPB bridge officer.

It was almost certain she had killed Sid Parsons' brother when he'd seen *something* he shouldn't have in her cabin back on Raleigh Station. That Luther had beaten him to the solution to the case was bad enough, but it was now a murder case Jameson would never be able to close.

Sid Parsons was taking the news about as well as could be expected. Jameson had been an only child, but he wasn't without sympathy for the man's loss, even though it seemed the man's brother had been an unpleasant sex pest, that wasn't a capital crime.

'What the spreff do you mean you're no longer investigating my brother's disappearance? Is somebody else doing it?'

'I know it's not what you want to hear, Mister Parsons, but the police are making no further efforts to locate your brother or to discover his whereabouts.'

'You're making it sound like he ran away, that he's gone into hiding because he's guilty of those things those dancers accused him of! You're basically sending a message that he's guilty! He had no reason to run! Those charges were never going to stick! Something happened to him, so why the chiff aren't you investigating?'

Luther had shafted Jameson very neatly. By filing a Discretionary Elision Docket on Ralph Parsons' killer, every detail of the case had become classified.

Jameson knew exactly who'd killed Parson's brother, but he wasn't even allowed to give him the closure of confirming he was believed dead. 'Procedure forbids me taking the matter further. I can't discuss it.'

'Well why don't I take it up with somebody over your head? You've done nothing, Jameson! Not a spreffing thing! I heard you were supposed to be one of the best investigators the police had. What the spreff use are you?'

'I can't give you any other explanation. My hands are tied. You can take the matter up with the Grand Marshal if you like, but his answer will be the same.'

'Well why don't I tell him how you let my station get turned into a war-zone while I'm at it? What do you suppose he'll think of that?'

'I don't trouble myself about what the Grand Marshal is thinking. On the other hand, I know very well what the Navigation Council would make of you running a commercial station rated at a 800 person capacity with no doctor, only one nurse, one med bed, and barely enough detention cells to handle the average bar brawl. This place wouldn't have turned into a war-zone if it weren't so pathetically under-equipped.'

Parsons' anger turned to frustration, 'You want to blackmail me to keep me quiet, Marshal? That's low.'

'It's not blackmail, Administrator. Please do pass your complaints about my investigation on to the Grand Marshal, because I'll be reporting you to the Navigation Council either way. If you don't have proper medical and detention facilities by the next time I pass through here, I'll be instructing the Navigation Council to have your operating status revoked.

'While your at it, you might want to make it a little harder for random visitors to eject sections of your station into the great black yonder.'

Parsons shook his head in disgust. 'You're a piece of work, Marshal. Take it from me, if the police ever need any help from me, they can go swing for it! Pass *that* on to Grand Marshal Balfour! Now get the hell out of my office!'

'Yes, I believe I will.' He stood and straightened the creases in his uniform, 'I'll be remaining aboard the station until a replacement Circuit Marshal arrives. The medical reports of all injured Police personnel, including Marshal Hurst, will be going in with my report to the council, this station's numerous inadequacies were a large contributing factor, after all. Oh, and if you think my wife will be doing business on a death-trap like this station, you can think again.'

Parsons watched the marshal walk out of his office, gritting his teeth in loathing. Turning to the adjoining door, he nodded at the man who walked in.

'You were right, Mister Griffith. He didn't tell me a spreffing thing about the singer, or about Black Fleet. He covered the whole thing up for them, just like you said he would.'

Griffith sat down and rested his palms on Parsons' desk. 'I'm afraid that's how it is between the Police and Black Fleet, Administrator. I'm very sorry your brother had to die for you to discover that.'

'Thanks,' he nodded, 'Well I tell you, Mister Griffith, I'm done with them. Done! From here on out, you get what I got. From my ears straight to yours, but not for free, understand? I get good information here, really good, and running this place isn't cheap. In case you didn't hear, I've suddenly got some heavy expenses coming up.'

'Of course, but why restrict your income, Mister Parsons? By all means be an informant for Black Fleet and the Police. Don't give them the *best* information, not as good as you give us, of course, but at least be reliable.'

'I don't get your angle?'

'Sometimes, it will be strategically advantageous for me if they have the wrong information, and you would be a very good conduit for me to see that they get it. As an added bonus, they'll be paying you to lie to them.'

Parsons chuckled, 'I like the way you think, Mister Griffith.'

'I quite like it myself. Now, as you say, you have some big expenses coming, so how about we start with a little something up front, in good faith.'

'I won't say no to that! How much did you have in mind?'

'Not money, Mister Parsons. I was thinking your status here might be made more secure with a state of the art medical unit and a new security station, with a full supply of riot gear, and, say, fifty holding cells? Oh, and I'll see you're furnished with a fully stocked pharmacy for the new medical unit, of course.'

Parsons jaw hung slack. He'd hoped for, maybe, fifty thousand Bucks, what he was being offered was worth over three million.

'We don't want the marshal's threats hanging over you, after all. Is that acceptable?'

'Yeah, yeah. That's good!'

Griffith nodded, seeming pleased. 'Don't you worry about threats from Leo Jameson, Administrator. As long as you're on my side, your operating status will *never* be revoked.' He stood and made for the door, turning an enigmatic smile Parsons' way, 'As long as you're on *my* side.'

Quiet snores of peaceful sleep greeted Qiang as she stepped inside her quarters. At some point Grace must have stopped vomiting and crawled into bed.

The bathroom was a small, peaceful, haven, and the results of her cafcaf binge were a pressing matter. She looked across at the dispenser next to the sink as a beaker was filling with a cloudy pink liquid. The readout above the dispenser beeped and displayed a message.

urine content suggests high stress levels

excess caffeine

diuretic dehydration

sleep deprivation

please drink

contains isotonic formulation

mild sedative

serotonin booster

She looked down into the toilet bowl, 'I can't even trust you to keep my secrets?' She shook her head, 'It comes to something when you get more sense from the computer in the toilet than the computer on the command deck.'

Freshening herself up as quietly as she could, she slipped into a clean uniform and sat at the table for a few moments of peace, listening to Pirie's soft snoring and sipping the sweet medicinal cocktail. Qiang didn't want to wake her, but in a few minutes her own watch would rouse her with her next shift assignment.

What the computer would do about assignments was anybody's guess, there were only enough people left aboard to run Black Wreath if they were running consecutive 25 hour shifts. They would have to hope Fleet had been told what had happened and that there would be a dreadnought to meet them at the patrol point, if not at the course correction point.

How much of the flight plan was controlled by the computer and how much input was needed from QM was a mystery to the cadets. If the computer had any issues operating with no commissioned officers aboard, there was no sign of it. Eventually it would need fresh orders, but for all anyone aboard knew that could be anything from a day, to a week, or a month.

Pirie's watch chimed at the same time as Qiang's, and she groaned herself to consciousness. Looking up at Qiang, blinking, she asked, 'What have you got?'

Qiang looked at her watch. The message stared at her. It wasn't commander, but it was the next best thing. Flight Executive.

'Flex. How about you?'

Pirie tried to focus her eyes on the display, 'Security patrol.' she sighed, 'We don't drop shell for another four hours, so that should give me plenty of time for a long nap.'

Qiang nodded. 'Got to get you there first. Let's get you up and dressed.'

Nodding, she lurched out of her bunk and looked around, slightly puzzled. 'Shouldn't Malcolm be back by now?'

Qiang didn't even know where Wrath would be now. If the reports of rioting that had got through before they'd left Beacon 505 were accurate, he could well be in a police cell, or maybe the infirmary, although there was something about Wrath, he had a strange kind of luck that seemed to keep him out of trouble, and even when there was trouble, he always seemed able to turn it to his advantage.

'It's a long story. He got left behind on Beacon 505, but knowing Wrath, he'll probably find a way to catch up to us.'

All eyes turned to a young and handsome PPB commander as he stepped into the barrack room, throwing the commandos a quick salute. Wrath felt Major Jaglan grab his wrist before he could return the gesture, noting that none of the commandos were saluting back. For whatever reason, it seemed PPB commandos didn't salute. The commander seemed to take this as normal behaviour.

'I'm Commander Guthrie, I'll be leading our assault on Black Wreath. I'll be leading from behind, obviously.' He seemed to find this amusing, there was no sign the commandos shared the view, 'We drop shell in a little over two hours, where the Savatara should be waiting for us. Timing will be tight, as we were delayed leaving Beacon 505, but we haven't stopped for course corrections, so we should beat Black Wreath to her destination, though we'll probably only have a couple of minutes to spare.

'I know some of you were supposed to be aboard the Savatara, but as I understand it they have a full compliment of commandos, so when we join them we'll have a fighting strength of over 80, and most of Black Wreath's crew were stranded aboard Beacon 505.

'The crew are cadets, so it should be a simple matter to exterminate them, but we can't allow them to scuttle their bird. Seizure of the vessel is our one and only goal, so we need to seize control of the power decks and the command deck as quickly as we can. We need to prevent the alarm being raised for as long as possible, so all crew are to be shot on sight.'

Wrath felt the tendons in his wrist flex and strain against Jaglan's grip, his fists tightening, trying not to let his face betray his reaction to this officer calmly talking about killing his crew-mates, matter of factly planning to murder his friends.

'We'll be boarding the breach-boat at 05:30 FST, so get yourselves ready. The breach-boats are unshielded, so due to the nature of the weapon we'll be using to make a breaching point, we can't launch until the weapon has been deployed to make us a soft spot to punch through the hull.

'The commandos from the Savatara will be the first *Rapid Attack Team* — designated Alpha RAT. We are Bravo RAT. We'll hook up to their breach-boat once they're in, using their breach point for ingress to Black Wreath. They will head for the command deck, and we'll take control of the power decks.'

He activated a holographic image of a Black Fleet dreadnought, which hung in the air in the centre of the barracks.

'Unlike our tower style vertical deck layout, Black Fleet uses a flat-deck system. This should make movement very easy for us. The corridors are staggered left-to-right with off-centre double doors every 20 metres, this gives them natural choke points that are easier to defend, but essentially, you can walk front to back of the craft without changing levels or using elevators, making it pretty straightforward to seize control of critical systems. In theory, anyway.'

Guthrie looked around the room, 'Now, what went down on Beacon 505 really made a mess of the unit assignments and the supply swaps. I know a lot of you guys may not know each other but I need you to work as a single unit, and I need you all to have what you need, so get to know each other, and share your gear if needs be, now's not the time to be cliquey. Get prepped, and be ready for muster at the breach-boat at 05:00 hours. That is all.'

Wrath's loathing began leaking out as he watched the door close behind the PPB officer. Jaglan leaned in conspiratorially, whispering 'There's going to be plenty of tags for everybody, so if you want us to leave that grubby specimen for you, just say the word.'

'What?'

'Commander Guthrie. He's your kill, if you want it.'

Wrath suddenly blanched at the thought, knocking the edge off his anger, abstracting the feeling. He'd played his part in yesterday's pirate junk bloodbath, but the pirate junk had been a shape on a screen, and he hadn't been the one who had pulled the trigger. He tried to focus his mind on the idea of shooting at people with live rounds instead of slap-rounds.

He swept his gaze around the barrack room, at Jaglan's squad, and the real PPB commandos, and he understood what he was in for. Every person here was here to *kill*. Up close, in person, real, *"stare them in the face and watch them die"* killing. Red Task.

He looked back to Jaglan, confused. In ordinary circumstances, he'd be aboard Black Wreath, totally unaware that at the next patrol point they stopped at they would be attacked, boarded, murdered.

The PPB commander, Guthrie, he'd talked about it like he was planning on doing some paperwork, or cleaning his boots. Surely Wrath should want to kill him? A strange, foggy mental numbness swept over him and he shook his head uncertainly.

'I don't know.'

Jaglan nodded, 'Well, keep it in mind, it carries a good tariff. In the meantime, try to avoid talking to anybody. My guys know the commando slang and their jargon, we can bluff our way through any awkward questions about commando training, what bases they get stationed at and so forth, which I'm guessing you can't.'

'I'll keep myself to myself, I can probably manage that for 90 minutes.'

No sooner had he said these words than his gaze locked upon a shaven headed, lantern jawed commando and realised he recognised the face, which after a moment, was itself touched by the spark of recognition.

'I know you!' the commando boomed, 'You're the Rothgill kid!' the smile that twisted its way onto his unfortunate face was as ugly as it was joyous. Wrath's heart sank as he responded with the sincerest fake smile he could push onto his face. 'Little Glen Rothgill! What a place to see you! Come on over here! We gots to talk!'

twenty one

Wrath's new best friend led him to the shuttle bay, full of questions, though thankfully none of them about his non-existent PPB commando training.

'How's your brudda? He moved to Viafrane? I bet he has. Always a great shooter, your brudda. I ain't followed the scene for a while, though.'

For a short while, when a young Glen Rothgill was starting his competitive career in the junior level comps, Salo Krupps had been quite something in the Gun-Grid scene on Pandale. Big for his age, he was an incredibly aggressive competitor in and out of the arena. Between him and his obstreperous, overbearing father the shoot judges were always wary of giving any decision against him.

A lot of people had been glad that he'd mysteriously quit the scene as soon as he turned eighteen. The assumption was the family had gone back home to Brocco in the eastern reaches of Pandale, where the accents were thick, and the money from gas mining was plentiful. Wrath was now figuring that Salo Krupps' disappearance from the shooting scene had coincided with his becoming old enough to join up with the PPB.

'Yeah, Gilbert's moving up the rankings pretty fast. The whole family moved there, except me.'

'You lost interest, eh? Me too, what was it with you? Stupid rule changes, right?'

Wrath nodded, 'Yeah, all the rule changes they kept rolling out, diluting the precision and going for wild action. Everything they do seems to make it more of a haven for pray-and-spray shooters. Skill doesn't seem to matter much now.'

Krupps returned the nod, sagely, 'It was going that way when I left. Who wants that, eh? Used to be a precision sport, right? Speed, tactics, and a steady gun arm. Not now, eh? That's why I prefer this. You shoot someone with this,' he tapped the muzzle of his assault rifle, 'they stay shot! Right?'

'I guess they do.'

'I heard they was even thinking of bringing in dual-wield shooting category. Can you imagine that? Knuckleheads waving their guns around and winning comps off lucky shots? Like some lame action movie. Dumb.' He shook his head in disgust.

'I guess we both had the same idea.'

Wrath noted the arrival of Commander Guthrie in the shuttle bay, he called over the sergeant of Krupps' unit, and Major Jaglan, who was also carrying the insignia of a PPB sergeant. The small huddle seemed to be going over tactics.

'Hey! My sista still asks after your brudda, you tell him she said "hi" next time you talk, okay?'

'Of course, yeah.' Salo's sister had been quite the looker, but Wrath was not sorry Gilbert had chosen to end the relationship with her. The Krupps family were best in small doses, certainly not people you'd want hanging around every Crissmuss.

Guthrie called them on and led the way up the loading ramp and aboard the breach-boat.

The interior was all bare metal and bare benches, with a single pilot's seat up front, and for the Commanding Officers a jump seat on either side. Guthrie took his place and waited for them all to get sat down.

'I tell you, I miss the arena some. You?'

Wrath shrugged, 'It seems like a lifetime ago.'

'Sure, your lifetime's not so long yet, though, eh?' Salo nudged him playfully, nearly knocking him out of his seat. 'I miss it some, for sure. When I quit the Navy I was thinking I might try out for the death leagues.'

Wrath visibly flinched, he'd always thought the death leagues were just a scare story. He'd heard rumours of people joining an underground circuit with live ammo, but the tall tales always had the ring of kids making big-talk. To him it had sounded like a bunch of brownhole.

'I didn't even know that was a real thing?'

'Oh sure. Big money. All run by Steimz fraternities. They make billions on gambling and subs for their shadownet broadcasts so the payouts are huge. It ain't that different from what we're doing now, when you think about it. Only in the death leagues, the people you shoot know what they're getting into! Not like the poor pups we'll be nixing today, right?'

Wrath forced a smile, turning his thoughts to Pirie, Qiang, Farr and the rest of the cadets who were going about their business, with no idea what was coming their way.

Wrath heard the loading bay door seal behind them and felt the subtle and fleeting twisting sensation of the on-board gravity systems taking over. Now they waited for the Sonya to drop shell. Waiting to launch the attack.

Whatever it was that Jaglan had in store for the commandos aboard this breach-boat, there were fifty more coming from the Savatara who would make it aboard Black Wreath before them, determined to sweep through the vessel killing everyone in their path.

Commander Rawlins had never been able to walk into a room with Captain Jowett without first taking a moment to just look at her. There was a mystique to the woman, an irreal aura of purpose infinitely greater than one's own. Her nickname at the naval academy had been "Diamond".

Small, beautiful, hard.

Not long after making it to the academy she had rapidly cultivated a cold hatred of Black Fleet, not through personal experiences or personal animosity, but simply because she was told that they were the enemy. For some people that is enough.

Jowett was silent, her eyes and her thoughts focused outside the window at the front of the newly built bridge.

The new bridge of the Savatara was as much a testament to the singularity of its task as the rest of the ship. Of aesthetic considerations, there were none. Of comforts, there were none. This was not a place for sitting, not a place for resting. The only equipment installed was that which related to combat.

No part of the ship had been spared in the efforts to turn her into a dreadnought killer. The old bridge had been in the way of the hyper-optic missile launcher, so it was stripped of equipment and eliminated.

Relocated to the very front of the Savatara, the new bridge was now in the least protected area of the ship. In Jowett's view, this was where it should be, irrespective of the necessity to site it here. A captain should not place their vessel in any greater danger than they themselves would risk.

'Captain?'

Jowett turned to her second in command, 'What is it, Rawlins?'

'I've done a masked sub-net poll of traffic movements to and from

Beacon 505. If they've skipped their course corrections and put in a hard burn all the way here like we did, the Sonya should be here with about 8 minutes to spare before Black Wreath is due to begin her patrol. The only problem is, without accurate course data that could mean them dropping shell anything up to thirty thousand klicks away from us.'

'It was never going to be range zero. We have no idea how close Black Wreath will drop shell to its patrol point.'

'It could mean a big delay for the Sonya's Rapid Attack Team getting aboard to help out Alpha RAT.'

'We're putting fifty battle hardened commandos up against a bunch of kids. The second team was only ever precautionary, and that was before we knew over half their crew would be stranded on Beacon 505.'

'Understood. The only other issue is getting in two missile strikes in succession. One hit isn't enough to soften the hull for breach-boat penetration. The Sonya's missile will be under its own power, which means it's a lot slower than ours, and our generator heads can't recharge fast enough to make an effective double strike ourselves.'

Jowett waved away Rawlins' concerns, 'We have two minutes from shell-drop to get in the first hit before their external monitoring systems are powered up. If the Sonya launches their weapon immediately, and we leave our strike until the last possible second, the Sonya's weapon should be able to strike soon enough after ours to open up a breach point. Relax, Commander. These contingencies are manageable.'

'And have you decided who'll lead the Rapid Attack Team?' Rawlins tried not to sound hopeful, though she relished the thought of being the first PPB officer to capture a Black Fleet dreadnought intact.

Jowett nodded again, 'Lieutenant Sullivan is our most experienced incursion leader, he's the natural choice.'

'Of course.' Now it was bitter disappointment she had to conceal from her voice.

Captain Jowett chose this moment to do something very rare, bridging an emotional distance she always kept from even the most senior crew and looking the commander straight in the eye. 'I need you here with me, Commander Rawlins. Let's not forget, we are a hunted boat now, the quarry of *all* space-going forces, even our own.'

It was the first time Rawlins had ever seen the Captain display anything but iron control and absolute confidence, an acknowledgement of just how high the stakes for this missions were.

Their only means of returning safe to the fold of the PPB Navy was to succeed in grasping their prize. Capturing the Black Wreath could be their salvation, anything else would be their damnation.

The assurances of Fleet had been oblique and dismissive. Qiang got no comfort from their vague confirmations that help for Black Wreath would come, eventually. Until then, they were to proceed as normal, and make the best of their situation by running emergency drills. They were told to practice fast power-ups, anti-incursion prep, and emergency scuttle procedures.

"Drills?" Qiang had never been Flex before, but she knew that any one of these drills alone was an overlapping sequence of complex procedures, with a large number of crew dedicated to the task. Running even *two* of these drills consecutively was unheard of, let alone all three, making the addition of scuttle procedures all the more chilling. *"They know what's coming but they won't tell us."*

By now the whole crew had seen or heard the news about the Savatara's part in the explosion that had disabled them during the Pandale ambush, but none seemed to have joined the dots yet. Qiang was the only one nursing a suspicion that the Savatara was now planning to finish the job.

If it was true, Fleet weren't admitting it, but their orders seemed pretty good clues. Fleet had mandated station-leave for all crew not on the immediate duty roster, including QM, and must have programmed new orders into the computer. The unexpected launch from Beacon 505 hadn't been an accident. Qiang's guess was they were hoping to evade the Savatara, Sabina and Sonya, and if they couldn't, then they'd at least limit their losses to around sixty cadets and one —from what Qiang had heard about Black Wreath— *very* old, training vessel.

Every remaining crew member aboard was on duty, even though some were on their third consecutive shift. Poor cadet Boyd, after pulling a full 25 hour shift as commander, was now with Pirie on his fourth shift, and probably the only person aboard who'd had even less sleep than Qiang.

With shell drop at the patrol point only moments away, she put a call in to Pirie.

'*What's up, Flex? Power gone to your head yet?*'

'Hey Grace, how's your guts?'

'*Great, the toilet told me all sorts of fascinating things about my puke and gave me some green goop to drink, full of peptides and electrolytes and that kinda thing. I actually feel pretty good.*'

'And how's Boyd?'

'*I think he's trying to break your record for the most cafcaf drunk in a single shift. His tongue has turned blue.*'

'Good, good. Stay sharp, we drop shell any minute, are you at the side dock, like I said?'

'*Who's in charge of security here?*'

'I know, but there could be some good merits in this, so run a good drill, okay?' Qiang tried not to give away her concerns, 'Treat it like it's real. Anti-breach protocols, weapons live, okay?'

'*We're set, Flex. Weapon up, right?*'

'Weapon up.'

'*You should say it like QM does, seeing as she's not here.*'

Qiang chuckled, 'Whuppunup Cadet!'

'*Whuppunup!*'

Qiang became aware of a presence behind her, acting commander Forlani cleared his throat, 'We all prepped, Flex?'

'As well as we can be, Commander. Twelve crew in the power room, the eight of us here in command, thirty cadets split into two squads on anti-incursion drills, and the final eight of the crew are in Double-Eight pods, top, bottom, left and right.'

'Heavy focus on defence, Flex? I thought with enough people in the engine decks we could have made a decent crack at beating our start-up record?'

'I'd rather be safe and slow than quick and dead, commander.'

'You're making it sound a little dramatic there, Qiang, but it's your call. There's probably plenty of time for more drills before Fleet can get a relief crew to us.'

'Let's hope so.'

Forlani started to nod, then frowned, shaking the thought away and turning back to the rest of the command deck crew, 'Dropping shell in thirty seconds, let's see how fast we can get this bird powered and prepped. We're all tired, but we're also well trained, so let's do ourselves proud, and see if we can earn ourselves a stack of merits while we're at it.'

Murmurs of approval greeted the sentiment. Forlani grabbed up the communications handset to address the rest of the crew. 'Dropping shell in ten seconds. On drop, power up, weapon up, go emergency scuttle drill. Three. Two. One. Drop.'

Qiang's eyes turned to the holographic sphere springing to life at the centre of the command deck. The sphere was blank, and would remain so until the external monitoring and weapons systems were powered, which couldn't happen until the generator head recovered. The power draw of the gravity systems during the trans-optic deceleration was massive, but it was the highest priority, keeping the human passengers from being turned into smears of blood on the front bulkhead.

The fastest power-up on record was 98 seconds, but with a dog-tired skeleton crew of cadets doing the work, they'd be lucky even to beat the two minute average.

Forlani paced slowly around the consoles, looking in at the holographic display, occasionally glancing at the elapsed time counter. He turned to Qiang. 'Want to put in a call to power control? Gee them along a little?'

'Having to answer a call from me would only slow them down, Commander. I'm sure they're giving it their best.'

Forlani shrugged, and Qiang turned her own attention to the elapsed time counter, hoping they might at least beat the two minute mark, if only to prove *her* right and Forlani wrong.

As the timer clicked to 117 seconds a flicker of an image began to resolve in the holographic sphere as the first LADaR pulse returned, and a flicker of a smile appeared on Qiang's lips, then she saw a vague ghost of an outline resolving and her blood ran cold.

The command deck shuddered, the holographic sphere vanished, and suddenly all light was gone. The command deck was in utter darkness, utter silence, as it had only ever been once before. They all knew this darkness, this silence, but the last time, they'd only been hit once.

Not this time. This time there was no simple shudder, damped by the powerful gravity systems, those systems had had no time to recover for a second blow. The full force, sound, and fury of the savage explosion smashed its way into the fabric of Black Wreath, and into the minds of her crew. Qiang's were not the only screams as everyone on the bridge was thrown violently sideways.

In absolute darkness, there was no way to know where she had landed. Waves of nausea swept over her. The gravity systems were struggling to work out which way was up, and so was she.

Slapping her uniform's chest panel, the high-intensity light built into it flared into life. As she moved around, the beam swept across shocked looking faces running with blood. Acting Commander Forlani was lying vertically against the wall, his head twisted underneath him in a way that was not compatible with being alive.

Fresh, piercing screams suggested people trying to move limbs that were no longer effective at being limbs. Another scream as more people remembered their own suit lights, and more beams found their way to Forlani's inverted, vacant gaze into the infinite.

Qiang was regaining her mental equilibrium. Tentative movements suggested none of her bones seemed broken, though she was tender. She made her way back to her console, jabbing at it, trying to prod it into life. Somewhere in her mind it occurred to her a dead man would not make a good leader in a crisis, and that she was the next link in the chain of command.

'Commander Forlani is dead,' she called out as calmly as she could, 'I am assuming command. Everyone who is alive and conscious, sound off.'

Five voices came back, Qiang looked around for who was missing, her light came to rest on a body lying crammed between his seat and his console. 'Is that Ginzu? Somebody check if he's alive.'

A dull redness lit the command deck as the emergency lighting system finally kicked into life.

'What happened?'

Qiang didn't try to identify the voice as her console was finally showing signs of life, her answer was for everyone. 'My guess is the Savatara is out there and she hit us with the same weapon they used at Pandale, only this time they had two of them.'

'Why did we get thrown around like that? The gravity systems are supposed to be able to absorb any impact?'

'We hadn't built up enough power reserve after the shell drop, it absorbed the first strike just fine, but the second sideswiped us before it could recover.'

Qiang's console was in recovery mode, running diagnostics. Her head was starting to throb and she could barely focus her eyes on the text. 'Diagnostics to audio mode.'

In keeping with the PPB's stance against artificial intelligence, it was a Protectorate-wide rule that computers weren't even allowed to sound human, and the report was made all the more chilling for the artificial voice that was reading it out.

'EMERGENCY POWER SYSTEMS ENGAGED. TOTAL CONTROL SYSTEMS FAILURE. TOTAL PRIMARY POWER SYSTEMS FAILURE. TOTAL WEAPONS SYSTEMS FAILURE. TOTAL EXTERNAL MONITORING SYSTEMS FAILURE. TOTAL INTERNAL MONITORING SYSTEMS FAILURE. TOTAL SHUNT COMMUNICATIONS SYSTEM FAILURE. TOTAL INTERNAL COMMUNICATIONS SYSTEM FAILURE. PARTIAL GRAVITY SYSTEMS FAILURE, RECOVERING. PARTIAL LIFE SUPPORT SYSTEMS FAILURE, RECOVERING. TOTAL PRIMARY LIGHTING SYSTEM FAILURE. PARTIAL EMERGENCY SYSTEMS FAILURE, RECOVERING. NOTICE: DEDICATED ANTI-INCURSION PROTOCOLS ACTIVATED. FURTHER DATA REQUIRES QQQZ LEVEL AUTHORIZATION. WOULD YOU LIKE TO REPEAT REPORT?'

'What was that about data that requires what authorisation?'

'YOU DO NOT HAVE ADEQUATE CLEARANCE FOR ANTI-INCURSION PROTOCOLS. ANTI-INCURSION PROTOCOLS ARE ACTIVE. WOULD YOU LIKE TO REPEAT REPORT?'

'No, I don't want to sit through that again. Just report any status changes as and when they happen. Can you prioritise any particular self-repair system?'

'ANTI-INCURSION PROTOCOLS CANNOT BE SUPERSEDED. SELF-REPAIR SYSTEMS CAN BE REPRIORITISED.'

'I need internal communications back. Highest priority. I also need bio-feedback monitors for all crew so I know who's alive, and what state they're in.'

'SYSTEM PRIORITY RANK UPDATED.'

Cadet Ginzu was coming around, and one of the cadets had laid Forlani's body in a more dignified position, having done him and everyone else the favour of shutting his eyes. Wondering who had screamed in the darkness, Qiang saw cadet Cabrera was being tended to by Maddocks, who had unzipped the leg of Cabrera's jumpsuit and was doing what she could for what looked like a severe compound fracture high in his femur. The level of blood-flow suggested there was no arterial damage. He'd live, or if he didn't, it wouldn't be the break that killed him.

Cabrera looked calm, his suit would have flooded his system with pain-killers as soon as his bio-monitors detected the break. At least, like last time, the PPB weapon had only affected Black Wreath's own systems, and their personal devices were still functional.

'INTERNAL COMMUNICATION SYSTEMS RESTORED'

Qiang grabbed up the comms handset, 'Power Deck, this is Commander Qiang, report status.'

'We're dead in the water, Commander. All power systems are out of our control and diverted to the self-repair systems. The generator head is in self-protect mode, we're just fighting to keep up with the power demands.'

'How about casualties, Chief? Bio-monitoring's not up yet.'

'Some nasty limb-breakages, but we're all alive, this is the safest place on this bird. Is this part of the drill? Because I do not approve.'

'This is no drill. How far did you get with scuttle procedures?'

'We've got more important things to worry about than training to blow our own vessel up, Commander!'

'Well that job might get taken care of for us. Keep an eye on the doors.'

'What?'

'We've been attacked, probably by the Savatara, and if they aren't going to vaporise us they're going to board us. Keep an eye on the doors, cadet, and if white uniforms come through, shoot to kill. Do not hesitate. Do not ask questions. Kill on sight. Confirm you understand.'

'I understand, but...'

'No *"buts"*, cadet. You've confirmed you understand, now confirm you'll do it. If you see a white uniform, you kill whoever is in it, instantly. Confirm.'

Qiang was prepared to lose her temper, but the cadet broke his concerned silence just before she was about to, *'Confirmed, I guess.'*

'Don't guess, kill. Acting Commander Forlani is dead. I doubt he's the only one, and don't forget the cadets, your crew-mates, that these spreffers killed at Pandale. Don't just agree to kill them, want to kill them. Comm out.'

The sentiment seemed to go down well with the command deck crew, she switched channels to pass the order on to the people who would be needing it first.

'Pirie?'

'Grace? ...happened? ...hurt, think some ...dead. ...ell broke loose!'

Pirie's signal was weak and sporadic, Qiang filled in the blanks. 'It's the same as at Pandale. Forlani's dead. I'm Commander.'

'Oh spreff! ...should we do?'

'How are your people?'

'Shaken up, ...said before, ...three of us left ...trapped, or dead. Whatever hit us ...like we were right by it. ...hot as the sun here. Helmet visors ...fried ...barely hear you ...with communications?'

'Grace, I think they're going to try to breach and board. They've made a weak spot they can punch through, you need to hold and defend your position. Fall back to the nearest corridor break and use the bulkhead door as a choke point.'

'...repeat, didn't copy any ...'

'Grace? Do you copy.'

'Please repeat, ...copy?'

'Expect breach and incursion! Fall back to the nearest corridor break and make a choke point. Shoot to kill.'

'Did you... shoot to...?'

'Pirie, do you copy?'

A harsh tone signalled the connection was broken. 'Computer, you said communications were fixed?'

'INTERNAL COMMUNICATIONS SYSTEMS ARE OPTIMAL. LOCALISED HIGH RADIATION LEVELS DISRUPTING COMMUNICATIONS IN AFT DOCKING BAY AREA. THIS IS OUTSIDE OPERATIONAL PARAMETERS.'

A soft thud and a sharp vibration silenced all noise on the command deck. Cadet Ginzu turned to Qiang, 'Have they hit us again?'

Qiang shook her head, 'That wasn't another bomb, the lights are still on.' For a moment the crew looked relieved but Qiang set them right, 'Don't look so happy, we're being boarded.'

Pirie was laid out flat by the impact, she felt Boyd grab at her waist, trying to raise her up, barely able to understand his shouting. Her eyes fell upon the sharp point of gleaming metal poking three metres into the corridor, heard the hull of Black Wreath screech as the point split open, forcing the softened metal apart.

She was barely able to keep her feet as Boyd dragged her backwards away from the breach boat.

'Wait!' She shouted, seeing her helmet lying on the floor where it had fallen. She'd been trying to get the visor working after the first explosion had locked the sensorupt protection into dark mode.

A man in white armour appeared from the hole torn in Black Wreath's flank. Men in white armour were supposed to rescue women, right?

The commando turned towards Pirie, transfixing her with his gaze, raising his weapon - his nasty and powerful looking gun - levelling it at her head. He was not here to rescue her.

Things seemed to move in slow motion, as the commando set his stance to absorb the recoil, steadied his aim, looked her right in the eye and pulled the trigger.

It took a moment that felt like a lifetime for them both to realise she wasn't dead. He pulled the trigger again, and nothing happened. As he pulled his gun up to look at it, she brought up her own, waited for him to look back to her, and gave him a triumphant smile, then gave him a three round burst that punched through his helmet and detonated inside his brain.

'Boyd!' she shouted, 'Whuppunup, stand your ground!'

She dropped to one knee, and began dropping commandos as they emerged. Boyd stood behind her, adding his own firepower to hers.

'Switch to intimidate!' she ordered, and they both flicked the audio report switches to maximum volume. Without her helmet the noise was deafening, but she wanted to scare them back into the hole they were crawling out from.

Questing gun muzzles poking around the side of the breach boat were met with a violent cacophony of noise and ricocheting ammunition.

'We need to fall back to a more defensible position. We've got them bottled up for now, but there's going to be plenty of them in there, and if they decide to rush us...'

'Understood.'

'Okay, backwards at 90 pace, maintain suppressing fire, we'll dig in at the next bulkhead, radio through to Qiang and wait for the second anti-incursion squad to get to us.'

Carefully stepping backwards, firing random bursts of gunfire at the opening in the breach boat, they didn't dare turn away to see how far from the bulkhead they were.

There were no more hopeful gun-muzzles emerging from the breach, but one flailing arm appeared. Pirie fired at it reflexively. Whether she hit it or not, she didn't know, her attention was drawn to the disc sliding along the floor towards her.

'Sensorupt!'

She tried to shield her eyes, but the blinding flash was too bright for her eyelids alone to protect her, the high frequency screech was deafening. She shot blindly, moving backwards as fast as she could, hoping not to stumble, blinking away the blindness.

Shapes began to form and the ringing in her ears subsided. She saw an officer step out of the breach, a handgun held out in front of him. She saw him pull the trigger, and again, there was silence, or was she just deafened by the sensorupt? She tripped and fell over something lying behind her.

It was Cadet Boyd, his faceplate had been open because of the same visor malfunction that had blacked out Pirie's helmet, what was left inside Boyd's helmet did not resemble a face.

She rolled away from him and heard an explosive round detonate where she had just fallen. The officer was lining up another shot, flanked on either side by PPB commandos, no longer carrying guns, but wearing arm-mounted magnetic flechette launchers.

Scrambling to her feet, spraying gunfire behind her, she began running for the protection of the doorway which was tantalisingly close. She ducked from side to side to evade the officer's pistol and the flechettes — terrifyingly long spikes of hardened steel, some of which were burying themselves in the walls alongside her.

Remembering what Wrath had mentioned on his first day aboard, about the craft being equipped with explosion suppressors, she understood why the commandos' guns hadn't worked. The officer's side-arm must have been a compressed air-pistol, and the flechette launchers would have a limited range too.

Pirie needed to tell Qiang as soon as she was clear, this invading force hadn't expected to find their guns ineffective, and the weapons they had that actually worked were very limited. They could be beaten.

Diving through the doorway Pirie slapped her hand on the closure panel. Leaning over to the closing gap, she wanted to get off a few more shots, to take down as many of the boarders as she could. She felt her head snap back, hitting the wall behind her, she tried to pull it away, but she couldn't move.

Qiang tried to ignore the expectant glances of the command crew. The bridge was still effectively shut down so there was nothing they could do but wait. They had armed themselves, as they were the last line of defence. What they, a bunch of cadets, could do against a PPB incursion squad was questionable, but they would do it anyway.

'BIO-FEEDBACK MONITORING SYSTEMS RESTORED.'

Qiang turned to her console to find out the worst, setting the system to rank crew who were dead or injured. She wanted numbers, not names. She couldn't deal with names right now.

It showed seventeen dead. The next page showed eleven injured. Then the number switched to ten. She frowned at the screen, and switched back to the list of the dead, which now numbered eighteen. At the sight of the name at the top of the list she let out a cry.

'No!'

She summoned all the strength she had to choke down tears that were trying to fight their way out of her, involuntary sobs trying to force their way out of her throat. She touched the name of Grace Pirie on the screen and trembled, squeezing her eyes closed as hard as she could, and whispering, 'Sleep tight, Princess.'

Ginzu spoke first, 'Are you alright, Commander?'

Hearing the title said out loud snapped closed the door on her devastation.

'Commander?'

Reminding her that she had to lead, she had to set this aside. Even then, her voice was close to breaking as she told them. 'They're aboard, and they're killing.' She shut down the bio-feedback display. 'We need to be ready. They'll be coming for us.'

twenty two

The commandos were hunched forward in their seats, mostly silent, though Wrath was being treated to a whispering, one-sided reminiscence about Pandale from Salo Krupps. Wrath could almost feel the air vibrating with the intensity of the anticipation filling the cramped confines of the breach boat.

Commander Guthrie turned away from the comms handset and looked at them, concern etching a crease in his brow. 'Alpha RAT are aboard, but they're reporting that the Black Wreath seems to have ship-wide explosion suppressors. Their rifles don't work, and ours won't either. Same goes for grenades. They've sustained minor losses and they'll be making slower progress than anticipated.

'You'll have to rely on your flechette launchers and shok-knux.' He took out his compressed-air pistol and examined the magazine, clicking it back into place, and slipping it back into his holster. 'This is going to be a dirtier fight than we anticipated.'

'Good!' said more than one of the commandos. Guthrie didn't look so keen, but faked a smile anyway.

'As soon as we're in, the breach boat is going to head back to the Sabina and bring back our own incursion squads for reinforcements with as many non-chemically propelled weapons as they can muster. Pilot says we are past the T-Point and at full neg-delta. We'll be connecting up to the Savatara's breach boat in three minutes. Sling your guns on anyway, in case we can find a way to knock out their suppressors.'

Salo Krupps turned to Wrath, 'Waste of your talents us not being able to use our rifles, eh? You any good with the flechettes?'

'I guess we'll find out!'

Krupps laughed and gave him a smile that seemed out of place with what Wrath had always thought of him. Behind that bluff and aggressive front there was something warmer, but most people probably never found it. Against all his instincts, Wrath found he couldn't help but return the smile, then flinched sharply as a fine mist of blood sprayed the inside of Krupps' visor. Krupps slumped over, as did several other commandos.

Sensing something was wrong, Commander Guthrie turned around, but the only thing he saw was a fist that landed square in his face, with the crackling sound of electrified shok-knux greeting the impact.

Another trooper dragged the pilot out of his seat, throwing him to the ground and dealing a swift and powerful blow, breaking his neck. The trooper took over his place in the pilot's seat.

Wrath felt a hand on his shoulder as Major Jaglan stood up behind him, 'Sorry about your buddy there, Wrath. Charming guy.'

Wrath looked down at the stream of blood trickling out of Krupps' helmet.

'What happened?'

Jaglan pointed at what looked like a small sticking plaster on the back of the helmet. 'Bang-patch. It's a stick-on, self firing bullet. Slap one of those on, you can trigger it whenever you want.' Jaglan held up a thumb trigger for Wrath to see. 'We've been slapping them on these guys for the last hour or so. One for each of our friends in white.'

Wrath nodded, 'I guess it's faster than fighting.'

Jaglan grabbed up his rifle and twisted the muzzle, pulling away the barrel. The gun split in half, revealing it was hollow inside. Within, packed in foam, was a smaller gun. Clearly a laser-fired weapon, it was bright blue, and unlike the graceless bulk of the commando's assault rifles, it had a smooth, flowing, sculpted look. It slotted into Jaglan's grip like it was made just for him, which it was.

'Crack 'em open.'

The rest of the squad split open their rifles, each with its own blue surprise inside. Wrath found himself copying them, he had switched his mind to autopilot.

Inside his own rifle was a blue gun, similar to the others, though not sculpted or shaped to his hands, it fit his grip well enough. Measuring its heft, he found it to be light and perfectly balanced.

He checked the magazine, 500 pellet-rounds, high-explosive only. These guns weren't for pacification or suppression.

'Arrival time?'

'30 seconds, Major,' the Pilot answered.

Jaglan nodded, raising his weapon in front of him and aiming at the docking bay door. 'Red Task. My callsign is set to Purge but callsigns are on hold. Call out tags only, leave the tariff attributions to the gun-cams. Weapon up.'

The squad arranged themselves around the doorway, by turns dropping to their bellies, their knees, crouching and standing - anyone on the other side of the door when it opened would see nothing but a wall of gun muzzles.

Jaglan turned an eye to Wrath, then to his gun, which was set perfectly at 46 degrees from horizontal. Putting his fingers beneath the gun muzzle, Jaglan pushed the barrel up flat and level, 'You're not in the Gun-Grid arena now, cadet. Weapon up.'

'This is a weird time to get deja vu, but I'm getting deja vu.'

The soft thunk of the docking clamps slotting in to place was followed by the soft hiss of air-pressure equalising.

One of the few people who'd been called by their name since he'd tagged onto Jaglan's squad was a toweringly tall woman. Sergeant Saskia, callsign "Sass," stood next to the airlock door, tapping keys on the control panel and examining the readout.

'No life signs aboard the Savatara's breach-boat, they didn't leave anyone to welcome us. They've probably thrown everyone forward to try to take the command deck.'

Jaglan nodded, 'Good,' he turned again to Wrath. 'We need to know how far they've got and where they are. I'd imagine your commander would welcome a friendly voice, chime in and let them know help is here.'

Wrath fumbled his watch out from under his armoured gauntlet and shook it to activate voice control. 'Emergency call to Command channel.'

The blunt reply was immediate, "NO SIGNAL"

Wrath frowned and turned a puzzled look to the Major.

'Comms may still be knocked out from the PPB weapon, or it could be local interference from radiation. We'll try again once we've got aboard.' Jaglan turned again to the sergeant by the control panel, 'Sass, open the doors.'

Sgt. Saskia keyed in the door code. On the other side, the Savatara's breach-boat looked much the same as the Sonya's, even down to a stack of dead PPB commandos.

Jaglan nodded appreciatively, 'Looks like your crew-mates scored some tags, Wrath! Probably nailed these guys before they realised their guns wouldn't work. How many do you count, Sass?'

She counted up the bodies, 'Nine tags. That'll lower the workload some.'

'It'll lower our tariff, too. Still, we shouldn't be short of tags today. Check the breach-way.'

'Breach-way is clear. They didn't leave anyone behind to guard the breach-boat. I wouldn't hang around either, there's quite high levels of radiation out there.'

'Makes sense, they don't plan on leaving. They're down nine commandos, with sub-optimal weaponry, they'll want to go for the command deck in full force. Someone grab Commander Guthrie's wrist-comm, I think Alpha RAT should know their reinforcements have arrived, I'm sure they'll be happy to tell us where we can find them.'

Moving away from the breach to try to get a communications signal, Wrath's early elation at seeing the stack of dead commandos vanished as they reached a corpse in a black jumpsuit lying on the ground.

'They got one of your guys, Wrath. Know him?'

Wrath saw the name tag and nodded, 'Cadet Boyd. He was...' some of Jaglan's squad moved the body gently out of the way. 'He was a nice quiet kid. Good kid. Cadet Boyd. I never knew his first name.'

'Sorry Wrath. There will be more.'

They started to move further down the corridor when Wrath heard a voice coming from his watch.

'Wrath? How are you here?'

The voice was Qiang's. 'Diana! No time to explain, you have a PPB Rapid Attack Team headed for the command deck, can you tell us their location?'

'Internal monitors are still stuck in self-repair, until then we're effectively blind.'

'Okay. I'm with a squad from Black Leopard, we'll get to you as soon as we can.' Wrath paused before sharing the news, 'We just found Cadet Boyd. He's dead, but it looks like he killed a few of them, so there's that.'

'I know. Bio-monitors came back on quite quickly. That's how I knew you'd got aboard. Lots of people are dead, Malcolm.' she took a moment to compose herself, *'Grace is dead, Malcolm. She's probably close by. Find her, please.'*

Wrath felt as if he'd been hollowed out, like a chasm had opened up where his guts used to be. He hadn't felt this way since he'd seen streaks of gleaming debris burning through the daylight sky and falling into the ocean on Pandale. The day he'd believed Yolande had died.

He'd been wrong that day, Yolande had been fine, and he found himself hoping this was wrong too, and that Pirie was okay.

The sergeant, scouting ahead, called back to them, 'Purge, got another dead cadet here.'

Wrath looked up and saw her, sat on the ground, an empty look of wonder in her eyes, her head pinned to the wall. She was not okay.

'We've got her, Diana. She's here. We'll...' his voice was almost a whisper as he looked at the sergeant, 'can you get her down from there, please?'

They started to pull her gently away from the wall. 'We're getting her down, Diana. She was just sitting there, nice and quiet. By the looks of it she tagged some of them too, I'm sure of it.'

'Thank you.'

Jaglan signalled for Wrath to end the call.

'I've got to go. We're coming, but they'll be coming too. Cut them down.'

'We will. We'll cut them to shreds.'

Jaglan nodded with approval, 'She sounds up to the job. I'll need my own link to your commander, set it up. I have another call to make first. Who's got Guthrie's communicator?'

One of the troopers handed it over. Jaglan fiddled with the communicator's controls and barked into it, 'This is Beta RAT. Alpha RAT respond!'

'This is Lieutenant Sullivan, Alpha RAT, why have you broken comm's silence?'

'Here's a better question, why did you leave the breach-boat unprotected? There were a bunch of cadets waiting for us as soon as we cracked the doors open! Our Commanding Officer is dead, and our pilot is dead!'

'If you've come through the breach-boat you've seen our casualties. We've had to throw everyone forward before their internal sensors are back online. Stop yacking and get to the power decks before they realise what's going on and try to scuttle!'

'The power decks are clear, after they sent out that ambush squad they only had five cadets left there. We ventilated them. Nobody is scuttling this bird.'

'Good. Now, can you find a way to turn off these explosion suppressors? It's going to be real tough going without rifles and grenades. These cadets have a significant range advantage, so we daren't move quickly.'

'Negative, the guy in charge down here said the suppressors can only be over-ridden from the command deck. He watched us kill his friends one by one then we cut a few body parts off him but his story stayed the same, so I believe it. If you can hold back until we can reach you then we'll attack them from all sides.'

'We can't hold off, we still have the element of surprise, we need to press every advantage we have.'

'The power decks are clear, we have no work to do here. Having us up there with you would double your numbers, what other advantage do you need? We're commandos. The men with you are commandos. We're fighting *cadets!* We'll fight and we'll win.'

Sullivan gave himself time to think before giving his doubtful sounding reply, *'Alright. The command deck is behind the for'ard stairwell on Deck 9. We've dropped to Deck 7 so we can undercut the command deck and come up from the other side. Head up to deck eleven and drop down using the central stairs, then we can hit them from above, below, in front and behind. Wait for our signal before commencing assault.'*

'We're on our way.' Jaglan tucked the communicator in a belt pouch and smiled, 'Internal sensors, who needs them? Wrath, what was your commander's name, Chan?'

'Qiang, Diana Qiang.'

Jaglan opened his own channel to the command deck, 'Commander Qiang, this is Purge, you don't know who I am, so I'm pulsing my authorisation through to you now. Got it?'

'I have it. I'm glad you're here.'

'I'm assuming control of your anti-incursion squad. Tell them to set up in the for'ard stairwell on Deck 8. The PPB incursion squad, Alpha RAT, will be entering from deck 7. Your team is to use fire & fall back measures to draw them into the stairwell. They are to fall back slowly but steadily heading up to Deck 9, then, when I give the command, they must exit and lock the doors. We'll move in behind them and we'll have ourselves a RAT trap. Understood?'

'Confirmed. I'll patch you in to their comms circuit so you can communicate directly.'

'Good. I need to be able to issue direct commands to your computer system. Are you able to link me up?'

There was a brief pause, *'It's done.'*

'You've done well so far, Commander. Just keep them out of there, we'll take care of the rest.' Jaglan waved his men forward.

'Weapons to silent. Ahead, pace 150.'

Wrath turned a last look to Grace Pirie's body before tagging on the back of the squad. In the red glow of the emergency lighting he could almost believe she was asleep.

He should be angry. He wanted to be angry, but the pain would not convert. It could have been him lying there, with Salo Krupps looking down at him. What would he have said to that?

"Hey! I knew this kid! My sista used to go with his brudda! Good job they split up, this woulda made Crismuss dinner pretty awkward, eh? HA!"

As he ran to keep up he thought of Salo Krupps back aboard the breach boat, crumpled on the floor with blood dripping out from under his visor. Salo didn't even know he'd been killed. Who was going to be angry about that? Krupps' father? There was a man who was never short of anger.

What about his sister? She'd eaten at Wrath's home, kissed Wrath's brother, and probably more. No! Wait. *Not* Wrath's brother, *Rothgill's* brother. Everything was becoming abstract in his mind. Was he Rothgill, or was he Wrath?

He was finding more than he expected to unpack from that question. The bomb that had brought him here, that was launched by the PPB, by the Savatara. He'd come here because he believed Yolande had been killed by that bomb, killed by pirates.

Had he joined up to kill pirates? Probably. But the bomb was fired by the Savatara, and now the Savatara was here, and had *really* killed people he cared about.

When he'd chosen this name for himself, *"Wrath,"* had he really been as flippant about is as he acted? So random? The word had jumped out at him and it had fit exactly what he'd been trying to suppress. Not sadness, but fury and vengefulness. On a level he hadn't confronted before, his reason for joining hadn't been about wanting a change of life, his motivation *was* wrath.

Somewhere aboard was the person who had killed Pirie. Wrath would likely never know which of the commandos had done it, but Pirie surely *deserved* vengeance. Someone should visit their wrath upon these thugs who'd been sent to kill a bunch of green cadets. That was only right.

Wrath couldn't locate anger, but for the wrathful, anger was a distraction.

The wrathful should be cold, intent, and ruthless. These things he could feel. These things, he was feeling.

Suddenly the weight and bulk of the PPB armour felt as nothing, his strides were as fluid and natural as ever they had ever been in the Gun-Grid arena. Mental and physical clarity unlike any he'd ever felt before, the visitation of pure wrath.

They were closing on the last corridor break before the for'ard stairwell, and he moved his hand to the selector panel on his gun, flipping the aural-report switch to the intimidate position. His forearms, his fingers, his mind, buzzing again with a fiery electric energy.

Jaglan pulled Guthrie's communicator from his belt pouch and raised it to his lips. 'Sullivan, this is Beta RAT, we are in position, will commence attack on your mark.'

'Confirmed. Alpha RAT is go. Commence attack now.'

'Confirmed.' He threw the communicator away and raised his own wrist-comm. 'Black Wreath Anti-incursion team, hostiles in motion, for'ard stairwell, engage on sight. Give ground slowly, don't let them sense a trap.'

He turned to his squad, 'Pace 100, light-foot, weapon up. Free-fire at my signal. Don't call tags. They don't know we're here, so cut them down quiet.'

The squad moved stealthily around the corridor break, the corridor widening ahead of them. In the distance, the commandos were making their way into the stairwell. Inside, the sound of gunfire and shouting greeted them.

Jaglan led them forwards, his left arm in the air and his right arm holding his rifle ahead of him. The squad were spreading out, pacing silently closer to the commandos, waiting to open fire as soon as the Major's arm dropped.

Wrath walked slightly behind, his mind feeling like a cold ball of fire, a sense of deep purpose energising his body.

Alpha RAT still hadn't noticed them, but they were close now. Jaglan's arm dropped and a silent storm of explosive pellets began to fly, punching through their armour, and detonating inside their flesh.

Wrath suddenly flinched at the sight, remembering the gel-dummies on the firing range, thought of the same thing happening to human bodies. Then he remembered Pirie, and the cold ball of fire consumed all other thoughts.

Wrath had yet to fire a shot, his thumb rested on the report switch, teasing it towards the silent position, and then the commandos finally realised they were being gunned down from behind, and the need for quiet was over.

Wrath forced his way through Jaglan's squad, weapon up.

Even with the ear-protection in the helmet, the clattering from the gun muzzle was cacophonous, designed to terrify anyone in front of it. Wrath strode towards the commandos, blasting out three shots a-piece to every face that turned his way.

'Cadet!' a voice from behind him shouted, the voice was Jaglan's, 'WRATH!'

"Yes," he thought, *"Wrath."*

'Spreff it!' Jaglan shouted over the sound of gunfire, 'Intimidate! Pace 120!'

If the noise had been loud before, the muzzle report of Jaglan's entire squad was a punishing aural assault. Wrath strode on, watching the commandos fall faster than they could emerge from the stairwell.

Out-gunned if not outnumbered, the commandos slammed the stairwell doors shut, heedless of the dead commandos being crushed as they closed.

Jaglan came rushing past Wrath, shouting into his wrist-comm, 'Anti-incursion team! Clear the stairwell and shut the doors! Computer, initiating anti-incursion protocol special measures, prepare gravity systems for G.A.P. in the for'ard stairwell, plus-ten, minus-ten, 30 second burst.'

Klaxons filled the air with a menacing wail.

'Anti-incursion squad, are you clear?'

'We're clear, doors sealed, but I don't think it'll hold them for long.'

'It won't need too, stand well clear of the doors. Computer! Special measures! GAP, GAP, GAP!'

Wrath suddenly felt strange, like the floor was flexing, and that he was getting lighter, then heavier, then lighter, and heavier again. From inside the stairwell came screams, smashing and banging, and a curious secondary noise, a soft wave, *vwoop, vwoop, vwoop, vwoop.*

The screaming soon stopped, but the vwooping sound continued, as did the thumps and bangs. Then there was silence, and a final crash, sounding like heavy objects dropping into a swamp.

Jaglan let out a long breath of relief. 'Anti-incursion squad, did any get out?'

'No, Sir.'

'I'm not "Sir", cadet, I'm Staff Major Jaglan. Take your squad and sweep the area. The commandos may have split up, so there could still be more of them somewhere. Check deck 11, but, I'd find another stairway if I were you, this one will need cleaning up.

The doors opened and a stream of blood ran out across the floor. Jaglan peered inside, 'You know, I've always wanted to see how that would work out in practice, but I never really thought about the mess.'

Wrath looked at the barely recognisable human debris within; a grotesque soup of armour, blood, guns, and gristle.

'What the spreff happened in there?'

Jaglan looked at him wide eyed, 'Wrath! Spreff it!' He shook his head and laughed, 'Frank Bull wasn't wrong about you, was he? I think you got five or six clear tags there, some assists, too,' he slapped him on the shoulder, 'I mean, tactically it was terrible, but I enjoyed watching it all the same. You've been shot, by the way.'

'What?'

Wrath looked down and saw two flechette spikes sticking out of his armour, a thin trickle of blood tracing red lines down the gleaming white belly plate.

'It won't be deep, most of the flechette is sticking out. Someone fix him up, eh?'

One of the troopers started to work at Wrath's belly. Whether through adrenaline, or the medical systems built into his jumpsuit supplying painkillers, he couldn't feel anything.

'Major, what happened in there?'

'Gravitic Anti-incursion Protocol.'

'Okay.' Wrath said, not disguising the fact this left him none the wiser. 'That's, what?'

'Imagine what would happen to you if I turned the gravity in here to negative ten.'

Wrath thought about it, 'I'd hit the ceiling, very, very hard.'

'And what if I then switched the gravity to positive ten?'

'I suppose I'd hit the floor, twice as hard?'

'And imagine if I did that every second for 30 seconds?'

Wrath looked at the grim viscera inside the stairwell and thought about what those 30 seconds must have been like for the commandos inside, 'People soup?'

'Warm and chunky. The bad news is, we should get to the command deck, and I'm not trekking back to the central stairwell, so we're going to get dirty boots.' Jaglan looked at the trooper spraying coagulant gel onto Wrath's wounds, 'Is he fixed up?'

'Almost as good as new.'

'Okay, let's meet your Commander Qiang, she sounds like my kind of girl,' he looked around him, 'Anybody got any idea where that Lieutenant Sullivan might be in this mess?'

Sass spoke up, toeing the body pile with her boot tip, 'There's a guy in an officer's uniform under some of these guys. I guess he was leading from the rear too. The cadet tagged him before he could make it inside the stairwell.'

Jaglan looked to Wrath, 'Junior officer! Good tariff boost. Good job he didn't get a chance to get into the stairwell, too, we need his communicator, and I didn't relish fishing through guns and gizzards to find it.

The stench in the stairwell was noxious, the steaming viscera of burst bodies was bad enough, without having to tramp through it. Wrath wanted to be out of this PPB armour, and back in black, so he couldn't see the splashes of blood speckling the bright white as it sprayed out from under the boots of the men walking ahead of him.

A new thought occurred to him, one he was surprised hadn't come immediately. 'Did we lose anybody?'

The trooper next to him shook his head dismissively. 'This is Jaglan's squad. He's never lost anybody. Nobody dares die on his team. He'd kill 'em if they did.'

Even though this was among the stupidest things Wrath had heard in quite some time, it was curiously reassuring, even if he had personally taken two flechette blades to the stomach, he only had himself to blame for that.

'Wrath!'

Wrath pushed through the men to get to Jaglan's side, 'Yes, Major?'

'Call your commander and ask her to open the door, and offer our apologies for breaching the dress code, if you would.'

'Qiang, it's Wrath. We're on Deck 9, but we're in PPB armour, so if you could open the doors and not shoot us, that would be great. You might want tell the anti-incursion squad to hold their noses too.'

'It's okay Wrath,' The doors slid open and Qiang stood before them, rifle in hand and blood on her face, a measured smile that spoke of gladness tempered by pain, 'I've got used to the way you smell.'

Jaglan stepped forward and shook her hand, 'not at your post,

Commander?'

'No, Major. It turns out my desire for command wasn't as strong as my desire to shoot as many of these spreffers as I could get in front of my gun, so I left cadet Ginzu in charge in the command deck. It's not like anything on this bird is working right now, I might as well have been left in charge of a rock.'

'I knew I was going like you, Qiang. Now we need to get your internal monitors working so we can see if we got all of the commandos.'

'We have, and we did. They're all dead. I almost don't dare believe it's over.'

Jaglan shook his head, 'It isn't over, Commander. The Savatara and the Sonya are still out there, and we have no idea how many of those missiles they might have left. If they suspect the incursion has failed they'll throw everything they've got at us, and we've got no way to escape, or defend ourselves.'

'So what do we do?'

'We call in reinforcements.'

'Does Black Fleet have any craft close enough to help?'

'We won't be calling in Black Fleet,' he held up Sullivan's communicator, 'we're calling in reinforcements from the Savatara and the Sonya.'

twenty three

Commander Rawlins looked at her captain, unable to keep the hope from her eyes. She wanted to lead the back-up team, and to be the one to capture Black Wreath.

The accent on the other end of the radio was thick, but the images were clear enough, as was the clatter of sporadic gunfire.

'Corporal Krupps, I need you to confirm that the explosion suppressors are shut down before I commit to sending that much weaponry and that many of my crew to help you.'

Wrath made a dramatic show of flinching at the sound of nearby gunfire, before shouting over his shoulder in as close an approximation of Salo Krupps' voice as he could muster, *'Oi! One of you spreffers chuck a grenade, eh?'*

An impressive blast soon followed, *'The field's off, but it's put a permanent spreff-up on our guns, they're still jammed up. Just send us your best blokes and a bunch of guns and grenades, eh?'*

'How many of you are left, Corporal?'

'Twenty five, Sullivan's dead, Guthrie's dead, both pilots are dead too so the shuttles are going to come back on auto. Makes more room for your blokes though, right? We need all we can get. They snuck a bunch of special forces goons from Black Leopard on here at beacon 505, sneaky spreffers crept up behind us and made mincemeat of us. But we've got 'em bottled up now, just need some extra hardware and some trigger-tuggers to go with it. Good blokes mind! If you send chumps they won't last a minute.'

'Alright, you'll have what you need.'

'Have 'em all in the docking bay ready so we can get 'em straight here, we can't be mucking about. The Sonya's still over a hundred chiffing klicks away, so they'll take ages to get here.'

'You would be well advised to watch your familiarity and your language when addressing a bridge officer, corporal.'

'Sorry, Cap. Bit fraught here, seen a lot of me bruddas turned to mush, no excuse though, eh?'

'Just send the breach-boats back, we'll send everybody and every weapon we can spare. Jowett out.'

Captain Jowett could no longer ignore the expectant look on Rawlins' face. 'Yes, Commander Rawlins, you can lead the team, but bring as many of our crew back alive as you can. We were already running with an absolute skeleton crew, this unwelcome extra jaunt is going to leave us critically under-manned.'

Rawlins smile was as much one of gratitude as victory, 'Thank you, Captain. I know how important this is. I... this means so much to...'

'Just go. The secondary incursion team will be waiting for you.'

Jowett watched her leave the bridge, wondering if her capacity to kill matched her eagerness to please. It had better.

Outside the front window the lifeless prize of Black Wreath hung motionless, dark, tantalisingly helpless on the outside, still dangerously hostile within. This prize was not easily won, and losing the best part of two squads of PPB commandos would make it a more sour victory for the admiralty who held Captain Jowett's fate in their hands. Commander Rawlins had to succeed. Everything depended on it now.

Wrath, along with the rest of Jaglan's squad had changed out of the bulky PPB commando gear and into Black Fleet incursion armour. He was feeling as lithe and light as a gazelle as he ran behind the big munitions sled being pushed at full speed out of the armoury. Jaglan ran alongside.

'I think your buddy Krupps would have enjoyed your impression of him, Wrath.'

'If you hadn't sprayed his brains all over the inside of his helmet, you mean?'

'Don't downplay that, Wrath, managing to hit a brain that small was a supreme piece of marksmanship on my part.'

They approached the breaching point and after some awkward shuffling managed to get the munitions sled inside the Savatara's breach-boat and aligned with the connecting docking bay door of the boat from the Sonya.

Wrath watched as they removed the protective shroud. Inside was a killstick missile. The sled was wheeled carefully inside the Sonya's breach-boat, barely clearing the docking bay doors.

'Spin it around towards the door and activate the gravity clamps. Then rig up the ignition sequence to the door controls.'

Wrath began to appreciate what would be waiting for the Sonya's secondary incursion team when their docking bay doors opened. A single killstick could turn the most heavily armoured pirate craft into scrap metal, and that was hitting them from the outside, this was going to be fired straight through the open docking bay doors and straight into the heart of the Sonya.

'You only brought one of these things, Major. What's going to be waiting inside this breach-boat for the crew of the Savatara?'

'Something much worse, cadet.' Jaglan smiled a dirty little smile, 'Us.'

Another sled was wheeled in, this one was smaller. Jaglan's team began to unfasten the crate it was carrying.

'Major, we've set the Sonya's breach-boat to return home on automatic. She's all set.'

'Send her on her way, if we time it right we should be docking with the Savatara just before the Sonya receives her payload.'

Wrath didn't recognise the... mechanism inside the crate. A sturdy trolley with a large round bar mounted on it. The bar was around 6 feet long, covered along its length with small pipes, maybe for delivering stun gas, or a maybe it was a heavy duty sensorupt rig.

Sergeant Saskia worked the control panel and the bar started rotating, making a harsh clattering noise as it turned. It came to rest vertically and the clattering ceased.

'The phalanx cannon is working fine, Major.'

'Okay, Sass, set it up.'

The device was hoisted up and the trolley wheels set in tracks they'd laid down in line with the docking bay doors. Either side of the bar they attached half-round plates of armour, each piece just a little larger than each of the docking bay doors.

The true purpose of the machine began to dawn on Wrath as soon as they started loading ammunition magazines into the back of it. Lots of magazines. They weren't gas-pipes running along the length of the bar, they were gun muzzles.

Jaglan was right, what was waiting for the team in the docking bay of the Savatara was even worse than a killstick missile.

Up until now, Wrath had no idea how thirty people were supposed to seize control of a Pallas-class PPB frigate, but now he understood the simple genius of Jaglan's plan. Captain Jowett was sending the very best fighters aboard her ship to wait in a small room, and as soon as the breach-boat's doors opened, this horrific machine would be wheeled in to greet them.

'Here,' Jaglan handed Wrath a strange looking black vest and a helmet ringed with a wraparound glass hoop. 'Put those on, cadet.'

Slinging on the vest, he recognised the layout of the controls of the small panel mounted on the vest's front. It was a much smaller version of the "Peggy" Personal Gravity Environment pack he'd used on his first night fixing the hull of the Black Wreath.

It made perfect sense. If the PPB used Gravitic Anti-incursion Protocols too, the P.G.E. would prevent Jaglan's squad from meeting the sort of messy fate that had ended the lives of the PPB commandos in the stairwell.

Slipping on the helmet, he was suddenly treated to a very disconcerting new point of view.

'Take your time with your first steps, cadet. Panagoggles take a little getting used to.'

That was an understatement, a full 360 degree field of view was downright weird. Tentative forward steps made things directly ahead move closer while things at either side moved further away, and even the slightest turn of his head was disorienting almost to the point of nausea.

'How am I supposed to shoot straight with this thing on?' he steadied himself by leaning against the Major, 'I don't even know if I can stand up straight with this thing on.'

'Your gun camera is linked into your visor, give the trigger a half-squeeze and you'll get a targeting reticle in front of your right eye. It's probably best to walk with weapon up and just use that view until you get used to the peripheral movements.

'Will that stop me puking?'

'Who knows? Better to extrude food than get shot in the back, though.'

'A good point, well made, but what do I do about not getting shot at if I'm on all fours lining the inside of my helmet with my breakfast?'

'You'll think of something.' Jaglan called up the command deck, 'Commander Qiang, seal the bulkheads around the hull breach, we're pulling out and you don't want all your oxygen to come with us.'

"Bulkheads sealed. Good luck, Major. I wish I was going with you."

'Another time.'

Wrath felt his helmet seal into place and a vacuum warning flashed up as the breach-boat's penetrating beak began to close. As the breach-boat tore itself free of the hole she'd punched in the hull of Black Wreath the ruptured poly-alloy superstructure screeched in torment before they tore free and silence returned.

Getting a clear look at the damage, it was significantly worse than it had been after the Pandale attack. Wrath didn't feel the same way about it, either. This time he wasn't looking at a vessel in need of repair, this time it was his home.

Just a few hours ago, he'd never heard the name Captain Miranda Jowett, but now, he was coming to *her* home, and she was going to see how she liked it when unwelcome visitors show up at the door.

Jowett watched the progress of the breach-boats with growing unease, worst case scenarios playing out in her mind.

It was only a matter of time before Black Wreath's offensive capabilities were restored. The best of her crew were going to be loaded aboard a single vessel, and it would only take one of Black Wreath's Double-Eight guns to knock them out of the sky with ease, and if they could load up and fire a killstick, the damage they could do was incalculable. Even a wounded Black fleet dreadnought was a mighty opponent. Learning to kill one had been hard enough, capturing one made that task look easy. Time was running out.

She lifted the comms handset, 'Weapons deck, load up our last missile and warm up the hyper-optic launch system. Target the hull breach in the flank of the Black Wreath. If I give the order, I need you to respond immediately and launch the weapon. In fact — belay that, transfer weapon control to me here on the bridge.'

'Aye Captain. The launch mechanism won't be up to power for at least seven minutes, after that, you can launch any time.'

Jowett flipped the comms channel, 'Power deck, this is the Captain. I know the hyper-optic missile launcher is a huge drain, but scavenge power from any and every system you can, I want you to prep for both ramming speed, and scuttling procedures.'

'Ramming speed, AND scuttling procedures, Captain?'

'I haven't decided which I might need. Hopefully neither, but prepare for both.'

'Aye aye, Captain. It can't be done in a hurry, but it'll be done.'

A flashing alert caught her eye, she glared with a quiet fury at the words on the screen.

LIFEPOD LAUNCH DETECTED

She'd vetted this crew over and over, shedding all but the most trusted; none of them had the makings of deserters. Checking the telemetrics for the crew, they were showing as still all being aboard the Savatara. Of course, there were more than just the crew here, the pirate armourers she had *acquired* from Woolfe Weapon Works were still captive. Except, it seemed they weren't. She checked the camera feed from the holding cells. Empty.

Had Rawlins set her lover free? Or had Anga-Kaska Woolfe put his genius to work on escaping all on his own? He was more than capable. The lifepod wasn't responding to overrides or destruct codes. He was a smart one, and she was in half a mind to let him go, but there was time enough to decide that. The pod would be easy to catch, and there were more pressing issues.

The breach-boats were about to dock, and Jowett was still troubled about the best fighters of both crews being left so vulnerable to attack on the return trip to Black Wreath.

Never mind the danger of being in the breach-boats, those fighters were *already* all in one place and vulnerable, all of them were in the docking bays, waiting patiently for two craft to arrive from a hostile vessel. Jowett was gripped by a sudden, deeper dread.

Fierce illumination flooded the bridge as outside the window, a dazzling flare of light consumed the breach-boat attached to the Sonya.

Jowett looked on in horror, the hull of the Sonya was rupturing from within, the entire vessel being consumed by a catastrophic blast.

Miranda Jowett's eyes darted to the screen showing the docking bay of the Savatara, of its doors opening and a large black tube appearing in the doorway.

'RAWLINS!' Jowett heard herself scream the name involuntarily.

The black tube erupted in fire and the screen went dead.

From inside the breach boat the phalanx cannon was ferociously loud, what it would sound like on the receiving end Wrath didn't dare imagine. The noise subsided and was replaced by the thin clacking sound of the firing mechanisms drawing on empty magazines.

Checking the scope, Jaglan was able to look inside the docking bay. 'Messy day today, PPB puddles to splash in everywhere we go.'

The savage weapon was pulled out of the way and once again

Wrath found himself stepping into a grim, crimson pond of human chunks. It was only a few hours since he'd first heard the term "Red Task", he'd had no idea just how literal it would turn out to be. He reminded himself again that everyone who had been in this room had been on their way to kill him and his friends, rapidly chasing away any doubts that might have crept into his mind about this ruthless slaughter.

Jaglan cautiously surveyed the room, checking no one had managed to dive for a safe little hidey-hole or some impromptu cover. He nodded, satisfied. 'Ignore the PPB purée, there's still going to be plenty of living people aboard this white slug, and by now they'll know something is very wrong. Our first job is to locate their mystery weapon and secure it, then lock-down the power deck. Only once we've done that can we think about taking the bridge.

'Sass, launch the scout drones. Squad, set your P.G.E.'s to adaptive gravity-neutral. Weapon up. Free fire. Shoot on sight. Call your tags. Pace 150. Go.'

The interior doors of the docking bay slid open and a dozen scout drones flew through, splitting up and heading off in different directions, dropping scores of micro-drones in their wakes. Jaglan was about to sprint after them when he stopped in his tracks, holding up his hand to halt the squad.

'Hold up! What the spreff?'

The inside of the Savatara couldn't be more different from what they'd seen aboard the Sonya. She looked like she'd been stripped out by pirates. Devoid of cladding, with missing walls, mesh flooring, bare metal, exposed trunking and ducts.

'Looks like they've done a little remodelling.' Sass said.

'They've converted to a flat deck layout, they must have completely stripped the interior and started from scratch. No wonder they wouldn't take on prisoners! They couldn't let anybody see this.'

'But why?'

Jaglan pointed ahead to the central elevator tubes. There were no doors, and the tubes had been heavily reinforced, and augmented with substantial power coils.

'It's just like the analysts guessed, they've ripped out the central elevators and used the shafts to build their hyper-optic cannon. That's how they're able to build up enough linear acceleration!'

'So if we follow the shaft all the way down it should lead us straight to their weapon?' Sass ventured.

'*And* straight to their power deck. Let's go.'

As they ran the address system resounded with the voice of Captain Miranda Jowett.

'*This is your captain. We have been boarded. Every available hand will arm themselves and head for the docking bay. The boarders will most likely be heading for the power decks and the bridge. Engage on sight, and punish them for violating our vessel. We must assume the attempt to capture Black Wreath has failed, therefore she will be destroyed. If these boarders are not eliminated our fate will be the same. I will not allow the capture of my ship. You are fighting for your lives, for your ship, and for me. Fight accordingly.*'

Jaglan called out, 'We've no time for room clearance! We have to stop that weapon launch and stop them scuttling the ship! Pace 180!'

The running pace moved up a notch, but the far end of the elevator shafts still seemed a long way off.

'Scout drones read armed PPB at the next junction on the left, blast them.'

All weapons were turned to the left but the running pace didn't slow. They broached the junction and a shower of explosive pellets felled a cluster of figures in white uniforms.

Various voices shouted out, 'Tag!'

'Drone counts 8 tags down, no partials, no survivors.'

Wrath could do nothing but run, he had no idea how they could sight on a target so fast, or even know that they'd scored a tag while sprinting past a junction at full speed.

For everything bad thought he'd ever had about "pray & spray" shooters in the Gun-Grid arena, any one of this squad would probably be championship material. His own obsession with trying to get the perfect shot didn't seem to be much use when the ammo was live and your opponents were actually trying to kill you.

'Drones have picked up tags behind, range point-two, sharp-shooters pick them off.'

Either side of Wrath two troopers stopped and dropped, something instinctive inside him had made the quick calculation that if anyone was a sharpshooter he was, as he found himself dropping to the floor with them. Sharp snaps signalled incoming rounds, the troopers lying prone next to him were shooting off rounds in return.

'Tag!'

'Tag!

'Tag two! Tag three!'

Wrath felt suddenly vulnerable between them, a magnet for a lucky shot that might miss the others. He found himself reaching for the control of his P.G.E. vest, and felt the gravity invert. He left the ground, spinning in the air, landing belly first on the ceiling.

He lined up his rifle and squeezed the trigger, the reticle appeared in his goggles and with the height advantage he could clearly see over a dozen PPB crew running towards them. He squeezed the trigger down hard and relaxed, squeezed and relaxed, squeezed and relaxed, hearing himself calling out, 'Tag, tag *two*, tag *three*, tag *four*, tag *five*, tag *six*, tag *seven*, tag *eight*.'

The rest of the pursuers dropped as the other shooters picked them off. Wrath released the trigger and rolled onto his back, looking down at the floor. His guts churned a little at the already weird 360 degree view from the panagoggles combined with the added disturbance of being upside down. He twisted the PGE control and fell to the floor.

'Ow!'

He hadn't allowed for the Savatara's own internal gravity pull, his landing was far less elegantly accomplished than it had been for the upward fall, 'I need to work on that.'

His fellow sharp shooters took a moment to look at him in amazement, then slapped him on the shoulder, 'Come on, cadet.'

They'd lost a lot of ground on Jaglan's squad, who were now getting close to the base of the weaponised elevator shaft and where they seemed to be engaged in a full-blown firefight.

The flash and wail of sensorupts accompanied by grenade blasts and gunfire grew louder as they got closer.

Wrath's helmet radio relayed the voice of Jaglan to him, 'Drones have picked another thirty troops behind us, tag them out!'

Wrath and the sharp shooters dropped again. These troops were closer, there was no time for gravity tricks or perfect shots. Whether he liked it or not, it was time for him to try his hand at pray & spray shooting.

A face loomed large in his targeting reticle, as did a gun barrel. As he fired off his shots he saw one strike the man in the neck just as the gun barrel flashed. On some level Wrath understood that being able to only see the muzzle itself meant the gun was pointed right at him, and that it had just been fired.

The realisation arrived slightly before the hot flash of pain. He may not have felt the flechettes in his belly when he'd been shot aboard Black Wreath, but he was feeling this. All his senses were swamped by the pain, too intense for him to even shout it out.

Through eyes streaming with tears, he could make out above him the blurry outline of a squad member holding something over him. The object flashed and he was aware of a powerful percussive force behind him, the forceful roar of an explosion overriding the intense ringing in his ears. Hands hauled him up and dragged him to the side. He could see a mouth, making words he couldn't hear. He tried to force his senses back into action.

'Cadet!' It was Sass, setting down a compact rocket launcher and looking intently and searchingly into his eyes.

'Yes?'

'Are you dead?'

He thought about it for a moment, 'I don't feel dead.'

'Okay, well let's go with that for now. Let me know if you change your mind.'

The same hands dragged him to his feet and through a doorway. Inside, Jaglan was waiting for them. He gave Wrath a slightly disapproving look.

'You got shot again? Is this a habit with you, Wrath?'

'Sorry. I promise I'll try to quit it.'

'Do. It's bad for morale.'

Wrath smarted as a medical scanner was pressed against his shoulder.

'It's not too bad, cadet,' the medic informed him, 'the round bounced off the side of your helmet and entered high in your neck, but there's no arterial penetration. It's embedded in your upper trapezius muscle. It's fragmented, but the puller will get all that out. Sit tight, this'll hurt some.'

Wrath looked around the chamber as the medic went about his business. A huge weapons-sled was slung high in the air, in a missile cradle suspended between four rails leading into the base of the widened elevator shaft. At the other end of the room a massive laser array and anti-light filter were aimed at a focusing plate mounted on the back of the launch-sled.

'Is this it? Is this their weapon.'

Jaglan nodded, 'It is, and it looks like it's the last one they have.'

The lights dimmed and a deep resonant hum filled the chamber.

'Get that missile out of there! They're powering up the anti-light cannon!'

Wrath could do nothing but sit and watch as the medic worked the shrapnel puller, flinching in pain as it darted in and out of his skin pulling bullet fragments from his neck, imagining the trajectory of this missile, set to perform its own invasive procedure, aimed squarely at the ragged hole punched in the side of Black Wreath.

Jaglan's squad were squirting explosive gel around the rails in front and behind of the missile cradle. Captain Jowett's disembodied voice filled the chamber.

"Prepare for ship-wide system shut-down. Anti-light cannon firing in 10 seconds."

Hurriedly the squad jammed remote detonators in the explosive gel and rushed for cover. The air began to rush out of the chamber as, far away at the front of the vessel, the barrel of this hyper-optic supergun was opened to vacuum.

"five, four, three, two..."

Jaglan's finger twitched, throwing the trigger, the blasting gel flaring into life and burning with a searing brightness.

"...one, firing."

The chamber was pitched into total darkness as the anti-light beam annihilated every photon in the room. The rush of air abated and dim illumination restored a faint light to the launch chamber. The cannon had fired.

Wrath looked at where the missile launch-sled had been slung, but it was no longer there, but nor were the rails that had held it. Looking down, laying on the floor was a smashed launch cradle and a very large, but completely intact missile.

Captain Jowett looked coldly on as the Black Wreath began a stately spin around her yaw axis. Where it should have delivered devastation, the long black finger of anti-light fog had simply given the crippled dreadnought a gentle nudge.

The slow spinning motion stopped abruptly. Jowett felt the cold chill running down her back intensify at the sight. The dreadnought was no longer crippled. Manoeuvring power was restored, and soon her weapons would be too.

'Power deck, this is the Captain. Please expedite scuttling procedures. As soon as you are able, destroy the ship.'

"Captain, the cannon requires a full shutdown to have enough power to fire, we've had to start scuttle procedures from scratch. It'll take at least a half hour to get the generator heads up to power for a blast big enough to destroy the ship, we may be able to muster enough power to gut her in twelve minutes. The Black Wreath's incursion squad is banging at the door, you need to send troops to hold them off, Captain!!'

Jowett closed her eyes and let out a long breath before answering. 'There are no more troops, chief. I sent everybody I had left, and now they're all dead. There's just me, and whoever is there with you.'

"We don't have any weapons in here, Captain. We will fight, though. We'll fight with our bare hands if we have to!"

She nodded, though there was nobody to see her do so, 'You will have to.'

She pulled out her air-pistol, carefully checking the magazine and the mechanism.

'Set for ramming speed, lock out the controls, then hold on for as long as you can. I'm coming.'

Jowett grabbed a portable communicator, straightened up her uniform and took a last look around her empty bridge.

What kind of a fight the engineers had put up, Wrath didn't know, but it hadn't lasted long, or made a lot of noise.

'Major, we have control of the power deck. Scuttle procedure has been aborted. They were building to ramming speed but we've cut power to the drives. Effectively, the ship is ours.'

'Not yet, Sass. Not until we have the bridge. Call back the scout drones. We'll leave a small squad here to defend the power deck and the weapon, the rest of us will go and relieve Captain Miranda Jowett of her command. We'll head out as soon as the drones get here.'

The medic finished dressing Wrath's wound, and Jaglan held out his hand to help him up. 'Come on cadet, you've come this far, you might as well take the ride all the way to the end.'

He was sore, but his legs worked fine, and his gun arm was still working. He took Jaglan's hand and got to his feet.

'That's what we like to see! You've been shot three times today but you keep on going. You're our kind of people, cadet! Although we tend not to get shot nearly as much as you do, but we can overlook that for now.

'Anyway, let's quit yacking, thanks to a certain arms reduction treaty it's been a very long time since Black Fleet got a new ship to play with, so let's keep hold of this one.'

The deathly quiet aboard the ship was disconcerting. Unlike the Black Wreath, the crude remodelling of the Savatara's interior had left no corridor breaks, just vastly long, echoing decks, over four hundred meters in length.

Wrath couldn't look away from the scattered bodies of the crew they had gunned down in their rush to secure the weapon.

'I told you we'd kill a lot of people together, Wrath.'

'Red Task, Major.'

'Red Task.'

He somehow felt remote from the whole process. Although some of these were certainly among those he himself had killed, there was a numbing sense of abstraction. 25 hours ago he'd never seen a dead body, now he'd seen more than he could count, although the level of physical disassembly of some of them had a lot to do with that.

Sergeant Saskia spoke up, 'Drones report a lone figure ahead, a woman in an officer's uniform by the look of it. Lightly armed.'

Jaglan squinted ahead, 'I have her. Range point-three-eight. Hold fire. Pace 120.'

The stride pattern stepped up as Captain Jowett's voice barked at them from the ship's address system.

"Black Fleet incursion squad. I'm coming to kill you. You don't get to have my ship!"

The sound of distant gunfire was followed by rounds ricocheting off the deck floor.

"Not my ship! You hear me?"

The gunfire drew closer and the shots were getting more accurate, they could almost hear her shouting without the aid of the ships speaker system now.

"NOT MY SHIP!"

Jaglan drew in his breath, 'Take her down, Sass.'

In a swift movement the corporal's rifle snapped up and snapped out three rounds. The shouting, and the shooting, stopped.

Jaglan's voice was a gruff whisper of satisfaction, 'Yes your ship.'

The squad didn't even slow as they marched past her body, but, catching sight of her Wrath *did* slow. He felt compelled to stop, wanting to see the face of this woman. Ultimately, it was her actions at Pandale that had changed his life. That bomb... no, that missile launched at Black Wreath, it had changed his name, his job, pretty much his whole life. He *should* see her.

She was beautiful.

He looked at her and thought of Pirie. They were actually quite alike. In ten years time Pirie might well have looked much like the woman who'd caused her death. Strange that their deaths should be so similar. Gunned down, then ignored. Just something to be swatted aside so a prize could be claimed.

Wrath knelt down beside her, staring at her.

'You brought me here,' he found himself saying, 'I had a boring little life on Pandale, and then you lit up the sky above my world, and it led me all the way out here.'

He almost wanted her to acknowledge it, this small consequence of her murderous plans.

'Just yesterday a friend of mine asked me if I was ready to be a killer, and I told her, no, I wasn't. She's dead now, because of you. And now I've killed a dozen or more people, because of you. I guess this is a weird thing to be doing, but I just thought I ought to tell you that, in case there's any part of you left that can understand.'

A sudden gurgling sound emerged from Captain Jowett's throat, quickly fading away into silence. He watched the pool of blood underneath her spreading slowly outwards, marvelling at how familiar such a sight seemed to him already.

A voice on his helmet radio broke his reverie, *"Wrath! Quit dawdling and get to the bridge, you'll want to see this."*

He closed Miranda Jowett's eyes and left her behind.

twenty four

From the bridge of the Savatara, Wrath had watched the arrival of the mobile dry-dock Black Chasm, watched her take the Black Wreath into her cavernous hold once again, back to the place where Wrath had first seen the vessel that he'd come to call home.

Now he was *back* home, in the briefing room of Black Wreath watching the battle-scarred hulk of the Savatara being pulled alongside as Black Chasm's clamshell was closing about them, hiding from view the devastated husk of Sonya, destroyed from the inside out by the killstick missile that had been waiting for Sonya's crew to open her doors and let in devastation.

Qiang stepped up onto the stage at the front of the briefing hall, turning off the giant screen, and turning to face her weary crewmates.

'This has been a hard 25 hours. We're in dry dock now, we're powered down and out of commission. I've turned the stupid computer off. Our injured have had their limbs set, wounds dressed and been transferred to the medical facilities aboard Black Chasm. There's no assignments, no shifts, no duties. We've done much more than just our duty today, so whatever you were scheduled to be doing, forget it.

'We rendezvous with the Black Leopard at around 0600 hours tomorrow, QM and the rest of the crew will be coming back aboard when she gets here. Until then, I think we should rest, eat, drink, dance, hump, or whatever else you feel like doing.

'I'm still commander for a few more hours, but these are the last orders you'll get from me. Let's put today out of our minds for a while. We're alive. We deserve to enjoy that to the full, for ourselves, and for our crew mates who didn't make it.'

There were some cheers and a small outbreak of applause that grew, then settled, then ebbed away. The few crew who were still aboard had no energy to make a real celebration of it. They filed out of the briefing hall quietly, leaving Qiang on the stage.

Wrath was waiting for her, 'Well said, Trooper.'

Qiang shrugged, 'I don't think it's going in the book of great military speeches, but I don't think anybody was looking for rousing words, just to hear it's okay to goof off for a few hours.'

'Well done anyway,' Wrath embraced her, and she took it as her due. 'The tactical advantages of goofing off are badly neglected in military history. I bet there's a whole chapter on it Sun Tzu's editor made him cut.'

'Yeah, "When your enemy is at bay, crank some tunes and crack open the booze." We kept that one to ourselves.'

'Is that a direct translation?'

'Verbatim. The man was a party animal.'

Qiang locked the briefing hall door and they began to walk back towards the cabins, both sorely in need of rest. Qiang looped her arm through his and let him do some of the work of holding her upright. 'I hear you got shot?'

'I did.'

Qiang studied his face, 'Did it hurt?'

He shrugged, 'The first two I didn't even notice. The third one, that hurt. That hurt a lot. The painkillers are keeping it down though.'

'You got shot *three* times?'

'I've got the holes to prove it.'

'I should be the one holding you up,' As guilty as she sounded saying it, she carried on leaning on him. 'As long as you're alright. I really don't want to lose another bunkmate.'

'Nor do I. When I came out of the stairwell and you had all that blood on you, I thought you might have been hit. You're okay, right?'

'No,' for a moment she felt a little heavier on Wrath's arm, 'I'm not okay. Princess is dead,' their walking pace seemed to be getting slower as they got closer to the crew quarters. 'I didn't get hit though. It wasn't my blood, it was theirs. I think I tagged four or five of them in the stairwell.'

'Glad to hear it. You should get a good tariff out of it.'

'What?'

'It's the same as killing pirates, there's a merit tariff for killing PPB.' Wrath hadn't even thought about it much when Jaglan had said it, now he did, it was a little disturbing. 'Does that seem weird to you? That they actually have a set tariff for killing PPB crew?'

'Yesterday it would have seemed strange. Now, I'm going to have to reassess what strange means, at least when it comes to the PPB, anyway.' She thought about the last few hours, the news report, the attack, the destruction of one PPB frigate and the capture of another, 'Are we at war now?'

Wrath took a deep breath before answering, 'The way those commandos talked about killing us, and the way Jaglan talked about killing them, I think we were already at war. Do you think they could keep a war secret?'

Qiang shook her head, not as a denial, but from resigned confusion.

They walked on without talking. From the sounds coming from the accommodation deck, the crew were taking Qiang's advice, and seemed to be working off her recreation suggestions like a checklist. There was no ignoring the uninhibited sounds coming from some of the sleeping quarters.

Qiang shook her head, 'I've never been able to do that aboard,' she told him, 'Not just because I share my cabin with two other people, although that hasn't helped.'

'It doesn't make it easy.'

'It's hard to believe I've been aboard this bird for nearly a year.'

They walked on in silence, seeming to walk more slowly they closer they got to their own cabin.

'How about you, Malcolm?'

'No, I haven't been with anybody since I've been aboard.'

'Sorry, no. I was a step behind myself. I meant did you kill any PPB?' Wrath didn't entirely believe that was what she'd meant, but didn't press it, 'You must have killed some of them, right? Staff Major Jaglan didn't take you along for nothing. You killed some?'

Wrath took some time to answer, processing what it meant to him. 'I did.'

'A couple? More than a couple?'

'More.'

'Five of them?'

This was not a source of pride for him, nor shame either, and he didn't know what Qiang was getting out of it. 'More.'

'Ten? Twenty? Fifty?'

'In my debrief they told me my gun-camera registered 14 unique tags to me, and some assists. One of them was a lieutenant. Apparently that has a good tariff.'

'Wrath, yesterday, she asked me,' she sighed, '*Grace* asked me, after that pirate attack, she asked me if I was ready to be a killer.'

'She asked me too. What did you say?'

'I said, if that's what it takes out here, then yes, I'm ready.'

'I guess you were right.'

'What did you tell her?'

'I told her I wasn't.'

'I guess you were wrong, then.'

'No. I lied.'

He felt Qiang stiffen a little before relaxing again, 'Well, you know that *now*, but you didn't know *then*. It's not a lie if you didn't know. How are you supposed to know until you actually have to do it?'

Wrath stopped and looked at Qiang, calmly, with certainty. 'No. I *did* know. I knew I was ready to be a killer, I knew it as soon as she knew she wasn't. Those pirates we blew into chunks, they were murderers, and they were going to go on murdering. I'm not a murderer, but I've no doubts. I'm a killer. I lied to Grace because it was what she wanted to hear. I *knew* I was lying.'

Qiang eyed him warily, 'Did you enjoy it? Killing?'

He shook his head dismissively, 'Not enjoy, no. But every one of them set out to kill me, to kill you, to kill Grace, and Boyd, Farr, QM, all of us. I didn't enjoy, but I didn't hate it either. It didn't feel enjoyable. It felt... correct.'

'It scares me, but I understand.' Qiang started them walking again, walking in silence on past the noises of their crew-mates making the most of it.

She stopped outside their cabin door and turned to him, placing her hands on his chest, 'The one who killed *her*, the commando who killed Princess, do you think you might have killed him?'

'I don't know. Maybe I did. Maybe you did? Or maybe whoever it was died in the stairwell. I'd like it if they died in the stairwell. I think they deserved a death that was, horrific and terrifying. I hope whoever killed Grace died confused, not knowing which way was up or down, and being smashed to spreffing pieces.'

Their cabin door slid open, but she stayed in front of him blocking the doorway, 'We... we did good, the both of us. We deserve to feel... good about what we did. I think.'

'We did. We do.'

She stared at him intently, 'We should...' she bit her lip, 'We should... this was a tough day. We should take... comfort to have come through it.'

Wrath nodded, 'You're right. We should'

'Okay. Good.' She stepped inside the cabin and slung her jacket up onto her bunk. Kicking her boots off and peeling off her shirt, she became aware he was still standing outside.

'Come in and shut the door, Malcolm. I'm not putting on a public show.'

Stepping inside, the door slid shut behind him. Wrath's deeply weary mind was aware there was more to this than her being too tired to get undressed in the bathroom like she usually did. His over-worked synapses weren't quite there yet, but something less cognitive was waking up to the possibilities.

He was transfixed as each item came off, and finally she looked at him with a perplexed smile as she tossed aside the last of her uniform.

'What are you waiting for, cadet? Weapon up!'

NOVEMBER

twenty five

Many things were not to the Chairman's tastes today. The loss of over two hundred Humana Faction and PPB sympathetic planetary Governors in last night's elections had started things off poorly.

The announcement that Sovereign Benoit's "temporary appointment" to the position of Sovereign was over, and that Edgar Phipps was now once again well enough to resume his position in sole command of the Focus Protectorate had definitely indicated a potential downward tilt to the Chairman's day.

The two hour call from Fathom, detailing the many ways in which Over-Admiral Connors might be gradually and painfully murdered over a course of weeks, or months, commanded his attention in truly nauseating and unwelcome ways - though some of them had sounded genuinely amusing, and mechanically ingenious.

All of this had come before he'd even had breakfast, which thanks to Fathom's illustrative descriptions he now had no intention of eating.

The PPB had already suffered huge damage over Project Snipe, neither the Chairman, the Committee, or the Admiralty wanted to give Black Fleet the added satisfaction of seeing Connors fired over it too, so he would survive in his position at the head of the Navy for a while, but not without a personal price.

The main problem for the Chairman was simply being here, in Over-Admiral Connors' stateroom aboard the PPB flagship Gisella, in orbit above Focus. Here representing the PPB as a loyal associate and signatory of the Protectorate Security Accords, waiting for the glorious return of Sovereign Edgar Phipps.

Phipps had already done this twice after his first and second investitures in office, forcing the PPB to come here in their most powerful vessel and doff their caps again was just rubbing their noses in it. But it was all televised, and failure to show up would have just been yet another public relations catastrophe. Better to get it over with with as much dignity as could be mustered.

The Chairman turned a look of distaste to the man he held responsible for this mess, 'When's he supposed to get here, Connors?'

Over-Admiral Connors stiffened at the Chairman's tone, which was so full of loathing it would take a full day's walk to get all the way back to merely disrespectful.

'Benoit touched down on Focus an hour ago at the Chamber of Governors and relinquished power to the Select Board. Phipps is due at Beacon 3 at noon, but he'll probably make us wait. I don't know if he'll come from the shuttle port or direct from the Chamber of Governors. He hasn't shown his face yet.'

'Captain Rourke is still alive out there, somewhere, maybe the *Sabina* will show up and try to shoot his shuttle down?'

Connors let the comment go, although he wasn't sure he'd mind so much if she did. 'Phipps can only serve another three years no matter what. There's only so much he can do in that time.'

'He can do plenty, Connors. Most dangerous of all things he can do now is, he can choose his successor. They'll let him, now. He can pave the way for someone just as bad, or even worse.'

Connors had had enough, his career was on borrowed time now anyway, 'You're a frightened man, Chairman Pierce. I don't think that's a good quality in a leader.' Deliberately ignoring the chairman's fully hyphenated name was a carefully calibrated insult, a long-term peeve of his superior.

'Leaders know the things that nobody else wants to know, Connors. Any leader who isn't scared is an idiot. I know how overstretched we are, I know how many varieties of moral, intellectual and financial bankruptcy we're facing, and I know how little control you have over the vastly expensive, over-staffed, under-competent, corrupt, and sometimes downright criminal Navy you lead. Don't make me wish I'd come down on Fathom's side this morning, Connors, and don't think that's something I couldn't change my mind about.'

A look at his watch showed it was nearly noon. He shook his head and sighed, 'About the only thing you can say about today is, with Phipps back in place, at least we're back to the devil we know.'

Outside the window, Focus's sun went dark, then vanished from view. A large sphere of anti-light fog evaporated and a vast black shape emerged, a softly rounded flat ellipse.

'What the spreff is that?'

Connors grabbed up the communications link to the bridge, 'Captain, identify that... vessel.'

"Navigation Control identifies the craft with Black Fleet tags, with a newly registered name, Black Sentinel. No classification given."

'How big is she?'

"We're calculating one-point-eight by oh-point-five."

Connors mulled the numbers – over treble the size of current Black Fleet dreadnoughts, and nearly twice the size of the ship on which he now stood, the largest PPB flag-class ship. Edgar Phipps was back in power all right, and how long had he had this behemoth hidden up his sleeve?

Connors turned to the Chairman and said with a sneer, 'The devil you know, eh? You think he had that made this morning? Last week? Last month? Benoit was never going to be allowed to stay in place. They've had this thing waiting in the wings, and for who knows how long?'

The Chairman said nothing, studying this new vessel, this ...what else could he call it but a battleship — taking in its magnitude with an appalled look on his face.

'I suggest you tell Fathom to get back to the drawing board, Mister Chairman. He's going to need to work out how the spreff we're going to fight these!'

The central plaza of Beacon 3 was resplendent with flags, pennants, streamers, bunting and balloons. The flags of every Protectorate world, interspersed with banners bearing the seal of the sovereign ringed each deck.

Every level of the hollow centre of the station was filled with chanting people, the central deck packed with planetary governors, dignitaries, military brass, and select members of the press corps, and all eyes were turned to the central elevators for the first sight of the new, old, Sovereign.

The chorus of cheering began to rise in pitch as the doors opened and the Sovereign's retinue emerged, then a positive roar erupted as Sovereign Edgar Phipps stepped into view.

As he got closer and cameras were able to get a better look at him, his face now filling the viewing screens ringing the plaza. His smile was youthful and relaxed, his skin aglow with a healthy tan, his stride confident and bold, he looked more like his old self than his *actual* old self ever had.

The crowd parted as his entourage led him to the plaza, chanting his name as he made his way to the raised lectern. He looked almost overwhelmed. The smiling game had never been a part of his political persona, but, here and now, he couldn't keep the happiness from his face. Waving and basking in this triumphant return, sharing in the audience's excitement, and their exultance.

He took his place behind the slender lectern, directing the crowd to sit, nodding approvingly as the noise began to abate.

'Honoured guests, welcome onlookers, citizens of the Protectorate, and those beyond, let's not pretend I haven't done this before.' His easy smile sent a wave of laughter and applause around the plaza, 'I'm still me, and we still live in the same Protectorate, but I've never liked repeating myself, so if you want to look up the speech I gave last time and pretend I said most of that again, we can all get on with our day.

'Of course, I am glad to be back. Back to health, and back to work. Sovereign Benoit had big shoes to fill, and I'm sure his efforts will not be soon forgotten. As I stand before you today, honoured to be reinstated as your Sovereign once again, he has earned my gratitude.

'Now, as I only have three years left to serve, time is a commodity I hold very precious, so I will answer a *small* selection of questions before I head up to my office and get back to work.'

Ben Cranford of Focus Vision News stood first, that is to say, nobody stood before he did.

'Sovereign Phipps, it's a privilege to be here to welcome you back to office, but your arrival took just about everybody by surprise. Your means of arrival, that is. What can you tell us about that huge black vessel out there?'

Phipps nodded, 'Thank you, Ben. Well, as is well known, the number of enforcement units Black Fleet is allowed to run and maintain is limited by an arms reduction treaty, and that number had been running down gradually for over three decades. However, there is no limit on the specification levels of those vessels. The Black Sentinel is the first unit off the line of the new Sentinel class vessels.

'As of today for every *two* of our obsolete craft that we decommission, they will be replaced with a single Sentinel Class craft, until we have met the limits set out in the treaty. This new platform means we minimise the loss in defensive capacity while bringing down our fleet size in line with the treaty.'

'Just what are the operating capabilities of these new craft?'

'Their capabilities are adequate to the tasks for which they were designed. If you want more answers you can direct your questions to Fleet, but they probably won't tell you anything I haven't, and maybe not even as much as that.'

Another reporter stood, 'Welcome back, Sovereign. I was wondering if you had any thoughts on last night's election results, and why they were so strong for Bradfordian candidates, and so poor for Humana Faction Governors, and Governor hopefuls?'

'I can only speak to what I believe motivated voter choices, and I believe the people chose to support the values and strength that have maintained peace and prosperity, freedom, and respect for every individual.

'I can't know the minds of every voter, I'm just glad so many like minded new governors will be joining the Chamber in the new year. As for why the Humana Faction and their fellow travellers have failed to attract the positive attentions of voters, that is something you'd have to address to them, although I'm sure they're asking themselves the same question right now. Just one more question now, please. How about you, Donna?'

Donna McGill of the Baxter's World Central News Agency stood, almost startled to be called on, though she was ready nonetheless, 'Sovereign, do you think this aggressive new weapons platform you arrived with today will be seen as provocative by PPB worlds? And don't you think this... battleship will be seen as using the letter of the Year 240 Treaty to defeat its spirit?'

Phipps gave her an icy smile, 'You wish to speak of provocation? Ask the crew of the Black Wreath about provocation. As long as so many in both the PPB hierarchy and the PPB Navy make loathing their peaceful neighbours their policy — free and successful neighbours who, reluctantly, have to contribute so much money to propping up their failing worlds and failing ideologies the PPB refuse to adapt to reality, anything other than giving them all of our money and crawling off to die is seen as provocation. The PPB is sick, and blames everyone but itself for what ails it.

'As for the Year 240 Treaty, the treaty has been limiting the ability of Sovereigns to protect their own citizens for over *thirty five* years, forcing us to pay subsidies to the PPB Navy for protection we only lack because of the treaty they bound us to. Recent events show that even that is not enough for some in the PPB fold, who decided to help us reduce the size of our fleet by their own means.

'When it comes to the PPB, the only provocative gesture I would ever fear to make is the provocation of being weak. That is a kind of provocation they will not receive while I am Sovereign. Thank you everybody. That will be all.'

Applause followed him all the way back to the elevators, and carried on long after he was out of sight.

The home of the PPB's spy network, "White" was concealed in the labyrinthine heart of White Satellite, a station locked in geosynchronous orbit above Baxter's World, looking down on the capital of the PPB.

Griffith sat in his office, gazing out of the artificial window at the view piped in from external cameras, waiting for a call from the only authority he obeyed, Fathom.

His intercom buzzed and his secretary spoke, *"I have Fathom for you."*

'Very well.'

Fathom's voice was never the same, a randomly selected vocal pattern, sometimes recognisable as someone famous, sometimes obscure, but, presumably, none of them actually belonging to Fathom himself, or herself.

"Good afternoon Mister Griffith. Are you well?"

'I'm always well, Fathom. How about you?'

"Yes. Always."

'You said you had a new task for me?'

"I do. I feel we are needful of broader tools of influence. The loss of Sovereign Benoit as both a supporter and an influencer is a blow, but may be a useful call to action for us."

'I certainly don't see us getting a friendly Sovereign in power again for the foreseeable future.'

"No. Sovereign Phipps will make consolidating a new power-base within the chamber, and on the Select Board an immediate priority. We will be needing something less political, and more direct."

'What's your thinking.'

"The news report of that young journalist, Linc Bostrom, was very effective in turning the tide of opinion against both the PPB and our Humana Faction sympathisers in the Protectorate."

'It didn't help us, that's for sure. He was probably supplied with the footage of the Pandale attack anonymously by Black Fleet. Only a spy boat would have been able to get footage that good from far enough away not to be knocked out by the weapon, and it wasn't one of ours.'

"Yes. Though we could, and have, replicated such leaks to journalists, it is difficult to do with enough frequency that it might be useful as a tool to shape opinion."

'So what's your idea?'

"We need our own broadcasting network."

'The PPB has over a dozen entertainment networks and news networks.'

"Broadcasting obvious propaganda for the most credulous people solely to PPB worlds, yes. This is of limited effectiveness and only reaches people who are already a part of the fold. What we need is something with reach

across the Protectorate, not just propaganda channels for our own worlds."

'That will take some setting up.'

"No. Darian Corvalis had just such a network, a sub-net channel called Gamma. Mostly it was illegal content, Death Leagues, pirate atrocities, exploitation material catering to a wide array of grotesque deviancies."

'I don't see that giving us much penetration into the kind of audience we'd need.'

"No. It will need a radical shake up, but everything is in place, and it already had seven billion subscribers, and probably many millions more with illegal access. All we need is somebody to take over programming and bring the network to respectability."

'Where will you find someone who can do that?'

"There is someone I have found is a match for any task."

'Who's that?'

"Why you, of course, Mister Griffith."

Griffith closed his eyes and let the news sink in. 'Of course.'

"We cannot risk further open exposure of the Griffith identity. It will still operate within the PPB sphere, but between Marshal Jameson and the fact Black Fleet managed to gain enough intel to seek you out, the Griffith identity is no longer safe for external use.

"You will need a new operating identity, one that won't attract questions. I have already planted rumours that Darian Corvalis is alive and operating under a new identity after extensive facial and physical reconstruction surgery. I have also started a rumour that Gamma has been purchased by a former pirate who made his stake and is seeking a legitimate business interest. More rumours are being rolled out at regular intervals. By the time you have decided on a new identity there will too many rumours for anyone to have a hope of working out who you really are, and all of them will be much more interesting and plausible than the reality."

'Very well. Forward me all of the details and I'll set things in motion.'

"I knew you could be counted on, Mister Griffith. Speaking of people who can be counted on, how is the creature?"

Griffith frowned at the term but said nothing, 'Fester is alive. He's about ready to be released from the healing mechanisms now. He shows no signs of lasting physical damage externally, that's due to giving him a completely new face, but he does seem physically sound. But his mind is a mystery even when he's conscious. They've kept him in a coma for nearly a month while he heals.'

"A remarkable specimen. I was doubtful when you decided to spare his life all those years ago. What of his charming infatuation with the singer? Can he be trusted?"

'I don't know. The girl is dead. He'll probably know I killed her. If he has a problem with that, I'll have to kill him.'

"Then a similar choice awaits you now as did when first you found him. Tread carefully. Goodbye, Mister Griffith."

'Yes,' he replied to an empty line. He switched to a new comms channel. 'Doctor Moody, I'm coming down. Get ready to open the pod. It's time to wake the monster.'

Griffith picked up the large hand gun from his desk, chambering a high-velocity, high-explosive armour piercing round. Fester was about the closest thing to a friend Griffith had left. For his own sake, Fester had better feel the same way.

Cleovald Dofstez waited for the elevator to open, treating the emerging Sovereign to a satisfied smile.

'You liked it, Clay?'

The smile widened considerably, 'Saving Donna McGill for last was perfect. Right for the throat, in with the teeth and out with the jugular. You're back on fine form.'

'That crone is an apologist for villains, anything less than instant attack would be a waste of time.'

The military guards led them through the blast-proof doors and inside the security ring, on the long walk to the Sovereign's office.

'And how are you feeling?'

'Well, that spa worked miracles, but be assured, I don't feel anywhere near as good as I look,' he drew his medical vaporator from his inside pocket and took a deep drag on it, 'nowhere near as good. I just hope I can last the full three years I have left in office.'

'Strange, I keep wondering if we can find a constitutional clause that would let us extend it out to another full five years?'

'Don't even, Clay. I wouldn't make it. I swear I wouldn't. No, we need another plan. A plan of succession.'

'Pickings are thin, Sovereign. We have some young people coming through, but they're not ready yet, and they likely still won't be in three years, either.'

'Shut up Clay, you know who I'm talking about.'

'Someone from the Select Board?'

'Of course form the Select Board, Clay. I mean you.'

Dofstez stopped in his tracks, unsure if he was missing some kind of joke, 'Sovereign, I'm a Goffa.'

'You can't help where you were born, and you've been a Protectorate citizen since you were thirteen years old.'

'But I'm a Goffa. There's never been a Goffa Sovereign.'

'Then it's about time there was. It's not like there's a law against it. Stop questioning it, Clay. It's happening. You're the next Sovereign, got it?'

Dofstez fell back in to step next to the Sovereign, 'Well if you put it like that. I guess you really were serious about provoking the PPB.'

The rotating door to the Sovereign's office lay ahead, turning gently and presenting its opening to them, sliding closed as they stepped inside. The door continued to spin around them as they waited in its hollow centre.

Dofstez decided he needed to broach a tricky situation lying on the other side of the door.

'Are you going to be nice to *her*?'

'You mean Veronica? The woman who got me fired?' Phipps regarded him coolly, 'Niceness has never been a factor in our professional relationship, Clay.'

'You know she's the reason you were able leave office in a way that meant you could come back. If she'd stood by and let you invade Steimz you'd be in jail right now, or maybe even strung up for the doghawks to eat for a Stipulation 3 violation. That's basically a charge of treason you'd have faced.'

'You know I know that, and that I don't need to be told any of it. She still got me fired, and left us all at the mercies of Sovereign Tobias Benoit. I'll be perfectly fair to her, don't ask for more than that. She was your teenage crush, not mine, and as much as I like you Clay, that cuts no ice with me. Frankly, it *shouldn't* cut any with you either.'

The door came to rest at the end of its circular path. Phipps took a good look at his office - the great circular desk set in the rich red carpet, the walls of deepest blue sparkling with the light of a simulated star-scape.

Either side of the desk stood a man and a woman: to the left, Sovereign Staff Commander Walter Torvus, Chief Supervising Officer of Black Fleet Staff Command and the Sovereign's Space-going Forces, to the right, Veronica, the Director of Triple-S, his spy-master. Both greeted him.

'Good afternoon to you both. Commander, I'll take your briefing momentarily,' he turned to Veronica, 'Director?'

'Yes, Sovereign?'

'Get out of my office.'

The Director paused for a moment, assessing the mood, and feeling the air in the room take a perceptible chill. 'Yes, Sovereign.' She took an awkward step, then halted, 'I'll speak with you later.'

'That's a rather presumptuous statement. Why are you still here?'

She walked towards the door of her adjoining office with as much composure as she could.

'Get out more quickly, Director.'

She turned a smile of frost and fear his way and raised her pace, catching a glance from Governor Select Dofstez, a look of pained sympathy.

Her door clicked shut and the Sovereign turned to Commander Torvus. 'I apologise for that little scene, Commander.'

'No apology is necessary, Sovereign. This is your office.'

'For now it is, you'll know Governor Select Cleovald Dofstez, I'm sure.'

'We know each other well, Sovereign.'

'Good. He will be the next Sovereign of the Protectorate. Do you understand.'

Torvus looked a little taken aback, but nodded.

'Do you have any objections?'

'Far from it. I wouldn't have dared hope for someone even half as capable as Governor Select Dofstez to be your successor.'

'Yes, Benoit has rather lowered people's expectations, hasn't he? From here on out, whatever I know, Clay knows. Quad-Q clearance across the board, strategy briefings, top level military appointments, absolutely everything. Understood?'

'Understood, Sovereign.'

Phipps turned to his heir apparent, 'What about you, Clay? Are you ready to find out how deep the chiff we're in really is?'

Cleovald Dofstez' head was spinning, but he was a man who knew how to roll with the blows and keep going, and was never one to duck a challenge. 'I await your instruction gladly, Sovereign Phipps.'

'Good. Let's begin.'

The Director took her place behind her desk, sitting in silence and pondering her future, wondering for how much longer this would be her office, her desk.

Sitting atop it was a stack of datasheets. Black Fleet Staff Command's pick of the new intake, and some of the more notable applications for officer candidacies. Despite herself, she couldn't help but start leafing through them.

She stopped dead as one name caught her eye. Studying the document, she saw the picture of a very handsome young man, a face with a bright smile, but tinged with the shadow of recent grief. His name was Ray Gibson. Her heart fell.

She'd sent so many people to their deaths that it shouldn't stand out, but something felt very wrong to her about the death of Melody Gibson. The psychological work-ups showed how close she had been to her brother, and seeing his face brought it much closer to home.

Maybe it wouldn't be so bad if Sovereign Phipps got his revenge and fired her. Maybe she hadn't lost all of her humanity yet. Maybe she could reconnect with her own family, such of it as there was left to reconnect with.

Maybe not.

Her intercom buzzed for her attention.

"Director?" The voice belonged to her chief of staff.

'What is it Commander Vassola?'

"Have you surveyed the candidates list I left on your desk? I'd like to discuss them with you."

She still had her job for now, and it still needed attending to.

'Very well.'

Vassola appeared in her office with almost indecent haste, and sat without waiting for an invite. Perhaps news of the Sovereign's curt dismissal had spread, or perhaps the precariousness of her position had been obvious to everyone already.

'You seem keen, Commander. I assume you have some favourites among these recommendations that you wish me to be aware of?'

'One or two, Director.'

'Don't lets waste our time, then. Who?'

'We've suffered some losses this year, Director. We need to be bringing through a different kind of Triple-S agent to be ready for the more aggressive PPB tactics we're seeing. This softly softly stuff isn't cutting it anymore.'

The Director hardened her look, 'Names, Commander, not talk.'

Vassola reached over and swept aside a few of the datasheets before finding the one he was after, placing it before her.

'Wrath? It says he's still a cadet. He's only been in the service a couple of months.'

'It's not unusual to recommend cadets who show early promise, Director.'

'He looks about 15 years old.'

'He's 19, and on his very first day he absolutely destroyed the Fleet record for firearms proficiency during a *demonstration* round. Then on his first *official* ranking shoot he actually broke the scoring system. We literally don't have a measuring system good enough for him.

'In just two days and three engagements he was jointly responsible for wiping out the entire crew of a pirate junk affiliated with the Gambala Clan, helped repel the PPB incursion squad on the Black Wreath, and scored multiple tags during the capture of the Savatara.'

'In the time it takes most cadets to work out how to put their uniform on he's put himself in the top ten of the Fleet Lethality Index. That's not just among his fellow cadets, that's across the whole of Fleet, including Triple-S agents, Black Task units, everything. The kid's a pure killing machine. I've seen his gun-cam footage and he was dropping battle hardened PPB commandos like they were targets at a shooting gallery.'

The Director half-heartedly flicked through the dossier, 'There's a lot more to spying than killing, Vassola.'

'I'm well aware of your ethos, Director, every death is a snowball and so forth, of course that's true. Be that as it may, the fact is you can train a good killer to be a spy, you can't train a dead spy to be a good killer. We need to move fast on this cadet. He was the personal recommendation of Sovereign Staff Commander Frank Bull.

'Staff Major Jaglan wants him for his blue-gun squad. If this Cadet Wrath takes the jump to the Staff command stream, we may never get him on Sovereign Staff, and he's exactly what we need. You don't need a reason to pick him for Triple-S, you need a reason not to, and it had better be a good one.'

The Director shook her head and looked through Wrath's paperwork, 'Reasons, reasons, reasons... here's a good one, he tried to sign up with the PPB before he signed up with us!'

'He was drunk at the time. I'd think killing over a dozen PPB and helping us capture a PPB frigate probably rules him out as having any sympathies for their cause. If that didn't, being shot by them three times and having his bunkmate killed by them should have.'

The Director pointed at the dossier again, 'Well here's another one, he's been in the service three months and he's already been shot three times. That doesn't speak well to his longevity.'

'He's *survived* being shot three times, and got up to keep fighting! You think we don't need that?'

'The fact is, Commander, he didn't sign up with us until *after* he tried to sign up with the PPB. This is Triple-S, Commander, QQ clearance is the basic level of entry, and it only goes up from there.

I'd need to see a lot more of him in action before even starting to consider him for a position with us. The fact he tried to sign up with the PPB at all should give anyone pause, if not be seen as an outright permanent grounds to never let him join Sovereign Staff. If that still isn't enough for you, well, he has a stupid made up name, and... he looks like my ex-husband. Let Staff have him, and good luck to them.'

Vassola was always respectful to the Director, but was running low on patience, 'I feel I should tell you, Director, these same recommendations will be going in front of the new Sovereign, who has indicated he will be taking an interest in this office's selections for Triple-S agents from here on out. It is the *Sovereign's* Security Service, after all.'

'Then I'll tell the Sovereign what I'm telling you. He is not what we should be looking for, and he's not what we need.'

'With respect, Director, what we need has changed. We've still got plenty of good agents who work your way, but we need something new. Frankly, with the open aggression we're seeing from the PPB what we need now are killers; fresh, fast, accomplished killers.' Vassola tapped insistently on Wrath's picture, 'This one is a born killer.'

One hundred steps led from street level to the concourse of the Viafrane Gun-Grid Arena; a towering amphitheatre of combat. Nobody ever died here, but careers had ended and reputations crumbled. Humiliation and failure for many was the inevitable price for glory of the few.

These hundred steps had always intimidated the young Glen Rothgill. He'd only ever competed here once when he'd turned eleven years old, and he'd acquitted himself well enough among his peers, but some people had made no secret of their belief he hadn't met the weight of expectation that came with his family name.

Today these were just steps. This was just a building. A very big building, alive with cheers and sighs from a crowd still out of sight but, maybe because he had spent the last few months living with a name that came with no expectations beyond those he had of himself, or because running around firing non-lethal slap-rounds seemed rather diminished in its significance, he felt a strong sense of remove from this place and this part of his old life.

'Glen!'

Reaching the final step, he turned in surprise at the voice calling to him, finding delight in the face he saw. The old man approached with a youthful fluidity to his stride.

'Frank!'

Frank Bull grabbed Glen's hand and pumped it gleefully,

'Should I still be calling you Frank?'

The old man looked puzzled at the question, 'Of course, Glen. What else would you call me?'

'What was it now?' Glen gave him a wry smile, 'Former Chief Supervising Officer of the Sovereign's Space-going Forces?'

'Ah!' Frank looked like he was considering his response, 'Somebody blabbed then.' He said, nodding. 'Well we both know a lot of people here, so as long as you don't want me calling you Malcolm Wrath, you can go right ahead and keep calling me Frank.'

'Yeah, about that.'

Frank held his hand up, a confessorial gesture, 'Glen, you are the only person I *ever* nominated for induction. Fact is I only did it because I think you needed a life change, and I thought it would be good for you, I wasn't expecting you to wind up joining a blue-gun squad in your rookie year, or for you to pick up multiple gunshot wounds, either.'

'Well, it seems some people figure your recommendation means I'm marked for greatness or something.'

'Seems so. There's no real data trail, but obviously word gets around, and it's already got back to you. I don't know how long your cover identity will hold, but my recommendation would probably make you a target for the PPB, and might make people in Fleet think you're getting preferential treatment. Neither of those things would be good for you.'

'Even without your name being linked to mine, I think I've probably done a decent job of making myself a target for the PPB if they have any intel at all about how they lost the Savatara.'

'Well that's true enough.'

'I suppose the name Malcolm Wrath means if I ever need to go back to being Glen Rothgill it should be a safe name to come back to.'

Frank nodded, 'That was the plan.'

'Anyway, today I get to be Glen again, for a while.'

'Yes you do! How's that going for you?'

'Alien. QM let me break out my old clothes,' he took a look down at what he was wearing, the same clothes he'd worn when he'd signed up, although the automated-purser had cleaned and pressed everything before it had been stored. 'It feels weird to be out of that flight suit to be honest. But there's far too many people who would recognise me around here for me to go around being anyone but my old self.'

'True enough. Speaking of,' He took Glen's elbow and led him towards the competitors entrance. 'Come on, let's be sociable, might as well catch up with some old faces while you're here.'

'Old faces sounds good.' Glen stopped in his tracks, "Did you hear about what happened to Salo Krupps?'

Frank nodded, 'I read the report, and that was a crazy coincidence.'

'A spreffing dangerous coincidence!'

'Yes, but there's a thousand worlds out there. How often do you think something like that is likely to happen again?'

'A friend of mine told me asking questions like that is usually the fastest way to find out. That would be a sticky hole to find myself in again.'

'Maybe, maybe not. You've always been good at thinking on your feet, and as I read it, you dealt with the Salo Krupps situation well enough, you'll just have to figure out how best to deal with it if these realities ever collide again.' Frank looked over Glen's shoulder, 'also speaking of...'

Glen turned as another familiar voice shouted to him.

'It is you!'

Yolande ran the rest of the way, and just as she'd done for years whenever she'd caught sight of him, she opened her arms and flung them around his neck, letting him scoop her up and spin her around in his arms. Suddenly he was very definitely Glen Rothgill in his totality, everything else fell away except the pure electric joy of this girl in his arms.

He set her down and looked at her with unconcealed gladness, 'Hey kiddo, long time no nothing.'

'Of course not, I haven't heard anything from you in months, you big goon! It was like you'd vanished without a trace!' She punched his arm, 'I heard a rumour from back home you thought I was dead!'

He gave her a reproachful look, 'Has Spoff been shooting his mouth off about me? You know you shouldn't listen to rumours.'

Frank Bull laid a hand on his back, 'Glen, I'll leave you two to catch up. We'll talk again.'

Glen nodded and turned his attention back to Yolande.

'Glen, Glen, Glen! So you've finally moved here where the action is! Are you staying with your parents until you find a place?'

'I haven't moved here, Yolande, this is just a visit.'

'Oh,' she frowned, 'Honestly, I thought you'd finally got over your thing with the new rules and wanted get back in the league. The pro season's just getting into full swing here, and with your connections you could probably get a wild-card qualification. I know you didn't like the newer rules, but rules change Glen, we've got to change with them.'

He rubbed her shoulder, 'I know, Yolande. Honestly, I think that's finally got through to me. I've seen the rules change a lot more than I ever thought they could, and I'm rolling with it, but I've got other stuff going on now. No more Gun-Grid for me, well, not exactly.'

He took a good look at her, not realising how much he'd missed her. He let out a sigh.

'What?'

He treated her to a bittersweet smile, 'I don't think I've ever told you how beautiful you are, have I?'

'Ha! Are you ill? Sarcastic remarks are more your thing. Admit it, you're only saying that because you thought I was dead aren't you.'

Wrapping her arms around his waist she pressed her head into his chest, 'See, I'm not dead, you big idiot.'

'Just dead annoying then?'

'That's more like it! You haven't changed a bit.'

He freed himself from her arms. Wasn't there any sign of it in him? Maybe the way he looked hadn't changed, but he was a killer. He was good at it, and he was fine with it. Was there no sign of it at all? He was glad she didn't know, but felt it ought to show in *some* way, somehow. He ought to seem... different.

He forced a smile, "Why change perfection, Yolande?"

'Oh of course. Perfect Glen! Everything has to be perfect for Glen. You really haven't changed one bit.' She looked him up and down again, 'Actually, you haven't changed. Aren't those the same clothes you were wearing the last time I saw you?'

'I got a little behind on my laundry.'

She looked over his shoulder toward the top of the steps, 'Is this your laundry now? Looks like your chauffeur's bringing it. I hope there's some fresh undies in there.'

Wrath turned to see a woman in a black uniform coming toward him, carrying a large, soft, kit bag. His eyes widened as he realised it was Trooper Qiang. Today was the day she was supposed to be catching her ride to the academy on Focus. In spite of Frank Bull's assurances, it seemed realities were about to collide again. A brief chill hit him as he wondered what name Qiang would use. She only knew him by one.

'Hey there!'

'Qiang? What are you doing here?'

"What hap, Killer?" she handed him the soft bag, 'I bought you some new duds. Good thing too, those don't suit you at all.'

Yolande looked on with amused interest, 'Killer? Is that why you dropped out of sight, Glen? Have you joined the Death Leagues?'

He thought about it for a moment, 'Not quite.' He set the bag down, hoping Yolande wouldn't pay it too much attention, 'Oh, Yolande, this is Diana. Diana, this is Yolande.'

'Hi.'

'Hey... oh!' Qiang did a double-take, 'It's you! The dead chick who's not dead!' She turned a smug gaze Glen's way, 'I told you she wasn't dead, you big idiot.'

'Glen!' Yolande looked on in phoney-surprise, 'you said you didn't think I was dead!'

'Nope, I said you shouldn't listen to rumours. That's just good advice.' He looked at Qiang, 'What you brung me, Diana?'

'Like I said, new threads, Killer. Trust me, you're gonna look sharp in that. Why the spreff you're getting it is way beyond me, but it's yours.'

Keeping the view to himself, he snuck a glimpse inside the bag and closed it quickly, turning a smile over his shoulder to Yolande, 'Good news. Fresh undies!'

'I don't even want to know!'

Qiang pointed at the bag, 'You might want to take a closer look at that.'

He pulled the bag open a little wider and took another, better, look inside, realising this wasn't just the uniform of a cadet trooper. It had the insignia of a full Staff Trooper, and attached to it was a transfer docket. He pressed his thumb against it and the words lit up.

STAFF TROOPER MALCOLM PRENTISS WRATH:
TRANSFER AUTHORISATION - BLACK LEOPARD
C.O. - STAFF COMMANDER RODHAM
REPORTING OFFICER - STAFF MAJOR JAGLAN
REPORT FOR DUTY IMMEDIATELY

He looked from Qiang to Yolande, and from Yolande back to Qiang. Two names were swimming in his mind. To one of these people he was a Rothgill, to the other he was Wrath.

'I've been told the transport's waiting for you. We're catching the same flight, we need to go pretty much now. Are you ready?'

To Glen Rothgill the desire to stay here with Yolande was a deep ache inside of him, but, Yolande Fenton didn't need a killer in her life. Malcolm Wrath... Wrath had waded through blood and gristle, he'd felt exhilaration at thumping explosive rounds into the bodies of people who had come to kill him and his friends. He had a choice, here and now, to be the kid or be the killer. If he wanted out, he was certain Frank Bull could make it happen, question was, *did* he want out?

His memory went back to the last question Grace Pirie had ever asked him, *"Are you ready to be a killer?"*

Ever since that day, every single day, when he got out of his bunk, put on his uniform and made ready to clip the deadly side-arms into his belt he looked himself in the mirror and asked himself that same simple question.

Knowing the life of Glen Rothgill was here waiting for him, just one day with a different answer was all it would take for him to be done with it, but today he'd answered the same way he always did. He turned away from Yolande, settling his gaze, steady and sure on Diana.

"I'm ready."

END